# SILENCE *and* SHADOWS

*Bantam Books by James Long*

FERNEY

SILENCE AND SHADOWS

# BANTAM BOOKS

NEW YORK  TORONTO  LONDON  SYDNEY  AUCKLAND

# James Long

# Silence *and* Shadows

SILENCE AND SHADOWS

A Bantam Book / March 2001

All rights reserved.
Copyright © 2001 by James Long.

*Book design by Laurie Jewell.*

No part of this book may be reproduced or transmitted in any form or
by any means, electronic or mechanical, including photocopying,
recording, or by any information storage and retrieval system,
without permission in writing from the publisher.
For information address: Bantam Books.

Library of Congress Cataloging-in-Publication Data

Long, James, 1949 Oct. 1–
Silence and shadows / James Long.
p.   cm.
ISBN 0-553-10863-8 (alk. paper)
1. Excavations (Archaeology)—Fiction.   2. Exhumation—Fiction.
3. Villages—Fiction.   4. England—Fiction.   I. Title.

PR6062.O5123 S57 2001
823'.914—dc21                                              00-060820

*Published simultaneously in the United States and Canada*

Bantam Books are published by Bantam Books, a division of
Random House, Inc. Its trademark, consisting of the words
"Bantam Books" and the portrayal of a rooster, is Registered in U.S.
Patent and Trademark Office and in other countries. Marca Registrada.
Bantam Books, 1540 Broadway, New York, New York 10036.

PRINTED IN THE UNITED STATES OF AMERICA

BVG   10   9   8   7   6   5   4   3   2   1

# ACKNOWLEDGMENTS

The research for this book allowed me to do something I had wanted to do for years, take part in a dig. Many thanks to Dr. Chris Gosden and Dr. Gary Lock for inviting me to join them at Alfred's Castle and for not minding when I used a notebook as often as a trowel. Tom Evans, Tyler Bell, Patrick Daly, Roger, and Rich helped make it memorable, and thanks also to Les, André, Debby, Sheila, Richard, Joe, and Paul, among all the others there. George and Birgitte Speake also helped tirelessly with research. Among the authors of the many books I have consulted, I would particularly like to acknowledge John Blair's *Anglo–Saxon Oxfordshire*, George Speake's *A Saxon Bed Burial on Swallow-cliffe Down*, and Hilda Ellis Davidson's *The Sword in Anglo–Saxon England*.

# SILENCE and SHADOWS

# CHAPTER ONE

ONE WAS A TIRED TRAVELER AT the end of his tether, fleeing from an annual act of penance. A gaunt shadowed man, the flesh burnt off him by guilt, his soul smouldered close under his skin. Old women sought to feed him. Young women sought to comfort him . . . until they saw the steel shutters behind his eyes.

Two more shared a house but that still lay ahead and he did not yet know them. He was as alone as it was possible to be and that was his choice. All the way on his headlong journey from the Welsh mountains he had avoided looking in his mirror, for fear of seeing ghosts. No speed he could reach proved fast enough to leave his past behind until the exhaustion that grief brings forced him to pull over. Then, as soon as the car had stopped, he had slumped in his seat, fast asleep.

The edge of the storm awakened him

three hours later, at that time when the body is closest to death. Sudden rain drummed on the roof and splashed his forehead through the open window, bringing him back to bones that ached from his curled posture and a head filled with the sour residue of his tears. He had climbed out of the car, standing with his face tilted up to the dark sky, taking the downpour as a further punishment.

Wales was behind him. Standing by the grave in the wet churchyard, it was no longer easy to apologize because he could hardly believe the person he had once been, the man responsible for this disaster of a headstone with its letters of accusation bitten into the hard grey slate. The man he had been—that guilty, misled man—was serving a life sentence in solitary confinement, locked in a cell somewhere inside his head where he never went anymore, leaving this other Patrick, rigidly controlled, to go on paying his dues for him year after year after year.

Back in the car, he emerged from under the edge of the cloud into that great glistening bowl where the rain had left its wet canvas prepared for the bright moon. Only now, in the safe English hills, did he dare to look back. On a country road winding down through the hills towards Oxford and the plain of the River Thames, he looked in his mirror and saw the wet tarmac worming behind him, a mercury river in which his tyres left their wake of spray.

The earth was soaked in light, puddled silver by the storm, an eldritch light meant for the eyes of foxes, as hard as a welding spark. The full spring moon, a handsbreadth up the sky, cast it cold across the ocean roll of hills, x-raying the bones around the heart of England. Sunsets are for the many, sunrise for the few; the moonlight that paints the land in shades of silver is a secret, a privilege to be observed alone with a sense of due unease.

The sideways moon etched the shape of the land in silver contours, precise in the washed, chill air. Those contours are the archive of the past, the record of ice, the signature of water and wind. Man walks on top of the packed sedimentary evidence of that past, leaving only dust and fragments to settle on top into the latest layer.

ON THE EDGE OF THE VILLAGE OF WYTCHLOW, A WOMAN SAT in the attic room that had been hers since she was born, wakened even earlier than usual by outriders of apprehension instead of the fresh-start joy that usually came with her dawns. She curled on the edge of the window seat, with the sagging window open as wide as it would go. The moonlight showed her the village as if it were a stage prepared for the first entry of the main characters and she alone had the rehearsal time to prepare herself. Against the faint brightness of the eastern horizon, the cricket ground was a shining lake, lapping up to the wooded island beyond, where the church held the high ground. Beyond that, out of sight, was the place where she would go into battle when the day began. In her whole life, she had never ducked a fight that mattered.

That woman was Bobby.

THE MOON'S THIRD WITNESS WAS OUT ON HIS WANDERINGS. Joe paced his life to need little sleep; he preferred to make his inspections in the hours when no others were about. A morning such as this was not to be wasted in bed—a morning when the moon shadow revealed with perfect lunar clarity the twisted history of the land. He swayed his feet through the glistening grass with delight, walking through the humps and folds of his ancestral land until he reached its crown and its core, and then he stood motionless in the top field, which wrapped itself over the brow of the hill like a grass handkerchief on a bald man's head. In these hurried times, those who still bothered with names for fields called it the Bury Field, but in the past, when field names were part of the vital navigation of the working day, it had been the Low Field. In time, people forgot what that really meant and decided the name made no sense for a field on a hill. That was what Joe's father had told him, the names and the tales strung through the songs that held them all together.

Joe thought of that man, long gone, with a pang of sadness. Out there on the hilltop, he sang a quiet song for his father, and the moon listened.

Under the earth there were others; he knew they were there, others from the frontier time who had looked out on just such moon secrets. Their history had blown away on the wind, no words set down to keep it, only the songs, his songs.

In the hour before dawn, these three people stared separately at what the moon chose to show them.

# CHAPTER TWO

O N THE LAST STAGE OF HIS
journey, Patrick played mind-
games to stay awake. When
he reached his flat, he would
still have to pack, so he ran
through the list of the things he must not
forget. Tent, sleeping bag, plate, mug, four-
inch trowel, hand cream. When that developed into its own soporific mantra, he
wound down the window to the point where
it always jammed, let the damp air wash his
face, and turned his attention to the outside,
looking at the signposts as he drove past,
playing with the names. The history frozen
in the roots of village names contains rich
pickings for archaeologists. *Archæologist.* The
word still had a foreign feeling, a label that
would not stick to him, however often he applied it. That was what he had studied to be,
way back when life was simple: an archaeologist. That was what he had returned to now,

from the moment when he had decided in despair it was easier to deal with those who were long dead. The time in between was a no-man's-land.

The sign to the village of Fawler occupied him all the way from Charlbury to the walls of the Blenheim Palace estate. Fawler from *faig-flor,* the term the wondering Anglo-Saxons had used for the mosaics scattered in the ruins left by the vanished Romans, forgotten artistry decaying into the Dark Ages—fifteen hundred years of slow metamorphosis into a name on a signpost. It was a suitable train of thought because mosaics were very much on his mind. The suspicion of a Roman mosaic was the reason time was tight, the reason he would have to pack in a hurry as soon as he got home. Right on cue, the sign to Wytchlow flared white for an instant in his headlights and he checked his watch. Twenty past five, and what might be dawn or just paler sky beyond the storm cloud was striping the east—four hours before he was due back here at Wytchlow again, packed and ready to start.

On the very last stretch into Oxford, past the airfield at Kidlington, the white line in the centre of the road began to repeat its painful trick, dividing in two as his eyes lost focus. He had to keep blinking abruptly awake to choose which one to follow. Kidlington, the fortified dwelling of the kin of Kidla, he supposed, long buried under a sprawl of modern housing. Five miles to go and sleep was claiming him. He turned to his last resort, the radio, and if there was an evil malignancy presiding over his affairs as he had begun to believe, it showed itself at that moment. A song was ending, a song from that closed past, a song he hated so deeply that he feared for a moment that his mind had thrown up the words and forced them onto the airwaves all by itself.

> *You can tell the truth to lovers but it's better when you lie.*
> *A puppy's just for Christmas, then you leave it out to DIE.*

The graveyard-shift DJ confirmed it was real, and not a trick of his punishing brain. "That was Nam Erewhon there with their infamous punk anthem, 'Wedding Vows,' requested by . . ."

Patrick's reaction was entirely involuntary. His left fist hit the radio so hard that it split the Off button and the tuning scale behind it into shards of plastic, which fell onto the old Peugeot's filthy floor to lie there curved and black, like fragments of cremated bone.

In the Cowley Road, a sodden pile of *Woman's Own* had been dumped on his front step—any secondhand value the magazines might have had washed out by the rain, which had left them dribbling pastel papier-mâché. Two feet away, a sign in the charity shop window scolded in vain: DON'T LEAVE DONATED GOODS OUTSIDE! Patrick unlocked the door and the whole pile slumped into his hall so that he had to bulldoze it all back outside with his feet. Until then, he had thought the linoleum was plain grey, but a pattern now showed through where the wet paper had wiped it.

In his days on the road, the moment of returning home had always been odd and often impossibly alien. In that lost past, the home to which he had been returning had started off as a soft, comfortable, welcoming place into which the only jagged intrusions were the ones he had brought with him. This place was not a home; it was just a space with nothing human in it to fight the short-term-lease squalor. There was not enough left of him to turn it into a pleasant place—and anyway, he knew he did not deserve to live in a pleasant place.

He slept, fully dressed, for an hour on a mattress that still smelt of some past tenant's spilt beer, then woke himself with a cold shower, not even trying the hot water because he was almost certain that the water heater wouldn't light. He had, for these last few years, got through his life by avoiding all possibility of disappointment. Fueled by a mug of strong coffee, he threw what he needed into a bag. In that old life it would all have been there ready, washed and folded for him. Now he had to retrieve his clothes from the corners.

There were two letters on the mat. One was an electricity bill, a final demand. The logo on the other envelope foretold something worse. "Colonic Music," it said, in gold over the silhouette of a broken purple guitar. It crossed Patrick's mind to leave it for his return but he knew it was already too late for that, and even unopened it would simply add another layer to the crumbling slag-heap of his past. He tore it open. Inside was another envelope, addressed to him care of the company and now forwarded. It started,

*Dear Paddy Kane,*
    *Can you settle a bet for my brother and me? He says that when*
*you punched . . .*

Patrick crumpled it up, threw it in the bin where the rest of Paddy
Kane belonged, and slammed the door of the flat behind him. He
was breathing hard. In this life—this cloistered, channeled life
where he went to bed each night with only himself, the very last person with whom he wanted to share a bed—Patrick could still be
harmed through such unguarded chinks. He treated that vulnerability by denial, by submersion in the safe, sterile dust of the ancient
past where the treacherous, lusty flesh had long been stripped from
more predictable bones.

Half an hour later, dry, locked-up Patrick was assaulted viciously
by love.

It happened like this. All the way out through the north Oxford
traffic, retracing his route of that same morning, he was less than half
a driver, earning the hooting disapproval of clock-racing sales reps
by his unsignaled lane changes. His head hurt from all his fears
about the days ahead, his first real test in this new professional role.
As a student, in the dim, simple years the far side of the gulf in between, he had learnt it all, the techniques, the terminology, the
minutiae of what to do and how to record what he had done. He
had learnt it and then immediately forgotten it when the last exam
was out of the way, and he had shed the gown and put on the ever-
more-wild clothing of an ever-more-wild life. Now he wore the old
clothing again. For the past two years he had buried himself in stuffy
libraries, trying to pick up the strands of all he had forgotten. A girl
had shown him the way back. A girl on a holy island had shown him
that if he tried, he might get back to the things that had once mattered and find some solid ground in his quicksand life.

All the money that had once poured through Patrick's fingers
had been drunk, snorted, and pissed away. What had been left was
not much by those standards but it was still a tidy sum. On one
of those early days after Italy, after Perugia, when he was full of
new, raw self-loathing, he had made out a cheque, put it in an envelope, and addressed it to one of those organizations that seek to undo
the harm done by people like him. The royalties still poured in,

unwelcome evidence that the songs he wished he'd never sung were still poisoning minds somewhere. Once in a while, he would use those cheques to fill a hole in his bank account, to keep him alive while he haunted the libraries. More often, they languished in their envelopes in his sock drawer until he found another good cause to send them to.

From today on, to sever that link, he intended to survive on a paycheck. He needed a new definition of himself. He had found what looked like being a steady job, that rare, rare thing in archaeology, and although it wasn't at all the job he wanted, as full of flaws and dangers as the airship *Hindenburg,* he was desperate not to lose it. Paradigm Site Check was one of a new breed of companies, operating on the profit-making edge of archaeology; the uncompromising, disquieting moral monitor who had come from nowhere to live inside his head was quick to point out each conflict of interest, each convenient perversion of the truth that went with PSC's commercial approach.

But this first field job was one Patrick hadn't been expecting and didn't really want, dumped in his lap by another man's bad luck.

"I know it's a bit early, but it's a jolly good opportunity for you to show us what you can do," John Hescroft had told him on the phone early Saturday morning just as Patrick was running out of excuses for delaying his departure to Wales.

Patrick knew immediately what that really meant. There was no time to find anyone else and they didn't want to spend the money.

"I'll see you have a good team ready when you get there," promised Hescroft.

It was too soon, the perfect opportunity to fall flat on his face. He'd expected to be number two on a series of digs while he found his feet. Trench supervisor was about his mark, not director. He knew this was beyond his knowledge and his capabilities.

Now the road to Wytchlow approached and demanded his fuller attention. A signpost read WYTCHLOW. 1 MILE, and the road it pointed down was narrow and twisting between high, banked hedges, crossing a threshold in the landscape. The road seemed to lift the traveler from the plain into the edge of the hills and move him back forty years. The main road had been crowded by bungalows, petrol stations, and over-rustic pubs, but this was immediately a

simpler land of bright spring hedges and soft fields sprouting with
an early fuzz of green. A steep rise led up through a dark filter of
old woodland towards a clean skyline which showed no sign of the
promised village. Then, around a sharp bend, the road was abruptly
lined by stone cottages, and the outskirts of Wytchlow leapt out at
him before he was quite ready.

No sooner had he registered the houses than Patrick had to
step on his brake as a woman burst out into his path from a gate—a
woman who was looking back the way she'd come, oblivious to him,
clearly upset, stumbling over the kerb.

He slammed to a complete halt as she banged into his door. She
bounced off it and he stared horrified through his open window,
shaking with shock as she staggered to keep her balance. Behind
her, a middle-aged man in a tweed jacket stood blocking a narrow
gateway by a sign that said WYTCHLOW PRIMARY SCHOOL. His face
was puckered up in a picture of prim distaste and his hand was held
up, either warding the woman off or demanding silence. She turned,
as if aware of the car for the first time, and bent to look in so that
Patrick was staring straight into her eyes.

Scientists who understand nothing now say that there is an un-
ruly cluster of chemicals, led by serotonin, that fully explains love.
These chemicals, they maintain, are entirely responsible for all the
feelings that accompany that first rush—the inability of any other
person, however beautiful, to hold the slightest sexual interest for
you; the dizzy, soaring vertigo that grips the lower torso; the impossibility of looking for long in any other direction when that person
is close enough to see; and the fretting, jealous distress when they
are not—feelings whose complete, total intensity cannot be accessed
by memory when time has passed and the firestorm they create has
burnt out.

Scientists miss the point. They are listing the messengers, not
explaining the message. They describe the mathematics of attraction
as if there were callipers and rulers to measure that fire of love—the
spacing of the eyes, the proportions of the face, the chemistry of the
pheromones. That gets a little nearer the point, but only a little.
Where does it leave all the rest of it? The thrilling complexity of
a voice, so rich with promise you are astounded that others around
you can carry on with life while it is speaking, that they are not as

stunned into silence as you are by the wonder of it. Then there is the way that this suddenly met, world-altering person appears as a rich larder, a vast library, the best gallery ever collected together, so that you cannot wait to step inside and start a long, proud exploration of her.

Thus when Patrick looked into the eyes of the woman who had so unexpectedly collided with his car, he was instantly overwhelmed. A flash flood of surging, sickening, pure emotion swept through the dry watercourses of his soul. If this had been love at first sight, it could have been the delicious redemptive moment at which his stalled life restarted, but it was not. It was love at second sight, an impostor—the cruelest trick that a cruel life still had to play on him—and in that instant he was lured towards the rocks of a wreckers' coast by a false light.

How can you describe a face? We are conditioned from birth to be swayed between love and hate, between fear and joy, by tiny differences in faces, by the way the muscles pull the flesh over the bone beneath. Faces are one thing and then another and then immediately another, constantly transformed by the humanity going on behind them and constantly informed by character. It makes more sense to say that what Patrick saw so shockingly was that rare thing, a perfect double—as close as an identical twin—of the face of a girl now locked in his far past, the girl with whom he had fallen instantly and completely in love at the age of nineteen.

What he saw first were the eyes—large and dark in a pale face under declaratory commas of eyebrows that owed nothing to makeup. The rest of her face was all complex curves bringing his eye down to full lips—lips that were now parted in shock, showing pure white teeth. Her hair was entirely hidden, tucked up out of sight under a woolen hat. He stared at her aghast for no more than two seconds as her eyes seemed to widen, then he wound up the window as if it were a drawbridge and drove away to safety.

He went only a couple of hundred yards, far enough to get out of sight around the corner, then stopped on the edge of an expansive triangle of village green. He stopped to try to put this ambushing genie back in its bottle, but instead the genie just went on swelling in the fresh air.

It was not entirely true to say that this woman was Rachel's double. Someone in their thirties cannot look just like a nineteen-year-old. What this woman with the huge, shining eyes looked exactly like was the Rachel of an alternate future—the Rachel who *would* have been, had her future been in the hands of a kinder lover. What she did *not* look like was the Rachel he had hacked out of that beautiful, promising start like a bad sculptor reducing lustrous marble to dust and chippings—that furtive, haunted, shadow Rachel who now seemed to be the sole, awful creation of his life.

That didn't help.

# CHAPTER THREE

WYTCHLOW SPLAYED around its central village green like a cleft stick. The road into the village split and ran down two sides of the triangular swathe, flanked by rows of low stone houses, some thatched, some roofed with rough stone tiles. A whitewashed pub was the only building to break the run of warm Cotswold stone. On the third side of the triangle, beyond the war memorial, a field stretched up a gentle slope to an array of old barns along the skyline. The village had a grassy heart. The two roads ran off the far corners of the triangle, curving down past a church on the right and heading into higher ground on the left. They looked like lanes to nowhere in particular, old lanes for feet and horses, not roads for tyres.

It was next to the war memorial that Patrick stopped to get his breath back. Unconsciously, he did what he had always done in times of trouble: He sought information to displace emotion. From childhood, words in books had been a refuge for him, opening safe rooms in his head. Now, his eyes drained the war memorial of information. Like every other village war memorial across the country, its list of dead from the Great War was ten times the length of the toll for the Second World War. The Flanders mud had taken thirty-six men from tiny Wytchlow, and the names pointed to the destruction of whole tribes of brothers or cousins. His eyes came to the bottom of the list. There were just four for World War II. Three men and one woman. The woman he had just seen began to push her way back into his head and he concentrated fiercely on the carved names to drive her image away. A woman killed? Was she in the armed forces? Was she a villager, the victim of a stray shot or some hit-and-run Heinkel? He wished the stone said more, and thought that this quiet place in the clear air above the plain didn't seem a stage for war.

He was wrong. Thirteen hundred years before, this had been a battle zone and thirteen centuries are no great stretch of time, just fifteen old men's lives laid end to end.

Time for hiding ran out and the clock forced him to drive on with part of his brain still locked into a baffled, looped replay of the sight of that woman's face, a moment of carnage. The left-hand lane led to the field at the far end of the village that was his destination; a gate gave access to a tight little square of rough grass, flanked on two sides by regimented ranks of foreign fir trees. The site looked far too small for the six houses that were planned for it, he thought vaguely. Undermined by what had just happened and timid at the prospect of what he now had to do, he drove into the field and realised with a sinking heart that he was going to have to stamp his authority on events right away. It looked as if some happy-go-lucky social event was just beginning. Tents were going up all over the place—garish polyester igloos being inexpertly erected across the field. Only one tent was where it was meant to be, a tattered, square marquee of patched camouflaged canvas, standing beside a pair of mobile lavatories like blue plastic sentry boxes along the edge of the firs. English reserve kept each of the campers well away from their neighbours, so that the tents were spread in a random straggle across the whole area of the grass, cars parked here and there amongst them.

The extreme irritation brought on by this sight helped to cata-pult Patrick out of his disabling ferment. He parked close to the fence and got out, clutching his clipboard.

"Stop!" he shouted. "Leave your tents, everybody. Come over here, please!"

The person nearest to him glanced up for no more than a mo-ment, then went back to the business of tightening his guy ropes. He was a crop-haired man with the battered air of a Spanish monk from some impoverished order, accustomed to finding the dust of woodworm on his bread and water. His forehead angled back like that of an Easter Island statue, and the lenses of his round glasses filled and sealed his gaunt eye sockets.

"A moment," he said in a burred growl, "I'll just be finishing this."

"Oh, no, you will not," said Patrick, almost as vehemently as he felt, "because if you do, you'll just have to take it straight down again and you wouldn't like that, would you?"

"I wouldn't at all," said the man, "but aren't you just the angry one today."

The others were straggling towards him across the grass, a bunch of encrypted strangers to be motivated only by him. He knew he would have to meet them and decode enough of them to make this human machine work; the thought of the effort ahead filled him with despair.

Their expressions showed a vague, trusting friendliness; they were a motley crew—a flock searching for a leader. Patrick searched their faces as they approached, looking hopefully for at least one who might be the lieutenant he badly needed, the one who would fill the gaps when knowledge or confidence failed him.

The only one among them who gave any impression that he had ever been in a field such as this before was a big, tough man of sixty or more, his grey hair bunched back in a ponytail. His black T-shirt said TERMINATE WITH EXTREME PREJUDICE across his barrel chest and his powerful arms were covered in tattoos. He walked across the field with an amused grin on his face and when Patrick caught his eye, he gave a conspiratorial wink. It was a straw and Patrick grasped at it.

The group formed a loose crescent around him and, to test his impression, Patrick looked at the tattooed man and said, "Have you put your tent up yet?"

He laughed and said, "Not me, mate."

"OK," said Patrick to the group. "Listen to me. I'm Patrick Kane. I'm the director of this dig and the first thing I have to tell you is that you're all going to have to take your tents down again."

"And why would that be?" asked the Easter Island monk. Patrick could not be quite sure whether his accent had once been Irish.

"Because you've put them up right over the top of the archaeology," replied Patrick evenly, and then the moment with the woman's face elbowed its way to the front of the queue in his brain so that he forgot what he meant to say next and had to stop short and glare hopelessly at them. As an accidental piece of theatre this worked well: All shuffled uncomfortably.

"We need the tents close together along the edge of the field—over there, by the catering tent. Put your cars next to mine at the far end."

"Couldn't we just dig in between them?" asked a small woman whose blonde hair was much younger than her face. She had bright red lipstick distributed over her teeth as well as her lips. "It's taken me absolutely ages to put my tent up. I've never camped before, you see." Her polished, gilt-buckled shoes and white trousers made this explanation unnecessary, and there was a loud guffaw from the tattooed man.

"What's your name?" asked Patrick, looking down at the list on his clipboard, the list that so far meant nothing to him. He wished it could stay that way. Strangers were best left as strangers.

"Gaye," she replied. "With an 'e.' "

"All right, Gaye with an 'e,' " said Patrick. "The answer to your question is no, we can't dig around your tent. You need to move it as soon as I've finished talking so that we can start to mark out the trenches. Understood?"

She looked doubtfully towards the field's edge. "If that's the catering tent," she said, "it's awfully close to the toilets. I think Health and Safety might have something to say about that."

Patrick ignored this comment. "OK," he continued, "as I say, I'm Patrick Kane, and I've only been working for PSC for a very short time so I'm sorry if there are some of you I *should* know and don't. Can I just ask which of you are PSC employees?"

Not a hand was raised.

*I don't believe this,* Patrick thought, although it was exactly as he had feared.

"So," he persisted, "what are you all?"

They looked back at him uncomprehending.

"Hands up if you're a volunteer," he said, and it seemed to him that every hand was raised.

Just to check, he took a deep breath and asked: "Are there *any* professional archaeologists here at all?"

The tattooed man lifted a hand the size of a leg of pork. "I am," he said. "Sort of."

Patrick, feeling suddenly glad for very small mercies, found himself lacking the energy to discover what "sort of" meant.

"Sorry, I don't know your name," he said.

"No need to be sorry, Pat," said the man. "Be a bit fucking amazing if you did, all things considered, being as how we never met before."

The blonde woman clucked at the obscenity and looked indignant.

"So what is it? And by the way, I'm Patrick, not Pat."

"That's all right, Pat. I'm Dozer. That's Dozer, not Sebastian." He was rolling a cigarette with one hand.

Patrick felt the exchange slipping away from him. "You mean your real name's Sebastian?"

"No, mate. That's what I just said. It's *not* Sebastian. You ain't listening."

He lit his cigarette.

"That's another thing," said Patrick. "There's to be absolutely no smoking near any of the trenches once we've started."

"I know that," said Dozer.

"Why is that?" said the monk. "We are in the open air, after all."

"What's your name?" asked Patrick, and the man reacted as if it were a prelude to some sort of punishment.

"Aidan," he said, uneasily. "I was only asking."

"Tobacco ash mucks up carbon dating. If there are finds, we need to know how old they are," said Patrick. "If you need to smoke, go downwind, the far side of the cars or right out of the field."

"Oh, no, I don't touch the stuff myself," said Aidan. "I was only wondering. . . ."

"Is there anybody else who's *not* a volunteer?"

A pallid scarecrow of a boy in a sun hat put up his hand. "I'm a student," he said. "Maxwell Muir. I'm doing this for my course. Fieldwork experience."

"Right."

"If we find things," the boy went on, "do we get to keep any of them?"

"How long have you been doing your course?" asked Patrick grimly.

"Since October," said the boy with apparent pride.

"Then you shouldn't need to ask that. Now, the rest of you," he said. "How many of you have worked on a dig before?"

Only three.

"Let's see." He looked at his clipboard in search of anything that might give hope. "Are we all here? I'll just do a head count." It came out at sixteen. There were eighteen names on his list. He ran through it and they all answered except for R. Redhead and C. D. Corcoran.

He looked around at his staff again and found himself exhausted by the unfamiliar experience of speaking more than one sentence to more than one person.

"I'm afraid I only discovered two days ago that I was running this dig. A colleague of mine at PSC named Toby Dixon was meant to be dig director, but he had an accident."

"Fibia, tibia, and lacerations," said a fat, bald man in the front of the group.

"I beg your pardon?"

"He's my next-door neighbour, Toby is. Fell through my conservatory."

"There's a coincidence."

"How do you mean?"

"You living next to him and being interested in archaeology, too."

"Can't say I am," said the man.

"Why are you here, then?"

"Your boss. What's his name?"

"Hescroft. John Hescroft."

"Yeah, him. He said he'd get my conservatory fixed if I came and helped."

Patrick strode away towards the far hedge, boiling with rage and reaching for his mobile phone. Halfway there he looked round to see most of them straggling after him and shooed them back like a herd of bullocks. A cloud moved across the sun and the temperature dropped sharply. He stopped at the corner of the field where a signal showing barely adequate reception briefly flickered on the phone's screen.

To the north, beyond the hedge, a field of short grass rose gradually to wrap itself over a rounded hill. On the skyline, a rock stuck up out of the grass, and then the cloud shadow swept by and in the sunlight Patrick saw it was not a rock at all, but a man, sitting stock-still and hunched up, arms pulling his knees to his chest, staring down at them. Patrick stared back but the man made not the slightest sign of movement or acknowledgment.

BEFORE THE TREES WERE HERE, BEFORE THE VILLAGE GREW, BEFORE THE WOODEN HOUSES TURNED TO STONE, THERE WAS ALWAYS A WATCHER ON THIS HILL, FOR THIS WAS A FRONTIER.

The phone rang at the other end and Patrick was put through immediately to Hescroft, who was effusively friendly.

"Patrick! Good to hear your voice. How are things going out there? I'm planning to pop out and see you. Few things I want to discuss."

"Such as?"

"TV," said Hescroft, putting an undertone of disconcertingly sexual pleasure into the two syllables. "Chance of a series, if we play our cards right. Do us no end of good. They're looking for the right sort of digs. Producer chappy saw your photo, thought you might be good material."

Patrick found himself mildly disgusted.

"I've got enough on my plate with this dig for now," he told Hescroft. "I'm a bit concerned."

"I don't think we need get too stirred up about this one, old boy. Pretty slender evidence to mount a Phase Two. Just do the bare minimum and let the poor bloody builder get on with it."

*That's it,* thought Patrick grimly. *That's all I need. A bent contract.*
Hescroft had no interest in finding anything here that would stop
the developer from putting up his houses. Was he doing someone a
favor? Probably. Patrick hadn't known John Hescroft long, but it
was long enough to know that he was more businessman than archaeologist, whatever his resume might say. The outcome of a dig
like this could make a huge difference to the value of a building site.

"Is that why I've got such a crap team?" he asked.

"What's the problem, old boy?" Hescroft sounded shocked.

"The problem is that there's nobody here who knows one end of a
trowel from the other."

"Surely not."

"They're all volunteers."

"Archaeology lives off volunteers."

"Not when a dig's being done by a professional unit on a paying
contract."

Hescroft retreated. "They're not *all* volunteers. You've got Phil
there, haven't you?"

"Phil?"

"Big man. Ponytail, tattoos."

"He said he was called Dozer."

"That's him."

"What about him?"

"Done thousands of digs. Knows it backwards."

"Qualified?"

"School of *life,* old boy. You can't beat experience."

"Are we paying him?"

"Sort of."

That phrase again. "What does *that* mean?"

"I'm getting his car fixed for him." Hescroft sounded uncomfortable. "It's tax efficient."

*Cheapskate* would have been a better choice of word.

"Look, John," said Patrick, "how am I meant to do the recording? How do I do finds? How do I look after the trenches? I'm going
to have to be everywhere at once. I can't leave this lot to themselves.
If they found Pompeii they'd dig right through it and out the other
side if there was no one there to stop them."

"Well, hold on there a minute. You've got CD."

"Seedy?"

"C. D. Corcoran."

"He's not here yet. Who is he?"

"Best in the business. One of these smart young Yanks doing his doctorate."

"So why's he not Dig Director?"

"You're staff, old boy. CD's contract. I told you, he's doing his doctorate. You'll like him. He takes this incredible bird with him everywhere."

"Bird?" said Patrick, thinking the last thing he needed was another hanger-on. He felt more threatened than relieved by the imminent arrival of a hotshot American, but an American with a girl in tow seemed somehow even worse. In the last two years nothing had hurt more than the sight of loving couples. Nothing, that is, except loving couples with small sons.

Small sons, old enough to walk, young enough to hold hands, pierced Patrick through and through. They didn't have to be black-haired, blue-eyed images of David. The way they walked, the way they *trusted* was enough to remind him instantly of what he had done.

He missed most of what Hescroft said next.

". . . black bird. Great fun."

Patrick was no longer listening. He was staring at the entrance to the field, at the man on the huge motorcycle now threading his way through the ruts and at Hescroft's black bird, clinging tightly to the rider's shoulder.

# CHAPTER FOUR

B Y THE TIME PATRICK REACHED
them, a knot of people had
already converged around CD
and the bird. The bike, a
Harley-Davidson, was resting
on its stand and a puzzling dialogue was
under way between CD and Dozer, on whose
shoulder the bird was now standing, cocking
its head at each of them in turn.

Dozer was pumping the younger man's
hand.

" 'Ow long's it been, CD?" he said.
"Where was it last, up the Orinoco?"

CD, a slight figure with thick glasses
and a mop of sandy hair disheveled by the
removal of his crash helmet, grinned and
replied in a soft accent, "That's right, you
old rascal. The Aztec treasure."

"Yeah, you owe me one for that," said
Dozer, and looked round at the rest. "Pulled
him out of the jaws of a crocodile, I did."

"Well, yes," agreed CD, "but wait until I tell them how you got me *into* its jaws in the first place."

"Can we save all this for later?" interrupted Patrick, before Dozer could protest. He held out a hand to the American, but the bird hopped onto it instead, digging its feet in painfully as it did so.

CD focused mild eyes, magnified by the thick lenses, on Patrick and nodded.

"You're not Toby," he said. "How is it that I leap straight to the conclusion that the admirable, reliable Mr. Hescroft has forgotten to tell me something?"

"I'm here instead of Toby. I'm Patrick Kane." A momentary flicker in CD's eyes alarmed him. "Can you persuade your crow to go somewhere else?"

"No, no, no, no, no," said CD, firmly. "Lesson one: Never call a raven a crow, they are very easily upset." He looked at the bird. "Edgar," he said. "Come." The bird leapt and flapped straight onto his shoulder.

"That's not a raven. Or a crow. It's a jackdaw," objected Gaye.

"I call him Edgar," said CD, "therefore he's a raven."

"What does that mean?" said Gaye, baffled.

"Edgar Allan Poe," contributed a smiling elderly man, whose hair was a mixture of grey and ginger. " 'Quoth the raven "nevermore." ' Yes?"

Gaye still looked baffled.

"Can we go and talk?" Patrick said to CD, feeling irritation rising again. "There's a lot to do and nobody much to do it."

CD blinked amiably. "That's cool," he said, and shared a sideways glance with Dozer.

"Just say the word, Pat," said Dozer, "I'll get stuck in. Want me to get these tents sorted?"

"Yes, that would help." The words "It's Patrick, not Pat" formed and died on his lips. "Come on, CD."

They walked down the edge of the trees until they were alone. Patrick knew CD was looking at him curiously.

"I've seen you before," said the American.

"Around Oxford?" suggested Patrick, though he knew his recent seclusion made that most unlikely.

Then CD stopped, snapped his fingers, and said far too loudly,

"Paddy Kane, you're fucking Paddy Kane! Sod this *Patrick* stuff. God almighty, Paddy Kane. My hero. Where's the hair gone?"

"Be quiet," said Patrick in a fury. "Keep your voice down. I am *not*." He couldn't even bring himself to say the name of who he was not.

"Don't kid me," said CD. "I know who you are."

"I'm doing a job here, like you are, just that."

CD took in the expression on the other man's face.

"OK, Patrick, if you say so," he said, but he went on staring. Then he shrugged. "So, tell me what we have here. No—I think I can guess. A bunch of amateurs?"

"Barely even that," said Patrick, suddenly anxious to smooth over and leave behind what had just happened.

"No digger, no site hut, not enough shovels, and no chance of doing it properly. That's Hescroft. Another contract stolen by undercutting the outfits with proper professional standards and the two of us desperate enough to take the job and compromise our immortal archaeological souls."

That forced a wry grimace out of Patrick. "Why are *you* so desperate?" he said, and in this man, for the first time in an age, he sensed the possibility of a real friend.

"Me? Shit. I have this loan to pay off. Do you have any idea how much I owe the U.S. Treasury for my studies? More than most third-world countries. It's OK as long as I go on studying. I only have to pay it back when I get a *real* job."

"So the loan just gets bigger and bigger?"

"I'm depending on that. One day it will get so big they'll decide it's a computer error."

"We'd better talk about the dig."

"Sure." CD looked at him curiously. "Been dropped in it, right? I guess you haven't done too much yet?"

It could have been a challenging moment with a different man, but Patrick found himself letting the mask slip with a vast sense of relief.

"No. I was expecting a gentler start."

"OK, buddy. Don't sweat it. I can help here."

"You should be the director, not me."

CD laughed. "Hey, you've missed the point. You're staff. Hescroft has to pay you anyway. I'm freelance. He doesn't want to shell out Dig Director dollars to me. I'm here for the beer money."

They talked until they saw the tents had been put in the proper places, CD skirting carefully around anything personal, then Dozer walked over to them. CD welcomed him with a grin.

"Three of us against the world, right, Dozer? All for one and one for one."

"Yeah, just like that time in Siberia, mate. 'Ere, Pat, who's doing grub?"

Patrick looked at the clipboard. "It doesn't say. All it says here is they've made arrangements."

"I hope so," said CD. "You have no idea how much free food matters to a starving archaeologist."

"Yeah, well, it's all in there." Dozer nodded at the marquee. "Boxes of this and that. Smells a bit rancid, though. There's gas rings there an' all. Just needs somebody to put it together. Anyway, there's something else you've got to worry about first."

"What's that?"

"Trowels. Absence of."

"How would it be if I give them the standard trowel lecture?" suggested CD, and Patrick agreed gratefully without the faintest idea what the standard trowel lecture was.

CD gathered them all round on the grass.

"OK, listen up," he said. "In a minute the director will be briefing you about the dig itself and what we're all doing here, but first it falls to me as his humble number two to do a bit of the basic stuff. So just to kick off, hands up, those of you who have a trowel with you?"

What they produced ranged from huge pointing trowels, still encrusted with old mortar, to tiny curved things of bent, coloured tin intended for brief flirtations with window boxes. CD held up his own.

"This is the only trowel to have. It's a four-inch WHS pointing trowel and nothing else will do."

"And why do you say that exactly?" asked Aidan the Easter Island monk, scowling. "It looks just the same as mine."

"Because it has a forged blade and handle," replied CD equably.

"I'm not in this for life," argued Aidan. "Eighteen quid they wanted for one of those. I got mine for three pounds ninety-nine."

CD turned to Patrick. "Will you excuse me if I get a little

metaphysical?" he asked. Patrick, who, thinking himself safe, had been abruptly engulfed by a fresh wave of violently mixed, indefinable love-sorrow, nodded.

"This is not just a trowel. It is an extension of your arm and your arm is an extension of your brain. When you are troweling in the earth, this is what tells you when you've found the finest of fine differences in the soil. The blade and the handle are all of a piece. Every little bit of information this blade meets goes on the fast track to intellectual processing. This is a blade that cannot lie."

"Oh, listen to that, will you?" remarked Aidan. "And me thinking it was just a thing for shoveling dirt."

"Soil, please," corrected CD, "never dirt. We are, after all, archaeologists. Soil has a million subtle varieties. It has a thousand colours. It tells us everything we need to know. You will form a deep bond with the soil. You will learn to taste it. Literally. When you find a piece of something that could be a pot or could be a rock, you will learn to put it in your mouth and see how it tastes on your tongue and on your teeth, because the mouth is the most sensitive organ."

"That's disgusting," said the blonde with the lipstick. "I shan't be doing that."

"Oh, you will, you will," promised CD.

A frightened-looking elderly woman at the back held up a very shiny trowel. "I say," she said, "mine's a WHS, but it's eight inches, not four. Will that do?" Her voice sounded as if she might cry if CD said no.

"Well, now, let's see," he said. "In many parts of the world that would do very well indeed. Here, I'm sorry to tell you, it is very definitely far too big."

Aidan, a man who clearly needed to test the truth of any proposition, wanted to argue.

"How could that be?" he demanded. "Surely you're not going to be telling us that the soil is so different here from elsewhere? Why would a big trowel do for one place and not for another?"

CD beamed at him benevolently. "Ain't about the soil, baby. Most parts of the world when you're poking about in a hole, you need something long enough to fend off the things that come out and *bite*." He opened a rucksack and started to bring out trowels. "I guess I've got enough here to go round. Five pounds to hire one. Fifteen to buy."

"They're old," criticized Aidan. "That's daylight robbery."

"Yup," agreed CD. "I have a Harley-Davidson and a hungry raven to support. Gather round afterwards and shower money into my hands—but first we have to talk about tools and sweat."

He paused and looked around him. "Archaeology is glorified gardening. Today we will be deturfing. That is unglorified gardening. You will hate deturfing. You will be using spades, shovels, and this kind of pick-thing you Brits call a mattock to get rid of the topsoil and—"

Aidan raised a hand and CD said, "Yes, what is it now?" with a comical sigh.

"I just wanted to ask, isn't it a bit easy to be breaking things with a mattock?"

"That just about hits it on the head," said CD. "It is extremely easy, as you say, to break things with a mattock. You might even say that breaking things is the whole point of a mattock, the core of its being, its *raison d'être*."

"But we don't want to be breaking things, not the sort of things we might be finding, surely we don't?"

"OK, time for one of CD's blinding insights, folks. Pay close attention here." He cleared his throat. "Almost everything that's in the ground's been broken for a couple of thousand years already. Hit it with a mattock and you don't do it much more harm than history already did. Break nothing, find nothing. Get good with your mattock and know when to reach for your trowel. Anyway, it's only modern Roman crap we're looking for here. I'm an Anglo-Saxon man myself, stains in the soil. This Roman stuff's all rubble, far too easy, so at this point I'll hand over to the director so he can tell you exactly why we're here."

There was a long moment of expectant silence before Patrick, who was back in that earlier whirlpool again, realized they were all looking at him. The awful miracle of the woman's face had shaken banned memories awake, memories of Rachel when she loved him, memories that poured petrol on the sparks of guilt.

"Um, this is a Phase Two investigation," he said. "There's a developer called . . ." he looked at his clipboard ". . . Roger Little who has applied for planning permission to build houses on this site. There was some historical evidence of tesserae being picked up in the plough-soil here." He saw that most of their faces were blank. "That's pieces of Roman flooring," he added. "Mosaic flooring? OK? They've done a geophysical survey and there is some evidence of a rectangular structure in the middle of the field." He glanced at his notes again, seeking refuge from this strangely unfamiliar, pompous, public voice of his.

"The field looks relatively unploughed compared to the surrounding fields, possibly because it seems to have been used as a village animal pound for many years, centuries maybe. That's a holding pen for flocks passing on their way to market. Before the construction goes ahead, we have to find out whether there is anything important here. You can all have an hour off to get sorted out while we mark out the trenches, then we'll get started. I'll tell you about all the procedures as we go along, but maybe the three of you who've done some digging can tell the others a bit about it while you're waiting."

He took CD and Dozer into the field with tapes, pegs, and a mallet, and they marked out the first trench from the information in the geophysical printout. While the other two were taping it, he walked away to the far corner to establish the line of the second trench and when he looked up, he saw the watching man was up there on the hillside again.

BEYOND THE RANGE OF MEMORY, ALL THAT SHORT TIME AGO, THE EASTERN SENTRIES OF THE HWICCA LOOKED DOWN FROM THEIR FRONT LINE AT THE VALLEY OF THE THAMES. THE RIVER WAS A FUNNEL THROUGH WHICH SUCCESSIVE WAVES OF MIGRANTS HAD STREAMED INTO THIS LAND, SPILLING OUT ACROSS THE NARROW SEA FROM THE OVERCROWDED HOMELANDS OF NORTHERN EUROPE, USING THE RIVER AS THEIR HIGHWAY INTO THE HEART OF THE LAND. DOWN THERE WERE THE GEWISSE, THAT WAS WHAT THEY CALLED THEMSELVES. "THE TRUSTWORTHY." ANY HWICCA WOULD TELL YOU IT WOULD BE UNWISE TO RELY ON THAT NAME.

As Patrick bent to push in a peg, thinking about names, about Patrick and Pat and Paddy, his keen ears caught a shred of words passing between CD and Dozer—familiar words, sung, not spoken, familiar hated words:

> . . . *Man's intended for deceiving, that's why Adam met the snake.*

He looked up at once, indignantly, and caught Dozer looking towards him, and CD guiltily looking away. Guessing what had just passed between them, he felt a hot wash of betrayal.

When they came over to join him, his first instinct was to make an excuse and walk away. But he knew it was a moment of crisis, a moment that had to be faced.

"Hey, Pat," said Dozer, "I thought—"

"No, me first," Patrick said. "I heard what you said and I can guess the rest. I want you to know that I just don't need it, right? You may think it's funny or something, but it's not."

"I don't think it's funny," said Dozer, "and it ain't anything to be ashamed of, either, as far as I'm concerned, chum. You were one of the greats."

"The punk Beethoven," added CD, thinking it was praise. "You wrote the words that made us all think."

"No, no. Not that song."

"Not just that song," said Dozer. "All of 'em. I'm no punk. I'm heavy metal, but we needed you. Bloody breath of fresh air, you were."

"You know nothing about it," said Patrick. "It's buried. It's in the past and I've got the right to leave it there. It's got nothing to do with me now. I'm asking you both to keep it to yourselves."

*Calm down,* he told himself. *You're handling this badly. First time out in public and you're blowing it.*

Dozer said, "All right, Pat, whatever you say," and Patrick was, for the first time, profoundly grateful he'd said Pat, fearing he might have said Paddy. Then the big man reached out a hand and squeezed his shoulder briefly, and Patrick almost cried.

"Finish off this one, would you?" he said, looking at the trench and struggling to keep his voice level. "I'll go and see about the cooking."

It was out of the frying pan into the fire. As he walked down towards the food tent, feeling their eyes burning on his back, he could see there was someone inside. The gas cylinders had been moved and he heard a voice singing a snatch from *The Marriage of Figaro*. It should have come as no great surprise, because of the nature of Fate, that when he went in through the flap, he found himself face-to-face, for the second time that morning, with that scalding reminder of his past, the woman from the road.

# CHAPTER FIVE

PADDY KANE HAD WRITTEN "Wedding Vows" in a drunken rage and almost immediately wished he hadn't. It became the single song for which his bawdy, violent band was best remembered, and the main marker of the breakdown of his life.

The story of how he wrote it became a rock legend in its own right—told first by a devastated Rachel to her caring but wholly indiscreet brother, then by him to a girl he was trying to impress at a party (as a useful way of dropping the fact that he was Paddy Kane's brother-in-law), and then by her straight to the *Sun* for a payment of two hundred pounds. It was out on the streets within eighteen hours of the writing, and this was the way it happened.

After the Frankfurt concert, Paddy Kane had been delivered home by a Colonic Music limo straight from Heathrow, following a flight that had tested the patience of the British Airways cabin staff. He had slammed in through the front door of the Georgian house on the banks of the Thames near Marlow, furious that the crude nude figure he had sprayed on the front wall had been covered up in his absence. Rachel was too scared of him by this time to have it removed but, unable to stand the sight of it, she had compromised by concealing it behind a trellis and a climbing rose.

Benny was the only one who ever took Paddy home. The driver was a trusted Colonic Music retainer who could be relied on not to give away the story of the Marlow house, the house that didn't exist, with the wife and son who didn't exist either. Benny was Paddy's confidant, the man who'd seen firsthand what two years in the clutches of the mandarins of punk had done to him.

"What's up, Pat?" Benny said from the front seat on the way back, because he alone in the company never called him Paddy. "Bad gig?"

The boy inside the man in the backseat wanted to cry.

"I'm fucked," the punk star said, and Benny knew what he meant. They'd dropped Vic Bogart off first and Benny had heard every word Colonic's boss had said, every bit of carefully polished pressure to push the image to extremes.

"Paddy boy," Bogart had said. "There's a sex thing in the way."

"What?" His voice was slurred.

"The rags are sniffing round. Why no pussy? they're asking. We got to slide a little skirt into the picture, kid."

"There's . . . there's Rache."

"Yeah, there's your contract, too. I'm talking glamour here, not childhood-sweetheart shit."

When Bogart got out, Benny drove a hundred yards, then took a risk.

"You don't have to do what he says."

All he got was a snort from the backseat.

"Tell him to stuff himself," Benny persisted. "Make that little girl of yours happy."

Benny knew he was wasting his breath. He'd heard the execs discussing Rachel when their star wasn't there. Living death, was the opinion; a sweet suburban wifey, the last thing Colonic wanted.

"What is it stops you, Pat?" he asked. "Onstage you're a demon. Then you come off and you let these old men push you around."

"Bloody don't."

"Yeah, you do. You got to learn to handle them."

There was a word from the back that could have been "Can't," then silence. Benny was worried because he knew the plan. Paddy Kane was on the ragged edge. Booze him up, hand out the powder, and Paddy'd blow away Rachel all by himself. When she'd gone, then maybe the manner of her going could be a story, just maybe—if it helped sell records.

Benny didn't want that. He'd liked young Pat Kane from the moment he met him, more than any of the already degraded young men who regularly passed through his backseat. Kane was intelligent, Kane was nice, Kane cared. Before they pushed the poison into him, Pat was someone you'd go a long way for. Now even Benny recognised he was possibly beyond saving, and Benny, well-paid, trusted Benny, was on the verge of quitting himself.

"You don't have to do it," he said again as he held the limo door open and got out the bags. "I hear what they're saying when you're not there. You're worth a cartload of money to them. Tell them to stuff themselves and they'll have to listen."

It was too late. Paddy had seen the trellis and the climbing rose and he'd lurched in through the front door, ready to direct his vengeance in an entirely inappropriate direction. Benny, unhappy, had to run for his next pickup.

The house into which Paddy staggered was silent, and that wound him up even tighter. After leaving the harsh house in which his dominating father had not tried to provide any of the warmth that would have made up for being a single parent, Pat had little chance to grow up and find his footing before the bewildering arrival of fame and adulation. In that short interval, when he'd been a student and she'd been starting teacher training, he had met Rachel at a dance. He was enjoying being a student, enjoying professors who took him for at least a partial adult, enjoying treading a path he had chosen for himself. Archaeology had touched something unsuspected in him.

They'd both been far too young, two nineteen-year-olds who had married a year later in a vague haze of sweetness with circlets of daisies in their hair.

Then the worst thing happened. In his final year, playing in his student band at a town pub, a scout had heard Patrick sing and heard the lyrics he'd written and had offered him a view of the world from a devil's high place. That wasn't all. The scout had seen the way he'd looked and the way the girls in the pub had looked back at him and the effortless command he'd had over them. When Pat moved, every female eye followed.

Pat had graduated with a record contract already signed and no fears about the future when he should have been filled with fear.

That was when the money-men of Colonic Music had started thinking about the savage end of rock. They'd seen how Pat's talent for words could be tuned to a new cutting edge. That was where the money was. They started to channel him in their direction, and his slender reserves of wisdom and experience had not been enough to keep him straight. His music had changed to a harsher post-punk beat. Every big cheque made it harder to say they were wrong. Rachel's invisibility had been an early, arbitrary part of the deal, poorly thought through—a madness foisted on him that became madder still when David was born. There was still plenty of Pat left to love David, and Rachel kept praying he would draw a line. When that seemed increasingly unlikely, she put her efforts into making a nest for their son; the gulf between Pat and Rachel grew daily wider.

When Benny dropped him off in his wild, sleepless, fueled-up state he had no idea that it was Monday and that, on Mondays, Rachel helped out at David's kindergarten. When shouting failed to produce any sign of her, he took a thick black felt-tip pen and began to write all across the white sweep of the kitchen wall. What he wrote was the first and final draft of "Wedding Vows."

An hour later, as the context of the house began to assert itself and the alcohol loosened its hold, it started to dawn on him that this might be a mistake. Finding a pot of white paint in the garage, he covered the wall and his clothes in a messy coat of obliterating emulsion.

When Rachel and David came home at lunchtime, he was somewhere deep inside himself, quiet and perhaps even penitent. Rachel tried to question him about the fresh paint but he wouldn't reply. She took this as only a small variation on his normal behaviour after a big gig, and left him alone while David sat on his knee for much of the afternoon, content to be there even when his father fell asleep with his arms round him. Rachel put David to bed and later, when she'd cooked supper, woke Paddy as one might approach an unexploded bomb.

It was halfway through a silent meal that she looked past his shadowed, staring eyes and saw dark shapes developing through the drying paint on the wall behind, the treacherous felt-tip lyrics shrugging off Paddy's attempt at obliteration. She read them over his shoulder with growing anguish while he stared at her, puzzled by her expression. When finally her face crumpled and he turned round to find a reason, he had no memory at all of writing the words that were branded on the wall.

> *A wife is there for leaving. Marriage vows are made to break.*
> *Man's intended for deceiving, that's why Adam met the snake.*
> *Adultery's for adults—faithfulness for fools.*
> *Monogamy's monotonous, even rulers break the rules.*
> *You can tell the truth to lovers but it's better when you lie.*
> *A puppy's just for Christmas, then you leave it out to* DIE.

Rachel's brother called in on his way to a party that evening, found his sister distraught and Paddy asleep, and copied the words down when Rachel wasn't looking, thinking—but not daring to say—that they were quite good. The girl at the party took them out of his pocket when he was asleep in her bed later that night. The newspaper printed every word of it. The band's keyboard player wrote the music the very next morning and Paddy walked in late to a rehearsal studio to find that his monster had taken living, breathing shape without any further help from him.

From that moment, Rachel lost her remaining faith that Paddy would one day be Pat again—the Pat she had met and loved with puppy-love the moment she'd first seen him. Neither of them understood that it was not just a matter of the band's success. It was not simply the increasingly jagged difference between Paddy's chaotic, adored life on the road and Pat's quiet life back home that was shredding the point where the two of them met. For a man like him, half-formed, a child is not just a blessing, it is also a huge shock. By the time their son was born and Rachel had won the battle to call him David, not Frodo, Pat knew how to change a diaper; he knew about helping with breathing during the contractions. He had even been

told by an uncle with unusual insight about the life-altering difference a child makes, a complete dependent who changes all your selfish priorities and makes a triangle out of a line. At the time, that had
seemed just words, strung together, with a meaning that did not
penetrate.

What he had not understood, what nobody told him, was the
heavy truth that came to sit, crushing his soul—the undeniable deep
awareness that he was mortal. David had come, and David, whom he
loved to distraction, had displaced him in the position of youngest of
his line. David's birth made it clear to him in the only real way it
could be made clear that he, himself, would one day die. Pat could
only hide from that truth, and the damage he did to Rachel in the
course of his hiding stripped the surviving fragments of joy out of
her so that what was left was no longer anything like the girl bride
with the daisies in her hair.

"Wedding Vows" was the theme to the destructive process by
which Pat transformed himself more and more into Paddy. It was so
much easier to be Paddy. Paddy was Pat with the brakes off, a man
with no need for responsibility, a man drawn to wild, fierce women,
not to sweet, quiet girls, and there was no shortage of wild, fierce
women following in the footsteps of a band like his. Paddy found he
was truly roused by women who could match him drink for drink,
drug for drug, who could laugh as loud and sleep as little—above all,
by women who reassured him that he could be someone else, a man
without a family, a man who was still immortal. Everything pushed
him further that way: Vic Bogart, his publicists, the nature of life on
the road with the band. The morals of a traveling man easily adopt a
blind freedom denied to the more sedentary. Paddy did not know
that there is a price for everything. It was only when the bill came,
the bill that was delivered to him on a sunny afternoon in Perugia,
that he recoiled. Then he abruptly left the band, cut his extravagant, dyed hair, abandoned his extravagant, dyed life, and became
Patrick—puritan, isolated Patrick—and tried to get back to his last
worthwhile point and do some growing up.

Until now, when he'd thought of Rachel he had thought of her as
she was at the end of their time together, not at the beginning. The
face-to-face encounter in the road in front of the Wytchlow school
had brought back the early Rachel, the lovely Rachel full of promise,
and uncapped the deep hole in his life. It was unbearable, and it

brought with it the thought of David, which was even worse than that, so he fought to put them both back in the darkness, out of sight.

In the transitional moment when he walked in through the flap of the catering tent and collided for the second time with the woman from the school, knocking a tray out of her hands so that slices of cheese fell all over the flattened grass around their feet, they both gave a little cry of shock. Hers was no more than a startled "whoops," but Patrick's was the disturbing groan of an anchor tearing from its bed far below the surface.

"Oh, sorry," she said, dropping to her knees and scooping up the cheese.

"I didn't know you were there," he said.

"Well, I was hoping you hadn't done it on purpose," she said, giving him a quick grin and brushing a slab of cheese with her hand. "It's only grass. I don't suppose it matters."

He stood there immobilized and tongue-tied.

"You can help me if you like," she said, looking up at him. "I don't want the boss to see me messing up the lunch before I've even got started. It *was* your fault, too, you know."

He knelt next to her and began to pick up the rough-cut slices of cheddar from around them. The surface of the cheese seemed as sticky as flypaper.

"I could pretend it's one of those herb cheeses," she said. "Do you think he'd believe it? I don't want to give myself away. I only told them I could do catering because I wanted to be on the dig. Have you met him yet?"

"Who?" said Patrick, lost in the sound of her voice.

"The boss."

"Oh, no. Well, yes, I'm him."

As he said the words, he found he didn't really believe them. He felt far too young and awkward.

"You're who?" she said, horrified.

"The . . . er, the dig director."

She scrambled to her feet with the tray. "Oh, God, that's not fair. I'm sorry, I didn't realise. You might have said something. You must think I'm really stupid. You don't look like a dig director."

"Oh. Oh, dear. Well, that's fine."

"I'm Bobby Redhead," she said, holding out a hand that touched double the normal number of nerve endings when he took it.

"Oh, right."

She looked at him strangely.

"And you are . . . ?"

"I'm fine."

"Good, I'm glad. But it was really your name I was after."

"Yes, of course. I'm, er . . . I'm Patrick," and he left out the Kane, which seemed too dangerous in combination.

"Look, don't pay any attention to what I said, I *can* do the catering, really."

He didn't care in the slightest whether she could or couldn't.

"I saw you earlier, didn't I?" he asked. "I was in my car. You were having a row with somebody at the school."

"Oh, was that you, too? I'm sorry. I was a bit upset."

Then Patrick knew that the huge moment in which they had stared into each other's faces had been an illusion, a one-way mirror. He had seen through to a ghost of someone else and she, perhaps, had not seen him at all.

A seeping chill of despair chased the thrill from his blood.

"You must think I'm really daft," she said, "first that and now this."

To distance himself, he tried to be professional.

"Have you got enough gas rings to do hot food in the evenings?" he asked, looking around to break the gravitational pull of those eyes. "The crew will need a hot meal at the end of the day."

"I thought I'd get it ready at home. Then I can bring it over and reheat it a bit."

"How far away is home?"

"You can see it from here." She reached past him and lifted the flap of the tent. "That's it, over there. Highbury Farm."

Patrick had to duck his head to see, and he could feel her breath on his cheek. She smelt of butter. Two fields away, a jumble of old buildings sat in a dip as if their thick stone walls had gradually pushed the ground down beneath them. A roof of lichened stone tiles branched and sprouted into dormers and cross-wings. Two barns formed the other edges of an open square, and while their walls were of the same gentle Cotswold stone, roofs of grey corrugated iron reinforced the message of the tractor in the yard. This was a working place.

"How much do you farm?"

"Not much—sixty acres."

"This wasn't your field, was it?"

Her tone changed sharply. "I wouldn't have sold it if it had been. The field went with the old wood and the estate. I didn't even know it was up for sale when Little wriggled in and bought it."

"You don't approve of this man Little, then?"

"I don't like Roger Little, I don't trust Roger Little, and I certainly don't approve of Roger Little, no. The very best thing that could happen to Wytchlow right now would be for us to find something so important that he couldn't build his damned houses at all."

"That doesn't happen too often, I'm afraid," said Patrick.

"We can but hope."

"Do you farm by yourself?"

"No, no. It's me and Joe."

Well, of course, there would be a Joe.

From outside the tent, a bass voice boomed, "Oy, Pat!"

Patrick ducked back out to daylight and safety. Dozer stood there jerking a thumb at a man standing talking to CD.

"Builder's 'ere," he said.

Roger Little was a huge man with a pugnacious jaw and a Birmingham accent who looked elsewhere when he talked as if he couldn't quite be bothered with you.

"You're not started yet, then?" were his first words.

"We've just marked out the trenches."

"Look, time is money, right? Your man, what's he called—Heskin? He said this wouldn't take long."

"That depends what we find. We're deturfing today and we'll see how—"

"By hand? You're taking the turf off *by hand*? For Christ's sake, I'll get a machine up here. Have it done in five minutes."

Normally, that would have been a welcome offer.

"No, thanks," said Patrick. "We can do it better by hand."

"Look at this lot." Little stared around him at the diggers who were sitting in the grass, gossiping. "They don't look like they've ever done a full day's work in their life."

CD, who had been standing there with the air of one who had heard all this before, laughed. "Appearances can be deceptive, Mr. Small."

"Little," said the builder.

"Whatever," said the American. His bird was perched on his shoulder, inspecting the builder with his head cocked to one side. "You're looking at the cream of British archaeology, here. You see Vera over there?" He pointed at the wispy woman with the eight-inch trowel. "She's a living legend. Found Tomb 218 in the Valley of the Kings. Dug it all by herself, shifted four hundred cubic metres of sand single-handed in eighteen days." He stepped closer to Little and lowered his voice. "She uses a trowel twice as big as any man I know. Then there's Dozer here. Former president of the UK Hell's Angels. I've seen him lift a two-hundred-pound sarsen stone with one hand."

"Pleased to meet you, Mr. Small," said Dozer, holding out a hand. Little turned to shake it, gave a gasp as his own hand disappeared completely inside it, and seemingly decided not to argue about his name.

"Well, why don't I get a digger up here anyway?" he said. "Then it's there to use if you want. I'll have a man for you any time you need to use it."

"We've got diggers," said CD. "Oh, I guess you mean a backhoe."

"I'll have a man for you any time you need to use it," said Little.

"Nah, just leave the keys. I'm trained," said Dozer.

"You sure?"

"Is the Pope a tap dancer?"

THE REMAINING TWO HOURS BEFORE LUNCH WERE HARD work. In that time they cut the edges of one trench and took the turf off half of it. The team rapidly divided into the stalwarts and the complainers, the latter led by Gaye, for whom nothing was ever right. She had some justification. The picks had splintery wooden handles, except for two new ones with plastic grips, which were much in demand. The spades had blunt blades which made tough work of slicing through grass roots, and out of ten wheelbarrows only two did not suffer from some combination of flat tyres, bent axles, and missing bolts.

Then there was Maxwell, the student.

Maxwell kept finding things. As every turf was hacked and

levered out to be barrowed safely out of the way of the trench, Maxwell, scarlet eruptions scattered across an otherwise chalky face, would kneel to scan the exposed surface as if the rim of the Holy Grail might well be poking through it. Work in the immediate vicinity would then have to stop while he pried a small piece of stone from the earth, rubbed it excitedly with his fingers and carried it off to show Patrick and CD and then, if he wasn't satisfied by their response, Dozer and anybody else who would listen to him. The first, second, and third times, they took the trouble to look at his find closely, explain that it was natural, and send him back to work with encouraging noises. The fourth time, CD held it up to the bird, which cocked its head, pecked at it, and chattered.

"What do you reckon, Edgar?" said CD. "Geology?"

Edgar hopped round through 180 degrees so that he faced backwards, lifted his tail, and excreted.

"Yup," said CD. "Thought so. Geology."

"What does that mean, 'geology'?" said Maxwell.

"Rock," said CD. " 'Archaeology' means things, 'geology' means rock."

The fifth time, CD took the proffered stone and, without even looking at it, hurled it over the hedge.

"That could have been important," protested Maxwell, aghast.

"Yup," said CD.

"You've thrown it away," pointed out Maxwell.

"Yup," said CD. "I guess we'll never know."

By the time they broke for lunch, CD had managed to establish a position with the others that Patrick deeply envied, an air of effortless expertise helped by humour. Dozer, too, had the attention and respect of the rest, but Patrick knew that he himself was far more of a mystery.

"Clear up your loose," shouted CD when Patrick called the lunch break.

"And what does that mean?" said Aidan, pushing his glasses firmly back into his eye sockets with one finger as he straightened up.

"Get rid of the loose earth. Put your tools on the ground, tip the wheelbarrows over to cover them up."

"Are we not coming straight back to them?" objected Aidan. "Why don't we leave them where they are?"

"OK," said CD wearily, "gather round for lesson two in CD's insights series."

They all came towards him.

He looked at them benevolently. "You do it because I say so, and I know more than you do," he said.

"Is that it?" demanded Aidan.

"Oh, you need reasons. You're a helluva man for the reasons, Aidan. OK, you're doing it to get into practice for when it matters, because if you get down to the exciting stuff and you leave the trench full of crap and it rains, then all you've got when you come back is mud, and we don't like mud because it washes the evidence all over the goddamn floor."

"So we put the barrows over the tools to keep them dry?"

"No, you put the barrows over the tools because if you step on a pick, I don't want to get sued."

They sat on the grass outside the catering tent, eating thick sandwiches of cheese and pickle. The other diggers looked exhausted by their morning's work and seemed too reticent to join CD, Patrick, and Dozer. Patrick knew he should be making the effort to get to know his crew, but he couldn't summon up the reserve of energy that would take.

Instead, he sat in his own reverie in the grass while CD and Dozer spun ever more apocryphal tales to each other of their imaginary exploits together around the world. He watched Bobby Redhead as she moved in and out of the tent, offering plates of sandwiches, baskets of apples, and jugs of orange juice to the diggers. An odd pang of jealousy hit him whenever she stopped to talk to any of them. She was still wearing her dark woolen cap and, in comparison, her cheeks seemed startlingly pale for a farmer's wife.

Gaye came over to him at a moment when he was miles away.

"You'll have to do something," she said, indignant. "We really can't be expected to put up with it. It's revolting."

"What is?"

"The wotsit. You know."

"No?"

"The . . . facilities. Those things." She pointed at the loos.

"What's wrong with them."

"Have you *been* in them?"

"Yes, why?"

"You can *see*."

"What can you see?"

"Everything. It's all just . . . well, *lying* there."

"That's how they work."

"It's repulsive."

"It's fine. They're full of special chemicals. They neutralise it all. It's perfectly healthy. You don't have to look."

CD put on a wolfish smile and Patrick suddenly knew that whatever he was going to say, it was going to make things worse.

"I like looking in them," he announced. "It's inspirational, it's ever-changing. The colours are fascinating. You wait until we have curry. Beef vindaloo is best. After that you get this rich sort of purple colour, and . . ."

Gaye had gone. She was replaced immediately by spotty Maxwell, who seemed equally indignant.

"I've been talking to the others," he said. "We all want to know when we're going to start *finding* things."

"Really?" said CD. "All of you? I thought there were some sensible people amongst you." Edgar hopped off his shoulder into the air and settled on Maxwell's head. Maxwell tried to bat the bird away, but he dug his claws into the boy's scalp.

"Keep still and he won't hurt you," instructed CD amiably. The jackdaw just spread out his wings for balance and stood there swaying like a heraldic crest on a knight's helmet. "Now, tell me, Maxwell," CD went on, "I guess you've seen the Indiana Jones movies."

"Well, yes," said Maxwell incautiously, "I have, all of them."

"OK, so that's got you all wound up and you just can't wait to find the secret chamber with the treasure in it."

"Oh, no, I know it's not going to be like that, but I just—"

"Come with me." CD stood up and the bird flew back to his shoulder. He looked around at the diggers. "Over here, everybody. Follow me. CD's insights number three."

He led them to the plastic lavatories, with Gaye lagging well behind. He opened the door of the first of the pair.

"OK, Maxwell," he said. "Stick your head down there."

"Where?" said the boy, appalled.

"Bottom left, below the door hinge, down by the floor. Read me what it says."

Patrick had tagged along with them to see what CD was up to. The stench, he had to admit, was terrible; Maxwell, crouched and twisted so that his head was distressingly close to the moulded plastic lavatory bowl, sounded as if he was gagging as he read the inscription.

" 'The Polyjohn Manufacturing Company, Wilmington, Indiana. US patent number seven five—' "

"Stop right there. That's enough. You can come out now."

Maxwell uncoiled himself rapidly. Someone moved into the edge of Patrick's field of vision. Bobby. He suppressed the temptation to look at her. An acute awareness of her presence gripped him like a static charge building in a thunderstorm.

"Listen up, everybody," said CD. "Patrick has asked me to tell you about *finds*." Patrick knew he hadn't done any such thing, but was profoundly grateful that the American was sensitive to his authority.

"Finds are nice," CD drawled. "Finds are fun, but mostly finds are useful because finds help give us *dates*. Finds are not what we are looking for. Information is what we are looking for. If we find things we do not rush to dig them up. Oh, no. We come and tell Teacher, and we are very, very careful to leave our find exactly where it is."

Aidan cleared his throat. "And perhaps you could tell us why exactly this young man had to stick his head down there so that you could tell us *that?*"

CD laughed. "Thank you for reminding me. Young Maxwell here has seen all the Indiana Jones movies. He would like to be Harrison Ford and he's kinda hoping the Ark of the Covenant is round here somewhere. As you know, archaeology Indiana-Jones-style is all about grabbing the treasure, escaping in a hail of bullets, and to hell with recording the context." He slapped the side of the blue portable toilet. "Well, this is the Indiana *John,* folks, and that's as close as you're ever going to get."

He looked at Patrick, tapped his watch, and raised an eyebrow. Patrick nodded.

"Back to work, folks. Tea break at three-thirty."

As they straggled off, Patrick heard Maxwell grumbling to Aidan.

"It's not really fair. He and Dozer keep going on about all the exciting digs they've done and Inca treasure and all that."

Aidan snorted, then said without bothering to lower his voice, "The only thing that worries me is how he *knew* that name was down there."

Because there is very little justice in life, it was Maxwell who made the big find later that afternoon.

## CHAPTER SIX

WHEN MAXWELL YELLED, Patrick had been staring westward for longer than was strictly necessary. On the western horizon, volcanic clouds were mushrooming, boiling up, borne ever nearer on wind. Between Patrick and the cloud fountain stood the catering tent, shivering and cracking in the rising wind, and through the half-open flap he could see glimpses of Bobby going about her business inside, oblivious to him. Patrick had learnt to worry about most things in recent years and the clouds gave him real cause for concern. Rain on a grassy field is just a temporary discomfort but rain on an opened trench is bad. You can't work underwater without risking destroying what you are looking for.

The yell came from the trench and spun him round, a yell that brought all the diggers rushing to the boy who had uttered it. It was too early for a find, they were still taking off the turf, but Maxwell had not followed the conventional, slow, patient ways of archaeology. Maxwell had dug his very own hole. There, delving through the rough topsoil where the turf had been lifted, was a small square pit a foot and a half deep with coloured fragments gleaming in the earth at its bottom. Piled at the edge of the trench were what Maxwell had taken out of his pit, a small stack of dirty slabs.

Patrick pushed his way through the cluster of craning diggers and saw a delighted, smiling face, the face of someone who knew he had just become a hero.

"What's happened here?" he demanded.

"Mosaic tiles. You know, your tesser things. See? I've found a floor," said Maxwell, as pleased as punch and failing to pick up any warning from the tone simmering under Patrick's question.

Patrick looked at the hole and the pile beside it, unable to believe that one overgrown teenager could do so much damage.

CD and Dozer, who had been at the far end of the second trench, arrived at a run and gazed down into Maxwell's hole.

"You took those out?" Patrick pointed at the dirty pile of slabs.

"Yup, and just look what was hiding under them."

"What did you think *they* were?"

"Those? I don't know. Stones?"

"That's a destruction layer, you little idiot. Roman roof tiles. All you're meant to be doing is getting the topsoil off. You've dug right through the context. I thought CD told you. We're not bloody treasure hunters. You've destroyed information. We need to know *how* this roof collapsed. You said you were an archaeology student, for God's sake."

"Yes."

"Well, haven't you learnt *anything* yet? We do it carefully, one layer at a time, not like a sodding bulldozer."

"I'm only a first year." Maxwell blinked at him as the tirade took Patrick's voice further and further into the spectrum of fury. "I have found a floor, haven't I?"

He had. It was true that at the bottom of that unforgivable hole, where he had pulled the tiles out in his haste to get to something below, there was a glint of rich colour, red and white and yellow, where a scatter of mosaic fragments poked through the moist earth. They were drying as Patrick looked, turning dull.

"We're not here to bloody find things. We're here to untangle the story of this place, slowly and carefully." Patrick, aghast at the damage, was on the verge of telling Maxwell to pack his tent and get off the site, when he saw a small, shining ball appear at the corner of the boy's eye and realised, after a second's mystification, that it was a tear. The part of him that could no longer bear to cause pain revolted.

"Oh, the hell with it," he said. "CD, give them a thorough lecture about contexts, will you? Assume none of them know *anything,* especially the students."

"OK, listen up again," said CD wearily. "A context is a context is a context. Get it? Shit no, 'course you don't, 'cos none of you know shit, right? What is a context, anyone?"

The older man with gingery grey hair answered. "It's the position of a find on a site and its stratigraphic relationship to its immediate surroundings."

CD blinked very rapidly. "Let me just run that one past myself. Er, yeah. I guess that's about the perfect textbook answer."

Patrick reached for his list. "I'm sorry, I'm still learning names. You are?"

"Peter Knight," said the man.

"And you are Emeritus Professor of Archaeology at which university?" said CD.

The man laughed. "No such luck, I'm afraid. I've been a bit of a bookworm all my life. Lots of theory, not much practice. I thought it was time I got my hands dirty."

Aidan had been looking from one to the other, frowning. "I'm glad you're enjoying yourselves, but I have to say that explanation was as much use to me as a stepladder in a sandstorm."

"A stepladder?" repeated CD.

"Whatever," said Aidan.

"OK. Well, in plain language, a context is a layer. It can wobble up and down but it's still a layer, right? A layer of time. Suppose it's a ditch. Then the surface of the ditch is a context. Supposing the ditch got itself filled in to halfway up, then that fill and anything that's in it is a context. When you're digging one context, whatever's sticking up out of the next one, even if it's the missing treasure of Eldorado, you don't disturb it until you've removed and recorded the whole of that context. *Ever.* OK?"

They listened with frowns of concentration on their faces.

A rising growl made Patrick look towards the road. It came in vertical rips of cannon smoke from the sky-battering exhaust of a large yellow tractor fitted with a backhoe, which crawled into view from behind the trees and turned to sway its way over the ruts into the field.

A large man walked in behind it with a proprietorial swagger; the man was Roger Little. At that moment, the billowing wall of dark cloud covered the sun, and in the abruptly muted light, Patrick caught a movement out of the corner of his eye. The watcher was on the hill again, nearer now. For the first time, Patrick could make him out, a man of middle age, powerfully built—an outdoors man in a dun-coloured shirt and heavy working trousers. As Little strode into view, the man on the hill made an abrupt lateral gesture with his arm, as if warding off something in disgust, and turned away.

IN THE UNRECORDED DAYS OF THE HWICCA, THE BLANK YEARS OF HISTORY AFTER THE LITERATE ROMANS HAD LEFT ENGLAND, THE WALLS STILL STOOD ABOVE A MAN'S HEAD, IVY-LADEN. ON A DAY JUST LIKE THIS, WITH TOWERING CLOUDS THREATENING RAIN, CUTHA HAD WATCHED THEM WITH CARE FROM HIS LOOKOUT POINT UP THE HILL. FOR MONTHS ON END, SOMETIMES EVEN FOR YEARS, THE FRONTIER COULD BE A PEACEFUL PLACE. YOU COULD ALMOST FORGET THE LAST BATTLE. TRADERS WOULD COME AND GO WITH GOODS FROM THE FRANKISH BOATS THAT SAILED AS HIGH UP THE RIVER AS THEY COULD REACH, BRINGING BROOCHES AND FINE METALWORK FROM THE FAR SIDE OF THE HOMEWARD SEA. CUTHA DIDN'T KNOW HIS OWN HISTORY EXCEPT THROUGH THE SIMPLIFYING SONGS AND THE EXAGGERATED SAGAS, EXTOLLING A GLORIOUS TRADITION. IN TRUTH, THE HWICCA WERE A MONGREL RACE, EASY ABOUT ABSORBING OUTSIDERS. SOME OF THEIR MEN HAD COME ACROSS THAT SAME SEA IN THE SERVICE OF THE ROMANS AND STAYED ON WHEN ROMAN DISCIPLINE, ROMAN BUREAUCRACY, AND ROMAN GOLD SHRANK BACK TO

THE BESIEGED COUNTRY OF THEIR ORIGIN. OF THOSE MEN, THERE WERE SAXONS FROM THE GERMAN COAST AND THERE WERE ANGLES FROM THE SOUTHERN END OF THE DANISH PENINSULA. THEY'D MINGLED WITH THE BRITONS, THE CELTIC RACE WHO HAD BEEN ROMANISED DURING THE FOUR-HUNDRED-YEAR OCCUPATION OF THE ISLAND WHEN THIS HILL, AS FAR FROM THE SEA AS IT IS POSSIBLE TO GET, HAD BEEN SAFE FROM THE SAXON RAIDERS, PROTECTED BY IMPERIAL MIGHT. FIFTY YEARS AFTER THE ROMANS DEPARTED, THE VILLA'S ROOF TILES HAD FALLEN IN, SHATTERING AS THEY FELL ON THE DECORATED FLOOR. IN THE NEXT HUNDRED AND FIFTY YEARS, THE TOP COURSES OF STONE HAD SLIPPED AND CRUMBLED IN THE WINTER STORMS, AND THE WOODEN BEAMS HAD ROTTED TO POWDER. THIS YEAR, THE TRADERS HAD STOPPED COMING AND THERE HAD BEEN SIGNS OF TROUBLE: MEN FROM THE VALLEY BELOW, GEWISSE MEN IN BANDS, PARADING WHERE THE HWICCA COULD SEE, OPENLY STEALING THEIR SHEEP, TESTING THEIR ALERTNESS.

CUTHA STUDIED THE ROMAN WALLS. THEY WERE A WORRY FOR THE WATCHERS, DEAD GROUND WHERE SOMEONE COULD GET CLOSE WITHOUT BEING SEEN. THEY'D HIDDEN THERE BEFORE.

Roger Little set the style of their encounter by glancing at Patrick, then walking away towards the trench so that Patrick would have to go to him. It was a game in which Patrick had, as yet, no stake. He didn't care one way or the other, so he went along with it and walked across.

"How are you getting on?" said Little as he arrived.

"Fine."

"Waste of time."

"Why do you say that?"

"There's nothing here. Never was."

A more experienced man might have kept quiet, but Patrick found himself blessing young Maxwell for the first time that afternoon.

"There is. We've already found it."

"Go on with you."

"It's a Roman floor, by the look of it. Just what we thought might be here."

"Where?"

"There. See?"

Little looked into the hole in silence for an uncomfortably long time. Patrick, unable to tell who was master and who was slave in this relationship, watched his impassive profile as the seconds stretched out.

CD was crouching in the trench below, cleaning up Maxwell's mess, and finally seemed to have had enough.

"It's OK," he called, "don't mind me. You're allowed to say something if you want to. Hell, it's your field anyway, Mr. Small."

"People often forget that," said Little. "Funny way to dig a hole. Straight down like that. I thought you lot did things more carefully. They don't do it like that on the telly."

"That's what we call a sondage." CD gave the word an exaggeratedly Gallic accent. "Used for getting us a baseline resistivity check when the barometric pressure variation might invalidate the ground-line reading."

Little clearly had no idea what CD was talking about, but then neither did Patrick—and nor did CD.

"What's that bird doing?"

"It appears to have just crapped down my back," said CD. "It often does that. That's how it expresses its opinions."

"So what happens next?" said the builder grumpily, losing interest in Edgar.

"We follow the lines of the geophysical survey," Patrick told him. "This shows up as a corner, so it looks like it confirms the indications that what we might have here is some kind of rectangular structure. Could be a temple, could be a villa. It's too early to tell."

Little squinted around the field. "Maybe I could build round it. Leave it as a garden. How far does it go?"

Patrick remembered the rough shape of the lines on the printout.

"I'll pace it out," he said, glad that the builder was showing some interest. "It goes off in this direction."

He walked twenty paces diagonally towards the far hedge, then turned at right angles and took twelve more. Little stood motionless, watching him as he completed the rectangle and came back to him.

"That's about it," he said.

"Nothing else in the rest of the field?"

"Nothing that's shown up on the geophysical survey."

"Could be worse. Move the plots around a bit, leave that bit in the middle as grass." The builder sniffed and squinted up at the clouds. "I'd better be off, I've got work to do. Does rain stop you?"

"Not unless there's a lot of it."

"There's going to be."

He was right. At half past four, the clouds brought a premature twilight and an icy, drenching rain which first washed the emerging layer of Roman roof tiles so brilliantly clean that every detail of their surface texture was clear, then filled the trench with an obliterating layer of muddy water.

The catering tent became a haven for the diggers as they huddled together inside, trying to avoid the dribbles leaking through its ancient seams. There was little room to spare around the edges of the rickety wooden table holding the gas rings, so the team was squashed together, welded unwillingly by rain, cold, and gallows humour. Patrick stood by CD, and the American tried to get him to open up, anxious to get a fix on this reserved, troubled man with the notorious past. He could get Patrick to talk about archaeology and about weather, but that was it. Bobby had gone home to cook their supper and Gaye could be heard complaining loudly about the conditions.

"You can't expect us to sleep in the tents in this, surely? Isn't there a guest house or something?"

CD stuck his head out of the flap. "Nothing wrong with this. Just a little local precipitation. That's all."

Gaye's tent blew away at five o'clock, dragged across the grass by the wind like a half-inflated balloon, ballasted by all her belongings jumbled together in a corner of it. Dozer guffawed loudly at the sight of the tent tumbling past the entrance to the catering tent, then looked at her stricken face and went out into the downpour to retrieve it from the hedge and put in all the extra tent pegs that she had left out.

At five forty-five, with the wind still rising, the old marquee reached some sort of geriatric canvas crisis and gave up the struggle. Water poured in simultaneously in a dozen new places at once. Mutiny was in the air. Patrick had no clear idea what to do, short of suggesting they all have a very early night in their individual tents,

but then help came from an unexpected quarter. A van with LITTLE
PROPERTIES emblazoned on its side drove into the field. Its owner
ran across to where they were sheltering.

"I would invite you back to my place," Little said. "I've bought
this old manor house two miles out, but I'm still doing it up, so that
won't do. What I have got is some dry sheds you can all sleep in. I
suppose I'm responsible for you one way and another. Get your gear
and pile in."

There was a murmur of relief from all around. The intricate
dance required to get out of the way of the leaks without overfamil-
iarity with one's neighbour had been getting under everyone's skin.
Edgar had crept inside CD's jacket to stay dry and could be heard
there chattering and grumbling. Every now and then CD would
jump.

"He pecks," he explained.

Considering the offer, Patrick looked at CD, who shrugged.

"OK," Patrick said to Little. "Thanks."

They piled into the back of the van and were driven through the
village and out the other side to what had once been a farmyard. Only
one barn survived and around it, dragging it down, stood a cluster of
small, square industrial buildings, surrounded by piles of bricks and
timber. Little unlocked one and opened the metal door. It was half-
full of tiles and sacks of cement, but the remaining concrete floor was
easily large enough for all of them and it was blessedly dry. It wasn't a
palace but compared to the alternative, it seemed like one.

"What are you doing about grub?" said Little.

"Bobby's cooking it."

"Bobby?"

"The woman from Highbury Farm."

"Oh, her," said Little. "She's crazy, that woman. Tell you what,
I'll get the grub brought over here, shall I? Then one of my blokes
can pick you all up in the morning. Forecast says rain's going to stop
overnight."

"He's changed his attitude," Patrick commented to CD when the
builder left them. "I never expected any help from that quarter."

CD gave him a delphic look. "I guess," he said noncommittally.
"Anyway, I'm not too good on concrete. I might just walk back
down to the field later on and sleep in that nice soft mud."

"Up to you."

If CD had stuck to his word, it would have turned out to be just another dig, but the American's intentions were fatally undermined by the dozen bottles of raw red wine that arrived unexpectedly with the food brought by a taciturn young man in the same builder's van. As a result, everything changed. Patrick was disappointed, even angry, that Bobby hadn't brought the food herself. He chose to think that was because she was shirking her responsibility, but the real reason for his response lay deeper. He had an odd, composite face lodged in his mind, part Rachel, part Bobby, and he badly wanted to see Bobby to remind himself which was which.

It was only the wine that allowed them all to fall asleep on that hard floor and when Patrick woke the next morning, the shed looked like a refugee camp, an untidy sprawl of bodies, jumbled together, heads resting on shoulders of people who had been perfect strangers the day before. He vaguely remembered raucous singing late into the night and CD filling his plastic mug repeatedly for him in a vain attempt to get him to join in. Patrick had poured all the wine away down a crack at the base of the wall and when the party got to takeoff point, horribly like old times, he had retreated into a corner of the shed, shunning the friendship and the songs, especially the songs.

His watch said that it was five past eight. He wriggled out of his sleeping bag, put on his crumpled jeans, looked aghast at Gaye, who was snoring loudly with her makeup smeared all over her face, and decided to walk to the field. He could see the church a mile or so away at the top of a long sweep of hillside, so he set off up the lane towards it. He was halfway to the village when a battered Land Rover passed him going fast the other way, braked, turned, and came back to him. A woman in a woolen cap jumped out. Bobby. His heart did another treacherous cartwheel.

"Get in," Bobby said. "You won't believe this. I'm so sorry. I should never have let it happen."

"What? What's happened?"

She was on the verge of tears. "Just get in. I *knew* it. I just thought you'd think I was being neurotic. . . ."

They were at the field two minutes later, but the field was utterly changed. The backhoe was standing in the middle of an ocean of mud. The tents and the cars were still where they had been along its edge, but out in the middle, desecration had taken place. A huge rectangle of grass had been carved away, dug down two feet or more.

Without looking any further, Patrick knew with appalled certainty that the hole more than covered the area of the geophysical survey, the area he had so obligingly paced out the previous day for Roger Little.

"Jesus Christ," he said, "I don't believe it."

"I slept through it." Bobby had tears of anger in her voice. "I think I half heard it but it kept turning into a dream. When I finally woke up I saw headlights, but I couldn't *do* anything."

"You went out?"

"Of course I did. I ran all the way. There was a truck just going away down the road. I wasn't even close enough to get its number."

"They were using Little's machine?" Patrick could see his career turning to ashes before his eyes. It didn't really surprise him. Everything turned to ashes.

"They'd finished with it. There was nobody here. It was standing right there where it is now."

"Did you go down by yourself?"

"Yes." She seemed surprised at the question.

"You didn't take Joe with you?"

"Joe? No, Joe was out somewhere. He goes off by himself a lot."

It was hard to know what to make of that.

"I'm an idiot," said Patrick. "Why didn't I stay with the tents? CD was right, but it was my responsibility, not his. Just look what they've destroyed."

They stared at it in silence for a few moments.

"Shall we go and see him? I know where he lives," said Bobby.

"You mean Little?"

"Of course I mean Little. Who else would I mean?"

"Well, what would I say. . . ?" He couldn't bear the way she was suddenly looking at him as if he had let her down.

"Yes," he said. "Sure. You bet."

Little was coming out of his garage as they drove into his yard. Carrying a bucket in one hand, he stopped and raised his eyebrows at the style of their arrival. Bobby was out of the Land Rover almost before it stopped, Patrick following her because he had no choice, propelled headlong into a confrontation for which he was not ready.

"We want to talk to you," said Bobby. "What you've done is inexcusable."

"What I've done?" said Little in mock astonishment.

"You know bloody well what I'm talking about."

"I don't think I do, and I don't like being addressed like that."

"You dug up the field."

"What, someone's dug it up, have they? You didn't leave the keys in the backhoe, did you? With all the kids round here? I hope they haven't done any damage."

"Kids with trucks?" raged Bobby. "Kids who cart all the earth away? Do you know what you've destroyed?"

"You be careful what you say," said Little. "You could get sued for saying things like that."

What happened next came as a complete surprise to Patrick, who found himself taken over as if possessed by another voice and another body. Both body and voice were shaking with the effects of a flood of adrenaline born from fury. This unexpected Patrick moved in between Bobby and the builder, boring into Little's personal space and pushing him back towards his door with the force of the words and the ready-to-snap tension vividly evident in every fibre of his body.

"Listen to me, you," he said. "Who else stands to benefit from wiping out that site, eh? Who else knew exactly which bit to destroy? Do you think anybody's going to believe it wasn't you?" His voice was getting louder and louder to cover that betraying, chemical quaver. "It's quite obvious what you've done and I'm going to make absolutely sure you pay for it. You took us for suckers, didn't you? Getting us out of the way? Well, if you think you're going to get your planning permission now, you've got another think coming. I'll see you're hauled into court for this."

They had reached the house, Little giving ground backwards all the way. Now the builder turned quickly, opened his door, and stepped inside.

"You can't talk to me like that," he shot back through the closing gap. "Get off my land. I'll call the police."

"Don't worry. I'll be calling them myself," replied Patrick.

In the Land Rover, heading back to the field, Bobby said, "You were fantastic," but all Patrick could do, instead of basking in the glow of her approval, was to sit there appalled by the knowledge that the old Paddy still lurked inside him, waiting for the slightest chance to get out.

# CHAPTER SEVEN

I N THE PUB THAT NIGHT, AN AN-
cient, wheezing stranger stuck his face
close to Patrick, fixed him with tiny
dark eyes from under the greasy brim
of his cloth cap, and opined that it
wasn't Friday, jabbing him on the arm for
emphasis and cackling with the mysterious
humour of it. The cackle sent a small cloud
of decay condensing around Patrick's face
from the brown stumps of the old man's
teeth.

It was the fourth or fifth time since the
diggers had taken refuge in the bar from the
renewed rain, that one of the locals had mentioned that it wasn't Friday, nodding as he
did so towards the far end of the bar, where a
stool, a guitar, and a mike stand were set up
on a platform.

Word that it wasn't Friday seemed to be
spreading round the village because every
few seconds the door would open, letting in
cold, wet air and cold, wet villagers in ones

and twos who would, immediately once they were inside, also give their opinion that it wasn't Friday and sometimes seek confirmation of that fact from the strangers huddled by the radiator in the corner. There had been no shortage of opinions expressed in the course of that day. By the time they all crowded into the pub that evening, Patrick felt he'd heard enough opinions to last him a long lifetime.

Dozer's had been the most painful and the most straightforward of all the opinions about the day.

"He'll get away with it, won't he? Must 'ave mates on the planning committee or he wouldn't have risked chucking his cash at that field in the first place. If we don't find anything else there and we can't prove it was 'im, they'll just roll over and let him tickle their tummies. It's the funny 'andshake mob, ain't it?"

"What do you mean? Freemasons?"

All that got in reply was a dark chuckle as Dozer took a long drag on the thin end of his homemade cigarette, lost in his enormous hands. Dozer's massive presence compensated for the fact that the rest of the group looked thin, insubstantial, and *unserious* somehow in that bar where they didn't belong and where most of the other inhabitants looked like proper working folk.

CD blamed himself. "That's why I planned to go back and sleep down there," he said. "I shouldn't have drunk that wine."

Gaye was looking on the bright side. "Does that mean we can all go home now?" she asked. "I could certainly do with a hot bath."

Hescroft had been the worst, preempting Patrick by turning up at the field while Patrick was still trying to get him on his mobile. Hescroft's opinions were uncompromising. Patrick had shown an extraordinary lack of judgment in leaving the site to the mercy of hooligans. There was very little hope of taking any effective action against Little without hard evidence. Anyway, what made Patrick so sure it *was* Little? The man had seemed a perfectly decent type to him. It wasn't a crime to be a developer, after all. It could have been anyone. After all, they *had* left the key in the machine, which was a childish mistake to make and one that could make them liable. He didn't say what they might be liable for. Above all, Patrick had let himself and Hescroft down by ruining the chances of a valuable TV series and that, Patrick sensed, was what mattered most to his boss.

"So what do I do? Kenny Camden's coming to see me tomorrow," Hescroft grumbled. "Talk about leaving me in the shit."

"Who's Kenny Camden?"

"The series producer. He's directing it, too. He's a very big name, Patrick. What on earth am I going to tell him?"

"Tell him we didn't find anything. What do I do with all my diggers?"

Hescroft had looked around at the despoiled field. "You've still got to write a report. Have them dig two trenches out at right angles from that hole. Just to make sure there's really nothing left. We'll be in it up to here with the planning department."

The new trenches had turned up three tessera fragments, a quarter of a roof tile, and a small piece of bent metal which might have once been a Roman boot clasp. It didn't amount to much. The only solid evidence they had of what had been there before was a single photo taken by CD of Maxwell's original hole, and CD didn't hold out much hope of that coming out well.

"All my photos look like mud," he said.

"This is mud," said Dozer.

For all that, they drew and measured and recorded as if nothing untoward had happened, but morale was so low by evening that there was little doubt, when it started to drizzle, that the pub was the right place to go.

The Stag was the whitewashed pub halfway along the green. It was a basic pub with curling beer mats thumbtacked to every available inch of the wooden beams that held up the ceiling and bright neon lights whose wiring snaked untidily across a bumpy, cream ceiling stained by years of smoke. Soon after they all arrived and ordered their beers, and in Gaye's case, their sweet martini, it became clear that word had gone out. There was a lot of background giggling going on at their expense, and whatever it was that made it not Friday clearly had something to do with them.

"What do we do now, Patrick?" asked Aidan. "Surely we don't just carry on digging with fuck-all there?"

"Excuse *me*," said Gaye.

"You're excused," said Aidan, "and what's the answer?"

"We finish those two trenches, then I guess that's it."

"Well, now, that's a disappointment, I must say. In my opinion, it's a—"

They never found out what fresh opinion Aidan had to add to all the rest, because the reason it might have been, but wasn't, Friday abruptly became clear with a loud guitar chord from the far end of the bar.

"Gawd almighty," said Dozer. "Take a look at Eric Clapton over there."

The man sitting on the guitar stool, fiddling with his tuning, wore a cowboy hat and a bright red waistcoat over a dirty shirt and mud-stained trousers. He strummed another chord or two then launched straight into a song, in a voice that started uncertainly but strengthened as he went on. All the locals stopped talking to listen with a near-reverence that seemed unwarranted by the quality of the singing. The tune was a simple variation on basic hoedown country-and-western, and as the words sank in, Patrick understood that it was the words they were here to listen to, not the music. The diggers had quietened down, too, in the general hush; it only took a few seconds for them all to realize that the words were about them.

> *They came up here to Wytchlow with their trowels all prepared,*
> *To search for Roman ruins that the centuries might have spared.*
> *They dug around all afternoon 'til it came on to pour,*
> *But they didn't like to get too wet so they all packed up at four.*
> *A nice man offered shelter in a barn a mile away,*
> *And they slept there like a pile of logs until dawn of the next day.*
> *When they went back to start again, they got a great big shock,*
> *Because while they'd all been sleeping, someone ran amok.*
> *They'd found the Roman pavement, but they didn't think too quick,*
> *'Cuz someone came there in the night and played a dirty trick.*
> *When they saw what happened, they could not believe their eyes,*
> *Next time they meet our Roger, they'll be a* little *more wise.*

The crowd roared its approval, and the old man in the cloth cap reappeared like a pantomime demon to make sure Patrick had got the point. "A *little* more wise, do you get it? Roger *Little*. A *little* more wise, eh?"

Patrick nodded wearily, realized that the whole bar was looking in their direction with grinning faces, and waved sheepish acknowledgment at them. He wanted to be somewhere else, where he didn't have to be a good sport. Being a good sport hurt. The door opened again. The colour and the temperature in the bar changed as Bobby walked in and everything else started to hurt, too. It was safer to look away but Patrick's treacherous eyes kept returning to her treacherous face and as she walked across the room, she dragged his gaze after her. She was still wearing her working clothes and that old woolen hat, and she looked as though she had come for a purpose, not for a drink. There was a chorus of greeting.

"How's the great struggle?" called a man in a Barbour jacket and a plummy accent.

"We'll win," she said.

"Bloody right," said someone else.

"Always done it, always will," opined the old man with the bad teeth. At the bar, a tanned woman in a glossy leather jacket started to whisper in Bobby's ear, clearly telling her what had just happened, because Bobby frowned, looked across at Patrick, and made a grimace that could have been an apology. It distracted him for a few moments from the knowledge that was slowly forming in his head, the knowledge that he'd seen the singer before, that if you took away the absurd hat and the waistcoat, you had a middle-aged man in working clothes, a middle-aged man who had been watching them in their field from his position up on the hill, a man who had been watching yesterday as Patrick had paced out the field and Roger Little had laid his destructive plans.

The full knowledge hit him. It wasn't only Little who had known what part of the field to dig up. This man, this sarcastic singer, had also known.

The bird had come out of CD's jacket and was doing tricks on the table to the amazement of the locals, playing tug-of-war with a beer mat. It was a dangerous game to play. Every now and then Edgar would let go of the mat and peck his opponent's fingers if he or she pulled too hard. Dozer offered Patrick another beer, but he wanted to make the cloudy pint last. He sought a glimpse of Bobby in the now-crowded bar, but all he could see was the top of her head, or rather the top of her woolly hat.

As if he'd read Patrick's mind, Dozer said, "Do you think she always wears that hat?"

"Scalp condition," said CD. "I knew a girl once, she had a scalp condition all over. Had to wear a chemical warfare suit. Never did find out what she looked like."

"Yeah," said Dozer. "That was my mother. She told me."

The singer drained his glass and picked up his guitar again. The bar fell silent once more at the first sound of his fingers on the strings; this was a different sound, a gentle, skilful arpeggio contrasting greatly with the crude strumming of the first song. The old pro that still survived in Patrick realised that this man could, when he chose, conjure some degree of magic from the strings. He played a long introduction and when he began to sing, it seemed that his voice was different too, softer and more lyrical, with a blur inside it that could sound at times like harmony.

> *I sing you the song of the German Queen*
> *With her hair dark red and her eyes so green.*
> *I sing you the song of the way they cried*
> *On the dreadful day when the fair Queen died. . . .*

In Patrick's teenage years, when he had been Pat, escaping from the house in Clifton, in the years when soft music had been enough, he had done the circuit of the Bristol folk clubs and the pubs, earning a few pounds a night playing all the old favourites to audiences who would spoil it by trying to sing along or by starting to clap just out of time with the music. In those days, music meant emotion, gentle emotion. Later, it started to come from another part of his head, when the hard, clever words got in the way. In all the days of the early folk songs, he'd never heard this one.

> *The eldest child of her father's line,*
> *A slender shoot from a sturdy vine,*
> *She kept his house from her early days*
> *Once her well-loved mother had passed away.*

The pub audience listened in reverential silence but Patrick detected that they were a little puzzled. It seemed to him that the first rough song was more what they were used to than this quiet ballad.

> *Her father wore the golden ring*
> *From the German lands where he'd been a king*
> *And, dreaming of what once had been,*
> *He called the girl his German Queen.*

*There came a time in that peaceful land*
*When their peace was marred by a roving band,*
*New arrived from the Saxon shore*
*With a grudge from home and an old, old score.*

*They climbed the hill on an autumn morn*
*And the first light gleamed on the swords they'd drawn.*
*High on the hill, that glint was seen*
*By the chieftain's girl with her eyes so green.*

*She ran to the wall with the warning gong*
*And she made it sing its arousing song.*
*Her brothers leapt from their wives' warm arms*
*At the first loud cry of its harsh alarm.*

*They met the raiders, blade to blade*
*In a spray of blood at the old stockade.*
*Outnumbered by them five to one,*
*The fight was led by the oldest son.*

*At the moment when they saw him fall*
*And his soul took flight to the warriors' hall,*
*The hills rang out to a chilling cry.*
*Their father saw the young prince die.*

Patrick let his guard down, flashing back to the first time he'd ever been on a big stage, to the awesome, terrifying, thrilling moment of walking out of the wings of the Apollo Theatre into a bombardment of howling applause. Four old friends and one new acquaintance, the drummer, a necessary evil, catapulted into this bear-garden by a recording session, some clever publicity, and a runaway hit in the charts. Rachel, worried, watching in the wings after losing her long battle to dissuade him. Pat out there onstage taking the first step towards being Paddy, tilted off balance by the first undreamed-of taste of massive, uncritical adulation. Patrick saw Rachel clearly in his mind's eye then, but it wasn't his mind's eye at all because this version of her was standing in the Wytchlow bar looking at the singer with an expression that seemed to have a little edge of apprehension in it. Patrick stared at Bobby for an age, pulling himself back into the present, as the man with the guitar sang on; then she moved her head and met his eye and frowned at the intensity of his gaze.

He blinked and broke the eye contact. As he became aware that he'd lost the thread of the song, he saw that the singer had got up from his stool and was moving through the crowd, coming towards him and his diggers, seated round their table. Like some intruding gypsy violinist at a restaurant table, the singer was standing as if he was directing his song straight at them.

> *Up on the hill on the sacred ground,*
> *They dug a grave in the ancient mound.*
> *They laid her there with her sword and shield*
> *In that older tomb in the Bury Field.*
>
> *Amber beads were round her head*
> *And she sleeps there still on her wooden bed.*
> *Her cloak secured with the royal jewel*
> *That had marked the years of her father's rule.*
>
> *Now leather and wood have turned to dust.*
> *The iron brackets are dark brown rust.*
> *The bed has lost its strength and weight*
> *But the burden on it's no longer great.*
>
> *The years and the plough have flattened the land*
> *Which she saved with a stroke of her valiant hand.*
> *Now silence and shadows mark the scene*
> *Of the glorious grave of the German Queen.*

He played a final sad sequence in a minor key, bowed his head to the applause, and turned back into the crowd around him. Patrick was left utterly astonished at what he had just heard. A song in a pub, a crude folk song, describing in detail something almost unknown except in the academic realms of archaeology? An Anglo-Saxon furnished bed burial correct to the minor detail? A wooden bed, with leather straps for a base, secured by iron brackets? A bed like the one at Swallowcliffe? A type of burial only recognised for what it was in recent years and now identified again at Edix Hill? Was it just chance? What had he missed in the rest of the song? He looked across the table at CD, who was draining his beer glass opposite.

"Did you hear that?"

"Well, yes. Having ears, I had little choice."

"No, I mean what did you make of it?"

"The chicken sword? Funny you should ask—"

"Chicken sword? What's a chicken sword? I meant the bed burial."

"Well, I don't know much about—"

"Hang on. He's going. I've got to talk to him."

The singer had taken off his hat and waistcoat and, bundled into an old raincoat, was making for the door, smiling and nodding his head at well-wishers he passed. It took Patrick a moment or two to push through the crowd after him, and by the time he got out through the porch, the man was just a dark shape moving across the village green ahead of him.

"Wait a minute," called Patrick. "Can I talk to you?"

The singer showed no sign of having heard him, and Patrick ran after him. The man must have heard his footsteps but he didn't slow down. Patrick found himself walking fast next to him as they crossed the edge of the green and turned onto the road.

"Stop just a moment," he said. "I want to know about that song you sang."

No response.

"I only want to know what it's called. Who wrote it?"

The man looked round at him and strode onwards.

"What's going on?" said Patrick angrily, trying to keep up. "Why won't you talk to me? Was it you who dug up our field?"

At that the man swung round, made an emphatic gesture of rejection in complete silence, and pushed Patrick in the chest.

"Don't you bloody do that," said Patrick, and grabbed the offending arm, only to have his own arm seized from behind and wrenched away. He swung round to face the unexpected attack and found himself confronting Bobby, panting with the effort of running after them and looking ready to kill him.

"Go home, Joe," she told the singer. "Go home. I'll sort him out."

The man looked at her, grunted, and walked off. Patrick stared after him aghast.

"That's Joe?" he said. "Your Joe?"

"Yes, that's Joe. What the bloody *hell* did you think you were doing, treating him like that?"

# CHAPTER EIGHT

H E WASN'T GOOD AT CONFLICT, never had been. From his earliest childhood days he had clammed up in the face of attack and raw emotion. At school he had been thought fair-minded, the epitome of the peacemaker, but that was only because of the pain conflict caused him. At home, his father's contribution to their sporadic conversation had been confrontational, an echo both of the successful prosecuting barrister he had been and of the maudlin drunk he was becoming.

Loving Rachel, the only truly joyous experience of Patrick's whole life to that point, excluded conflict entirely. For that short time, he loved everything in his life, studying during the day in a haze of well-being, returning to her from the libraries to tell her about ring-ditches and pottery fabrics and urn burials and all the other things she cared nothing about but loved hearing his beguiling voice telling her, because he had so obviously found something that touched his soul. She was amazed that she had won this golden boy. She was proud to walk down the street and see the other girls' glances, and equally proud that he took no notice of them. Then the music burst out and built a wall across that path he should have taken, and he took the other way instead.

There was no slow build towards maturity in that life, no limits to what was acceptable. Instead, there were older men who praised him more the further he went, where being sexy and being dangerous were the way to get approval, and where his own self-critical faculties were undermined by the booze and the drugs and, above all, the mindless adulation.

That way lay ruin.

When conflict came at him from behind, out of the night at the end of this damaging day, it was more than he could deal with. His head spun with the anger in her voice—anger aimed, bizarrely and undeservedly, at *him*. Now she didn't just look like Rachel; she sounded like her, too.

"I didn't know that was Joe."

"What difference does it make who it was?"

"I was only trying to talk to him." He recognised and despised the whine of self-protection that had entered his voice.

"You weren't. I saw you. You were pushing and grabbing at him. What sort of person are you to do that to *him*?"

*My God,* he thought, *I wish I were Joe to have a defender like this.* "I thought he was being pretty rude, if you must know. He wouldn't answer."

She stood back and laughed derisively. "He wouldn't answer? He *couldn't* answer, for God's sake. He doesn't talk. You must know that. Didn't anybody in the pub tell you?"

That made no sense. Were there two Joes?

"Joe doesn't talk? Come off it. I've just heard him singing."

"Yes, of course you did. He sings. That's what he does, that and the odd poem, and only when he's performing. He doesn't talk apart from that, can't get any words out. Even to me. He hasn't talked for years."

*How do you two communicate?* thought Patrick. He didn't say it.

"There's no reason to go bullying him like that." She was calming down a little.

"Bobby, I had no idea." It was the first time he had said her name. He had to do it, to establish for himself who she was. "I didn't know any of that." He didn't even understand it, couldn't really believe he was having this odd conversation with this profoundly disturbing woman on this cold, wet village green in the pitch darkness, with only a damp tent waiting for him.

"You really mean nobody told you?"

" 'Course they didn't. I wouldn't have gone chasing after him if they had."

Silence.

"Why is he like that?"

She made a noise of exasperation, the sound of someone who had been asked that question far too many times.

"I don't know. Nobody knows. He talked when he was little, then he just stopped."

"And he doesn't talk to you, either."

"He writes me notes."

"I don't understand about the singing. How can he do that?"

"That's his way. He puts on his clothes and he's someone else. He's a performer, he's not Joe anymore. Maybe he just needs to be somebody else. I suppose I should be able to explain it if anyone does, but I can't. It's pretty hard to understand."

"No, it's not," said Patrick, thinking just how much he knew about the lure of being somebody else, about changing clothes and changing beliefs on a big stage with the world looking. In the dark, with the moon not yet risen and only the lights from the pub to pierce the thin drizzle, he could just see the shine of her wide eyes, turned on him. A door opened and closed somewhere behind him and the slight, brief light showed him her face, framed in dark hair, the hat gone, and she was not Rachel because Rachel was blonde.

"I heard . . ." she said, and stopped.

"What did you hear?"

"Nothing. It can wait."

"No, come on. What did you hear?" Without wishing it, there was a harsh edge in his voice.

"That you . . . you used to sing."

"Who have you been talking to? CD? Dozer?"

"No, no. It was one of the diggers, the guy with the round glasses."

"Aidan?" Jesus. Did everybody know?

"Listen, Patrick, I didn't mean to upset you. It's none of my business."

They were both silent as the echoes of discord died away into the darkness.

"That song he was singing," said Patrick, driven by the need to say something as well as by the need to know. "The German Queen and all that. Do you know it?"

"I've heard bits of it," she said, and there was relief in her words—acceptance of the olive branch.

"Was that the whole song?"

"I don't think so. I've heard other verses. I think he missed out a lot in the middle."

"Do you know where it comes from?"

"I think Dad taught it to him."

"Your father?"

"I think so. Joe used to have a terrible stutter. Dad taught him old songs to help him talk, but then, after Dad died, he stopped talking completely."

"You and Joe were brought up together?"

"Of course we were." He could see the pale disk of her face tilt. "He's my brother. Didn't you know that, either?"

A younger sister protecting her damaged older brother. Bobby and Joe, sister and brother. The Bobby side of it began to make more sense. She hadn't felt like half of a couple.

"No, I didn't. . . . Do you think he'll sing it again? In the pub?"

"I don't think so. It was quite unusual. He usually sings his own stuff. It's how he manages, see? All week he saves up the things he's thinking and all the things he wants to say, and he makes them into songs. People come to the pub just to hear what he's going to sing next. Betty, she was the old landlady, she loved it. I'm not sure about this new one, but I think it's pretty clear what her customers want. Just once in a while, when he's had his say, he'll sing one of Dad's old songs. You can't really ask him to do it. He's not very biddable, Joe. He sticks to his routines."

"He didn't tonight. It's not Friday."

"He sang tonight because of what's happened, because of you, because he wants the whole village to know it was Roger Little who did it."

"Hang on. You weren't there for the first song. He wasn't having a go at Little. He was poking fun at us."

"I heard about it. That was just his way. It wouldn't do to take your side openly against a villager, even a newcomer like Roger Little, not just like that. Think about it. His real message was that Little did it, and that's what people will remember. Did you mind?"

"Yes."

"I think he realised that. I think he sang the other song as a sort of present, to make up for the first."

"So it wasn't Joe who dug up the field?"

"Joe? Why on earth did you think it was Joe?"

"He was up there watching. I paced out the area we'd surveyed, exactly the same bit that got dug up. Little was there, but Joe saw it, too."

"So you leapt to the conclusion that he'd done it? Is that what you thought? Why would he do that? What about the trucks that took the earth away? How would Joe do that?"

"No, you're right. I didn't know who he was. I do now."

"Listen to me: Joe would sooner cut his own arm off than damage anything from the past. He was beside himself when he heard what Little had done."

"OK. I understand. He spooked me a bit. I kept seeing him up there watching us."

"That's the other thing Joe does. He keeps an eye on things."

A thought struck Patrick. "Did he *see* Little doing it? Do you think he was there?"

"I don't think so. He's out and about a lot at night. He could have been anywhere."

"Thank you, Bobby."

She was silent for a few seconds, still a little suspicious. "For what?"

"For explaining."

"I'm sorry I had to. Trouble with a place like this, you get to think everybody knows all the same things you know."

"What was all that other stuff about? The business at the school yesterday?"

"Oh, that." A gust of wind blew drizzle at them. "I'll tell you sometime."

"There might not be a sometime. We'll pack up tomorrow, I expect."

"Really? Damn."

"Why damn?"

"I've been looking forward to this dig."

"We'll see how it goes tomorrow. You will be there?"

"You'll still want hot food, won't you?"

"Oh, yes."

"One more thing. Will Little get his planning permission now?"

"Not my department. Quite possibly. It might make a difference if we could prove it was him."

"Oh."

"Time I went back," Patrick said, and because it was so very dark, he added, "Shall I see you home first?" and was discomfited when she burst out laughing. She cut her laugh off with a hand over her mouth.

"I'm sorry. I didn't mean to be rude," she said.

The night hid his flush. "I just meant it's very dark. There are no streetlights."

"Yes, I know. I've lived here an awfully long time. I've managed all right so far." Then, as if to take the sting out of her words, she went on, "All the newcomers who move in here, it's always the first thing they want to change. They always start asking for street lamps. We've managed to fight them off so far. One night, they look up and notice all the stars, and after that it's all right. They get the point."

He watched her as she strode away and the hermit in his head managed to pull the door shut again. Groping his way back to the field, lost in his thoughts about mute singers, old songs, and fiercely protective sisters, he crawled into his tent and climbed into his clammy sleeping bag fully dressed in an attempt to get warm. Lying there feeling miserable, it was with mixed feelings that he heard the first faint noise of feet and voices. The diggers were coming back from the pub, the diggers who, it seemed, all knew about Paddy Kane, thanks, he supposed, to CD and Dozer.

The noise swelled and broke into individual voices as they came to the tent line. They didn't seem to be going to bed. There was much to-ing and fro-ing, and then a flickering glow through the walls of the tent, which grew into an intense orange light as branches were snapped and fed into crackling flames. Next came unwelcome footsteps close to his tent, and a familiar American voice.

"Patrick, old bean. Are you awake?"

He pretended not to hear and CD just cranked up the volume.

"Patrick. Yoo-hoo, Patrick."

"What?"

"Are you awake?"

"I am now."

"Come and join in the fun."

"Not tonight. I'm tired." What he meant was, *Not tonight, not after you've blown my cover to the whole gang, not after the day that's marked the lowest point of all the low points of my new life.*

"Don't be a party-pooper. Guess what I've got in my pocket."

"I don't know," said Patrick wearily, who also didn't really care.

"Just a bottle of eight-hundred-year-old Glenboggy malt, kept for an occasion such as this, that's all."

"No, it's OK. Enjoy yourselves. I'm tired."

"Hey, listen up. I know it's only the second night, but it's kind of like our last night, too. They'd like to see you. Gaye's got made up specially."

"What?"

"Yeah, she got pissed and fell in the mud. Face-first. She thinks it's funny. Hey, listen, Patrick, *I'd* like to see you. Come on out of there."

So, reluctantly, Patrick joined the diggers round the fire, the group of disparate people who should have been on their way to becoming a team, his team, but now looked like staying just that, a group of disparate people. Tomorrow would see the end of it. They made space for him, on one of the logs they had dragged up to the fire.

"What happened with the singer bloke, Pat?" asked Dozer. "Saw you chase out after him."

"Nothing really. He's not a talker," said Patrick.

"Thought he'd lifted yer wallet, the speed you was going. Saw wotsername, Bobby, chasing out after. Did she catch you?"

"Er, yes. Well, that is, she's his sister. She went off home."

"Yeah. They gave us the background in the pub. Weird, eh? Him not talking. What did you want him for?"

"That song. Just something I wanted to know."

"Beds," said CD. "You said something about a bed."

"Well, yes. I just had an idea that the song was about a bed burial. It seemed pretty unlikely."

"Listen, my period's the Romans. I like solid chunks of *things,* not all this modern Saxon shit. Jesus, you know the way it is on an Anglo-Saxon dig. You get really excited when the dirt changes colour 'cos maybe you've hit a hole. It's just like the song—'Silence and Shadows.' I mean, a hole makes it a big day if you're into Anglo-Saxons. Give me something you can bounce a trowel off any day."

"Hang on. I'm sure you said the opposite yesterday. You said you hated all that Roman stuff."

"Yeah, that was yesterday. Whatever I'm doing, I like the opposite best."

"You don't know about bed burials?" asked Patrick, feeling pleased that there was at least one area where he knew as much as the American. "Have you read the Swallowcliffe report?"

"Nope. So tell us the story."

"Yeah, tell us a story, Daddy," said Dozer.

Patrick took the bottle that was passed to him and tried a small swig, using his tongue to block the neck so it would look like a big one. A corrosive liquid seared his throat and kicked his brain from underneath.

"Jesus, what's that?" he gasped.

"You've not tried Glenboggy before?" said CD. "Well, as they say in the traditional distilleries of the South Bronx, there's always a first time but there's not often a second time. Go on with your story."

"I've got this thing about place names," said Patrick, "so I like this story. Not the bit about beds so much, that's pretty straightforward. This guy Speake went back over the notes for a dig someone did years ago and never published. Speake put it all together from the finds and the dig notebook. Everything had been stacked away in dusty old boxes for heaven knows how long. It was a Bronze Age barrow down south of Stonehenge, and in it they'd found an Anglo-Saxon woman, surrounded by all kinds of iron brackets. They realised she had been buried on a bed, and they managed to work out what it had looked like."

"That's why you got excited in the pub?"

"Well, yeah. The leather straps and stuff. The way the song described it, that was pretty much the way it was."

"So what's the business with the place names?"

"On the old charters, this burial mound was always called Posses Low. So everyone thought the obvious thing, that someone called Poss had been buried there. Thing is, in among the finds were all kinds of bits of gold and silver and bronze, and when they put them together, they realised they made up a really elaborate shoulder bag, a satchel. A pretty distinctive bit of kit. So anyway, that's when they realized that *pusa* is the Old English for 'bag,' and Posses Low might have literally meant 'the grave of the bag lady.' "

"Nice," said Dozer. "*Low* as in Wytchlow."

Patrick became aware that a silence had fallen and that people were moving closer to their end of the circle to listen.

"What would the *Wytch* bit be?" someone said out of the darkness.

"Maybe a personal name."

"You have to beware of *dindshencus*," said Peter Knight.

"Well, yes, of course," said CD. "I was saying so only yesterday. Those things have a nasty bite."

"Never mind him," said Patrick. "What is whatever it was you said?"

"It's what the Irish call it. *Dindshencus.* I just used it because it's the only one-word encapsulation of the concept."

"Which is?"

"It's the process of creating a false tradition from the name of a place. For people who couldn't read and write, it was a bit tempting sometimes. They kept doing it in the Anglo-Saxon Chronicle, you know. They invented this man Port and his sons who landed at Portsmouth, when the name came from the Latin *portus*. You know the story of Berinsfield? It's a salutary lesson."

"Which is . . . ?"

"There was a big cemetery excavation not that far from here. Anglo-Saxon. The archaeologists got all excited because the place next to it was called Berinsfield and they took that to come straight from burial field. Then someone told them the truth. It was a new village, more of a housing estate really, and they'd invented the name in 1960-something because Saint Birinus was supposed to have spent some time round there. Nothing whatsoever to do with graves."

"Well, anyway," said Patrick lamely, "it sounded to me like the song was about a real burial. I expect it was all just chance."

"I don't think so," said CD. "It wasn't just the bed, was it? There was the sword, too. Could be there's an archaeologist out there writing songs. Maybe it's a whole new style: archo-rock."

"I dig it," said Dozer to a chorus of groans. "All right, fuck off, then," he added amiably.

"I didn't hear the bit about the sword," said Patrick. "What was it? Something about a chicken?"

Aidan, sitting in the lotus position on the wet grass with his round glasses reflecting flames, spoke in a lilting voice.

" *'The robber band, they quaked and ran before the wrath of a righteous man, leaving their dead where . . .'* What was it now? *'Where they'd been laid by the slashing edge of that chicken blade.'* "

"Hey, that's pretty impressive," said CD. "Can you do the rest of it?"

"What do you think I am?" snapped Aidan. "A tape recorder? That verse just stuck."

CD looked around the rest of them. "Anybody else remember?"

"It was just about fighting and that," said young Maxwell. "I didn't pay it much attention."

Nobody had. They'd sat and let it wash over them. Aidan's solitary verse and a few scattered phrases were all they could assemble.

"So what's this chicken blade, then?" said Dozer. "Something you kill chickens with or what?"

"Or what," said CD. "Definitely or what. You wanna hear my story now?"

There was scattered agreement from the darkness.

"You better all have some more Glenboggy," said the American. "This could be a long night. The tale I am about to tell makes shaggy dogs look clean-shaven. It is *decidedly* far-fetched and there's nothing like Glenboggy to dull the critical faculties. I make it myself specifically for that purpose."

"I bet it's not as far-fetched as that time you an' I got stuck in the Aztec tomb with the bats," said Dozer, reaching into the fire for a stick to light another cigarette.

"It comes close," said CD, "pretty close." Owlish behind his pebble glasses, he looked at Patrick.

"OK, here goes," he said. "Peter, if you know anything different, keep your mouth shut. Now, it just happens that the first thesis I ever wrote for my doctorate was all about the evidence concerning sword manufacture in the old Norse myths."

"Fine," said Patrick, uncomfortably aware that he hadn't yet written a thesis about anything.

"So don't laugh, OK? I swear I didn't make any of this up."

All the diggers had squeezed in close to the fire, to hear better. Stifled chokes betrayed the course of CD's bottle through the darkness.

"There's an old Norse myth called Thiorik's Saga," CD told them. "Thing is, just so you don't all think I'm some sad guy who enjoys reading stuff like that, Thiorik's Saga is kind of compulsory reading for anybody who's interested in old swords, on account of the fact it's just about the first detailed description of how they made them. Boring as shit, right?"

"Go on."

"Making strong swords was really big stuff, hard to do it well. There was a lot of crappy iron in those days and most people didn't know the difference. A good smith would pick the right iron and twist bars of different grades together so that when they were heated and hammered in the forging, you'd get a really good blade that could take a sharp edge. If a bad smith screwed up, the blade would bend halfway through a fight. Now, this was not good news for the guy holding the handle. There's descriptions in the sagas of people stopping fighting to put the blade on the ground and bend it straight with their boot, which was fine if the other guy was prepared to wait, but patience and gentlemanliness were not qualities for which your average Norse berserker was most noted. Where was I?"

"Thingy's saga. Thoracic or something," said Dozer.

"Thiorik. Right, well, in the saga there's this smith called Velent or Weland. He's probably old Wayland who crops up whenever there's a forge around in a Norse saga, and he promises to make his lord a really strong sword."

Gaye turned round and was very noisily sick into the grass just beyond the fire. There was a chorus of disapproval from those next to her and a sharp, acid waft of vomit, thankfully obliterated by a swirl of smoke. Patrick looked towards Gaye and saw, beyond her, someone else sitting. The figure was not in the circle but well back in the gloom, almost beyond the reach of the firelight. Patrick wondered briefly who it was, but as soon as Gaye recovered, CD went on.

"So Velent makes this sword called Mimming, because they gave their swords some pretty strange names in those days, and when he finishes it, he takes out his file and starts filing away at it. Nothing odd in that, because when you forged the iron, the bad stuff came to the surface so you always filed it back to the good metal. Only thing is, Velent didn't stop at the good metal. He just went right on filing, right on until the blade was all gone."

The bottle had come full circle and CD paused to take a swig.

"Oh, brother," he said. "Next time I mustn't put so much water in. You want to hear the rest of the story?"

"You can't stop there," said Aidan. "Go on with you."

Patrick looked again at the figure in the darkness; it looked as if he had moved a little closer. He nudged Dozer.

"Who's that out there?" he whispered.

Dozer looked across and shrugged.

"So, Velent files the blade away until it's just a pile of shiny filings lying on the floor of the smithy, then he sweeps it up and mixes it with grain, OK? After that, he starves his chickens for three days—"

"Cruel man," said Gaye indistinctly from a prone position in the grass.

"—and then he feeds them the mixture of filings and corn and keeps those hens shut up for a while. Then guess what he does next?"

"Roasts them," said Dozer.

"He collects their droppings. That's the nice way the polite books say it, right? He collects the chicken shit, guys and gals, the poultry poo, the rooster doo-doo, and he shapes it into a blade and he forges it all over again, and there he has it, a nice shiny, hard blade. But he doesn't stop there. Oh, no, remember this is Velent we're talking about. You don't get into sagas by doing things the easy way, even if they're mad things. He did it *three times*. If I'd been one of his chickens, I'd have gone on hunger strike, or started being a lot more careful about what I pecked, but anyway, in the end, Velent has this amazing blade that's much smaller and as strong as hell, which he inlays with gold, ready to give to his boss-man."

"Who goes out and kills lots of people with it, thereby precipitating the first arms race?" suggested Maxwell.

"I guess you haven't read too many Old Norse sagas," said CD thoughtfully. "That would be just a little bit simple for your average Norse saga. No, what Velent does then is he makes an exact replica of the sword, but he makes it out of really crap metal and he gives *that* one to the King."

"So what happened next?"

"No idea. I lost interest about there. I guess the King got killed and his kids sued Velent under the Sale of Goods Act. Then he would have lost all his customers and wound up sleeping under a bridge in Valhalla, looking in the garbage for empties with a few drops of ambrosia in them after the gods had finished feasting. That guy had a lot to learn about marketing, I guess."

Aidan was in a questioning mood. "It's got to be a load of shit, right? I mean, it's not a serious story, for chrissakes."

"A load of shit is exactly what it is," agreed CD affably, "chicken shit from beginning to end; but get this, that same story comes up completely independently all over the place. There's the Arabs, too, right? Some writer, Al something or other, Al-Biruni, I think. He says almost exactly the same thing, except it's ducks and geese, not chickens. Same thing in the old Asian stories, with ostriches."

"But it doesn't make sense, does it?" objected Aidan. "I mean, you couldn't actually *do* that."

"*Au contraire,*" said CD. "What does chicken shit smell of? Ammonia. That's because it's full of nitrogen, and when you forge iron with nitrogen, you get nitrides, and that is just exactly what you want for a good strong blade. By the time you get to the Spanish sword makers in Toledo, they were all at it. Those Spanish dudes used to mix up honey and flour with a good dose of bird shit and smear that all over the blade while they were forging it."

"So the chicken blade could be true?" said Dozer.

"Could be," replied CD.

Before he went to his tent, Patrick looked past the trees. The darkness hid the village as it had always done. There should have been no mystery to its name. The double "c" of *Hwicca* has a *ch* sound. To the west lay the remains of the great forest of Wychwood, the Hwiccas' wood. Wytchlow's roots were plain enough, but his mind was on other things. He turned and looked across the field, but could see no sign of whoever it was who had been sitting listening out there in the darkness.

# CHAPTER NINE

THE SHADOW OF THE SUN ACROSS dew-soaked grass showed it was just past six in the morning. The shadow was man-shaped, stretched out and tapering to a tiny head far away. The man from whose feet it stretched would have served well as a sundial, so still did he stand, taking care to keep this shadow of his off the tents, for fear of waking the wrong people. The man had no feeling for what counted as early to those who are used to modern life regulated by electric light and thick curtains, but he was content that they should go on sleeping away the daylight—all of them except one, that is. He studied the ravaged field, fixed his eye on the dark green tent at the end of the row, and decided it was time.

Patrick woke abruptly when the tent collapsed on him, catapulting him out of a warm world in which for once everything had seemed to be vaguely all right, to find himself smothered in damp polyester and horizontal tent poles. He struggled to get out of his sleeping bag, enmeshed in a tightening cocoon of cold tent fabric. His fingers found the zipper for the tent flap after a struggle, and he slithered out onto wet grass, leaving his sleeping bag behind in the wreckage of the tent. His heart was racing, because he knew it was impossible that his tent could collapse so suddenly and comprehensively without the intervention of some outside agency. It was the igloo type, supported by an interlocking structure of glass-fibre poles, curved in arcs and slotted into sockets at each corner of the tent. These tents didn't come undone easily, not even when you wanted them to.

He climbed out expecting to see a large animal standing there, a stray cow, even, but there was no visible explanation. The rest of the campsite was silent and in good order. The corners of the tent were still pegged to the ground, but it was undeniable that somehow, the ends of the poles had all come out of the eyelets into which they fitted, so that the poles lay with their ends protruding from the fabric in a flattened cross. Perplexed, he bent down to put them back and, as usual, it was a wrestling match. The poles didn't go back into place any more easily than they normally came out of it, which worried him all the more. Somebody's idea of a practical joke? He wouldn't put it past CD and Dozer, but the psychological moment when they would have jumped out laughing had already passed. Giving up, he crouched to creep back in, hoping for another hour's sleep; as he did so, there was a noise from behind him like stone striking stone. Only then did he do what Joe so much wanted him to do and look round, up at the hill beyond their field, where the man he had last seen outside the pub was now standing, just the other side of the fence.

Patrick stared at him, frightened by the sudden knowledge that for reasons he could not fathom, Joe must have come to his tent while he slept, must have crouched next to his head, separated only by the flimsy fabric, and pulled his tent poles apart. Was this a reprisal? A punishment for his own aggression last night on the village green? He stared across at the older man and it felt as if they were the only two alive in the whole world, then Joe lifted a hand in a summoning gesture and, turning his back on Patrick, began to trudge slowly up the hill.

Entirely unsure what to do, dressed only in the T-shirt he'd slept in, which was barely long enough to cover his crotch, Patrick stood staring at Joe's retreating back, trying to make sense of it. The other man stopped and looked round and repeated his beckoning gesture even more emphatically and Patrick found himself raising a hand in acknowledgment and pointing at his tent as if to explain he needed clothes. He groped inside for jeans, socks, and boots, pulled them over his wet feet with difficulty, and looked up to find that Joe hadn't waited for him and was now well on his way up the hill.

He seemed to have no choice.

The barbed wire strands snagged his shirt as he wriggled through the fence. The field beyond was rough pasture with tussocks of grass that tricked his feet as he climbed the gentle slope, so that he was forced to look down. Whenever he looked up again, he saw Joe standing waiting for him up ahead. "Joe wouldn't hurt anybody," he said to reassure himself. Joe was on their side, as angry with what Roger Little had done as he was himself—but why, if the man couldn't talk to him, was he summoning him? What could happen when Joe stopped at wherever it was they were going to?

It was steep only at the bottom of the hill and the rise was deceptive, rolling over gradually so that the shape of the land didn't reveal itself until he'd got to where he'd last seen Joe. He was on a gently domed plateau of the same coarse grass, with undulating fields and woodland to the west and the land falling away towards Oxford to the southeast. Joe was a hundred yards away, but he was no longer leading Patrick onwards. He stood there facing him, stock-still, and when he was sure Patrick was looking at him, he jabbed his hand down emphatically, pointing at the earth by his feet. He looked hard at Patrick, then repeated the gesture and walked rapidly away in the opposite direction.

Patrick watched him go, wondering, then tried to fix the spot with his eyes and, when Joe had disappeared out of sight into a copse of trees down the far slope, walked slowly towards that spot. There was nothing remarkable to see, just a swelling of earth that made up the very top of the hill. He walked around it, looking down, then crouched and ran his fingers through the short grass. There were molehills scattered here and there but he could see no sign of human disturbance, and he had no idea what he was looking for.

He would have walked away but he had a sudden strong feeling that Joe hadn't gone, that the man was watching him from down in the trees. Moving thirty paces to one side of the spot, he got down on the ground and did four slow push-ups, his head raised, staring at the place Joe had indicated. It was an old trick, shown to him on his very first student dig, but it worked. The change in perspective as he lifted himself up and down, just a foot off the ground, gave him an exaggerated view of the small changes in the topography of the land ahead.

Close to the earth, smelling the bruised grass under his hands, he suddenly knew what Joe had been pointing at.

The very top of the hill had a shape all of its own, rising just a fraction more steeply than the natural curve of the land, a flattened dome maybe fifteen yards across. He followed the line of it as closely as he could, estimating the height. It was probably no more than two feet at the most above the natural lie of the land. He moved to one side and did the push-ups again, and he could almost persuade himself that there was the ghost of a ring-ditch all the way around the low dome. The surviving evidence was slender but after he'd looked carefully at it for several minutes, he was convinced he was looking at a barrow, a burial mound, flattened by the slow erosion of wind and rain from the Bronze Age days of its building.

Patrick felt a sudden keen disappointment and was immediately angry with himself for his lack of logic. A Bronze Age barrow was interesting enough, especially if it had never been spotted before. In his preliminary work before coming on-site, he had seen no evidence of such a barrow on the maps. But it did not fit with Anglo-Saxon bed burials. All the way up the hill, there had been an absurd hope at the back of his mind that Joe's song had meant something, that maybe at the end of this mysterious journey there would be a clue to the last resting place of his German Queen. Instead, there was something here, but it was a something that predated what Patrick wanted it to be by well over a thousand years.

He sat down on the ground on the very top of the flattened barrow mound and looked down at the Thames valley below, wondering again why Joe had got him out of bed so early and so uncompromisingly to bring him to this spot. It was the first moment he'd had for reflection since this doomed dig began, and reflection wasn't what Patrick most enjoyed. In the stifled, quiet years since he had reformed his life, he'd spent a lot of time, indeed almost all of his time, by himself, but reflection had taken the shape of self-accusation more than anything else. Something had changed here, and he put it down to the fact that, despite himself, he was enjoying the company of these people—CD's nonchalant wit, Dozer's solidity, even Aidan and Maxwell. For a moment his mind brought Bobby into the equation, but Bobby was a dangerous diversion from the straight and narrow, a shortcut back to lost Rachel.

He swore to himself, and only when a crow flapped away from its place in the field beside him did he realise it had not been to himself at all. He didn't recognise the truth, which was that in the past two days, he had started to become a real person again, and the process was painful. It wasn't just a question of guilt. Blame had helped him through the last few years. Sharing the blame for David. Bobby took him back to a Rachel he still loved, a Rachel he could not blame.

David would have run down this hillside. David, his dark, liquid hair flying behind him, would have leapt on his stocky legs and tumbled over without minding and rummaged in the grass for sticks and stones to produce like jewels. The earth was always full of treasure for David.

All this time, Patrick had been fiddling, running his fingers through the loose soil of the molehill on which his right hand was resting, playing with the tiny loose stones and letting them trickle through his hand. But as his thoughts took this painful turn he let everything go except one larger stone, which he turned over and over in his fingers like a worry bead, taking comfort from its cylindrical regularity.

Gradually the quality of that regularity forced itself through to the front of his mind and he opened his palm and looked down at it. Geology is always playing cruel tricks on over-optimistic archaeologists. Many an experienced eye has been misled by a freakishly regular piece of natural stone, but not many stones are shaped like cylinders with a tubular hole running through them from end to end. Patrick spat in his palm, rubbed the surface of the little cylinder with his finger. Colour, man-made colour, burst through its coating of grey soil-dust; bright yellow greeted the matching morning sun for the first time in centuries.

Had it been a piece of pottery, he would not have been immediately sure of its period, but it wasn't pottery. It was opaque yellow glass, decorated with thin red lines in the characteristic crossing-wave pattern, finely worked, beautiful, and as precisely dateable as you could wish for.

Anglo-Saxon. Seventh century. He'd drawn Saxon beads by the hundred for practice in his studies. He knew them backwards and this one was perfect—an extraordinary thing to find right where the tongue-tied singer had brought him—a bead you might easily find in a seventh-century burial. Joe's song had said something about beads, amber beads around her head, or something like that. This wasn't amber, but it did very well for a substitute.

Patrick scrambled to his feet and looked down at the wood where Joe had disappeared. He could have been standing there, hidden in the trees. It was impossible to tell. Patrick waved and gestured, wanting the man to appear, to come and look at this miraculous find, to find a way to tell him more. No one came out of the wood.

It was still early. There was a far buzz of commuter traffic heading for Oxford on the A40. In the foreground, an occasional car drove down from the village to the plain. Patrick moved to sit down again but found he could not. The grass he had sat on before was now undeniably someone's grave, someone who had owned this bead. He sat down instead where he judged the faint impression of the ring-ditch to be, looking again at the bead in his hand, not as an artifact heading for measurement, recording, and a glass case, but as a messenger, bursting out of the earth with a tale to tell. Seeking to postpone the moment of returning to the start of what looked set to be a bad day down the hill, he clasped the bead in his hand and stared down towards Wytchlow, the village mostly hidden down under the curve of the land.

Wytchlow. The name jumped at him. As Dozer had picked up last night, *low* often meant a burial mound, *low* from the old Saxon *hlaew,* as in Posses Low. You had to be careful with such names. In some parts of the country it was used just as often for a natural hill, but not here, not in Oxfordshire. He'd said last night that *Wytch* could be a personal name, so this could be Wytch's low, the place where Wytch was buried, but there was Wychwood, too. The Hwicca? Something else was nagging at him, something he had read. It wouldn't come back.

Patrick thought again of the owner of the bead. Were they fresh from their homeland on the north German coast, pushed out by

rising sea levels in front and rising population behind, taking to
their boats for a fresh start? What had they made of this alien landscape? He looked down towards the ruined field. The remains of
Roman buildings would still have been a dominant presence across
that seventh-century landscape, littered with the walls of collapsing
villas and disintegrating temples left behind in the fifth century
as those who organised Roman Britain fled for home. The Angles
and the Saxons didn't use stone. What would they have thought of
these alien, almost magical, constructions that were thick on the
ground right through the valleys of the Evenlode, the Windrush, the
Cherwell, and the Thames, the favoured locations for great Roman
estates? Anger rose in him again as he thought how long it had
lasted, that mosaic floor of which they had caught only a glimpse—
of how it had ticked away the centuries undisturbed until it had got
in the way of a greedy man's plans.

In the back of his mind, the inner voice that never left him told
him he, too, had been greedy; he, too, had despoiled; he shared that
same sin to the full.

The bead, intricate and vibrant, distracted him. It was safer to
sink into the bead's history than his own. The Germanic tribes—the
Angles, the Saxons, and the Jutes—used up their creative energy
more often in their possessions than in their housing. A Roman
would have poured this energy into the intricate decoration of his
walls and floors, using the wealth harvested from the skilful organi-
sation of great farming estates to build them so well their artistic
message would last a millennium or more. No Anglo-Saxon would
have bothered with that. Postholes for their houses, most of them little more than timber tents, were the only lasting evidence of their
construction efforts. Civilisation had crumbled fast in the two hundred years between the Romans' departure and the burial of this
bead. Literacy had vanished with the Romans. Four hundred years of
occupation had taught the Britons how to enjoy the Roman way of
life, but not how to maintain it when the teachers left. Then, unprotected and faced by waves of pagan invasion, they brought in their
own pagans, the first mercenaries from the German coast, not knowing they were inviting in the Dark Ages, as the floodgates opened to
their invading kin.

How would it have been for the bead-wearer, living here? Patrick
knew what the archaeology showed. *British* and *English* were not

synonyms then, far from it. *English* meant Angles, the Germanic invaders, worshipping Thor and Woden and the rest of their pantheon. *British* meant Britons, the Celtic people who'd been here long before the Romans ever came and who had blended their gods into Rome's new Christianity. He looked toward the scarred field below. The archaeology showed that these incoming English and their neighbours, the Saxons, skirted round the Roman remains for a hundred and fifty years. It told him that these people displaced the British who were here before by some unknown mixture of violence and integration. It also told him, most fascinatingly of all, that quite suddenly, after 600 A.D., Anglo-Saxon attitudes changed. They began to annex the old Roman sites with new confidence, using the now picturesque ruins as burial places for the most important among their dead, borrowing their gravitas. At the same time, they began to use the much more ancient earthworks, too, inserting their cuckoo-dead into these old nests. Archaeology told him all these things but it didn't tell him *why,* and that was what he wanted to know.

Patrick studied the just-discernible shape of the mound. It had been someone else's glory that the Anglo-Saxon burial party had usurped, some much older warrior whose bones had been shoveled aside for the new occupant. That change in attitude fascinated him. He was interested above all in why people change, and he had good reason.

The sun was higher now, starting to drive the dew off the grass. Soon he would have to go down the hill again and preside over the sad laying-to-rest of his ruined project. Not yet, though. It wasn't even seven o'clock. There was time to sit here awhile yet and consider this bead and this barrow. Then he remembered what it was that was nagging him about the possible origin of the name of Wytchlow.

Something he'd read, some dissertation on Oxfordshire place names, picked up during a long afternoon in the dusty peace of the Ashmolean library, had suggested the village might once have had a longer name. On the slender evidence of an old and almost indecipherable charter, the writer had suggested an older name for the village, "Wytchamlow," and that was suddenly much more interesting.

*Wicham* in its various forms was a name the Anglo-Saxons started using soon after their arrival. The place-name expert, Margaret Gelling, listing the place names that included it, showed that they were mostly associated with old Roman sites, often near major Roman roads. She took the logical approach, suggesting the names survived because the sites still had a use for the Saxons, as markets or as land boundaries. Patrick had a wildly illogical idea, a gut feeling. He thought the word *wicham* had a superstitious overtone, a name you might use to describe ruins you would pass with a shudder, keeping to the other side of those old straight roads, walking quickly and muttering a prayer to your own gods. Stone walls, even walls that were overgrown and tumbled, would do that to you if they were outside your own timber experience. Fragments of paintings on the walls, vivid pictures on the floor, bearded men with thunderbolts would terrify.

A *wicham* would be a place to shun in the dark.

*Wytchamlow,* the burial mound by the Roman ruins. It made sense. And who, he wondered, was the Saxon cuckoo in the old mound on which he was now sitting? The Saxon whose burial bead he was holding? Could it possibly be Joe's valiant German Queen on her wooden bed?

THE WICHAM LOW WAS A GOOD THEORY, BUT QUITE WRONG. THE MOUND THAT TOOK THE NAME OF "HWICCA'S LOW" PREDATED THE HWICCA, OF COURSE, BUT IT WAS A PROMINENT FEATURE OF THEIR LANDSCAPE, A BUMP THAT MARKED THE SKYLINE AS THEIRS FROM THE EAST, FROM THE DIRECTION OF THEIR AMBITIOUS NEIGHBOURS.

ONLY UNBRIDGEABLE TIME SEPARATED THE PLACE WHERE PATRICK SAT FROM THE PLACE WHERE HILD, CUTHA'S SISTER, SAT WAITING FOR THE END OF HER WATCH. THE MOUND SHE SAT ON WAS STEEPER AND, IN HER HEAD, SHE HAD POLITELY ASKED THE SPIRIT OF THE MOUND FOR PERMISSION TO USE IT AS HER SEAT. LIKE CUTHA, HILD KEPT A CAREFUL EYE ON THE WALLS BELOW. WHEN SHE WAS YOUNGER AND A TOMBOY, SHE HAD DARED THE BOYS TO GO IN THERE. THEY CLAIMED IT WAS A HOUSE OF THE *PUCA,* THE GOBLINS, BUT SHE KNEW THERE WERE NO GOBLINS THERE, ONLY ELFEN, AND THE FAIRIES DID NOT FRIGHTEN HER. SHE KNEW THE BRIGHT GLASS BEADS SHE WORE PLEASED THE FAIRIES. IT WAS POLITE TO WARN THEM WHEN

YOU WERE COMING, SO SHE SANG WHENEVER SHE WENT TO THE PLACE OF THE FLOOR-PICTURE.

SHE SQUINTED AT THE SUN AND WORRIED. THEIR FATHER HAD SAID HE WOULD SEND SOMEONE ELSE BY NOW, BECAUSE THERE WAS A GREAT DEAL TO DO AND A SHORT TIME TO DO IT. EVERYTHING HAD BEEN WET FOR DAYS AND THE FLOOR OF THE BEORNAS HALL, THE GREAT HOUSE OF THE WARRIORS WHERE THEY LIVED, WAS A MISERABLE MESS OF DAMP RUSHES AND THE MUD THAT CAME IN FROM THE YARD ON HER BROTHERS' FEET. THE THATCHED ROOF OF THE DRY STORE WHERE SHE KEPT RUSHES THROUGH THE WINTER, HAD SPRUNG AN UNSUSPECTED LEAK SO SHE'D SPENT EVERY SPARE MOMENT OF THE PAST TWO SUNNY DAYS SPREADING THE RUSHES OUT ON THE GRASS, TURNING THEM TO GET THE DAMP OUT. SHE LOOKED ANXIOUSLY AT THE CLOUDS. IF THEY BROUGHT RAIN BEFORE THE END OF HER WATCH, ALL HER EFFORT WOULD BE WASTED AND THE FLOOR WOULD CONTINUE TO BE A QUAGMIRE. NOT THAT ANYONE SEEMED TO NOTICE EXCEPT HER.

SHE HAD A SPECIAL PRAYER TO OFFER THAT DAY. DISTURBING RUMOURS WERE MAKING THEIR WAY UP THE HILL WITH THE OCCASIONAL TRADER WHO STILL CAME FROM THE RIVER. THE SPIRIT OF THE MOUND WAS A POWERFUL SPIRIT, AND HILD HAD DECIDED TO OFFER A SUITABLY POWERFUL GIFT. THERE WERE SIX BEAUTIFUL BEADS ON HER NECKLACE AND SHE WOULD STILL HAVE FIVE, SO, THOUGH THE LOSS HURT HER, SHE SLIPPED ONE OF THEM OFF AND RETIED THE LEATHER THONG. SHE TRIED SCRAPING THE EARTH AWAY WITH HER FINGERS TO BURY IT, BUT THAT ONLY MADE A SHALLOW SCRAPE; THEN SHE SAW A TINY HOLE MADE BY A MOUSE OR A VOLE. SHE DROPPED THE BEAD IN, PUSHED IT DOWN OUT OF SIGHT WITH A GRASS STALK, AND SAID A FERVENT PRAYER FOR PEACE.

# Chapter Ten

PATRICK HAD COME BACK DOWN the hill at quarter to eight with a secret in his pocket and a wild idea. He went straight into the catering tent where Bobby was serving porridge and poured himself a mug of tea from a big aluminium pot. She looked startlingly fresh against the frowsy queue of camping-crumpled diggers, and she had a smile for everyone, which seemed to be making up for the shortcomings of the porridge. Patrick took his place in the line, enjoying watching her, and when he held out his bowl, she stared at him curiously, her eyes bright. Unsettled, he ran his fingers through his hair and surreptitiously checked his fly. There was nothing wrong. He could not guess it was just that he looked fully alive for the first time since they'd met and he was moving with the assured purpose of someone who had rediscovered his direction.

"Morning," she said. "How are you?"

"Good morning," he answered, smiling. "I've been up to the top of the hill." He gestured towards it. "That is your field up there, isn't it?"

"Yes," she said. "And the field beyond."

"Do you plough it?"

"No, it's just pasture, really. There's hardly any soil." She wondered why he looked so pleased. She had been wondering about him and the diggers' rumours of his past for much of the previous twenty-four hours. This seemed a different Patrick who faced her now, a Patrick with someone there behind the eyes, someone who looked straight at you, whose responses came quickly, not a heartbeat late. He had a powerful enthusiasm about him; she vastly preferred this version. They said he'd been a legend. Until this morning it had been hard to see how that could be.

He left the tent as abruptly as he had come.

Knowing the odds were stacked against him, he dialed John Hescroft on the mobile phone from the far end of the field, well away from other ears. He knew that if Hescroft asked the right questions, he would find it very hard to justify what he was about to suggest. Before he dialed, he rehearsed the conversation.

*"I've found a probable Anglo-Saxon burial. I want to look at it while we're here."*

*"What's the evidence?"*

*"A song I heard in a pub and something I pulled out of a molehill."*

That wasn't even the tough part.

*"Who's going to pay for it?"*

That was the real question, but as it turned out, it was a question Hescroft never asked, in a conversation that was not at all what Patrick expected.

It started off on predictable lines.

"We're wrapping up this afternoon, John."

"Nothing else on the site?"

"Nothing that counts."

"It's a big disappointment, Patrick. I don't need to tell you. There's going to be a fuss about this. All that effort and planning gone for nothing."

"Well, there is one other thing. . . ."

"What's that?"

"I think I've found another site."

"What do you mean?"

"Could be a good one—a possible Saxon furnished burial in a barrow just up the hill. Unknown, I'm sure." He must be mad, he thought, to be inflating this slender evidence so far. Hescroft would surely burst his bubble at any second. Anyway—and this was the big difference between PSC and a proper, university-based archaeological unit—why should PSC care? It was in it for the contracts, for the money, not for knowledge for its own sake.

Hescroft didn't burst his bubble. There was a thoughtful silence, then a wholly unexpected response. "Really? Now, that's something else. Whose land is it?"

"Bobby's. The woman you hired to cook."

"And you think it might be the real thing?"

"Too early to tell."

"But you think so, or you wouldn't have mentioned it?"

"Well . . . yes."

"Would she let us dig?"

Us? "I'm pretty sure she would."

"It's not a protected monument?"

"No, it's not listed. It's a plain old field."

"I'll be out in an hour or so."

Patrick ended the call in a state of pleasant bewilderment, astonished that Hescroft hadn't dismissed his idea out of hand.

He would have been less pleased if he could have seen the scene in Hescroft's office, where, replacing the phone on its rest, his boss looked across the desk at the man opposite, a white-haired man in an expensive black leather jacket who reeked of old cigarettes, and said, "You're going to like this."

Oblivious to what was going on in Oxford, Patrick was standing with the phone in his hand, gazing up at the hill in thought, when a hesitant voice behind him said, "Patrick?" and he looked round to see Bobby there, wiping her hands on a tea towel.

"Yes?"

"I didn't mean to disturb you. It looked like you were thinking. It's just I want to know how many more meals you'll need."

When she talked, it wasn't so bad. She didn't sound like Rachel. The worst times were when she was silent, and he was answering, looking straight at her. Then he found it hard to concentrate.

"I don't know yet," he said, "but it might depend on you."

"How do you mean?"

"Joe woke me up this morning. I think he wanted to show me something. He led me up the hill."

She frowned. "This hill?"

"Yes. Did you know there's a burial mound at the top, an old barrow?"

"No, I didn't."

"Joe pointed it out to me."

"Are you sure?"

"Yes, I am. Completely sure. It was as plain as anything."

"I can't think of anything up there that looks like a barrow."

"You hardly notice it unless you know where to look. It's there right enough, and what's more, I found something there."

"What was it?"

"Have a look."

Patrick showed her the yellow glass cylinder and watched with pleasure as she turned it in her fingers, entranced by it. "It's Anglo-Saxon," he told her, "much more recent than the barrow. I think there must be a later burial there."

"Just because of this?"

"No, there's more. I went on looking after I found that. There are some molehills and an old rabbit hole, and in the edge of the rabbit hole I found these." He brought out of his pocket two short grey pieces of what could have been dry wood.

"Bones?" she said, looking at them. She took one from him. "Human toe bones."

"Yes. How did you know?"

"Oh, I know some things. They're pretty distinctive." She gave it back. "So when you say it might depend on me . . ."

"I mean, I'd like to get my boss to agree to let us dig a trial trench up there, while we've got everyone together. It seems a waste not to. Also it would make it a bit less of a disappointment for everyone here. You would have to give your agreement. It's your land."

"Mine and Joe's—not just mine. He'd have to agree, too."

"I think he would. After all, he showed me the place. That must have been what he had in mind." Patrick wondered whether he could voice what he really felt and decided to say it anyway. "The song he sang . . . the song about the German Queen. I thought maybe he took me there because it was about that place."

She just raised her eyebrows, that was all, but immediately the bottom dropped out of his certainty. If it sounded absurd to her, Joe's loyal sister, then how much more absurd would it seem to anybody else?

"I'll ask him if it's all right," she said, "tonight."

"You'll *ask* him?"

"Yes. We do communicate. I'll mention it to him and he'll let me know one way or another if he doesn't agree, believe me."

OHN HESCROFT CAME INTO THE FIELD, NOT IN HIS OWN CAR but as the passenger in a huge black Toyota Land Cruiser with metallic red logos on the doors. Patrick read the words written below the logos, "Belwether Productions, Film & TV," and began, belatedly, to smell a rat.

Hescroft had a wide, public-relations smile on his face and slapped Patrick on the shoulder with his left hand while shaking hands with his right.

"Want you to meet Kenny, Patrick. Kenny Camden from Belwether. Kenny, this is our new young superstar, Patrick Kane."

And what did Kenny Camden say, smiling a tobacco-stained smile, long white hair flowing in the wind, but, "Hi, Paddy. It's a great pleasure to meet you again. We've got a lot to talk about."

*Again?* thought Patrick. He had no recollection of ever having seen the man before. "It's Patrick," he said stiffly.

Kenny gave a conspiratorial wink. "OK. Patrick. Got it."

"What about this new site?" said Hescroft. "Give us the lowdown."

"New site?" said CD, walking up. "Hi, John." Then he stuck his hand out to the TV producer. "Hi, I'm CD. Mr. C. D. Corcoran, if you want to be formal."

"Kenny Camden. I read your piece on the Ridgeway hill forts."

"Wow, that makes three—you, me, and my mother."

"No, no, I was impressed," insisted Camden smoothly. "What do you think of this burial mound of Patrick's?"

CD looked quizzically at Patrick for a moment and Patrick saw that this was the point at which everything would fall to pieces. He'd said nothing to anyone except Bobby. He hadn't even shown CD the bead. What an idiot. What a way to treat a friend.

"Too early to tell," CD told Camden, "but you never know, do you? Better let Patrick talk you through it. I'll just listen. I'd love to hear it all over again." He turned a beaming smile on Patrick, who blessed him from the bottom of his heart.

"There's a local tradition of a burial site at the top of this hill, an Anglo-Saxon burial inserted in an older mound." Patrick picked his words carefully. "I was shown the place early this morning by someone who's lived here a long time. There's clearly the remains of a small barrow there with a ring-ditch around it. Possibly Bronze Age. It looks to me like it's been eroded, not ploughed out. There's been rabbit and mole activity, and I found this in the waste soil." He brought out the bead.

Hescroft whistled and picked it off his palm to show to the producer. "Look at that, will you? Typical Anglo-Saxon."

"Ain't she a little beauty?" said CD, just as if he had seen the bead before and was merely confirming the judgment.

"Then there are these," Patrick said quickly, hoping the bones really were what he thought they were. He had a sudden illogical fear that they might be something else entirely.

"Human," said CD after the briefest of glances, "definitely human."

Hescroft and the producer exchanged significant looks and the man in the black leather jacket nodded.

"Well, now," said Hescroft. "Kenny and I have been discussing this programme idea, and he wants to shoot a pilot to see if he can get one of the majors interested in a series. We were going to suggest shooting the Roman dig, until certain—well, certain untoward events got in the way."

"This is better," said Kenny. "We'll be in from the start."

"There might be nothing there," said Patrick faintly.

Kenny shrugged. "It's only a couple of days' shooting to find out, right?"

"I can't say that for certain," Patrick objected, but felt Hescroft's arm creep round his shoulders.

"Two days should do it," said Hescroft firmly. "You and I will have a little talk afterwards, Patrick."

"It'll make a great show," enthused Kenny. "I can see it now. The wild man of rock puts down his guitar and picks up a trowel."

"What did you say?" said Patrick.

"Whoa, no offence."

Patrick swung round on Hescroft. "What have you been telling him?"

"Nothing," protested Hescroft, astonished. "I don't know what he's talking about."

"Let it go, Paddy," said Kenny. "He didn't tell me. He didn't have to. You've got a short memory. I shot your second video. Don't you remember?"

Of course he didn't. That sort of thing happened somewhere out in corridors, the hazy corridors of his life then. You just hired people to do things like that. They weren't people you noticed.

"The *Devil Dream* album, for Christ's sake," said Camden. "OK, you've lost the hair, but you're not hard to spot. You did the greatest disappearing act since Elvis. Everybody wants to know what happened to Paddy Kane. You don't forget Nam Erewhon that easily."

"Nam what?" said Hescroft.

"You really don't know," said Kenny, looking at him in surprise. "You mean you really don't know who you've got here? The man who told the prime minister he was a power-mad war criminal? The man who wrote 'Wedding Vows.' The man who—"

"That's my business," interrupted Patrick. "I don't want all that brought up. I just want to forget it, OK?"

"Not OK, no," said Kenny. "This show stands or falls on human interest, on you being in it, and don't tell me it makes any difference if we call you something else. You haven't changed that much, chum. People are still going to notice you even if we don't tell them. It takes a celebrity to make a show like this tick."

"No way," said Patrick. "Absolutely no way!"

"Don't shout," said Hescroft, alarmed.

"I don't give a shit."

"John," said the producer, "let's you and I sit in the car and talk this through. Then we'll all get together and have a little talk with your boy here when we've hacked out the details."

Patrick stalked back down the field with CD. The American cast around for something to say that would ease the furious isolation of the man next to him.

"Listen, it doesn't matter."

Silence.

"He's just a TV jerk."

A slight bounce of the head.

"Patrick, what difference does it make? Everybody here knows you used to be famous."

"How do they know that? Because you told them?"

"No way."

"Dozer, then?"

"Dozer wouldn't do that—not when he saw it mattered. One of the other guys recognised you."

"Which one?"

"That doesn't matter. Old Doze and I, we did our best. We—"

"What do you mean—you did your best? You mean you two have been going round talking about me?"

"Hey, now, that's enough, mister. You can't have it both ways. Yeah, we did. We went round asking people to lay off you. Do you have a problem with that?"

"Yes. I'm not a freak show. I'm not there for people to tiptoe round me, gossiping when I can't hear."

"The jury's out on that one. Because that's just the way you're behaving."

"What way?"

"Like some kind of freak show."

Patrick swung round on him, furious, then saw CD's eyes, enlarged by the bottle-ends of his lenses. The eyes had nothing but concern in them.

He exhaled noisily. "I'm sorry. Maybe I've got this a little out of perspective."

"That's OK. Look, I don't know what you've been through, but if you want to talk about it . . ."

Patrick had constructed his recent life around not talking about his past, not seeing anyone from his past, not putting himself in any surroundings where that past might come back and bite him. The offer was kind, but it hurt.

"I'll be all right."

"Ding, ding," said CD. "That's the noise my not-entirely-true detector makes."

"CD," said Patrick, "I know you mean it well, but there is nothing, absolutely nothing in my old life I want to talk about. I wish none of it had happened. I would dearly like it to be . . ." He was about to say "buried" but the image of the two graves in Denbigh churchyard punched him in the stomach.

". . . forgotten."

"People won't forget you," said CD. "You can change the way you look, but you can't change the way you sound."

"I don't sing anymore."

"You talk. You've got a hell of a distinctive voice however you use it. That's how people know it's you."

"Oh, shit. Really? I didn't know that."

"Really. Plus one other small thing. Your face."

"I don't look the same."

"If you say so. And by the way, just before you consign it all to history, I would like you to know that I think you were one of the all-time greats."

"CD, that is no comfort, believe me. No comfort at all."

SITTING IN THE LAND CRUISER, KENNY CAMDEN WAS SPELLING it out to John Hescroft.

"That's amazing," he said. "You promise me you really didn't have any idea?"

"I don't know about that sort of music," Hescroft answered. "I can't even remember what he said he'd been doing all that time. Traveling, I think. You get a lot of these ex-hippie types in archaeology. They bum round the world and do a bit here and a bit there. The great thing is, they all love what they do. You can employ them for peanuts as long as you promise to feed them."

"But he wasn't just anyone. He was famous. Paddy Kane."

Hescroft shook his head again. "No. Why did he give it all up?"

"I can't remember, but I'll soon find out. Something went wrong. He left the band and what was left didn't amount to anything when he'd gone. They broke up completely. Now listen, John, you've got to talk to the boy. Make him understand. He knows about publicity."

"What do I say to him? You heard him."

"You say to him, 'You want to dig this barrow, that's the price you pay—take it or leave it.' "

"What price exactly?"

"That he fronts the show."

"You mean, you make it clear he was this . . . this rock star."

The producer considered and grinned. "You don't have to spell that out. Tell him we'll let him just be Patrick Kane, archaeologist." *The hell we will,* he thought. *This one is going to leak, and then watch the ratings.*

S O PATRICK WAS CALLED BACK AND PUT ON THE SPOT, AND though he knew he was supping with the devil, in the end he had little choice. The song and the bead had got him and he could not leave the mound alone. The only way they could dig on the hill was if Kenny Camden was shooting it for his pilot. Hescroft had stars in his eyes, and he'd pay some of the bills if he had incentive. TV was the incentive. Publicity for PSC was the incentive. Money was the incentive. After supper had been served in the catering tent, Patrick caught Bobby in the middle of clearing up and said, "I need to talk to you about the barrow. When will you see Joe?"

"As soon as I get this lot back." She indicated the stack of dirty pans. "He'll be waiting for his own supper."

"What shall we do?"

"I'll come back and tell you, if you like. Probably not until about nine-thirty. Are you going to be here or at the pub?"

It was a fine evening, warm and clear. "Here, I think."

"I'll see you later, then."

When she'd gone, Patrick called everybody together.

"You know this dig's over," he told them, "and I'm very sorry about the circumstances. Some of you, I know, are disappointed not to get the chance to do a proper dig. Well, I don't want to raise your hopes too much, but there's a possibility we could go on and do another dig very close to here. John Hescroft's asked me to point out that it will be entirely a matter of volunteering. There's no money available."

"So what else is new?" said Dozer.

"I won't be able to tell you much more until tomorrow morning, but think about it." He was about to let them go. Then, on the spur of the moment, he decided there was, after all, something more to say.

"Also . . . I know that some of you have picked up the fact that I used to be, um . . . well, involved in the music business." It would have been good to make some sort of joke out of it, a flip, disarming comment, but humour was unknown in the mental Siberia that made up this part of his past. "That's ancient history. It's something I've left behind, so please, if you don't mind, allow me just to be an archaeologist for the purposes of this dig, and nothing else."

They all seemed to be looking at him very hard. Aidan nodded slowly, and Gaye looked around at her neighbours with a disconcertingly conspiratorial expression on her face.

The crew went to the pub; Patrick found it easy to resist their invitations to come, too. He suspected that they needed a break without him, to discuss him in all probability, and he found he didn't really care what they said. There was nearly two hours to kill, so when he was sure that they'd gone on ahead, he walked down the lane into the centre of the village, crossing the green well away from the pub. At the far end, near the apex of the long triangle, there was a low brick building with notice boards in front of it. It had the look of a village hall, and there were lights on inside it. He stopped and looked in. Newspaper was spread across the floor and two women were on their knees in the middle of it, painting an old cart in glossy black. It had two wheels at the back, a smaller one at the front, and a long wooden handle to tow it along. Inside was a seat of cracked and desiccated leather. A Victorian Bath chair, he thought, designed for pulling the aged, the infirm, or the just plain pampered around the streets. It had seen better days. Where the hood would once have been, there were hoops of wire, arching over the seat. Its wheels were bright red.

He was lost in thought, inspecting this strange vehicle, when hands grabbed at his legs. He looked down in shock to see a small devil tugging at his knees, cackling. It was half his height, but its face was no child's face. It was dark and deformed, covered in disturbing, crawling shapes.

"No, stop that," he said, alarmed, putting his hands out to fend off the thing. "Leave me alone."

A woman's voice from inside yelled "Mikey!" and the little creature rushed out of sight round the corner, still cackling with laughter.

Patrick took a deep breath and walked away, heading back to the camp wondering just what he had been looking at, glad to leave the village behind. Back at the tent, he dragged one of the catering tables outside, set up a folding chair, and lit a candle inside a jam jar. When Bobby came quietly back to the field an hour later, she saw in the candlelight that his cheeks were wet.

# CHAPTER ELEVEN

PATRICK HAD NOT BEEN PRE-pared for the flood of pain that came when he moved the candle.

Most things that hurt eventually blunt themselves by their repeated assaults on a defended mind, and he had become good at defences. After Perugia, when his wanderings ended and he was persuaded by a stranger to go on living, he knew he didn't want disciples anymore, although disciples seemed to hurl themselves at him as soon as he opened his mouth. He chose isolation to avoid that, and spent the next seven hundred long evenings sitting alone immersed in academic tasks, reading textbooks or dig reports where human life was safely sterilized, the flesh stripped from the bone. It didn't take him back to the happiness of his student days, but it did occupy his mind and build a bulwark against the derailing influence of others. This time round, he was a student only by his own definition. He had his degree already, he'd just forgotten it all. Living a very quiet life on a tiny portion of his royalty cheques, he set himself a two-year course of intensive reading, and although he used the same libraries as students, he wasn't part of their lives. He didn't share tutorials and lectures with them, didn't have a college, and when they set their books aside in the evenings and went to the pub, he stayed with his books.

One or two girls tried very hard to reach him during that time because he was a fascinating figure, the cause of much speculation. If they caught his eye there was often a momentary flash of something extremely exciting before he looked away. Imagine him with hair and he'd be quite like Paddy Kane, one or two of them said. One brash American girl, confident in her powers of attraction, tried to get him for weeks. In the end, driven to desperate measures by her lack of progress, she put a note in front of him which simply said "Fancy a fuck?" and out of some sort of bemused politeness, he followed her out of the library at lunchtime to her dorm room. There was a robotic quality about the love he made, and she told friends afterwards that she'd never had to work so hard at anything in her life, but he said little and his eyes seemed to be looking at the past, not at her, so that was the end of it.

I N THE PEACE OF THE DESERTED CAMPSITE, HE WAS TRYING TO draw the Anglo-Saxon bead on which his entire theory rested; all he had done was drag the jam jar closer to light his sketch pad. As he moved, the flame flared as hot wax spilt, sending a brief splash of light out through the jar's lurid label—pastels of red and green and blue across the white sheet of sketching paper, and instantly, unprotected, he was back in Italy.

In Perugia Cathedral, in limbo between his betrayal and the retribution that immediately followed, he had watched a small boy playing on the marble floor, entranced by the spangle splashes of colour dashed across the stone by the Italian sun through the stained glass. This evening, the memory of that boy, that little Italian stranger, had conjured David out of the darkness just as it had at the time. David, brimming with trust and love and promise, stood there in the unreachable shadows. When Bobby came out of those shadows instead,

Patrick's cheeks were wet and Bobby, walking silently up to the table, staring at his face, wasn't sure if he even knew she was there.

Stopping at a distance, on the edge of the candle glow, she waited until his head moved fractionally towards her, then she spoke softly.

"Hello, Patrick? I just came to tell you that Joe's very pleased. I told him what you said and he did a little dance."

There was more silence because Patrick was dragging himself back from where he had been and didn't yet trust himself to speak. What the candle flame had just done to him had come out of the blue. Until then he had found himself in an unfamiliar state of anticipation mixed with apprehension, knowing Bobby would be coming back.

"You can start when you like," she said, to fill the gap. "I suppose you'll have to move all the tents out of here but there's a track into our field at the other end, and there's a good flat space at the top of the hill. Well, you've seen it, I suppose. It can be a bit windy but it's well drained up there. I can move stuff with the tractor and trailer if it would help." Another silence but now at least he was looking up at her.

"I don't know how easy it is to move things like those loos but I'm sure we could manage if everyone . . ."

" 'How beautifully blue the sky, the glass is rising very high,' " said Patrick.

"What?"

" 'Continue fine I hope it may, and yet it rained but yesterday.' "

"I think I'm missing something here," she said cautiously.

"Gilbert and Sullivan," he said. His voice sounded normal to him now. "It's a song the chorus sings to fill up an embarrassing silence. Is it *The Pirates of Penzance?* I can't remember."

"You could ask Peter. He'd probably know."

"Does he know about everything else, too, as well as archaeology?"

"I think so," she said. "He knows about field drainage and cattle diseases anyway. Was that what I was doing, filling an embarrassing silence?"

"Wasn't it?"

"I wasn't embarrassed. I just thought you needed a moment or two."

"Yeah, I did. Thanks."

"You're an odd man."

"Sit down and tell me about it. Hang on. There's another chair somewhere. Would you like a glass of wine? It's pretty horrible."

"I only like horrible wine," she said.

And so they sat there on opposite sides of a flimsy wooden table with the candle between them, and the low yellow light of the candle lit one side of Bobby's face in a new and startling way so that he saw just ivory curves and deep shadows and she saw an El Greco face, even more haunted than the one he usually presented to the world.

"You're not wearing your hat," he said. Her hair was tied back, dark in the dim candlelight, a small mercy, banishing Rachel.

"I'm not working right now, nor in the pub with the farmers. I do get a bit of time off."

He looked for safe ground. "I saw something odd in the village. They were painting this old cart."

"Ah. That's not just an old cart. That's the May Queen's carriage. It's May Day in nine days."

"What happens on May Day?"

He knew at once that this might be safe ground for him but it wasn't for her. There was a new note of bitterness in her voice when she replied.

"Normally something lovely. This year, maybe a revolution."

"Meaning?"

She sighed. "There's a squabble going on in the village. It may sound a bit trivial to an outsider but it's one of those really divisive things. Anyway, it seems huge to me."

"Tell me."

"I'm up against the headmaster. There's a tradition here, going back heaven knows how long. It's quite beautiful, really. Every May Day, the schoolchildren sing all round the village. They go to the houses of all the old people who can't get out and about. It takes up most of the day. There's a procession and it centres round the old Bath chair. Everyone gets up at dawn on May Morning and we all go out into the meadow down by the river, we call it Claim Meadow, and we pick the flowers while the dew is still on them. The children put the dew in little bottles for their mothers because if you put May Morning dew on your face, you lose your wrinkles. Did you know that?"

"I didn't."

"After that, there's a big breakfast in the Reading Room—that's

the place where they were painting the chair—then we all decorate
the cart with flowers and we push the May Queen round the village
in it before the maypole dancing."

"So why the squabble?"

"It's absurd, isn't it? There's a new headmaster and he's one of
these educational hothouse types. You know the sort."

He feared for a moment that she was going to ask him if he had
children, but she didn't.

"He thinks school holidays are far too long and he's really into
exams and grading and all that. He's banned May Day this year. Says
it's got to happen at the weekend out of school time because the Na-
tional Curriculum doesn't leave any time for it. I mean to say, what
harm would a few hours do? That's all it takes. He must be mad. It's
only a *junior* school."

"Isn't there anybody else you can go to? What about the School
Governors?"

She shook her head. "They're on his side. It's a Church of England school. We had a great vicar up to last year, the Reverend Jim,
but he's gone and now this awful old man has come in who acts as if
he owns our souls. He's straight out of Trollope, a double-barreled
name and a single-barreled mind. I think he was an army chaplain
or something, but he's extraordinarily narrow-minded. He says May
Day's a pagan festival and it's un-Christian to celebrate it."

He wondered for a moment which Trollope she meant, Joanna or
Anthony. Probably Anthony. "I suppose technically he's got a point."

"Oh, yes? Christmas was a pagan festival, if you want to be a
purist. But really, what does that matter? What does it matter compared to the fact that this has been happening year in and year out for
as long as anyone can remember? Certainly for a century or more,
probably much more. Even the war didn't stop it. It goes down the
generations. There are old ladies of eighty in the village who remember when they were May Queen. You should see their faces when the
cart comes past their doors. I'll remember when I was May Queen to
the day I die." Her voice trailed off for a moment. "Do you know
why he really hates it? Because there's a lovely old carving that they
put on the front of the cart. It's a sort of wooden mask with lots of little holes in. They push the stalks of the flowers into the holes so it
comes to life. You should see it. It's a face with two birds flying out
of the mouth and a sort of beard made of leaves and fruits."

"I *have* seen it," said Patrick, remembering the little demon tugging at his knees, suddenly quite sure that the boy shouldn't have been racing round with the mask. "Is it a Green Man?"

"That's what the vicar says. He says it's pagan. Well, you get Green Man carvings in churches all over the place. He's just got some real beef against anything that's fun. I can't stand him."

"What about the other governors?"

"Guess who's the chairman?"

"Well, I don't really know anyone from round here except . . . Ah. Roger Little?"

"Precisely. Anyway, he's not from round here. He's only lived here three years. Came down from Solihull or somewhere. His children go to private school, for heaven's sake. The vicar says it's good to have a businessman as chairman. What rubbish."

"So what are you going to do?"

"Mass disobedience. Most of the parents are on my side. They're going to take their kids out of school that morning and do it anyway. Colin Campling—that's the headmaster—says he'll suspend any child for a week who's not in school that day as a punishment. It's absurd. He's threatening to suspend five-year-olds!"

"So that was what was happening when I nearly ran you over? But tell me, why are you so involved in this? Have you got children in the school?"

"Oh, God. No, of course I haven't. Don't say that. That's what Campling keeps saying."

"I'm not attacking you." He wished he hadn't said it. There had been a touch of anguish in her voice. "I was just wondering."

"I *was* a child. I did that procession every year I was in the school. I think it really matters. That bloody man's got no sense of the history of it."

"Would it really make a difference if you did it a couple of days later?"

"Would you mind having Christmas the following Thursday?"

"I wouldn't really care," he said.

"You haven't got kids?" Now she had said it.

He breathed out sharply and his throat closed up on his reply. He just shook his head.

She moved her head slightly to one side. He had been staring at the half outline of her face, mesmerised by the effect of the candle glow. Now the light spilt into her eyes as she moved and, dismayingly, the distancing hair lost in the shadows, it was young Rachel looking at him again, concerned and too close.

"Do I get another question?" she said. "You've had quite a lot."

With an effort of will, he could speak again. "If you want. I don't promise to answer it."

"I was never into that sort of rock," she said, and he flinched. She went on anyway. "So I only know a bit about your band and your songs, but you don't strike me as the sort of person who would do anything terrible."

"Is that a question?"

"Well, this is. There's a lot of you that's buried, I reckon. I don't understand your contexts, so you can't complain if I get my trowel out. Why are you so harsh on yourself? What is this enormous price you've decided you have to pay?"

He tried to deflect her. "You don't know I'm harsh on myself."

"I have eyes and ears. I've rarely seen someone suffering as much as you are, Patrick. When I see suffering I usually try to help. It's in my nature. You can tell me to go away and leave you alone, but you can't tell me you're not suffering."

He turned sharply to one side so that he didn't have to look at her because her face, through pure accident of history, was the fiercest accusation of all. "If I am, I deserve it."

"That's hard to believe."

"You can't say that. You don't know."

"Patrick, you've got a hair shirt on every second of the day. You jump down the throat of people who want to help you. You look like a drowning man. No, that's wrong. You're too *dry* for that. It's more like you're burning yourself to death from the inside. What did you do to deserve that? Did you kill somebody?"

He jerked his head back to stare straight at her and, looking into his horrified eyes, she was appalled to realise that, trying to suggest the worst impossibility, she had hit on some sort of central truth.

Something was changing in his eyes as the strict guardian inside him, his last line of defence, tried to slam the doors on her. *You've let her in under your guard,* it said to him. *Don't do that. You should have learnt by now.* Until then there had been just the two of them in their alternative candlelit world. Now the spell had broken and his history had come rushing in. As if he were falling away from her, she reached out then and clasped both his hands in hers. His eyes opened up again, startled and vulnerable, and he gripped her hands tightly in his, speechless. It was an overwhelming moment in which there was nothing to say.

Someone did say something. Behind them, Maxwell, unsteady on four pints of beer and coming back to his tent for more money, said, "Well, look at you two, then."

T HE NEXT DAY, ON THE WAY IN TO BREAKFAST, EVEN BEFORE Patrick had got inside the food tent, he got a knowing smile from Gaye and a smirk from Maxwell. He stopped abruptly at the tent's entrance and walked round the back to collect himself. Two of the other diggers were sitting on the grass behind the tent, talking in low voices, a rabbity man called Martin and the woman with the huge trowel whom CD had labeled Vera. Patrick had no idea whether that was her real name. Both were drinking coffee and chatting and they didn't see him coming.

". . . holding hands. He saw them. That's what he said."

"Really? That's hard to believe."

"I know. He's not exactly your warm type, is he? Rather sweet, though."

Patrick stopped again and turned back. With nowhere left to go, he went into the tent. Bobby looked up from the gas ring where she was frying eggs and gave him a wide smile.

"Good morning," she said. "How are you today?"

There were half a dozen people inside the tent assembling their breakfasts. CD was feeding pellets of bread to his pseudo-raven. Dozer was putting together a massive sandwich. A middle-aged man, another one Patrick couldn't yet name with any certainty, was poking a wooden spoon suspiciously into the porridge pan. Patrick felt as if every eye was upon him.

"Oh," he said, "I'm fine." Then, for camouflage and out of embarrassment, he said, far too abruptly, "Can we get your tractor and trailer over quite soon, do you think? We need to get this lot moved as soon as possible."

"Er, well yes," she said, disconcerted. "As soon as breakfast is over."

"Thanks," he mumbled, helped himself to coffee and cornflakes, and went outside without meeting her eye again.

All that day, he kept away from her, believing that everyone was watching them and hating the feeling of vulnerability it gave him. He told himself that he was here as a professional, as a leader, and a leader should not be the butt of gossip that put him on the same level as the youngest and silliest of his diggers. It was a busy day, and it took much longer than it should have to move camp. The catering tent was a cumbersome thing, all knots and heavy wooden poles, and the canvas which had proved too thin to stand up to the downpour was still heavy enough to resist their attempts to manhandle it into place.

When it was all done it was late afternoon, and the new camp was a much nicer place to be than the old one. They were just over the brow of the hill, fifty yards beyond the barrow, on a small, almost flat plateau. The portable loos were set up a hundred yards farther down, to Gaye's satisfaction, and they cut the turf back to make a big campfire a safe distance from the site.

The site itself was another matter. CD and Dozer had looked at it closely as Patrick showed them what he had seen and where he had found the bead. CD tried the same trick, lowering himself to the ground and doing push-ups, Edgar fluttering up in the air indignantly, but he looked less than convinced when he finished.

"Jeez, I hope you're right. I'm not sure I can see it."

"It's the light," said Patrick. "In the morning, the sun hits it at the right angle. It's much easier to tell then."

Dozer was sifting through the earth where the moles and rabbits had dug, looking closely at two or three tiny fragments that he picked out of the soil, but each time he shook his head and tossed them away.

"This *is* the right spot?" he said. "Where them toes came out?"

Patrick was already feeling his neck was stuck too far out when the TV crew arrived with Kenny Camden, eager to shoot.

"Can't you do a bit of planning or something?" Camden asked, clearly disappointed that they weren't ready to start. "What about you guys walking round and deciding where to put the trench?"

That was something Patrick had intended to do by himself, later in the evening, anxious to think through the whole process without other people there to see him stumble, but to his surprise it went well. CD was in a generous mood again and contributed some thoughtful ideas phrased in such a way that it always sounded as if he was agreeing with something Patrick had already said.

"You're absolutely right," the American agreed. "We need to do it in quadrants. If we start a trench about *here,*" he scratched a mark on the ground, "and take it through to, say, *here,*" another mark, "we should catch the edge of the ditch and get into the centre of the mound. That's assuming they buried him in the middle."

*Him?* Patrick almost said. *It's not a him, it's a her.* But he stopped himself in time, aware of how whimsical that would sound on film.

They pegged it out, took careful measurements, and called it a day. Queuing up for supper, Patrick made sure he was in animated conversation with CD about the need to get some proper paperwork together, skeleton record sheets and stuff like that, just in case. He avoided looking directly at Bobby even when she poured stew into his bowl. He wasn't going to give anybody the slightest excuse for gossiping about him.

That night nobody went to the pub. Bobby took the dirty dishes back to the farmhouse to wash. Dozer, putting them in the car for her, said, "Come on back after. We'll have a few bottles round the fire," and she smiled at him and said she might, but she didn't.

Her brother came instead.

They didn't know he was there at first. They'd used the tractor to bring in a load of wood from the farm, and around a blazing fire, fueled by the wine, the diggers had been singing old Beatles songs, accompanied by CD on an improvised bongo made out of a catering tin of baked beans.

There was a gap at the end of a loud and muddled version of "Hard Day's Night" when Patrick was almost enjoying himself, forcing some sort of sociability out of his depths to contradict that dreadful verdict from the morning, that he wasn't exactly a warm type.

In that gap, unexpectedly, someone strummed a guitar in the darkness behind the fire and every head swiveled towards the sound. It was hard to see into that darkness, and in the sudden complete silence, there was another sequence of chords, thin on the wind.

"Come and join us," CD called. "We need a guitarist. In fact, we *badly* need a guitarist."

It seemed to Patrick that the dark shape did move nearer and when the guitar sounded again, it was much easier to hear, but the person playing it was still all but invisible to them. When he started to sing, the voice was Joe's and the tune was vaguely familiar but the words were not.

*At the dawn of the years, when we made our home here*
*Near the ruins the Romans had built,*
*The Smith wrought a blade, the best ever made*
*Then he ground it right back to the hilt.*

"Hey, CD," said Aidan, "it's—"
    "Shut up," said CD with unusual ferocity. "I'm listening."

*He had sweated for hours at twisting some bars*
*Of the purest and best of the metal,*
*Then hammered it hard til the surface was starred*
*And patterned with leaves and with petals.*

*He'd a bet with his Lord that he'd conjure a sword*
*That could never in battle be beat*
*So he worked through the day til he'd ground it away*
*Then he summoned his chickens to eat.*

*He spread corn around on the filings he'd ground*
*And the chickens ate up every bit*
*Then he shut them up tight for two days and a night*
*And gathered up all of their shit.*

*With their droppings he made the shape of a blade*
*And put it once more to the heat.*
*As it melted and burned, so the silver returned*
*Then the blade on the anvil he beat.*

*The Smith did it twice more, attacking that core*
*With his rasp until it was gone,*
*Then watched as his hens ate the filings again*
*And reforged their shit til it shone.*

*When the process was done, he knew that he'd won*
*The wager his Chieftain had laid.*
*The blade sliced through bone and iron and stone,*
*The best sword that ever was made.*

They gave him a cheer and a clap and called again for him to join them but no one came out of the darkness and when Dozer went off with a bottle and a mug in hand to give him a drink, the big man soon came back, shaking his head.

"Buggered off," he said. "What about that, eh?"

"He heard what you were saying the day before yesterday," said Gaye, turning to CD. "It's obvious, isn't it? He was listening when you told us about the sword, and now he's gone and made up a song. It's quite sweet, really."

"There was something in that song that I'm sure I never told you," said CD.

"What?"

"He said the blade was patterned. Something about stars and leaves and petals. That's exactly what you got in the days of the great swordsmiths with a really good blade."

Peter said, "Of course, the Arabs were real experts at that, but you find it in some northern swords as well."

"True," said CD, "too true. Far too true. Yes. But anyway, I never mentioned that, did I?"

"That's just a coincidence," said Gaye.

"It couldn't be a really old song," said Aidan. "The words were modern and if he'd changed them, they wouldn't rhyme anymore, would they?"

It kept them all talking until a cool wind rose and they drifted off to bed, leaving Patrick. He walked down to what he profoundly wanted to be a burial mound. He crouched by it and hoped for his own sake that the man with the guitar knew what he was singing about.

Time twists any tale.

# Chapter Twelve

She was halfway across the yard to start the milking, anxious to get that first task out of the way before all the rest of them piled up. It was a full enough day without all the extra work she had taken on up the hill. A bellow from beyond the house stopped her.

"Hild! Where are you? Come."

She thought of ignoring it but no one ignored Cuthwulf for long, so she put down the wooden pails with resignation and went to find him. Round the corner of the hall, the huge figure of her father, still in his long nightshirt, stood with his back to her, staring up at the eaves.

"I'm here, Lord," Hild said.

"Sodding bloody hut-dwellers," he said, without even glancing at her. "They haven't a clue about building

PROPERLY. YOU WOULDN'T HAVE PROBLEMS LIKE THIS WITH
SAXONS. LOOK AT THAT." HE POINTED UP AT THE CORNER
OF THE ROOF WHERE A SHORT SECTION OF THE TIMBER
FRAME UNDER THE EAVES WAS HANGING OUT AT AN ODD
ANGLE. THERE WAS A GAP BETWEEN IT AND THE THATCH.

"GET IT FIXED," HE SAID, AND SHE HAD TO BITE BACK A
REPLY.

*WHO'S GOING TO FIX IT,* WAS WHAT SHE WANTED TO SAY.
*YOU KEEP FORGETTING YOU'RE NOT ACROSS THE SEA NOW. YOU
HAVEN'T GOT FIVE HUNDRED SUBJECTS ANYMORE. YOU'VE GOT
ME AND THE BOYS AND A COUPLE OF DOZEN HWICCA WHO DON'T
KNOW HOW TO BUILD THINGS THE WAY YOU LIKE THEM BUILT.*

"I'LL TRY, LORD," SHE SAID INSTEAD.

HER FATHER TURNED AND LOOKED AT HER THEN, AND
SHE FELT A SUDDEN RETURN OF SNEAKING AFFECTION FOR
THE OLD BEAR WITH HIS SCARRED FACE AND HIS BROKEN
TEETH. IT WAS NO ACCIDENT THAT THE PRICE FOR JOINING
THE HWICCA HAD BEEN TO TAKE UP RESIDENCE ON THIS
EXPOSED HILL. CUTHWULF'S REPUTATION WAS KNOWN
EVERYWHERE WHERE TALE-BEARERS WENT. HE WAS FEARED
BY EVERYONE HE HAD EVER MET, EVERYONE EXCEPT HER
MOTHER WHEN SHE WAS ALIVE AND, SOME OF THE TIME, HIS
OWN CHILDREN. SOME, BUT NOT ALL OF THE TIME.
IT MIGHT HAVE SHOWED IN HER FACE BECAUSE HE HALF
SMILED, A DREADFUL SIGHT, AND SIGHED.

"ONE DAY SOON, HILD, WE WILL HAVE A PROPER HALL
AGAIN, A PROPER SAXON HALL, TWICE THIS SIZE. ONE DAY
SOON YOU WILL HAVE ENOUGH SERVANTS, MY LITTLE
QUEEN."

HE TURNED AND LEFT HER AND SHE LOOKED UP AT
THE DAMAGED TIMBER AND WONDERED IF HE'D DONE THE
DESTRUCTION HIMSELF IN ONE OF HIS LEGENDARY BURSTS
OF RAGE. AS USUAL THERE HAD BEEN PLENTY OF NOISE IN
THE NIGHT, CUTHWULF'S GRUNTS AND A SCREAM FROM
WHICHEVER ONE OF THE UNFORTUNATE HWICCA WIVES HE
HAD TAKEN TO BED WITH HIM. AT THAT MOMENT, TORN
BETWEEN RELIEVING HER ELDEST BROTHER, ON WATCH UP
THE HILL, OR TRYING TO ORGANISE REPAIRS, SHE ALLOWED
HERSELF A SMALL DEGREE OF RESENTMENT THAT HE DIDN'T

OFFER TO TAKE A TURN ON WATCH. THE ONLY TIME
CUTHWULF EVER WENT UP THE HILL THESE DAYS WAS WHEN
HE TOOK HIS SONS TO PLAN HIS FAR-OFF BURIAL IN THE
SPIRIT'S MOUND. HE HAD GRANDIOSE PLANS FOR THE SCALE
OF THAT BURIAL, QUITE IMPOSSIBLE TO ACHIEVE WITH THE
WORKFORCE THEY COULD COMMAND HERE.

HILD WOULD HAVE GIVEN A GREAT DEAL TO BE BACK IN
SAXONY AGAIN WITH PEOPLE TO RUN AROUND FOR HER.

WAS THIS ALL REALLY WORTH IT? ALL THIS, JUST FOR A
SWORD?

By teatime that day, the first day of digging on the barrow, Patrick
was getting sideways looks. Lifting the turf felt like pulling back a
curtain, and he longed to see clear signs of a feature—a grave-shaped
patch of different soil to prove immediately that a later burial had
taken place here. It wasn't just the usual unquenchable optimism of
the young archaeologist he was feeling. This was the unhealthy self-
delusion of the gambler, knowing the ball will lodge in twenty-
seven when the wheel stops spinning and then, when it doesn't,
seeing how obvious it was that it was never going to. What he saw, as
he should have expected, was a horribly uniform surface of earth and
small stone, and his internal doubts began to grow and grow.

"OK," he told the diggers, "let's get on with cleaning this up."

When Kenny Camden tried to get him to tell the camera what it
was they were looking at, he couldn't put together any words that
were halfway convincing or in the slightest bit hopeful. All they'd
found in the first few hours was an area of disturbance where the rabbits had dug in for some way, a couple of bullets, and a fragment of
pottery in such bad condition that it was impossible to date it to
within a thousand years.

Dozer twiddled one of the bullets between a thumb and a cal-
lused finger. "Three-oh-three," he said. "World War Two, I reckon.
Angle they were at, probably came from aircraft machine guns. Some
dogfight."

Camden liked that and Dozer was encouraged to speculate far
too freely on camera about the type of plane they might have been
fired from.

"Spitfire, possibly," he said, "or a Hurricane."

"Or someone out shooting foxes," said Patrick, under his breath.

"Always the romantic, eh, Dozer?" said CD.

"Hey, CD," said Dozer. "Remember that time we were digging in Sumatra and I had to defuse that unexploded bomb?"

"No," said CD, "not Sumatra. That was Guadalcanal."

"Saved your life, though, didn't I?"

"Yeah, that's another one I owe you."

Maxwell had stopped troweling, and sat back on his heels as he listened, goggle-eared, believing every word of it. Jack, the cameraman, smiled and switched off. He'd been around a good long time and he didn't say much.

In the afternoon, just after the tea break, CD's bird made a painfully clumsy landing on Patrick's knee as he sat on a stool, writing up the trench records. It dug its claws in, flapping its wings to get its balance, and in the ensuing argument between Patrick and the bird, Patrick's pen and the notebook fell in the grass. Patrick picked up the notebook; Edgar picked up the pen and flew off with it, landing on the grass a few steps away and looking back as if he were a dog playing with a ball.

"Sorry," said CD, running up. "I'll get it. He knows better than to mess around when I'm here. Good ravens don't do that, Edgar. Put it down."

The jackdaw spread his wings, flew down over the crest of the hill, and disappeared into a large tree on the edge of the wood below.

"OK," CD told Patrick, "leave it to me. I know which tree it is. On second thoughts, have *my* pen."

They were stopped in their tracks by a bellow from Dozer at the trench: "Over 'ere, you two!"

"Another red herring?" Patrick said quietly, although it was the sound he most wanted to hear.

"I know that tone of shout," the American replied. "Dozer gets overexcited just to keep his spirits up when there's nothing happening, but he knows what he's doing. I smell blood in this one."

They walked back to the trench only because dig directors don't run, and they both knew from what they saw on the way that something impressive was going on. The other diggers were gathering around Dozer, hanging back at a little distance and gazing at the earth intently. Whatever he'd found, this was no machine-gun bullet.

They made a space for Patrick and CD. Patrick stared avidly at the ground. Dozer, looking up at him with an expression of proud ownership, said, "Take a gander at this." He was kneeling, using the very tip of his trowel, and then he put his face close to the earth to blow the loose soil away.

He straightened up, nodded at Patrick, and pointed at the ground. Then Patrick was able, with deep satisfaction and huge relief, to see at last what he meant and what he'd found. Showing through the earth was a flattened, irregular disk of rusty iron.

"Shield boss?" Patrick said.

"Looks like it," said Dozer. "There's your Saxon."

The relief was enormous. The shield boss was just as it should be, the surviving central part of a wooden shield that would have been laid close to the corpse at the end of the burial. A shield boss increased to near certainty the chances that there was a burial here and that there would be more to find. Then Patrick's satisfaction was overshadowed by a pang of regret. A shield boss meant a shield. A shield meant a warrior. A warrior meant a man, not a woman, not a queen. Whatever they had found, it was not the grave of the German Queen.

"Sorry, folks, I missed that," Jack the cameraman said. He was a decent man, a lot less pushy than his boss, so he made his request with a certain measure of diffidence. "You couldn't do it again, could you?"

"How do you mean, do it again?"

"Well . . . just maybe put a bit of earth back over it and sort of discover it again. Just for the camera."

They had to do it three times before he was sure he'd got it right, and a little bit more of Patrick's self-esteem dribbled away each time. It went against everything he'd ever learnt. You didn't mess about with contexts, not for the camera, not for anything. He was acutely uncomfortable and all the more so when they asked him to describe to the camera what they were looking at.

"It's an iron shield boss. More or less shaped like a cone." He pointed out its shape in the soil. "There should be a flange around its base with holes where it was attached to the wooden part of the shield. It covered the hole in the middle where the hand grip went."

"Change the shot," ordered Camden. "Pull out a bit. Paddy, give us a bit about what this means. You know, what it tells you about the burial?"

"Turn the camera off," snapped Patrick, furious. Camden nodded at Jack.

"Is that off?" Patrick asked.

"Yes."

"OK. Get this. Do *not* call me Paddy. If you do that to me on film, I'm not letting anyone do any more digging until you're out of here, understand?"

"Hey, listen. Calm down. Nobody's going to hear my words," said Camden. "We cut those. It'll just be you talking, right?"

"Ah," said Patrick, discomfited. "Well, all right, but that's not the point. Just don't call me that, right?"

"OK, OK."

Patrick, now more than a little embarrassed, did his best. It took three takes and was greatly helped by some asides from CD between the second and third takes about the complexities of shield bosses.

"You know much more about this than I do," Patrick said to him quietly. "You should be doing the interview."

"I'll bet you Peter knows more than we both do," CD whispered back. "That's not the point. You're the director is the point."

"The shield boss," said Patrick on the third take, "indicates the probability that this is indeed an Anglo-Saxon burial site. It's the first important find we've made since we started digging, and it's the right way up for a typical burial where the shield might be laid flat, sometimes on the arm or across the chest, sometimes across the legs. It's, er . . . it's a very good thing to find in a burial, because the design of these bosses developed steadily throughout the period, so it should help us date the burial fairly precisely. From what we can see of it so far, the shape looks as if it could be what's called a Group Six boss. It's too early to tell, but that would date it from somewhere between the middle of the sixth century and the middle of the seventh. Oh, and of course, we can now be pretty sure that this is a male, that is if it is indeed a burial, because shields and weapons are always associated with warriors."

"Very good indeed," said Camden.

"Nice one," said Jack. "I could do with a close-up."

"Right," agreed Camden. "Can you just do that bit again where you pointed out the shape of the shield, something about Group Six? We'll just shoot the close-up."

Patrick couldn't remember what he'd said so they had to play the tape to find out and he found it far harder to do it properly when he had to memorise his words even when they'd been his own words in the first place. He was halfway through his fifth try when he ground to a halt.

"What's wrong now?" said Camden.

"Nothing's wrong," said Patrick, looking intently at what was showing through where he'd just knocked aside a small lump of soil with his pointing finger. "I think we've found bone."

He pulled his trowel out of his back pocket and, with huge care, moved the soil, crumb by crumb, out of the way. Unmistakable yellow-brown bone ran across the bottom of the indentation he'd made. The arm that had held the shield in battle still held it in death.

KENNY CAMDEN WAS DELIGHTED WITH THE DAY'S WORK when he and Jack drove off an hour later, leaving the diggers erecting a large square frame tent as a cover over the grave for temporary protection. At seventy-five miles an hour on the back road to Woodstock, Camden lit a cigar with both hands while he steered with his knees and blew a cloud of smoke at his passenger, who resented both the smoke and the risk the man was taking with his life.

"Listen, Jacko," he said. "If we get another wobbly like that one, keep shooting, right? Even if he makes me agree to turn off, just pull out wide and keep the camera running. Act natural so he'll think it's off."

"Mmm," said Jack, who didn't much like being called Jacko, either.

TWELVE DIGGERS GATHERED ROUND THE FOOD TENT THAT night in an extraordinarily cheerful mood. Six of the less enthusiastic volunteers, including the fat man with the broken conservatory, had elected to quit when they moved to the new site. There should still have been thirteen left, but CD was missing. Patrick looked at his staff, singing and joking, united by the thrill of having found something. He spun out the job of writing up the records, sitting on a separate chair, being busy. He was still on his guard with Bobby, feeling any signs of friendliness he displayed could be misinterpreted by anyone who saw them. Being separate from them all made it less noticeable that he was separate from her. He watched Bobby when he thought no one was looking and noticed that everyone smiled when she was talking to them. CD arrived after they'd finished the tomato soup and were just being handed bowls of a brown mixture that looked and smelled very like the previous day's stew. He was limping, disheveled, and bleeding from a scratch across his cheek.

"Hi, guys," he said.

"Been in a fight?" said Dozer, looking hard at him.

"No," he said, "no, no, no."

"What, then?"

"I walked into a door."

"Dunno if you've noticed. This is the open air. It don't come fitted with doors."

"Good point. Very good point. Couldn't have been a door, then."

"You've got a leaf in your hair." Dozer reached across and pulled out the leaf, which came with a small twig attached. "You been through a hedge?"

"Up a tree, actually," said CD, "then down it again. Faster. Until I stopped." He paused. "At the bottom." He sat down and winced. "Suddenly."

Patrick walked across and inspected the visible damage to CD's face. "Not the tree where Edgar took my pen?" he asked.

"That's the one," replied CD. "The very one."

"For heaven's sake," said Patrick, "it wasn't anything special. You shouldn't have done it. I'd rather have a live archaeologist than an old ballpoint."

"It's not just the pen," said CD between gritted teeth. "He took the keys to my Harley."

"Your bike?"

"My bike."

"I'll sort it, mate," said Dozer. "Remember that time in Salisbury? I can crack a Harley lock in three seconds."

"I'd rather you didn't," said CD stiffly. "That time, if you remember, you not only cracked it but you rode off on it, too. I know exactly where my keys are. Believe me, that bird is in big, big trouble when he comes back."

"He's still up there, is he?"

"He's talking to a crow, and if I was that crow, I'd be hanging on to my wallet with both hands."

The meal was cleared away and nobody seemed inclined to move.

It was a mellow evening, with twilight halfway to closing the day's account. Everyone was sprawled on the grass, Patrick watching from his chair. The wine had come out, and CD and Dozer were telling old war stories about digs they'd done.

"So there we were in this punishment pit, miles from sodding anywhere," Dozer was saying, "eight feet down in solid chalk. Baking bloody sun, just the two of us 'cos the director didn't much like us, and this git sticks his head in the top of the hole and says, 'I say, my good men, you're not meant to be doing this. This is han hancient monument. Hit his protected, don't you know.' So old CD here, he looks up at the geezer and says, 'Bugger off. We're British Gas. We're looking for a leak.' Worked like a charm."

Patrick laughed with the others, then caught a movement out of the corner of his eye and turned to find Bobby standing at his shoulder.

"Could I have a word with you?" she asked.

He became acutely aware of how close she was standing. It seemed to him that silence had fallen, though it could have been a natural pause in the stories. He suspected that everyone was looking at him.

"Of course you can. What about?"

"Catering and things. I don't want to break up the party. Shall we talk somewhere else?"

"Right. Lead on."

The last of the sun's glow slipped from the base of the western clouds as they left the circle. In the sudden gloom, Bobby walked ahead of him to the gate where the farm track started, then waited for Patrick to catch up with her. They heard the conversation pick up again.

"Not here," she told him. "Farther away. Come down to the house," and she was off down the track before he could argue. He thought he detected an unsettling edge to her voice.

Patrick walked down the hill after her, wondering what aspect of the catering could demand the journey. Bobby knew the track towards the farmhouse and he did not. Ruts and potholes kept tripping him up in the deepening darkness so that he fell farther and farther behind. Ahead, dark shapes of trees were limned with light from the farmhouse beyond them. As the track turned sharp left around a barn, into the entrance to the yard, he saw Bobby waiting for him, arms akimbo, in the open gateway. Only then did he realise that she was really angry.

He walked slowly up to her. She made no move to get out of the way and he came to an uncertain halt.

"What's wrong?" he asked.

"What's wrong? I'll tell you exactly what's wrong. What's wrong is that I've never felt so humiliated in my life. You seem to have singled me out specially for the cold shoulder treatment, and I must say, I'm not quite sure what I've done to deserve it, apart from listening to you last night. So what's going on?"

"Ah," he said, and she waited.

"Is that it, just 'Ah'?"

What could he say? That he'd let his guard down and she had slipped in under it? That she'd undermined defences he had learnt to rely on utterly? That he'd been embarrassed that others had seen evidence of his weakness?

"I . . . um, I made a bit of a fool of myself last night."

"In what way?"

"Well, you know. When Maxwell came back and . . ."

"You mean when you were upset? He saw you upset and that's enough to make you think you have to be some kind of shitty, aloof bastard to me all day?"

"I didn't mean to—"

"You didn't mean to treat me like I wasn't there? Like I was some sort of scullery maid? Just because he saw you when you were upset? What sort of person are you? Why do you have to be some great big macho iceberg all the time?"

"It's not that."

"Well, what the hell is it, then?"

"He spread it around. I heard everybody talking this morning. They think . . . well, you know."

"No, I don't know."

"They think we've got something going."

"Something going?"

"They think I fancy you."

"Oh, I see." She nodded a couple of times. "Well, do you?"

"I . . . well, I mean, that wasn't the point. Maxwell misunderstood the situation, didn't he?"

"So, all because of that, you think it's all right to behave in this stupid way all day? If you want to look *really* childish, just go right ahead."

There was a stone trough next to him and he sat down on the edge of it and put his head in his hands. "I'm sorry. I'm very, very sorry. You're right."

She sat down next to him.

"What is wrong with you?" she said, and the words sounded much less harsh. "You've got everybody wondering. You stand out like a sore thumb. Just relax a bit. Stop putting yourself out in the cold."

"I'm not very good at authority. I need to be in charge here. That's what I'm here for. It doesn't come naturally."

"You don't do it that way. You can be yourself. If you're halfway reasonable with people, they'll respect you."

"Oh, God. Believe me, I can't be myself. That's one thing I'm trying very hard not to be."

"What does that mean? You were going to tell me about it last night, before Maxwell turned up."

"Was I?"

"Well, I thought you were."

"I don't think talking helps. I don't even think I *can* talk about it."

"Patrick, I think you *have* to."

"Don't I have the choice?"

"No, I don't think you do. If I saw someone bleeding to death in the street, I wouldn't give them the choice. I'd try to stop the bleeding. I told you that before."

Side by side, two feet apart, he could look straight ahead and not be disturbed by her counterfeit face.

"I lost someone."

"Well, yes. I know that." There was something in her voice he couldn't identify.

"How do you know?"

"I found out."

"You found out?"

"Don't sound so surprised. You may have forgotten, but you were quite famous. I looked you up."

"Where?"

"On the Internet, if you want to know. There's pages and pages about you."

"Are there?" He was genuinely astonished.

"Of course there are. Every song you ever did. Pictures of you on-stage, though I don't think I would ever have recognised you. Reams and reams of stuff about you quitting your band. Nothing since then."

"Well, thank God for that, at least."

"It says you had a wife. It says no one knew until you quit."

"When I quit," he repeated softly, and each word was a doubt-ful step towards what might be an abyss, "I didn't have a wife any-more."

She didn't ask the obvious direct question. As if she knew the shape but not the precise nature of the jagged tear in his soul, she skirted round it.

"Why didn't anyone know?"

"The record company didn't want them to. They wanted me to keep her tucked out of sight. It was one of those stupid ideas some-one has and then they can't let go of it because they're in too deep. You know how it is. They want you to be an object of lust. It's the myth of availability. I got married young. We came as a package and they didn't like the package. Rachel . . ."

There, he'd said her name out loud for the first time since the fu-neral. A million times inside his head and once out loud. "Rachel was too . . . I don't know. Normal? Not glamorous. Anyway, she got in the way, they said, so before I knew what was happening they told the world I was single. It was just plain dumb."

"Did she mind?"

"I think she minded every single thing that happened to her from then on."

"Patrick," said Bobby, and a tiny hesitation warned him she had been building up to this. "What happened in Perugia?"

"Oh no, hold on a minute. What do you know about Perugia? Does it talk about Perugia on the Net?" He sensed her flinch away from him. He hadn't shouted, had he? He didn't know for certain. There was no loud echo coming back at him from the barn walls. He *wanted* to shout. *Is the most secret stuff of my life plastered across cyber-space?* That was what he wanted to shout.

"All it says is that you quit your band in Perugia, after a concert. It says what happened was tied up with . . . Well, I don't know. Something pretty bad, the end of your marriage. Was that when Rachel left you?"

He stood up. "Enough. That's enough." He couldn't see her face—only a pool of shadow under the woolen hat.

"Patrick. I just want to help."

"Look, Bobby. It doesn't help. I don't want to go there. I have to go back to my tent and the dark night and find a way to just go on *being*. You think this is good for me. I know what's safe and this isn't safe and it's me who has to live with it, not you. We've got a dig to do, thanks to Joe. That's all I'm going to think about. Maybe we'll talk when it's over."

"All right," she said helplessly.

"I'm sorry I upset you. It wouldn't have happened if you hadn't turned up when you did. I usually keep things to myself. From now on, I'll try to treat you exactly like I treat everybody else."

She nodded, looking down at the ground, and as he turned to walk out of the light into the darkness again, he said, "Bobby, I hurt people like you."

# CHAPTER THIRTEEN

I T WAS ONLY FIVE MINUTES IN THE
stumbling darkness from one end of
the track to the other, but he did not
want to be at either end. Behind him
were Bobby's acute and painful questions. Ahead of him, up the hill, were the
diggers. The wood smoke on the wind was
streaked with thin fragments of their songs.
He was afraid of what would happen when
he walked into their circle, blighting their
evening. They were dwellers in a different
world. They would stop talking when they
saw him, coming back in from Bobby's darkness to cast his own shadow over them all.
What could they do then but wonder about
him and about what he had been doing down
there? The track lifted over the fold of the
hill and, a hundred yards ahead, the campfire
bloomed—black backs in front, then orange
flames and yellow faces beyond.

Patrick could not go nearer. It was a
foreign bubble of inaccessible warmth. He

stopped at the field gate and stared towards the fire and wished from the bottom of his soul that he could turn the clock back and just be one of them. A normal person with a normal history of no great interest to anyone. The woman down at the farm with her face and her questions had brought home to him the fact that he'd only been fooling himself, thinking he had managed to duck out of the spotlight forever.

Perugia was his private hell, not another peg for public speculation spread round the world by cyber-gossip.

In Perugia he had watched the little boy playing in the spangles of cathedral light. He had seen the boy's father move on a few steps, then stop and turn when he realised his son wasn't following. Instead of calling to him to come on, to leave the wonderful stained-glass splashes the sun was making, the man had sat down on a bench and watched the child, smiling in unhurried tolerance. Patrick, in an anguish of repentance for what he had done onstage the night before—a three-cock-crow betrayal on worldwide television—had sat there and watched him and seen how a boy and his father should be. He had seen the little boy, with the same glossy hair as David, the same stocky build, and the same wide smile, lost in his simple child's world. He had seen the boy's father respecting that world and giving him all the time he needed, centring his day on his child and not himself.

In that moment, Patrick had vowed to be more like that from then on, vowed to be a better father to David and a better husband to Rachel.

He was coming down from the effects of the concert and the chemical cocktails of the past twenty-four hours. Perugia was nowhere, just a stopping place along the way from Rome to Venice, and the Cathedral was just a safe place to get away from the rest of the band, the rub-you-raw, never-know-when-to-stop rest of the band who were in a bar, oblivious to the town's medieval ramparts and winding backstreets. They would never think of coming in here. He knew them intimately and he knew them not at all: Now they felt like willing accomplices to his destruction.

Along the far wall of the Cathedral was a row of confessionals, open-fronted, priests sitting inside in full view. Patrick longed to confess, but he had no God to confess to. He watched in awe to see how it was done. A man sat in a wheelchair, astonishingly at ease with the priest, gesturing, even laughing. The priest leaned forwards with his elbow on the sill, nodding and smiling. Perhaps confession would not be so painful. Then Patrick saw the light above the booth was on where all the rest were off, and he realised that this was no confession—this was just what it seemed, a chat between friends while the priest waited for his next customer. Confessions were certainly taking place, but they were in the other booths with their lights out, and they were being conducted in huddled, sober, awful secrecy.

Unable to speak Italian, unable to believe in God, unable to share his opinion of himself even with a priest, he closed his eyes and made his confession to himself in that huge stone box of thought. The tourists' footsteps were replaced by buzzing silence, and he tried to tell himself what he felt and what he feared but it came out with excuses attached to it.

*I've been selfish,* he said to the listener inside his head. *I needed the space. I've betrayed the people I care about most . . . but she's pushed me into it. She hasn't understood where I have to go.*

Something about the place stopped him, blocked his evasions, and brought him closer and closer to the inescapable truth. And the truth was that if he was to save anything from this, if he was to give David all he wanted to, he had to leave the band and had to do so now. That truth lodged in his head and wouldn't let him go, and it was *so* big that he had no choice but to get to his feet and walk out of the cool cathedral into the sunlight to where he had left the band's manager, Don Claypole, sitting at a restaurant table on the edge of the square. He was heading for Don to tell him it was all over, fin-ished, canceled here and now, and he meant it. He had a contract but it didn't matter one bit. He didn't care if it cost him all the money he had, because the patient father and the boy who played in the light had made him see himself for what he had become. He still had David's love, and he would get Rachel back from the wasteland in which he had thrust her. For David's sake, he would get Rachel back and, who knows, there might still be something for him there, too.

The scene was clear in Patrick's memory and always would be. His eyes, assailed by the remnants of abuse from the day before, protested at the bright lunchtime light. The steps down to the piazza were an indistinct white slope, and coming up them to-wards him through the dazzle was a dark stick-man right out of a L. S. Lowry painting, who was saying in Don Claypole's voice, "Ah, Paddy, there you are," and Patrick was saying back to him, "Don,

I've got something to tell you," and the stick-man replied in that awful voice, "No, mate, I've got something to tell you first. . . ."

The sudden eclipse of the campfire as a figure passed across its light, coming towards him, pulled him out of the memory. The approaching person spoke with CD's voice, saying, "Patrick? Is that you?"

"Yes."

"What are you doing out here? Are you by yourself?"

"Yes, of course I am."

"So, just taking in the night air, I guess?"

"Just thinking."

"Did you sort things out with Bobby?"

"Sort things out?"

"Er, yeah. The catering, or whatever it was."

"Oh. Yes."

"Right." CD came right up and leaned on the gate next to him and there was a long silence.

"Happy?" said the American in the end.

"God, what a question."

"You want to hear what my mammy taught me?" He went on without waiting for an answer. "She taught me not to leave my rocks near any hard places. Also to avoid animals with horns in case they turned out to be savage dilemmas, and always to beat some other guy's back, not my own, on the grounds that other guys' backs are easier to reach and the wrist action is slicker."

Silence from Patrick, not trusting himself to reply and not wanting another sermon.

"You've got to learn to zigzag. You got to know your snakes from your ladders. If you go one step forward and two steps back, you just say, That's great, I'm waltzing. OK?"

A small grunt came that could have been assent, or amusement, or just an indication that Patrick was listening.

"OK," said CD, "that's good. You're in there somewhere. Now, let's talk about this."

"It's late." Everyone wanted to talk. Everyone except himself, Patrick thought.

"It's only six o'clock on the East Coast. No need to panic. I'm only talking archaeology here. I guess that's allowed?" CD saw Patrick give a little nod against the night sky's gleam.

"So, let's look at this guy we're digging up. He was born. He died. A thousand years later, all we have left is the hard bits and a few knickknacks. Maybe he was a happy guy. Maybe he was a sad old Saxon bastard. In the end it made no difference. We sure as hell can't tell, and he tasted the same to the worms. The world still turns."

"I thought that was what we were here for—to tell." Patrick's voice was low and reluctant, but for all that, he had been plucked to safer ground by this outstretched hand of conversation.

"Oh, sure, we can tell a few little things. Ain't we clever? We can tell if he broke his leg when he was a kid or if he had syphilis or maybe even if he had bad toothache, but we can't tell if he was a good guy or a bad guy. We can't tell if he was the life and soul of the party or if he cried himself to sleep every night."

"There's grave goods," persisted Patrick. "They tell us a bit."

"Is that right?" said CD in mock wonder. "Yeah, those swords and shields, they sure tell us a lot. They tell us men used to fight. Well, now, there's a revelation. Anyway, grave goods are what other people put in their graves for them, not they themselves. They were too dead to choose. Maybe they would have preferred a cuddly toy but their relations wanted young Aethelfric to go to meet his ancestors as a valiant warrior, not let them down by greeting Granddad in the Valhalla entrance hall with a teddy bear in one hand. That's why they gave him a sword even if all he ever did was trip over in the mud and impale himself on it. Burials aren't the time for honesty."

"They can be," said Patrick, and his sombre tone caused CD to pause a moment before replying.

"Tell me about it," he said. Then he waited out a long silence, so long that the young man next to him was eventually forced to break it.

"I went to one," he said in the end, "where they told the truth. Believe me, that's a very bad idea, especially if you're on the receiving end." He straightened up. "Sorry I mentioned that. Let's not talk about it."

CD saw his opening slipping away and tried a new angle. "I read this article, all about the psychology of archaeologists. Did you know we're just a morbid bunch of voyeurs?"

"Yes, I think I probably did."

"No, you have to say 'no' so I can explain why."

"All right. No."

"Seems we're only one step away from people who go out to look at plane crashes or the guys who slow down on the road to see the bodies in the car wrecks. Apparently we get our biggest kicks out of digging up the dead and wondering how they died. It's acceptable because there's no flesh. Flesh, you're a voyeur—dry bone, you're an archaeologist."

"Maybe."

"Now, what the article also said was that these people, the ghouls, the crash gapers, they're after pretty much the same experience as guys who drop an Ecstasy tablet at a rave. Synthetic love. Instant, artificial pleasure with a bit of danger to it. All the thrill of the twisted metal without having your own flesh torn. Vicarious pleasure."

Twisted metal and synthetic love were uncomfortably close to Patrick's blackest depths.

"Sounds like crap to me," he said forcefully.

"Yeah, me, too."

Patrick's denial had been too strong, but its momentum carried him on and he turned that momentum to the safer parts of what CD had said. "I don't buy the rest of that stuff, either. We just never had the tools before. Surely you agree with that? We can find out much more now than we ever could before. Given the right resources here—which, of course, we won't be—we could find out a huge amount about this burial. OK, I grant you we won't know if he died happy."

"That doesn't matter. All I was saying is you only get one chance and you're dead a long time. You might as well be happy, Patrick. In the end, no one gives a shit."

"I hoped it would be a woman," said Patrick. "I know it's silly, but I really did."

"Me, too," said CD. "Maybe there's a woman there, as well."

"Unlikely. This one looks like it's dead centre in the barrow."

"Well, dead anyway. Could be there's another one. I did some digging in France," said CD thoughtfully. "Champagne Ardennes. We found these incredible burials—men and women together. Some of them were holding hands. Some had their arms around each other."

There was a tiny noise, a swallowing or perhaps a gulp, in the silence that followed.

"Are you OK?" asked CD.

Silence.

"We all cried like babies," CD told him. "Dozer was there. Ex-president of the Hell's Angels and there he was, down on his knees, using his trowel like he was uncovering the crown jewels, tears pouring down his ugly face."

Patrick found his voice again. "He really was a Hell's Angel? I thought that was just a story you made up for Roger Little."

"No, no. Old Doze? He was the Boss. The toughest of the tough. Even back then, when he was still biking, he used to go on digs. Been digging since he was twelve. Two sides to his life. Door tight shut between them."

"It's a survival skill."

"For some people, I guess. For others, could be a trap."

"We're not going to find another burial in the barrow."

"I guess not. So much for our friend and his weird song. If there really is a German Queen anywhere up here, she didn't have a shield buried with her. That's for sure."

"Yes."

"Shame."

"It is rather."

"I would have liked to find the chicken blade."

Patrick laughed.

"Hey, anyway, Patrick. These diggers. Maxwell and the rest. We could do something for them, you and I. Make it more real."

"How?"

"Put it to the test. In public. See how much we can *really* tell. Every night when we finish and the cameras have gone, we could do a bit of speculating round the campfire—put together some guesses."

"I thought that's what our report's meant to do. All in its proper place. Considered, scientific research."

"Dry as dust. Why don't we do it for fun? Pin some humanity on those old bones. All very scientific, of course. We've got the TV people trying to do that whether we like it or not. It would help turn these guys into proper diggers—get them involved."

"I don't see why not."

"That's if they *are* bones."

"We've seen them."

"We've seen one. Could be just a shield and an arm some Anglo-Saxon buried for a joke."

Patrick looked up. The crowd round the fire was thinning out. His devils had left him, and he felt drained and inexpressibly weary. "Time for bed."

"OK," agreed CD, well content. His prime objective had been satisfied. Bringing Patrick and his team together through a nightly session round the fire might help bridge the chasm between them. It might also help engage Patrick's attention so that the pained, distracted vacancy faded from his eyes. That, CD thought, would be good for everyone.

He had no way of knowing just how far the process would go.

PATRICK WOKE IN THE MORNING TO FIND THEY WERE ON AN island. A tide of mist had swept in across the Oxford plain, and the hill rose out of it as if there were nothing else in the world. The fog suited the way he felt. CD's words had warmed his dreams and coloured the memory of the last few days, so it felt all at once that this hilltop had become home in a way that nowhere else had been for years. It seemed to him that his greatest fear was that the dig would come to an end. An encroaching outrider of the mist had collected in the dip where Joe and Bobby's farmhouse sat, so that only the roof and chimneys emerged from it. Patrick envied—indeed almost resented—the way her life was rooted in this spot.

ONCE AGAIN, IT WAS DOZER WHO MADE THE NEXT FIND, soon after they started, with the camera conveniently pointing at him so there was no question of having to fake it for a second shot. The trouble lay in what it was that he found. The wood of the shield had long since dissolved into the soil, outlasting the flesh by no more than a century. The huge man, kneeling on planks stretched across the trench, was gently teasing the grains of soil out from where the shield would have been, exposing the rib cage below with unlikely patience. There, lying across two of the ribs, was a large circular object fully eight inches across. It was caked and encrusted with dirt and corrosion, but at its edges, intricately decorated metal betrayed its origins, and those origins, quite clearly, were much, much older than the shield.

Patrick had entrusted the main job to his most experienced

diggers. CD and Dozer were working on the area around the shield boss while the others were kept out of the way, extending the other trench towards the edges of the barrow. All spent as much of their time as they decently could glancing enviously towards the two men digging in the centre of the mound. When they'd started that morning, Gaye had found a small curved piece of something unidentifiable. She made the mistake of showing it to Dozer.

"Go on," he said, "taste it."

She put it to her mouth with utmost reluctance.

"Now, put it against your teeth. That's the way to tell."

He kept on at her until she scraped it with her teeth for a fraction of a second.

"That's amazing," she said. "You can tell it's not stone straight-away. Is it pottery?"

Dozer took it from her and looked at it. "Nah," he said, "that's bone."

A stricken look came over her face which he pretended not to see. He rubbed at the piece and peered closer. "That's interesting," he said. "Look at those marks. Very characteristic."

"What of?" Gaye said, faintly.

"It's a toss-up," he said. "Syphilis or leprosy."

She screamed and rushed from the trench, spitting and wiping her mouth until Dozer's laughter brought it home that she'd been had.

Finding the disk brought all work to a complete halt and took Kenny Camden, who had arrived just in time to see its uncovering, to the point of rapture. Bobby had walked across from the catering tent when she saw something afoot, and stood at the edge of the trench staring down at it. She stared at the disk, frowning, then she turned and went back to preparing their lunch.

For Patrick, the trouble started when Peter looked at what they'd found and confirmed his own fears.

"Look at the edge decoration," he said. "That's not seventh-century Anglo-Saxon, is it? Roman, surely. It's got to be at least four hundred years older."

CD agreed and, after a quick and disturbing conference with the two of them, Patrick had to find something sensible to say to the camera.

"This is, um, definitely a bit of a surprise," he said, looking into the camera's eye. "It's not at all the sort of thing you would expect to find with an Anglo-Saxon burial. In fact, at first sight, judging by the workmanship, it appears to be Roman." After that he just trailed off into silence.

"What do you think it is?" Camden prompted, off-camera.

"I haven't a clue. We'll have to have it cleaned before we know."

"Look, Pad—Patrick. You've got to say *something* that makes a bit more sense than that. Viewers expect some sort of narrative. You can't just duck out."

"Well, all right, but we *don't* have a clue. It's completely unexpected."

"OK, well, say so then, but do it with a bit more force and go on a bit longer."

Patrick tried again. "This has come out of the blue, something that really shouldn't be here at all. We don't know what it is yet. It needs a lot of cleaning, but it's clearly highly decorated, some sort of plaque perhaps, apparently laid across the chest in the burial, something with ceremonial value. It seems to have copper in it. And the strangest thing of all is that it is very obviously not Anglo-Saxon. Our best guess at the moment is that it's Roman workmanship, so what it's doing here, in the middle of this burial, is a complete mystery."

"Very good," said Camden. "Just the ticket. You're a natural."

Patrick found himself loathing the praise.

"How soon can we get it cleaned up?" Camden pressed.

"Well, that's up to John Hescroft. That would be in the post-ex."

"The what?"

"Post-exploration. When we've finished. If there's any money. Sometimes the finds just hang around in boxes for years."

"No, no, no. That won't do. I'll sort it out." Camden started tapping numbers into his mobile phone, walking off towards his car. When he came back, he had a triumphant grin on his face.

"Hescroft's fixed it up. The lab is going to get into it straightaway. He said you'd know where to take it."

"How did you do that?"

"We've got a deal. We'll throw in a bit of cash if we have to. I'm getting a good feeling about this. We could be on to a good one."

## CHAPTER FOURTEEN

IT TOOK THE REST OF THE MORNING to expose the disk completely, record it, and lift it carefully out of the trench. Maxwell, clearly wishing he'd found it, had more than half his attention on what was happening in the next trench instead of on what he was doing himself. That was why, using a shovel where the change in the colour of the earth should have prompted him to bring out his trowel, he completely missed seeing an edge of flattened metal protruding from a lump of earth. The lump went into a bucket, then into a wheelbarrow, then onto the heap with all the rest, taking its story with it.

As that wheelbarrow trundled past him, Patrick straightened up from the trench, looked down the hill, and saw the mist was still there around the house.

MIST OFTEN COLLECTED THERE,
ALLOWING ONLY THE ROOF OF THE

HALL TO SHOW THROUGH IT. A YEAR AFTER HILD HAD
DONE THE BEST SHE COULD WITH THE REPAIRS, CUTHWULF
WAS STILL COMPLAINING ABOUT THE DRAUGHT. WHENEVER
THE MIST CAME HE MADE A SMALL SACRIFICE TO PROTECT
THEM FROM WHATEVER MIGHT COME UPON THEM UNDER
ITS CONCEALMENT. THAT HADN'T STOPPED TWO OF THE
SHEEP GOING MISSING AND CUTHA GETTING HIS ARM BADLY
SLASHED, A WOUND HILD WAS STILL TENDING.

"DAUGHTER!"

"COMING, LORD." IT WAS ORDERS ONE MINUTE AND
QUEEN-LANGUAGE THE NEXT. YOU NEVER KNEW WHERE
YOU WERE WITH CUTHWULF.

"WHICH IS THE BAD WINE?" HER FATHER WAS IN HER
STOREROOM, HOLDING A BULGING SKIN IN EACH HUGE
HAND. SHE RESCUED ONE OF THEM.

"THAT ONE, LORD," SHE SAID, "WITH THE WHITE MARK
ON THE SKIN. SHALL I POUR IT AWAY?" THEY HAD FOUND AT
THE MEAL LAST NIGHT THAT ONE WHOLE SKIN HAD TURNED
TO VINEGAR.

"I HAVE A LIBATION TO MAKE," HE SAID. "IT WILL
SERVE."

"SHOULD THE GODS NOT HAVE GOOD WINE?" SHE ASKED,
SHOCKED. "I CAN USE THAT FOR COOKING!"

SHE WONDERED IF SHE HAD GONE TOO FAR WHEN SHE
SAW HIS SCOWL.

"THAT IS A MATTER FOR ME. GO AND GET MY SWORD. NO
MAN SHOULD GO INTO THIS MIST WITHOUT A SWORD. WHO
IS ON WATCH?"

"CYNELM."

"TELL ONE OF THE OTHERS TO GO HALFWAY UP THE HILL
AND USE THEIR EARS. CUTHA'S GOT GOOD HEARING.
CYNELM COULD BE SURPRISED AT ANY MOMENT UP THERE."

*NO,* SHE WANTED TO SAY. *HE'S IN BRIGHT SUNLIGHT UP
THERE. YOU'D SEE IF YOU EVER BOTHERED TO GO MORE THAN
TWENTY PACES FROM THE HOUSE.* BUT LIFE WAS TOO PRECIOUS
TO SAY THAT SORT OF THING TO CUTHWULF.

SHE WENT TO GET THE SWORD FROM ITS HANGING PLACE
AND STRAPPED ON THE BELT FOR HIM WHILE HE STOOD

WITH ARMS RAISED. HE TOOK THE WINESKIN AND STRODE OFF, DISAPPEARING INTO THE MIST.

THREE MINUTES LATER, WHILE SHE WAS CUTTING THE ROTTING PARTS FROM THE VENISON, WORRYING IF WHAT WAS LEFT OVER LOOKED A LITTLE SMALL FOR THE EVENING MEAL, THERE WAS A SCREAM AND A LOUD ROARING OUTSIDE. HER HEART RACED. SO OFTEN IN RECENT TIMES, AS THE TENSION GREW, SHE HAD FEARED THIS MOMENT, WHEN THE RAIDS WOULD SPILL OVER INTO SOME FULL-SCALE ATTACK. SHE SEIZED THE KNIFE AND RAN TO THE DOOR, HEARING ANSWERING SHOUTS AND FEET RUNNING FROM THE DIRECTION OF THE HUTS. HER BROTHERS WERE COMING TO HELP. NO HELP WAS NEEDED. CUTHWULF EMERGED FROM THE MIST HOLDING A MAN IN EACH HAND, BANGED THEIR HEADS TOGETHER HARD, AND DROPPED THEM ON THE GROUND, WHERE THEY LAY INERT. HER BROTHERS FORMED A CIRCLE AROUND THEM.

"KILL THEM," CUTHWULF ORDERED HIS SONS. "THEY TRIED TO CREEP UP ON ME."

"WE KNOW THIS ONE. IT'S WOTSISNAME." CRIDA PUT OUT HIS FOOT TO PROD THE NEARER MAN IN THE RIBS. "YOU KNOW, THE BLOKE THAT BRINGS THE HONEY."

"STEAN?" SAID HILD. "OH, NO! I'VE BEEN HOPING HE'D COME. HE'S NOT DEAD, IS HE?"

CUTHWULF SHRUGGED. "SHOULDN'T HAVE CREPT UP LIKE THAT. SHOULD HAVE WAITED TIL THE MIST CLEARED. WHAT DID HE EXPECT ME TO DO?"

"HE'S BREATHING," SAID CRIDA. "I'LL GET A BUCKET."

THE WATER WASN'T NEEDED. STEAN OPENED HIS EYES, GRUNTED A BIT, AND SAT UP.

"WHO DID THAT?" HE DEMANDED.

"I DID," REPLIED CUTHWULF. "WHAT DO YOU MEAN BY WALKING UP TO ME LIKE THAT?"

"LORD. FORGIVE ME," SAID STEAN HASTILY. "I WAS BRINGING YOU A MESSAGE FROM YOUR KIN."

"WHAT MESSAGE?"

"THEY SAID TO TELL YOU THAT THE BROTHER BAND OF YOUR ENEMY HAVE SAILED FROM THE OLD HOMELANDS

AND ARE NOW SEARCHING FOR YOU, WITH CYNEGILS'S
APPROVAL."

"THOSE CRAPHEADS? SO?"

"THE GEWISSE HAVE TOLD THEM YOU CAME ACROSS THE
FRONTIER. THERE ARE MANY OF THEM AND THEY HAVE
SHARP SWORDS."

"NOT AS SHARP AS MINE," SAID CUTHWULF, ROARING
WITH LAUGHTER. "NOT AS SHARP AS MINE AND THEY KNOW
IT." HE SLID THE SWORD FROM ITS SCABBARD AND WHIRLED
IT OVER THEIR HEADS.

"DOES CYNEGILS KNOW WHERE I AM?" HE SAID, THEN
HIS MOOD CHANGED ABRUPTLY. AND HE GRABBED STEAN
BY THE THROAT WITH HIS OTHER HAND. THE TRADER
STRUGGLED, HIS FEET OFF THE GROUND, FLAILING HIS ARMS
UNTIL CUTHWULF SET HIM DOWN AGAIN.

"HE KNOWS YOU'RE WITH THE HWICCA, LORD. THAT'S
ALL."

"BUT YOU KNOW I'M HERE AND YOU'RE GOING BACK. I
THINK I'LL HAVE TO KILL YOU."

"YOU CAN TRUST ME, LORD. I BRING YOU HONEY AND
SALT AND SWEETMEATS."

"DOES HE BRING THOSE YELLOW SWEETS?" SAID
CUTHWULF TO HILD.

"YES, LORD."

"ALL RIGHT THEN, JUST KEEP YOUR MOUTH SHUT OR
THE CHICKEN SWORD WILL OPEN IT RIGHT ACROSS."

THE OTHER MAN STIRRED AND CUTHWULF LOOKED
DOWN. "OH, YES," HE SAID, "I'D FORGOTTEN ABOUT HIM.
WHO'S HE?"

"HE'S GOING ROUND TELLING PEOPLE ABOUT A NEW
GOD," SAID STEAN, GRATEFUL HE WAS NO LONGER THE
FOCUS OF ATTENTION. "HE'S WITH THE ITALIAN."

"A NEW GOD?" SAID CUTHWULF, AND THE MAN TRIED
TO SAY SOMETHING. CRIDA THREW THE BUCKET OF WATER
OVER HIM AND HE SAT UP, GASPING.

"WHO'S THIS NEW GOD, THEN?" SAID CUTHWULF. "IT'S
NOT THOR'S GRANDSON, IS IT? WE KNOW ABOUT HIM."

"IT IS THE ONE GOD," SAID THE MAN INDISTINCTLY.

"TALK STRAIGHT," SAID CUTHWULF. "CAN'T UNDERSTAND YOU. WHAT ARE YOU, A FRANK?"

"I HAVE COME TO OFFER YOU SALVATION," SAID THE MAN, GETTING UNSTEADILY TO HIS FEET. HE WAS OLD AND THIN, DRESSED IN A LONG BROWN ROBE, AND HE HELD UP SOMETHING ON A CHAIN AROUND HIS NECK.

"OH, GOOD," SAID CUTHWULF, EYEING THE NECKLACE.

"YOU MUST GIVE UP YOUR FALSE GODS AND TURN TO THE ONE TRUE GOD, WHOSE SON DIED FOR YOU SO YOU MIGHT LIVE."

"NO, NO," SAID CUTHWULF, AND A CASUAL BACKHAND SWING OF THE CHICKEN SWORD TOOK OFF THE HEAD OF BIRINUS'S EMISSARY TO THE HWICCA, SPLASHING CUTHA AND HILD AND STEAN WITH SPOUTS OF ARTERIAL BLOOD. WHEN THE THRASHING HAD STOPPED, CUTHWULF REACHED DOWN AND PULLED THE REMAINS OF THE THING THAT HAD BEEN ON THE NECKLACE CHAIN FROM THE STUMP OF THE MAN'S NECK.

"FALSE GODS INDEED," HE SAID. "PRESENT FOR YOU, QUEEN," AND TOSSED IT, COVERED IN HOT BLOOD, TO HILD, WHO QUICKLY DROPPED IT IN WHAT WAS LEFT OF THE WATER IN THE BUCKET.

"YOU'VE ALL GONE A BIT QUIET," SAID THE HUGE OLD MAN, THEN HE LOOKED ROUND. "HERE, WHERE'S THAT STEAN GOT TO?"

When the heavy Roman disk had been lifted from its place in the earth, Patrick packed it in a box he found at the back of the tent, still lacking any of the proper paraphernalia for tending the finds. He took it into Oxford in his car, surprising himself by the extent to which the world outside their hilltop came as a shock—a place full of noise and hurrying people, where he became aware of the grass stains on the knees of his jeans. He saw the disk safely into the hands of the conservation specialists. With long experience at seeing the forms that lay beneath encrustation, they confirmed it as Roman in a matter of moments, but anything else would have to wait until the painstaking process of cleaning it had taken its course.

It was after five when he drove back up the hill into Wytchlow and past the school where Bobby had first rushed into his life. He looked at the gate, almost hoping for history to repeat itself, but it was long after schooltime and there was nobody there. A large piece of cardboard had been taped to the school railings. On it, someone had written KEEP MAY DAY ALIVE in big red letters. Suddenly unwilling to drive straight back into the life of the dig, Patrick took the other road, the right fork down the side of the village green, and pulled into a small lay-by at the end of a pathway up to the church. A Victorian redbrick vicarage stood on a bank above the road on one side of the path and a short terrace of thatched cottages lined the other, two sides of a funnel drawing him towards the lych-gate.

The churchyard promised another brief limbo between demanding worlds, and Patrick had spent much of his recent past seeking limbo. The church proved to be old and simple, a mixture of Norman and Gothic. It was full of spring flowers, as if he had arrived hard on the heels of a wedding, but between the sprays of white and yellow, sombre remnants of medieval frescoes loomed on the walls, great patches of them obliterated by time and damage. The surviving figures painted on the plaster were grim, judgmental. Patrick preferred to look at the flowers, and as he did so, it was as if he stood in another, even older church. A clear memory came back to him from the weeks immediately after Perugia—the weeks when he had wandered through Britain's lonely places, seeking isolation, explanation, and then, when that failed, obliteration.

He'd escaped from the house at Marlow and the press siege, had his head completely shaved by a barber in Slough who failed to recognise him, then swapped his Mercedes for a small camper-van at a roadside car lot whose proprietor couldn't believe his luck. He'd headed north, crossed the Tyne at Newcastle, and kept on driving into the night until he was deep into Northumberland, near the Scottish border. He went to sleep in a car park on the coast with no idea where he was. At dawn, he was awakened by the rhythmic thunder of wild surf, and looked out of the camper's window to find himself under the walls of Bamburgh Castle. He gazed out across the long curve of the beach to where the waves were breaking on the black bones of the Farne Islands, and in that unpeopled coast, he saw somewhere that fitted his immediate need. It looked like a place where he could be a hermit if he chose, and then perhaps it could be the place where he could make a grand, silent end of himself, swimming out, head-butting those huge, curling waves until the sea sucked him under or flayed him on the reefs.

For the next two days it was as if he was counting down to that final moment. He found himself in no great hurry, quite calmly walking and driving up and down between the remote sea-castles, towering fortresses against long-gone invaders. He spent one whole day in the skeletal, gull-mewing wreck of John of Gaunt's Dunstanburgh, going over his entire life in painful detail, clearing the decks for that one-way swim, which seemed the only remaining possibility now that he had rejected all the others.

What saved him was a place and an extraordinary event. The place was Lindisfarne or Holy Island. It had seemed the right setting for his last performance. He never considered for a moment that it might also provide him with a last chance. He had waited at the landward end of the causeway until the tide's retreat let the first gleam of the road surface show through the waves. Then he drove out through the sea, long before the safe moment, defying the waves to clash together and drown him. He left behind him a queue of other cars, their occupants horrified by his rashness. Following the moon's pull as it sailed off round its orbit, the sea began to withdraw across the flat sand beyond the rescue tower and the stakes marking the old foot-passage, leaving behind only a threat of fanned-out sand and seaweed wreaths to remember it by. He drove onto Holy Island, a low place of rough grass and sand dunes, a halfway place between one world and another, with a growing knowledge that this was the right setting for what he planned. He could not imagine ever driving back across that causeway.

Lindisfarne village held no attraction for him. He left the camper and walked to the castle on the seaward side. There the sea again exerted its hypnotic pull, frothing over the reefs and roaring in backward-splashing arcs up the pillars of the channel markers as a small fishing boat dipped and reared its way back to safety. The harbour held his attention for a short time—old wooden boats upturned and bisected into sheds for fishing gear, tarred dull black against the weather.

Last of all, and it was the very last thing of all for him because he had nowhere else to go after this, he turned in to the ruined priory and read of Cuthbert, the Christian saint, and his lonely death on that same island of Inner Farne that Patrick had seen when he was looking out from Bamburgh Castle. Thirteen centuries had passed since that death.

Ruins suited his mood, and the priory's miraculous archway, a diagonal thread of masonry still arcing across from pillar to pillar when all the rest had fallen, came to him as an omen, a signal that in all great ruins, something precious may still sustain. The moment was immediately spoilt by the influx of a horde of tourists. They were the families who'd waited for the tide to clear the road, a shrill army wrapped in bright plastic, irreverent and banal, grandfathers joshing fat daughters while sullen children pulled at stroller handles. They came like a biblical plague to separate Patrick from any thought of salvation. To avoid them, he hurried into the tiny church which stood facing the priory ruins.

Inside that church, an old man in vicar's black smiled at him and, getting no response beyond a wild stare, left him to himself. Patrick sat in a pew, reading the church's history from a pamphlet, praying that the man in black, the carer for souls more willing and less lost than his, would leave him alone. What he read occupied that small part of his brain that still engaged with the world. It also gave him sudden insight into the psychology of ruins. This unassuming building, its central part dating back more than a thousand years to the Saxons, was far older than the infinitely more glamorous ruin facing it. Yet because its walls and its roof still stood intact, the world beat a path to the priory and largely ignored St. Mary's Church. Paddy Kane had been a glamorous ruin for the last three years of his band's riotous success, and many had come to share his ruined glamour. Ruins got more attention than they deserved simply for being less than whole. It seemed time for one ruin, his ruin, to slip quietly into the sea. In this godly place he could still find no God to talk to, no God to stop him, only his unbearable self and the trail of damage he had left. In Perugia he had come face-to-face with a god of sorts, but only as an accuser. It seemed to Paddy, in that hushed church on its part-time island, that he had committed a sin that was irredeemable, that the crucified Christ on the altar might well have died for sinners but not for sinners as bad as him.

It came to him, too, that a new noise outside was not the waves but the roar of a sudden downpour and then, signaling the end of quiet thought, the entire group of sightseers, noisy as gulls and dripping wet, streamed in through the door for shelter and filled the narrow aisles, chattering away as if this space had no right to command silence.

That was his signal. He got up from his seat and headed for the door with no other destination in mind except the sea, knowing that in the rain, it was less likely some watcher would be there to interfere. He reached the back of the church where the vicar stood watching with resigned tolerance as his church filled up. There he got no farther. There was a new influx of wet tourists, but these were different. A group of seven or eight teenagers burst noisily in through the door, dressed in exuberant rags, their hair knotted and braided. In the lead was a girl with a face of fragile beauty and purposeful intent. Her cohorts, all boys in their late teens, had eyes that seemed to Paddy to be entirely accustomed to trouble. At any concert, the bouncers would have been keeping a close eye on them. The vicar stiffened as the teenagers entered, and watched with growing anxiety as they pushed their way firmly through the milling tourists, heading for the central aisle, then made their way towards the altar.

"My goodness," murmured the vicar. "What are they doing?"

Paddy had stood next to him, watching, because he could take in this small moment of theatre on a level that barely touched him. There was no reason not to stand and watch it develop. The vicar took a few steps up the aisle, prepared to try to stop the youths if they tried to abscond with the candlesticks, but that was not their intention at all. They filed into the front pew and knelt to pray amid the hubbub. After a few seconds, the girl stood up, a colourful angel in rags, framed by the white flowers in vases in the archway ahead of her. She held her hands out to each side and turned her face up towards the ceiling. She seemed to take total command of that stone enclosure of time and space and as the tourists nearest her became aware of the silence she was generating, it caught hold of them and spread from person to person until all the noise that had filled the church moments before drifted down to a whisper.

The girl held her stance long enough to create a tension in the silence, all eyes focused on her and no one willing to stir until she did. Then, the boys next to her got up off their knees, and as she let loose a long high note, they joined in, singing in harmony to some ancient, unfamiliar tune with words in a foreign language. It was a song of high spirituality and soaring power and at the end, there

were little noises of appreciation throughout the church. The tourists'
conversation, when it started again, was subdued; the notes of the
song seemed to hang in the air between the beams of the roof.

The girl turned and came back down the aisle, followed by the
boys, with everyone in the church watching them, and she smiled at
Paddy and the vicar next to him. The vicar put out a hand and
stopped her.

"My dear," he said, "where are you from?"

"From the old eastern part of Germany," she said, "just by the
frontier."

"What you just did was very special," said the old man. "Would
you tell me why you did it?"

"This is my brother," she said, "and these are my cousins, and
since we were born we did not see each other until the Wall came
down. I made a promise that if my brother and I could see our
cousins, I would one day make . . . what is it? *Eine Wallfahrt.* I do not
know the word."

"A pilgrimage?"

"Yes, I think so. I said I would come here and give thanks for it,
and that is what I have done. I am glad they wanted to come, too. I
am sorry it has taken me so long. Money was not easy."

"Why here?"

"Oh. I had a postcard on my wall for all the years, a very old
postcard of your church and your beautiful island. I always was
thinking that it looked a good place for new beginnings."

Paddy had turned abruptly, seeking only an ending, and left
them to talk, leaving the church as the rain stopped and striding out
past the priory ruins, past the beach of the little harbour littered
with the bones of the fishing boats, out to the rocks where the waves
waited. He sat down to stare at the sea until the moment of certainty
came but what came instead was the German girl. She sat down beside him and asked in her accented English what it was that troubled
him so much. While her brother and her cousins kept a distant
watch from the harbour's edge, she sat there with him and listened
with intense concentration while he unaccountably told her the
whole story. The words tumbled from him. Then, instead of anything banal, she nodded and said that, yes, the waves might be a perfectly good choice under such circumstances, but it was hard to be

sure because the future is not written yet and perhaps he had a lot to give in exchange for all that he had taken.

"I do not like to think of you drowning yourself here in my special place," she told him. "You will spoil it for me if you do, and I will never be able to look at my postcard again. If you must do this, please do it somewhere else. Your ghost would stay here, you know. Others who come here for healing or for thanksgiving may not hear or see you, but a little part of them will know always that you are here. Please do not do that. You are right: You have done bad things. Better to throw away just that part of you, not the whole of you."

Then she kissed him on the cheek and went back to her family and talked to them while he sat on his rock and discovered that the impulse to self-destruction, which had seemed strong only because nothing opposed it, had now acquired a counterbalance. When he got to his feet, they were still there watching him from a distance and the girl waved to him, and when he walked slowly as far along the seaward shore as he could, taking a new interest in the shape and sound and smell of things as if he had just awakened, they were always somewhere off at the edge of his vision. When, eventually, he returned to where he had left his camper, he saw their VW van, with its German plates, parked in the same road. He was surprised when they showed up that afternoon at the same campsite near Berwick-upon-Tweed, but he shouldn't have been. If he'd been watching in his mirror he would have seen their van shadowing him, far back down the road like a faithful sheepdog. After that, by common agreement, they continued in convoy for the next week, wandering through the Lammermuir Hills, spending their time walking, sitting, talking. The boys' English wasn't nearly as good as the girl's, so she and Patrick spent most of that time talking together. She was called Beatriz and during that entire week she never once mentioned a single thing that he had confessed to her on their rock beside the water. Instead she fanned the faint embers she detected deep in him, the embers of past enthusiasms, forcing him to dredge his memory for facts about the history of the land they were in, about borders, about castles and kings and, in the end, when she found his true centre, about archaeology.

"You know about these things," she said. "You care about them. Maybe you should go back to take an interest in them. It will, I think, help you to heal. You have no god you recognise, so believe in something. Do you know what I have to believe in?"

"Your postcard?"

"Mathematics."

"Oh, come on."

"No, listen to me. Don't be so silly, you quick-judging Englishman. You will never see a truth if you answer so fast. Mathematics is beautiful because there are solutions and it is not just numbers. For me, mathematics can be philosophy and poetry, but it has a frame and a system and when I feel very bad, I can use it to remind me that there are ways. You have something, too."

"What do I have?"

"History and your digging-up, your detective thing. Looking at the signs in the earth."

"Bea, I don't see how that helps."

"You have told me yourself," she replied indignantly. "You look at the marks on the land and you don't tell me about ditches, you tell me *why* the people dug them there. You have the clues to *what* people are. Go on digging. You should have a trench around you for a while yet, I think."

A less devastated man might easily have fallen in love with her for what she did, but that part of Patrick was deep-frozen. All the time, she kept reminding him that the sea was still there, that if he found no source of beauty and interest left in the world despite all this, he could still consider it as an option. Just not on Holy Island, she said, not at Lindisfarne.

By the end of that week, when they all drove together back to Harwich and he waved them off as the Hamburg ferry sailed away, he was a few paces back from the brink and set on the path that led him to his new life.

DIGGING HAD STOPPED WHEN HE LEFT THE WYTCHLOW church and returned to the hilltop. By some TV-influenced miracle, they had acquired some of the trappings of a proper dig during his absence. A small hut had been delivered to protect the finds, and a portable shower unit now stood next to the loos. Bobby served another variation on the theme of brown stew and mashed potatoes, but they swallowed it with enthusiasm. Even Gaye ate it. Until now, she had been picking at the food, then eating from private supplies in her tent, unaware that the lantern inside gave a shadow show to the outside world as she spooned the contents of cans and packets into her mouth.

Bobby brought her own plateful and sat down at the table opposite Patrick.

"You're eating with us tonight, then," he said, and immediately regretted that he had stated the obvious.

She raised her eyebrows and smiled. "Looks like it. CD told us about the discussion session. I thought I'd like to be here."

"Discussion session?" said Patrick in surprise, then remembered what the American had suggested the evening before. "Oh, right. That."

Temporarily, in the low light of early evening, she wasn't so very like Rachel. Just as the candle had transformed her by lighting her from underneath, so the evening sun accentuated the planes of her face—more curved than Rachel's—the fuller light of day highlighted the similarities, the spacing of her eyes, the shape of her nose and chin. Or perhaps, he thought, it's just that Bobby looks serene and Rachel never looked serene.

"I'm sorry?" he said. He was suddenly aware that she'd been talking to him.

"I said, when are we starting?"

Everyone always thought he had a plan. He had no plans.

"I don't know. When we've cleared the table?"

So they did. They washed up using the cold water from a newly erected stand-pipe and an entire roll of kitchen towels, then they got the campfire going. After that there was no more delaying possible, and Patrick found himself facing an expectant ring of faces as if he were some kind of professional lecturer. He realised too late that these things need thought and preparation. Playing for time, his mind a complete blank, he looked for CD to rescue him, but the American sat there smiling amiably back at him with all the rest, his bird perched on his shoulder. Edgar was cocking his head and looking around as if searching for something else to steal.

"OK," Patrick said when time had stretched just beyond that elastic point where normal behaviour ends. "Um, I thought we might, er . . . Well, we might go over what happened today and well, you know, talk about it."

Lame start, he thought instantly.

"As you all know we found an object this morning which doesn't quite make sense. We know this is an Anglo-Saxon burial."

Aidan put up his hand as if this was some sort of schoolroom, and Patrick blessed him. Anything that got other people talking too was a help.

"How do we know?" the man said in his direct way.

"Well, we found the shield boss. It's diagnostic. That means it gives us a date. Bosses are very typical of their particular period."

"Yes, that's all very well and good, but now you've found something Roman. So maybe it's the shield boss which shouldn't be there, not the other thing, you know?"

"You mean maybe someone buried the shield there later, on top of a Roman burial?"

"And why not?"

"Well, the Romans didn't usually bury people in the middle of old barrows. That's definitely more of a Saxon thing."

Aidan pushed his glasses back into his face, looked around, and sniffed as if he was reserving judgment on that.

"Well, just suppose it was someone later altogether who happened to like old things and got himself buried there?"

"A bit unlikely."

"What is this Roman thing anyway?" asked Gaye.

"It's too early to tell," said Patrick. "We'll have to—"

"It's always too early to tell," cut in Maxwell. "You're always saying that, you know. Too early to tell."

CD smiled. "That's the way it is, kid. You better learn those words. It's archaeologist speak for 'I don't have any idea and I'm not going to guess until I have to.' Consider yourself privileged to be here tonight for a rare event. This is guessing time. Tonight we can all stick our necks out. Just don't hold it against us when we're wrong."

"So let's hear your guess, then," said Gaye.

"OK," said CD. "It's more or less round. It's too big and heavy to be a brooch and it looks too lumpy to be any kind of dish or plate. If it is part of the burial, then it seems to be in a pretty prime position, central, lying on the chest. I think it's most probably a clutch-plate for an early Roman Chevrolet."

"Early Roman Chevrolets had automatic gearboxes," said Peter. "It looks more like a Ford to me." His face was deadpan and it was a moment before the laughter started.

"Some kind of medallion, ain't it, Pat?" said Dozer. "Something a bit ceremonial. Looked a bit like that to me."

"It's too—" started Patrick, and the rest of them joined in a chorus, "—early to tell!"

They all burst out laughing, and after a slightly affronted second, Patrick joined in. With delight, CD watched his scheme starting to work.

"Supposing it is an Anglo-Saxon burial," said Bobby's rich voice from the growing darkness beyond the fire. "And supposing this other thing is Roman. He could have found it. Couldn't he? The man in the grave. Maybe he just liked old things, so they buried it with him."

Patrick, insulated from the disruptive effects of her face by the gloom, said, "Interesting thought."

"I dunno," said Dozer. "Pretty serious business staying alive back then. They didn't 'ave time to go collecting, did they? Shelter and food and not getting a spear between the shoulder blades, that's what they thought about mostly."

"Bullshit, Doze," said CD amiably. "They made beautiful things, those guys. Look at the Alfred jewel or the Kingston Down brooch or anything at all from Sutton Hoo. They knew about beauty. Why couldn't they collect it? Maybe this guy found it when he was digging up potatoes one day and thought, 'Hey, cool, I'll keep that to be buried with.' "

Dozer levered himself round to stare at the American.

"Shows what you know, you dopey four-eyed git," he said. "They didn't 'ave potatoes. Thought you'd know that, you being a clever clog with a college education."

"Oh, right, so that invalidates my whole thesis, I guess. Potatoes, turnips, whatever. Go sic him, Edgar."

The jackdaw flapped onto Dozer's head.

"I give in," said the big man. "No call to start bringing in air support. Call your effing vulture off. 'Ere, Bobby. Can't your Joe sing us another song? Something about the Roman thing. Tell us what's going on."

"Joe sings when he wants to," said Bobby. "I can't tell him. I don't even know where he is tonight." But she looked round and stared into what was now full darkness on the hilltop.

"Does he know about it? About the Roman thing?" asked Maxwell.

"I told him," she replied.

"Of course, the real question," said CD, "the real question is, why do we like all this old shit anyway? Who do we—Whoa there, hang on just a minute. Was that a bottle I heard? The gentle slopping of some sublime liquid in some vessel of the clearest crystal? Is that indeed the product of a far-off fermentation that I smell over there in the darkness beyond the fire? I think it's singing to me. Come on, bottle. Come to Daddy. Cast your Glenboggy on the waters, as they say, and it shall be returned threefold."

Bottles emerged from the shadows like the loaves and fishes on the mountain. Wine began to circulate.

After a while Aidan said, "Go on, then, what's the answer?"

"Answers? I don't have answers. I have enough trouble with the questions," said CD. "I go on pulling this shit out of the ground because it's what I do and I can look at it and kind of be surprised and not be surprised. You know how it is, you pull a lump of Samian-ware out of the ground and you're the first person to see it since some Roman matron smashed it in the year 300. You know it's Samian-ware and that's half the thrill, but you look at it carefully because it might just be some kind of pattern nobody's ever seen before and then everyone will start saying, 'CD? Sure, isn't he the guy who first identified the Samian-ware toothbrush steriliser?' Hey, am I starting to sound like Maxwell?"

"And what would be wrong with that?" demanded Maxwell.

"I can imagine that Anglo-Saxon finding his Roman clutch-plate," said Patrick. "He wouldn't know where it came from, would he? He probably wouldn't even know how it was made. Maybe it seemed like magic."

It was the first completely unforced sentence he had uttered in four years, but before that dawned on him, a guitar chord came out of the darkness like a warning round the blind bend of time.

# CHAPTER FIFTEEN

IT WAS FRIDAY, BUT JOE HADN'T SUNG in the pub, he'd sung to them up here on the hill, sung, then stopped and disappeared while they sat waiting for his next verse. When he'd gone, their world had narrowed itself back down to the circle of firelight and the ceiling of stars, and then the argument had started.

"Come on," Gaye kept saying, "it's too obvious for words, isn't it? He's just made that up. He knows we found something today and he's made it up. No offence, Bobby. I suppose it's quite sweet, really, but honestly, you don't want to start putting any faith into things like that."

"Hang about, Gaye. You stop being the cynic," said Dozer. "That's my job. It's what I'm known for, good looks and cynicism."

"And your slim figure, I suppose?" she scoffed.

The tune had been familiar and was what

they all wanted to hear—another installment of the song he'd sung in the pub, the song of the German Queen. This time, however, he started somewhere in the middle, the words coming weakly through the cooling air.

*A month went by while they mourned the son*
*And marked the bold deeds he had done*
*By laying his shield across his chest*
*As they put him in the grave to rest.*

*That was when they came again*
*In the hooded night, those murderous men,*
*Feet wrapped in cloth and swords honed keen*
*But they didn't allow for the German Queen.*

*She stayed awake while her brothers slept.*
*Moon-shadows moved in the watch she kept*
*And when she heard a skittering stone,*
*She beat the gong with a great leg bone.*

*Three brothers only faced the foe*
*And they made their stand by the witch's low.*
*They stood surrounded, back to back,*
*Against the waves of the night attack.*

*Their sister raced to summon aid,*
*To bring the King with his chicken blade.*
*But the King's old legs brought him there too late.*
*His last three sons had met their fate.*

*The King's hot blade was slaked in blood.*
*Six traitors lay in the hillside mud.*
*Down that hill they carried their own*
*And buried them round their valley home.*

*The King turned to his daughter dear*
*And spoke to her of his dreadful fear.*
*"You, my Queen, are the only one*
*Left of my line. You must bear a son."*

Joe had seemed to falter there, playing an extended instrumental passage, stopping and starting again as if uncertain where to pick up the tale. Then he came to a decision and launched into a new verse, but it was clear he had jumped ahead in the story.

> *At the village under the witch's low*
> *The Queen and her children came to know*
> *A time of peace, a time to mend,*
> *A time they thought would never end.*
>
> *She filled their home with the things she found*
> *Given up by the riven ground,*
> *Sharp axes chipped from ancient stone,*
> *A stag's head carved from an old thigh bone.*
>
> *When others shunned the Romans' stones*
> *She dared inspect their resting bones*
> *And there, when winter turned to spring*
> *She found what proved her favourite thing.*
>
> *He came to her from the deer-delved earth*
> *As if the land had given birth*
> *And what she saw beneath the sod*
> *Was the leafy brow of the woven god.*

There was another long pause, as if Joe was not quite sure what came next. When, eventually, the silence stretched too far, one of the diggers swung the beam of his powerful torch around the field and there was nothing to be seen except the brief red gleam of an animal's eyes.

"What's a woven god?" said Aidan.

"I haven't a clue," Patrick replied. "Do you know, Bobby?"

"No. I've never heard that before."

"I thought he said woden god," said Maxwell. "That would make more sense, wouldn't it? Wasn't there a god called Woden? Or maybe he said wooden. A wooden god."

"He made it up," declared Gaye. "He must have. He heard us going on about this silly idea that people collected old things back then and he made it up."

"And the rest of it?" said Aidan. "It's a hell of a story."

"Hell of a songwriter, too, if Gaye's right," said CD. "Hears us talking and makes up a song to fit, just like that."

"Doesn't fit, though, does it?" argued Dozer. "He's still going on about a *her*. What we've got here is a *him*."

That was undeniable.

"Come on, Bobby," said Maxwell. "You're the expert. What's the song about?"

"Oh, don't ask me. He's my brother and he's a good man, but I don't know how his mind works, really. I'm quite sure that he always has the best of reasons for what he does. I think maybe it's some sort of parable."

"What does that mean?"

"Well, I don't mean this to sound disloyal to him. What I mean is, I don't suppose it's meant to be literally true. The axes and the stag's head, I know where they come from. They're on our mantel-piece at home."

"There you are," said Gaye.

"What sort of axes?" said CD.

"Old hand axes. My father—our father—used to collect old bits and pieces."

"Stone axes? From where?"

"Just round and about. People say he was a great one for seeing things. He'd walk the fields after ploughing and he'd bend down and pick up stuff nobody else could even see. He knew what he was look-ing for."

"Didn't you know him? You said 'people say.' "

"He died when I was pretty young."

"Who ran the farm after that?" asked Gaye.

"My mother and Joe. Joe was almost sixteen then. I was a bit of an afterthought. Then when my mother died I came in with Joe, because he does need a bit of looking after. Not domestically, but business things. He doesn't talk on the phone. That makes life a bit difficult."

Patrick had been staring at Bobby, fascinated. "So your father was a bit of an antiquarian?"

"Oh, yes. I suppose I take after him. I find things, too, but the trouble is, I don't often know what they are."

"You could take them to the museum."

"If there were world enough and time," she said wryly. "There's not a lot of seconds left over in a struggling farmer's day for that sort of thing. You start off with the milking and the rest of the day just fills up. I'm taking time off to come up here, but that counts as my first holiday for five years and probably my last one for the next five. I've had to get some extra help in, and a farm like ours only just makes ends meet, you know."

"It's not exactly a holiday for you, is it?" asked Patrick, feeling suddenly that perhaps they had all been taking her efforts rather for granted. Bobby somehow seemed too translucent, too high-spirited to be bogged down in a life sentence of hard rural grind.

She didn't answer, because Dozer broke in. "Someone's coming," he said, and certainly a torch was probing in their direction from the track.

"Hello there! Are you the diggers?" called a querulous male voice.

Bobby groaned.

"No, we're Diana Ross and the Supremes," said Dozer.

"Yes, we are," Patrick called back hastily. You often got local visitors on digs. People loved to come and stare into your trench to see what they'd been walking over unsuspectingly all these years. They didn't usually come in the dark.

He stood up and the figure came up to the fire, shining the torch directly into his eyes.

"Are you the feller in charge?" said the new arrival.

"Yes. I'm Patrick Kane." Bright afterimages of the torchlight were dancing across his sight.

"I am the Reverend Augustus Templeton-Jones," said the new arrival, finally switching off the torch.

From the ground, Dozer said, "Blimey, I thought there was only one of you."

"What?" said the visitor.

"Nothing, mate," said Dozer. "Just asking my pal here for a fag."

"What can we do for you?" said Patrick. "I'd offer you a chair, but there isn't one."

"I won't stay. I heard in the village that you might be in need of my services."

"In what way?" said Patrick, puzzled.

"You've found a body, I understand."

So the news had got out already. Who'd been off the site? Patrick wondered. One or two of the diggers had been down to the village. They must have told someone.

"We've found a possible burial, yes."

"May I take it that you are going to observe proper procedures?"

"I'm not sure what you mean."

"Oh, I'm sure you are, Mr. Kane. As you well know, it is a requirement that any Christian remains that are disinterred should be given proper Christian reburial, preferably at the earliest suitable opportunity. I belong to a group within the Church which feels that, over the years, far too many gross liberties have been taken with the dead in the name of archaeology. I trust you agree with me?"

"Um, Mister, er . . ." Patrick couldn't begin to remember his name. "Reverend, that is . . . what we have here is almost certainly a pre-Christian burial. I'd say it's probably sixth- or seventh-century Anglo-Saxon, and—"

"Augustine came to Kent in the year 597, young man. Correct me if I'm wrong, but that was the sixth century."

"I'm sure you're right," said Patrick, floundering.

From the darkness, a voice—Peter Knight's voice—said, "Saint Birinus didn't convert Cynegils of the Gewisse until around 639, and this would be on the very edge of the Gewisse's territory."

"That's right," said Patrick. "In any case, this grave doesn't show the usual signs of Christianity. It's not orientated east-west. It's a bit too early to tell—" There was a titter around the campfire and the visitor looked round sharply. "—but the evidence so far is that it's a pagan burial."

"Well, that would suit some of my parishioners," said the vicar with a sniff. "I doubt you can be certain, however, and if there is any doubt, then I shall insist on all the proper ceremonies being carried out."

Peter cleared his throat. "There was, of course, the pagan reaction to Christianity during the reign of Æthelbert's son, Eadbald, to take into account."

Someone clapped quietly.

"Who?" said the vicar.

" 'Scuse me, governor," put in Dozer in an unusually innocent tone of voice; Patrick gritted his teeth, wondering what was coming.

"If it's not a Christian, is it all right if we just chuck the bones in a box?"

"That would be a matter entirely for you," said the vicar.

"Suppose it's a Roman?"

"As I say, that would be a matter entirely for you."

"But weren't most of the Romans Christians?"

"I think you're trying to trip me up," said the vicar crossly.

"Have you been God for long?" said Dozer unforgivably.

"What did you say?"

"I said have you seen Godfrey Long?" said Dozer. "He's a mate of mine. I thought you might have passed him on the way."

"No, I have not," said the vicar angrily, and turned to Patrick. "Have you informed the authorities of your find?"

"What authorities?"

"The Coroner's Office. I gather that is a requirement when you unearth human remains."

"Well, I know it is, in theory. In practice, they tend to get a bit annoyed if you ring them up about bodies that have been dead for over a thousand years."

"I can see that none of you can be trusted to follow proper procedures," said the vicar. "I shall be keeping a very close eye on your activities. I bid you good night." He turned away, switched on his torch, and stumbled over a rabbit hole, to the barely suppressed delight of the diggers round the fire.

"God almighty," said CD when he'd gone. "There go the genes that made the British Empire what it was. Why is it that the words 'total dickhead' somehow spring effortlessly to mind."

"That's the man I told you about. Our dear open-minded vicar," said Bobby. "The one who's causing all the trouble at the school over the May Morning procession."

"Would you like him killed?" said Dozer. "I've got a mate does it on the side. He's a chiropodist the rest of the time. A hundred and fifty quid, and he gives discounts for bulk."

"No, thank you, Dozer. But it's tempting."

"You sure? It's the only thing that gets through to people like that."

"Speaking of bulk," said CD, "he's right about the burials, you know, which is annoying considering he's a complete asshole. If it's

Christian, you have to do it right. I was doing all the post-ex on a dig last year. We hit the edge of the old paupers' burial ground in Saints-brook. Two hundred and ten bodies in red coffins."

"Why red?" asked Gaye incautiously.

"Warning of disease," said CD. "TB, typhoid, syphilis, that sort of stuff."

Gaye went rather quiet.

"Anyway, I went along to the crematorium and asked if they gave a discount for more than one body. Guy there puts on this pious face and asks how many of the deceased are in question. That's how he put it. 'How many of the deceased are in question?' Two hundred and ten, I say. Was it some sort of crash? he says, so I say 'No, I've just got a very bad temper,' and I can see him starting to look at the phone out of the corner of his eye."

"Did he give you a discount?" said Dozer.

"Yeah, but it still came to twenty grand."

"What did you do?"

"Found a friendly vicar and put them all in a big hole when they were digging his drains."

"So what's going to happen to our bloke here, then?" asked Maxwell.

"There'll be tests and stuff to do. We look at his bones and decide what killed him and if he had any diseases, then they go in a box somewhere in case anybody wants to have another look at them later on."

"Unless he's a Christian."

"If he's a Christian, I'm a boiled egg," said CD.

"By the way, folks," put in Dozer, "keep your mouths shut. If everybody 'ears we're finding things, we'll have every Tom, Dick, and Harry up here sticking their noses in."

"Don't you believe in the public's right to know?" said Aidan. "Surely the local people have a legitimate interest?"

"It's their illegitimate interest I'm bothered about, sunshine," rejoined Dozer. "You'd be amazed what gets nicked when you have the hoi polloi sniffin' around."

"I'd better go," said Bobby. "You don't want to be kept waiting for your breakfast in the morning."

"Up the revolution," said CD. "Anything we can do to help, just say the word."

She stood by the flames, looking towards where Patrick and CD sat, and the same magic lighting from the fire painted her a new face. "Thanks. Come and join the May Day march. It's next week. The vicar's going to have an empty school whatever he says." Then she was gone.

"She's a great kid," commented CD. "I didn't know farmers ever came with built-in beauty and culture. Maybe I should be a farmer. I could marry her and settle down. Farming's only archaeology with added manure."

"Nah, she wouldn't 'ave you," said Dozer. "Anyone can tell she's only got eyes for one bloke."

"And who's that?"

"Me, of course," stated Dozer. "You're too effing ugly."

Before they turned in for the night, someone started singing the inevitable songs that any group of people with a bottle or two round a campfire tend to sing. CD noticed with satisfaction that Patrick sang along with them, although he kept his voice so low they could barely hear him.

Early the next day, Patrick dressed and crawled out of his tent into dew-laden grass, and the world felt as if he were the only person alive in it. There was a gauze curtain across the land below the hill again, but the sun was already warm and a lark's thin song was sparkling down through the spring air. The mist would not last. He walked straight to the mound, where a makeshift wooden frame covered by a plastic sheet protected the exposed bones, and found that someone had been there before him. A tin can rested on the grass next to the trench; in it was a bunch of wildflowers. Someone, he thought, was apologising to the warrior for the mess they were making of his grave. He lifted the grave cover carefully off and the bones curved out of the earth, just the forearm and a few ribs so far, the merest hint of the complex person whose framework this was. When Patrick was a child, he had been so frightened of skeletons that even seeing the word in the pages of a children's story was enough to make him scream. On many nights in that house where no one ever came when he cried, he would lie in bed with the light on, trying not to sleep, sure that darkness would bring them, eye sockets searching and finger bones reaching. In the worst days after Perugia, he had seen the skull under the skin of every single person who inflicted themselves on him—the police, the lawyers, the music company flacks, and Rachel's family, Rachel's awful, accusing family. Rachel.

In a reverie, gazing at the earth, following the curve of the ribs into it as if he could see what was down there, a shadow fell across the grave. He twisted, startled, and an accusing ghost climbed up out of the mist, staring at him.

"Rachel," he said. "Oh, God. Rachel."

Rachel wore a woolen hat. Rachel stared, then reached out to touch his arm and said in a voice that was not Rachel's, "Patrick. It's all right. It's me, Bobby."

The touch of her hand shocked him. He jerked his arm away and she looked down at her hand as if in wonder.

"What happened?" she said.

He wrestled his control back. "I didn't hear you coming."

"I'm sorry. I just wanted to come up while it was still quiet. I didn't think anyone would be here."

"We're not the first." He pointed at the flowers. "Was that Joe?"

"Maybe. I don't know. It's not like him." She tilted her head and he looked away, down at the bones.

"You called me Rachel," she said. "Did you really think I was her?"

"I suppose I did."

"Do you still see her?"

Patrick stared at her, suddenly aware that his life wasn't such an open book as he had recently come to think. Bobby knew he'd lost Rachel, but she clearly had no idea what form that loss had taken. An unfamiliar need to confide came over him but he couldn't find the right words.

"No, she's not . . . I mean, she's . . . No, I don't."

"Why did you think I was her?"

"I don't know. I was miles away."

She started to say something else, then thought better of it.

"Do you think we'll uncover him today?" she said finally.

"You have to take things like this very slowly," he answered. "Bones may look strong, but they can crumble on you just like that. If the soil's too acid they get eaten away. It's quite dry and chalky here, but it's not like that all the way through. There's a wet patch at the end of the other trench. I think maybe you've got a spring or something."

"These bones look quite strong."

"I hope so."

"Thank you for last night," she said.

"No need for that."

"Will you go on doing it?"

"The discussions? Maybe."

"You must."

"I will if Joe keeps coming. Those songs are extraordinary."

"I'm glad you think so. He's not being a nuisance?"

"Anything that makes the Maxwells of this world think is not a nuisance."

"Are you enjoying this dig, Patrick?"

He was surprised. "Enjoying it? I suppose I am. At least I'm starting to."

"I'd better go and get the kettles on."

She was gone and the mist was lifting so that, down the hill, walls and chimneys showed through. He looked after her and found he *was* enjoying it. For a man who had fully expected never to enjoy anything, this came as a surprise. He looked back at the bones and found in them a rational explanation. This was already a significant dig. The Roman plaque or whatever it turned out to be had made sure of that. Television, he reflected, was an irritant, but without Kenny Camden's cameras, the dig wouldn't be happening at all.

H E FELT A BIT LESS GENEROUS WHEN CAMDEN AND HIS CAM-eraman arrived two hours after they started digging and instantly brought work to a halt. Earlier, over breakfast, Dozer had got a metal detector out of his car and run it over the spoil heap.

"Just checking," he said. "Can't be too careful with plonkers around."

The detector buzzed and he waved it backwards and forwards, then dug around with his trowel until he found a small lump of earth with a metal edge showing.

"Well, that's a pity," he said, bringing it back to the tent.

They all gathered round as he carefully freed the object from the caked earth.

"That is indeed a pity. Which of you threw it away, I wonder?"

"It could have come from *your* trench," said Maxwell. "Why are you looking at me?"

"I don't miss things like that," said Dozer.

"What is it, anyway?"

It might have been a pendant or a fragment of a brooch and seemed to have three short arms, one of them folded over where something had hit it. Shooting it and describing it for the camera took half an hour, glossing over the details of how it had been found.

"Could it be a cross?" Camden asked while Jack was filming. "If you unfolded it?"

"It's just possible. One of the arms could have been cut off. We won't know until it's been cleaned." Patrick waited until he saw the camera switched off. "Anyway, don't tell the vicar. We'll never hear the end of it."

Patrick had wasted enough time that morning already, kept away from the trench by a series of lengthy phone calls from John Hescroft about nothing in particular. Now he took Camden aside.

"Look, if we have to keep stopping just because you're not here when we find things, this could take years."

"Paddy, old son—"

"Patrick, please."

"Patrick. Ease up. You know how it is with filming. Anyway, I'm the bearer of good news."

"What?"

"Don't sound like that. I'm bearing gifts and I have no Greek ancestry. I'm well on the way to getting proper money fixed up, a real budget for the pilot, not the spare change I've had so far. If your boss agrees, we can both throw in a bit more, go halves and put something together, then I can do things for you."

"Like what?"

"I don't know. Things you need. More lab work. Whatever."

"So long as you get what you want for the show?"

"We're going the same way, you and me. You want to find interesting things. So do I. If it needs a bit of cash to get them cleaned or whatever, we're up for it. That's all I'm saying."

"Hescroft hasn't agreed to this yet, then?"

"Well, not yet, but you and I, we can persuade him, can't we?"

"He's not known for being lavish with his cash."

"A matching contribution, that's all I'm asking."

"We'll see."

While this conversation was going on outside Patrick's tent, CD had left the trench and strolled over, waiting politely for them to finish. Camden looked at him.

"Did you want something?" he said.

CD indicated Patrick. "Just a word with the boss," he said. "Private matter."

"Sounds interesting," said Camden.

"Yes, it is. It's Maxwell. He's got terrible diarrhoea, so I was thinking, in case it spreads we should get a stool sample and send it off for analysis, so I need a jar and, I don't know, maybe a clean stick to—"

"I'll leave you to it," said Camden.

When he'd gone, Patrick looked at CD. "What?" he said.

"Smokescreen," said CD. "Well, more like riot gas, really. Worked, didn't it?"

"OK. You were saving me from him, was that it?"

"No," said CD, "I need to tell you something and I didn't want him to hear until you had a chance to think about it."

There was a serious tone in his voice that Patrick hadn't heard before.

"Tell me."

"We've found more bones."

"Yes?" said Patrick, thinking that was what you might expect to find when you were digging up a skeleton. "So?"

"I'm afraid they're the sort of bones you might not really expect to be there."

# CHAPTER SIXTEEN

PATRICK LOOKED ROUND THE hilltop. Camden had wandered off to the mound and was watching Dozer. A man with a van was sucking out the contents of the chemical loos. The diggers were digging and Bobby was somewhere inside the catering tent, singing old Joan Baez songs. She had a good voice, a lush contralto which had been tugging at him to join in. He nearly didn't see Joe, who could have been a gatepost or a small bare tree, so well did his immobile form blend into the landscape. Bobby's brother was standing well out of the way, beyond the site hut, watching, and when Patrick lifted a hand in uncertain greeting, there was no discernible response.

"What are you talking about?" Patrick asked CD.

"You'd better see for yourself. You're not going to believe me if I tell you."

When Dozer saw the two of them walking

back, he got up out of the trench, beckoned the TV man over to him, said something, and then walked off with him towards the Land Cruiser, where Jack was doing something to his equipment involving batteries and much rummaging in bags in the back of the big Toyota.

"He's running interference for us," said CD. "Good old Doze. Always there when you need him, and quite often when you don't."

"What do you suppose he's telling him?"

"Some load of bullshit. I don't care as long as it keeps them occupied for a minute or two."

They reached the mound. The other diggers were busy extending the outside trench, fired up by that morning's tiny find.

"OK," CD called. "Early coffee break. Clear up your loose."

"I hope Bobby's ready for them," said Patrick.

"I hope she's not," replied CD. "The longer they take, the better."

The diggers went without a backward glance, and the hairs on the back of Patrick's neck began to prickle. Finds were usually noised aloud. The others had no idea that CD and Dozer had come across anything out of the way.

"Unexpected bones, you said. Where are they?"

The cover was back over the skeleton and CD left it in place. "First, let me walk you through the way it's gone. We've uncovered the side of the skull, all the rib cage, and enough of the legs to be pretty sure the body is lying supine, stretched straight out with the arms crossed at the wrists over the pelvis. The skull's tilted to one side and we've exposed the top surface of the pelvis."

"Sounds fine."

"Well, it's not." CD sounded rattled. "Take a good look."

He lifted the frame away carefully and Patrick stared down at what was now a recognisable skeleton, partly emerging from a bed of dark soil. From what he could see of the skull, it looked in fine condition, with the side of the jaw, the temple, and cheekbone area intact. That was all he could see of it. At a quick glance there was nothing else to see; the rib cage, the arms, and the top of the pelvis looked completely normal. The skull made it much more of a person. He suppressed an urge to say hello.

"I don't see any extra bones," he said. "What do you mean?"

"You have to get down close."

"OK." Patrick knelt on the soil, taking care where he put his weight. He was searching around the edges of the burial, wondering if perhaps the man had been buried beside or even on top of someone else.

"Not there," said CD. "Look just above the pelvis."

Patrick did as he was told, looking at the skeleton itself. When he turned his gaze properly, two tiny bones, thinner than the thinnest part of a chicken's wishbone, reared out of the earth.

"Oh, I see. Rodent? Could be rabbit ribs. Maybe some bunny died in its burrow." *I hope it didn't damage anything if it burrowed here,* he was thinking.

"You don't get it, do you?"

"Get what?"

"Those bones," said CD. "They're not from an animal. They're human."

"Oh, come on. They can't be. They're far too small. They're like a baby's . . ." Patrick's voice died away.

"They're exactly like a baby's," said CD, "because that's what they are. This warrior of ours was pregnant. Congratulations, young Patrick. Against all odds, we seem to have found the German Queen."

Patrick stared at him, then back at the frail bones. Elation was swiftly followed by a sense of something approaching horror, a conviction that he was not up to this. There was too much to be explained. There was Joe's impossibly undeniable song, but there was also something unique in archaeological history. It meant that this was a huge dig, one that would attract enormous interest, one that would have to be done just right. It also meant that sometime soon, two worlds were going to collide. Joe's song could not be kept in the dark for long. Archaeology was science. Joe's song seemed more like magic. The two could not easily coexist.

"Christ, CD. What do we do now?"

"Me? Why ask me? I'm having trouble believing my eyes. I guess we need a bit of time and a clear site. Why don't we send them all off field-walking? Get the TV crew to go with them, then the three of us can have a good think about what we've got here."

"Good. Let's fix it."

That was what they did. The diggers, somewhat reluctantly, went off across the hilltop in a long straggling line, searching for ancient artefacts that probably weren't there, looking for any signs of further human habitation on the hilltop, where there was no reason at all to find any. Maxwell accumulated a pocketful of oddly shaped stones. Gaye broke the buckle on her sandal. Aidan saved the day by finding a Tudor coin that had nothing at all to do with their dig but distracted everybody nicely. Jack the cameraman got several minutes of fairly unexciting pictures. It all bought enough time for Dozer, working with infinite care, to expose the eggshell fragments of a tiny human skull, crushed by the weight of the earth above it.

Then everything happened at once, too fast for them to keep the top on their delicate jar of secrets. They covered the skeleton as the diggers came back, but as they did so John Hescroft drove up to the tents, and Kenny Camden jumped in the car before he could get out. Patrick stared at them talking animatedly in the car, and wished he could lip-read.

It was just as well he couldn't. Inside the car, Camden said, "I don't know about this. I'm not sure we're getting enough to swing the real money. Your boy's a bit bloody difficult, John."

"Not playing the game?"

"It's all there. He just doesn't loosen up and let it show. He's so bleeding telegenic it hurts, but he opens his mouth and all you get is dusty fumbles. Have you seen him moving?"

"What do you mean?"

"He's got the movement. He can't help it, never could. He's so sexy I've half a mind to shoot him moving round and stick a voice-over on top. You know what I mean?"

"I'm afraid studying the movement of the male body has never been of great importance to me," said Hescroft huffily, and Camden roared with laughter.

"I think you're missing the point here. Anyway, you don't mind if I have a go at him?"

"In what way?"

"I gotta get him to play ball—let me do the rock star bit. We need to get a flavour of Paddy Kane into this."

"He doesn't want that. He said so. I don't think you should—"

"It's either that or you shell out ten grand to fund the rest of the pilot."

"Well, I suppose he probably wouldn't really mind."

THEY SAT IN THE CATERING TENT, THE THREE OF THEM, Hescroft, Camden, and Patrick, while Bobby buttered bread in the background. Hescroft and Camden had briefcases and piles of paper. Patrick, empty-handed, picked a sheet of paper off the table next to him. It said, *Tonight's menu: soup, meat stew, vegetable stew, pudding.* He folded it and held it in his hand. It seemed necessary to have a piece of paper.

Hescroft's face had the closed expression it usually wore when money was at issue. He looked like a golf club chairman about to blackball a membership application.

"Kenny," he said, "Patrick. We're faced with a tough decision, I fear, about where we go from here, and I think we need to put our heads together to sort it out. Patrick, first of all, how far have you got?"

"We've got a skeleton, partly exposed, perhaps a third of it thus far. The skull's turned towards the left shoulder. There's a shield boss, as you know, and this morning . . . we uncovered what may turn out to be a sword in the second trench."

Camden showed surprisingly little interest in that.

Hescroft barreled right along. "Right. Well, I should tell you that Kenny has made a suggestion about funding the rest of the dig, which requires us to make a fairly substantial contribution to costs. Now, I don't need to tell you that it isn't the sort of thing we usually do, although there is of course the publicity aspect to consider. We would perhaps have hoped that the television side of it might have covered a higher proportion of the total." He looked at Kenny Camden, who was lighting a cigarette. Camden took a deep drag.

"Unfortunately——" he began.

"Unfortunately, you'll have to put that out," said Bobby from behind him. "This is a food preparation area."

Camden raised his eyebrows and looked at Hescroft, who shrugged.

"I'm afraid she's right," said Patrick.

Camden bent down reluctantly to stub it out in the grass.

"Could you give us a few minutes?" said Hescroft to Bobby.

"Not if you want lunch ready on time," said Bobby.

"We have to discuss some delicate matters."

"Your choice. Go outside and I won't hear you. Stay inside and I'll try not to listen."

They stayed inside.

"As I was saying," said Camden, "the reaction I'm getting, unfortunately, is that there isn't anything very earth-shattering about an Anglo-Saxon burial. You know very well how much TV archaeology there is these days. There's bones shows everywhere. It's in danger of being done to death. We're looking for something new. Personalities. Now, you've got Dozer and CD, and they're both good on camera, but it's not enough to make anyone sit up and take notice, so there's a limit on what we can invest at this stage."

"Well, I'm afraid I don't think my company can afford to fill the gap," said Hescroft. "It's a shame, really."

*This is a setup,* Patrick thought with sudden certainty. *They've stage-managed this.*

"I suppose it would be different if you could do the ex-rock-star angle," he said innocently.

Camden, who had been staring at the ground in the pose of someone who was reluctantly heading for a tough decision, lifted his head a little too sharply.

"Well, yes," he said, "it certainly would, but I thought that wasn't really an option."

"It's not," said Patrick, his suspicions confirmed. Bobby had paused and was standing stock-still with her back to them.

"I don't know there's a lot else that can save it," said Hescroft a little too eagerly. "Shame, really."

"I mean, I have considered other angles," said Camden. "Don't think I haven't."

*Oh, yes, I'm sure you have,* thought Patrick. "Such as?" he asked.

Camden was clearly groping. "Well, there's this strange business of the song. . . ."

"What song?" said Hescroft.

"There's some weird old man who sang a song about this burial," Camden said, and Patrick saw Bobby's back stiffen. "Apparently that's the main thing that brought your guys up here. Didn't you know?"

"Is that right?" said Hescroft to Patrick.

"Up to a point." He looked at Camden. "I didn't know you'd heard about it."

"It doesn't work, though," said Camden, "not in TV terms. It would just look wacky."

Patrick chose his words very carefully. "Oral history has an important place. Archaeologists need to listen to it. People do remember the really big stories."

"What? Over a thousand years?"

"It would certainly tail off, that's true. The first few generations, everyone would know it. Storytelling was the main entertainment, after all, songs and stories. After fifty generations, who knows? But it's quite possible there would still be one person who knew the old tales."

"But it's crap, isn't it?" retorted Camden. "It's just some daft old bugger. Apparently he can't even talk properly."

Patrick saw Bobby turn round. In her hands she held a bowl of lettuce. From the expression on her face she looked quite capable of emptying it over Camden's head. He shook his head at her fractionally.

"Why exactly are you so sure it's crap?"

"Oh, come on. For a start, what you've got here is a male burial."

"What's all this about?" asked Hescroft, bewildered.

"This guy, this old farm bloke, sings in the pub," said Camden. "He sang this song about a woman who was supposed to be buried up here. All about how she died trying to save her village or something. That's how your friend Patrick here found this grave. Only thing is, it's not true."

"Is that right?" Hescroft was looking at Patrick with a shocked expression. "You didn't tell me that. I think that's extremely unprofessional. You could have had us all on a complete wild-goose chase. Have you any idea how much this sort of dig costs?"

*Virtually nothing, the way you do it,* thought Patrick. He felt like a poker player holding all four aces.

"No," he replied. "In fact, that's completely wrong."

"Which bit?" said Camden angrily. "The song?"

"No, the song's right. The song by itself wouldn't have made me want to dig. Finding the bead convinced me."

"Just as well," said Camden, "considering the song was about a woman. It is a man, after all."

"Well, no," said Patrick, "it's not."

Everything was suddenly utterly clear. They were trying to present him with stark alternatives. Insist on privacy and have the dig canceled, or agree to be ex-star Paddy Kane playing at archaeology and carry on. He decided the time had come to play his ace in the hole, the third option.

"It's not what?" Hescroft asked.

"It's not a man. It's a woman."

Bobby gasped.

Hescroft made a tutting sound. "Come off it. How could you possibly know that for certain? You know as well as I do, at least I hope you do, that you need a proper examination of the whole skeleton for that." He held up a hand. "I know what you're going to say. I've heard it a thousand times. The shape of the skull, right? No pronounced brow ridges? Rounded upper margin to the orbit? That never gives you a definite answer. People get misled that way all the time. You haven't even had a bone specialist in. It's not even fully dug. For God's sake, Patrick, don't go off on some flight of fancy. You've got *weapons*. There are no female Anglo-Saxon burials with weapons. It's adult males only."

"Apart from Cologne," said Patrick, blessing CD's knowledge and hoping for Hescroft's ignorance. That wasn't an adult male. It wasn't a woman, either, it was a boy, but Hescroft wouldn't know that.

"Well, yes, apart from Cologne," said Hescroft, clearly improvising, "but that was different, wasn't it?"

Camden was watching him, apparently enjoying the show.

"Nevertheless," said Patrick. "It is a woman. There's no doubt about it. I'm not going by her skeleton at all. I'm going by someone else's skeleton."

Hescroft made a derisive noise. "How can someone else's skeleton tell you anything at all about this one?"

"It's the bones of her baby. She was pregnant."

Bobby dropped the bowl.

"Christ," said Camden. "A pregnant warrior-woman. All right! Now we've got a show."

He had a faraway look. He was thinking: *All that and a twitchy rock star back from the dead.* Patrick mistrusted that look, but not nearly enough.

"That's extraordinary," said Hescroft.

"We haven't told the diggers yet."

"We'd better have a look."

"Why don't you tell them now?" said Camden. "We'll shoot it. Nice scene."

Patrick let them leave the tent first then turned to share the moment with Bobby—two people joined in a sudden, jubilant conspiracy.

They took the grave cover off and the diggers, realising something was in the air, gathered round. Hescroft knelt in the earth in his smart linen trousers and stared in absorption at the bones, nodding.

"No doubt about it," he murmured. "Absolutely extraordinary."

Jack set up the camera, and Patrick, forgetting entirely that it was there, told all of them what it was they had found that morning. For the first time, his words came out with fire and honey; no one had any option but to listen in fascination. When he finished, he expected a string of impossible questions, but there were none. They all stood staring at the tiny skeleton, still nestled inside its mother, in complete, sombre silence.

The questions came that night round the campfire when the TV men had gone.

"Is everyone here?" said Patrick.

"Gaye isn't," said Dozer.

"Yes, I am," she said, stepping into the firelight. "Sorry, I dropped my lipstick down the loo."

"Did you get it back?" asked Dozer.

"I decided no one needs lipstick *that* much," she said primly.

"Blimey, Gaye, you're going native," he said, and she joined in the roar of laughter.

CD lay back on the grass staring at the first stars. "I hope you guys all realise," he said, "that you've lucked into one of the greatest digs of all time. I mean, not only have we got good food and comfortable beds"—there were loud groans—"but we've got a dig that's going to be in all the textbooks."

The shape of the frame tent over the grave made a yellow filtered square against the last of the twilight.

"Facts first," said Patrick. "One female skeleton, pregnant with what seems like a very fully developed foetus, though we'll need a proper opinion on that. She definitely had a shield across her chest. There's a small bone-handled knife, though the blade's mostly gone, plus at the upper end of the outer trench about six feet from the feet of the skeleton, Gaye has uncovered what looks very like a section of a sword blade—a very good sword blade."

"How do you know it's good?"

"It's still there, that's why. The metal must have been fantastic.

It hasn't all corroded away. That's remarkable because it's in a little pocket of damp clay."

"Nitrites," said CD. "Remember, it's the chicken blade."

Patrick looked at him sharply.

"It's evening," said the American. "I'm allowed to be silly. Anyway, what's silly about that? Joe sang it. That's good enough for me. If he can sing a pregnant warrior woman into existence, he can manage a chicken sword. I believe it. In the evenings, anyway. Daytime, I turn back into a scientist."

"Leaving that aside for the moment, just in case anyone still thought we were wrong, there's what looks like the remains of a chatelaine."

"Which is what exactly?" asked Aidan.

"It's usually a ring or a brooch, which is a sort of a toilet kit, with things hanging on it like tweezers and little picks. It's quite damaged and dirty, so we'll have to see."

"The significance," CD added, "is that chatelaines only come with females, if anyone was still in any doubt. Hairy-assed Anglo-Saxon males did *not* take their toilet kit with them."

"Don't you find yourself wondering what she was called?" said Gaye.

That would have produced some sort of wisecrack before today, but as it was, everyone knew what she meant—and that was the instant at which the woman in the grave started to become something much more than an assembly of old bones in all their minds.

"Names are so rare," said Peter. "Before 40 A.D. there's nothing, then the Romans arrive and there's four hundred years of occupation when there's names everywhere, inscriptions, bureaucratic lists of this and that, written history. Then the Saxons come and names are just spoken words that die with the lips that spoke them."

"I'd like to know," said Gaye. "I'd really like to know. She's a she, not an *it*."

"So, where do we go from here?" said Patrick. "We have an enormous question to answer and that means we are going to have to be very careful indeed about how we do this dig. Everything we know about the period tells us that they were very hierarchical. Men fought; women didn't. The oldest son got the father's weapons."

"The oldest son was dead," said Bobby. "So were the others. The song said so."

"I don't remember anything about the oldest son."

"He sang it in the pub, the first time," said Aidan. "You should have been listening."

"Can you remember it?"

"I can," Bobby said. "There are one or two verses I know. I just never realised it was all part of the same song before."

"How do they go?"

She spoke them slowly but with a lilt that set the tune humming in their heads.

> They met the raiders, blade to blade
> In a spray of blood by the old stockade.
> Outnumbered by them five to one,
> The fight was led by the oldest son.

> At the moment when they saw him fall,
> And his soul took flight to the warriors' hall.
> The hills rang out to a chilling cry.
> Their father saw the young prince die.

> He burst on them, this vengeful lord
> And he whirled the blade of the iron sword.
> They fell at his feet like stalks of corn
> Harvested for his dear firstborn.

Patrick, who had earlier been such a passionate advocate of oral history, now found himself backpedaling. "We've got to avoid putting too much faith in the song."

"Why?" demanded Maxwell. "It's been bang on the money so far."

"Well, I know, but what we do here is going to be under intense scrutiny. If it appears that we're being led by the song, we'll just look stupid."

Bobby, of all people, backed him up. "My father taught Joe the song and I expect he got it from his father. I don't know for sure."

"Surely," said Aidan, "he couldn't be singing it word for word the way he first heard it? No one could do that. He probably knows all the details of the story and roughly how it goes, but he must rewrite it in his head when he wants to sing it, wouldn't you say?"

"I'm not so sure," said Bobby. "He's got an amazing memory, and I sometimes hear him practicing in his room."

"That must be weird," said CD.

"I like it," she said. "It's the only time I ever hear his voice in the house," and Patrick caught a sudden glimpse of how lonely life must be for her, too.

"I wish I'd listened more closely," he said. "Come to that, I wish he'd sing it all again." There was no sign of anybody out there in the darkness tonight. He sighed. "What else have we missed?"

"I know a few more bits of it," said Bobby. "I think it's probably a very long song, but she tries to save her people from these raiders and they kill her brothers and then in the end, she's killed, too, so I suppose under those circumstances, they would give her an honourable funeral, wouldn't they?"

"Who knows?"

"What surprises me," said Vera, the woman with the huge trowel who normally kept herself to herself, "is that a woman would fight. She'd have been better off running away."

"You don't know that. Maybe she'd had enough of running away. You have to hold your ground sometimes," said Bobby. "You can't tell me people have changed that much."

"What do you mean, changed?" said Vera.

"Well, haven't you ever felt angry enough to attack a man?"

"Oh, no, I don't think I have," said Vera rather primly.

"Well, I have," said Bobby.

"So have I," said Gaye, looking meaningfully at Dozer.

"I would have picked up a sword if I'd had to," Bobby went on. "At least, I hope I would, if someone threatened the people I loved. So would lots of women. You're not trying to tell me that wasn't true in those days, too? If a woman felt strongly enough, she'd have done it. Peter, what do you think?"

"Me? About female power in Saxon times?"

"Yes."

"Well, I suppose there's the precedent of Boudicca in Roman times."

"Who's Boudicca?" said Maxwell.

"Queen of the Iceni, an East Anglian tribe, Celtic. She led a rebellion against the Romans in 60 A.D."

"Oh, you mean Boadicea?"

"That's just the Roman version. Probably neither of them were her real name. Boudicca is more or less the name of the Celtic goddess of victory, you see. It was probably just the name her supporters gave her."

"Well, if she could take up arms and be that sort of queen, so could our lady here," insisted Bobby.

"Maybe." Peter sounded cautious. "But Boudicca was a Celt. The Saxons seem to have been much more hierarchical, more male-dominated—but then, we don't know for certain."

"Well, I would have done it," said Gaye vehemently, "so I'm sure she would have."

"Quite right," agreed Bobby, while the others looked at Gaye in some surprise.

"Do you think we'll be able to find out much more about her?" asked Aidan.

"I suppose that's the good side of having the cameras around," said Patrick slowly. "Sounds like they're going to pay for a bit of work."

"What sort of work?"

"We haven't discussed it yet but there's a lot we could do. It's funny, isn't it? Bones used to be just old calcium. You could measure someone's height and usually you could tell their sex, but that was about it."

"How *do* you tell their sex?"

"The pelvis," said Gaye with an "Isn't that obvious?" tone. "We are a bit different in some respects, you know."

"Not just the pelvis," said Patrick. "The skull shape, too. The shape of the forehead, the brow ridges, that sort of stuff."

"I've got a very female skull," said Dozer.

CD sniggered. "And you keep it—"

"—under the bed!" they chorused.

"Go on," said Aidan, who didn't appreciate that sort of distraction. "What else can we tell?"

"Marks of diseases on the bones, injuries, places where infections have eaten away the bones, that sort of stuff. Then there are the marks of the muscle attachments. That gives some clues about build and strength. Now we've got facial reconstruction and DNA testing and all that. There's oxygen isotope analysis."

Patrick trailed off. Aidan said, "And what might that be, exactly?"

Patrick was trying to remember, wishing he'd never mentioned it, but CD stepped in.

"You can take a sample from a tooth. It tells you roughly how far north or south someone came from."

"How would that help?"

"I guess it wouldn't make much difference for our friend here. She's from northern Europe, one way or another. But it does help with Roman stuff. You can tell if they're the real thing, fresh up from the Mediterranean, or whether they're just upwardly mobile local Brits putting on the Roman lifestyle."

"Facial reconstruction sounds good. I've seen them doing that on the TV. Wouldn't you just like to see her face?" said Aidan.

*I would. I certainly would,* thought Patrick.

No one seemed to want to go to bed, and the talk moved in vague, pointless circles until one o'clock, when a sharp chill descended and drove them to their tents. Patrick couldn't sleep. After half an hour, he got up and carried a torch over to the burial site. The sky was on fire with stars, a night sky that seemed full of significance and wasted on mere sleeping. He paused for a time outside the square bulk of the frame tent protecting the grave, then opened the zipper with an illogical fear that he was intruding into a private room. The woman showed white in the torchlight, and he knelt on the strip of grass beside the trench and stared at her. The methodical, disciplined part of his brain was doing his preparation for the following day, when he would need to take full responsibility for the way the dig proceeded and when, in the spotlight of television, there would be no excuse for sloppiness. Concentrating on that, he pushed aside the warnings from the other part of his brain, the part that was running riot with guilt and with associations, until it pushed back, forcing him to recognize that he had stood beside a grave just such as this only a week ago.

# CHAPTER SEVENTEEN

THE WANING MOON HAD JUST risen, an usher's torch to show Patrick his escape route from the open grave. He stumbled towards it across the rough hilltop until a gate stopped him, the same gate where CD had found him shunning the fireside two days earlier.

In his mind's eye he saw the well-worn movie of the Denbigh funeral. Rachel's father came at him yet again, yelling accusations through that frosty, frozen crowd of mourners, who drew aside to let him come because they all wanted to see blood. He saw one hand reach out for his neck and the other, clenched, pulling back for the blow.

At the back of Patrick's mind a small voice expressed disgust. *You should get beyond this,* it said. *You shouldn't keep crawling over the broken glass of your past.* The voice didn't allow for the fact that when survival has demanded that a man should dam up the watercourses of emotion, he is bound to be ill-prepared when they start to flow again. He had his eyes tight shut, leaning on the gate, sucking sobbing breaths of air that bore the grave-chill of night. The bodies in this old grave, the woman and her child, showed him what the earth of the Welsh churchyard concealed when he stared down at its impassive surface. David's bones would be more substantial than this never-to-be-born Saxon child's, but that was all David was now: bones and a tear-pricking memory.

On that black screen of his closed eyes, Rachel's father rushed at him through the funeral crowd, so solid that he heard his footsteps. There *were* footsteps.

Patrick opened his eyes and in the moonlit night that was now not then, the image did not go away.

Out of the darkness, a man was coming for him.

IN THE MOONLIT NIGHT, THE BROTHER BAND HAD CROUCHED BELOW THE HILL AND RELUCTANTLY DECIDED THAT VENGEANCE WOULD HAVE TO WAIT FOR DAWN. BOOTS WRAPPED IN RAGS, FACES AND BLADES SMEARED BLACK WITH SOOT MIXED INTO GREASE, THEY HAD SENT A SCOUT AS FAR AS THE OLD WALLS AND DISCOVERED IN TIME THAT THERE WAS A WATCHER ON THE HILL. THEY HAD PULLED BACK QUIETLY OUT OF RANGE OF EYE AND EAR TO WAIT FOR MOONSET. THE LEADER OF THE BROTHER BAND WAS HARNA, OLDEST SON OF THE DEAD HARDRAD, AND DELAY WAS THE LAST THING HE NEEDED. HIS MEN WERE NERVOUS ENOUGH ALREADY. HE COULD HEAR IT. THEY WERE BREATHING TOO HARD.

"CUTHWULF IS NOT A DEMON OR A GOD OR A BEAR," HE TOLD THEM. "HE IS A MAN, AND WE'VE GOT RIGHT ON OUR SIDE."

"AND HE'S GOT THE SWORD," SAID A QUIET VOICE FROM THE DARKNESS; IT SOUNDED LIKE HIS YOUNGEST BROTHER.

"BUT THAT SWORD IS OUR FATHER'S SWORD. REMEMBER THAT. THE BLOOD OF THAT SWORD IS OUR BLOOD, AND WHEN IT COMES TO IT, THE SWORD WILL NOT LET ITSELF BE TURNED AGAINST US."

"YOU'RE SURE OF THAT, ARE YOU?"

"HE KILLED OUR FATHER FOR IT AND HE SHOULD NOT HAVE TAKEN IT. THAT'S WHY WE'RE HERE. JUST REMEMBER THAT."

"IF IT'S SO EASY TO SORT OUT CUTHWULF, WHY HAVEN'T THE GEWISSE ALREADY DONE IT?" SAID THE YOUNGEST BROTHER. "WHY DO THEY HAVE TO WAIT FOR PEOPLE LIKE US TO SHOW UP?"

"TELL THEM, STEAN," SAID THE LEADER. "TELL THEM WHAT YOU TOLD ME."

THE HONEY-SELLER, RICHER FOR THE SERVICE HE WAS PROVIDING, DIDN'T SOUND ANXIOUS TO OBEY. "THAT WAS FOR YOUR EARS, LORD."

"MY EARS MIGHT NO LONGER BE ON MY HEAD BY THE END OF THIS BUSINESS. TELL MY BROTHERS SO THEY UNDERSTAND."

"THE HWICCA ARE A WEAK LOT," SAID STEAN, "AND MY PEOPLE, THE TRUSTWORTHY GEWISSE, HAVE BEEN HAPPY TO LEAVE THEM ALONE UP HERE. BUT NOW THERE'S OTHER THINGS TO CONSIDER. YOU KNOW WHAT'S HAPPENING IN THE NORTH? NO? DOES THIS SORT OF NEWS NOT GET ACROSS THE SEA? YOU KNOW OF THE MERCIANS? COME ON, YOU MUST KNOW THEM FROM THE HOMELAND TALES, THE ANGLIANS WHO BURN THEIR DEAD? YES, I THOUGHT SO. WELL, THEY'VE DONE WELL UP NORTH FROM HERE. THEY CALL THEMSELVES THE FRONTIER-FOLK IN THEIR DOG-LANGUAGE. THEY HAVE A KING, PENDA, BIGGER THAN ALL OTHER KINGS IN THE SPAN OF HIS POWER, AND HE'S COSYING UP TO THESE HWICCA. PENDA WILL USE THEM AS A BACK DOOR TO OUR LAND. THE HWICCA ARE JUST PUPPETS. MY LORD CYNEGILS SAYS IT HAS TO STOP AND THE RENEGADE CUTHWULF SHOULD NOT HAVE BEEN GIVEN SANCTUARY BY THEM."

"SO CYNEGILS WANTS US TO GET RID OF CUTHWULF?"

"TO BE TRUTHFUL, YOUR ARRIVAL WAS CONVENIENT, SHALL WE SAY. FOREIGNERS WITH A LEGITIMATE GRIEVANCE, A FAMILY SCORE TO SETTLE, STOLEN PROPERTY TO RETRIEVE. PENDA COULD NOT ARGUE WITH THAT. THERE'S THIS CHRISTIAN BUSINESS, TOO."

"Meaning?"

"You saw him, didn't you? That Roman, Birinus, the old bloke in the white cloak. He was at the court when you were."

"Of course I did."

"Well, then, you know he's persuaded Cynegils to give up the gods?"

"We heard, but what's that got to do with Cuthwulf?"

Stean snorted. "Cynegils told Birinus to try converting Cuthwulf. Some chance. I brought one of his priests up here, and Cuthwulf took his head off."

"With the sword?" said the youngest brother.

"Yup. Whop. Clean off. Hardly had to try."

"Enough of that," said their leader. "It won't be so easy when he tries to turn it against its rightful owners. It is not Cuthwulf's sword. He got it by treachery. Just remember, it was our father's life he took."

"Birinus says his priest is a martyr," said Stean. "That's a bit like a sacrifice, I think. Personally, he looked just plain dead to me. I beat it before I joined him."

"Today we will protect you."

"Oh, I'm not going up there," said Stean. "Not with that bloody maniac around. I don't mind the rest of them. The sons are just blokes. A bit loud—typical Saxons, saving present company—and the daughter's a dish, but I'm not going near Cuthwulf."

"You stay here, then," said the leader sourly. "You'll miss out on the spoils."

"If there are any. Cuthwulf calls himself a King but he's living in the past, that man. He's got sod-all up there."

"He was never a King," said the leader. "Not by right. Our father was the King, until that bastard murdered him."

"YEAH, YOU TOLD ME."

"HE'S GOT NO OTHER FAMILY AROUND, HAS HE? JUST THE SONS AND THE DAUGHTER."

"NOT ROUND HERE. APART FROM HIS WIFE'S LOT."

"WHAT WIFE? DID HE TAKE ANOTHER WIFE?"

"NO, THE DEAD ONE. THE FIRST TIME HE WAS OVER HERE, HE GRABBED HER AND TOOK HER BACK HOME WITH HIM. SHE CAME FROM ROUND HERE. ABBANDUN WAY."

"I DIDN'T KNOW. ARE THEY POWERFUL?"

"THEY HOLD A LOT OF LAND."

"WILL THEY HELP HIM?"

"THEY WEREN'T EXACTLY PLEASED TO SEE HIM BACK AGAIN WHEN HE CAME RUNNING WITH THE SWORD. I THINK THEY WERE HOPING HE'D STAY YOUR SIDE OF THE WATER. THEY'D HAVE BEEN MORE WELCOMING TO A MAD DOG."

"SO THEY WON'T BE LOOKING FOR A BLOOD FEUD?"

STEAN LAUGHED DERISIVELY. "THEY'D THROW YOU A FEAST, I RECKON."

THE LEADER LOOKED UP THE HILL. "MOON'S DOWN," HE SAID. BUT IT WAS NEARLY DAWN BEFORE HE JUDGED THEM READY FOR THE FIGHT, AND DURING THE LONG WAIT, THE SOOT HAD RUBBED OFF THE YOUNGEST BROTHER'S SWORD BLADE. THE FIRST RAY OF DAWN FLASHED OFF IT AND GAVE WARNING TO THE WATCHER ON THE HILL, WHO SAW A MAN MOVING OUT OF THE GLOOM AND RACED TO SOUND THE ALARM.

Out of the night, a man was coming for him, rushing at him in the same way Rachel's father had rushed at him, so that he recoiled, horrified, and yelled and put his arm across his face to ward off the blow.

No blow came this time, but neither did any reassuring word. In the silent darkness his eyes had to do the work of recognising Joe— Joe, who could only stare at him with profound sorrow on his face. Patrick brought his sobs to a shuddering halt but could not control the whooping breaths that replaced them, and he stared back at Joe as if he had no idea how either of them could be there.

Joe's face was a moonlit monochrome print of pity. He looked into Patrick's eyes as if testing his soul, then reached out a tentative hand, palm raised, and touched him with flat, coarse fingers on the centre of his forehead. It felt to Patrick like something you might do to a frightened animal; his breathing eased as Joe vaulted the gate and walked rapidly away down the track towards the farmhouse without looking back.

Patrick shivered, and the funeral came back to claim him again. Rachel's father's punches hadn't hurt nearly as much as his words of denunciation, delivered standing over his fallen son-in-law. Patrick hadn't tried to defend himself, knowing he agreed with him. After the assault, he had lain motionless on the ground, his head crushing a bouquet of roses so that the smell of the blood from his nose mixed sickeningly with a hothouse waft of bruised petals, hearing the man tell the unwavering truth of what had led to this. Maurice Jenkins, whose only daughter now lay beneath their feet, ready to dissolve into the soil, told all those grim, suited men and their sombre, tailored women about the Rome concert, and he made it sound like the final straw in a planned process of destruction. At the end of his passionate speech, not one person from Rachel's tribe stepped forward to help Patrick to his feet. Patrick's cousins, the only members of his own thin family present, faded away with them: He was left to rise and slink away from them all on a one-way trip out of their lives.

Again there were real footsteps in his ears, here in the Oxfordshire night, but this time they were light and fast and before he could even consider retreat, Bobby coalesced out of the black into the silver, running towards him. He barely had time to put up his defences.

"Who's there?" she called. "Patrick? That is you, isn't it?"

"Yes."

"Joe woke me."

"He shouldn't have."

"He was worried. I could tell."

"How?"

"Never mind. I could, that's all. What's wrong?"

She was close to him, staring at him as her brother had done. She was dressed in a long coat and boots and the moon gave her a third face, not the Rachel-face, nor the candlelit madonna, but something else, something inscrutable, the farmer out to do her job.

A measure of pride surfaced in Patrick, something he hadn't felt for a long time.

"I'm not playing this game, Bobby. Go back to bed. I'm not some lost sheep you have to save."

"I think you might be. Patrick, tell me what's wrong."

"All right," he said, stung, and trying to drive her away with the brutal truth, "since you ask, I'll tell you. I'm here because I'm not a nice man. I'm here because that grave up there has made me remember something I did which no nice man would ever have done, okay? Do you want to hear about it?" He heard no reply. "Do you?" he insisted savagely. "Because if you don't, then just go back home and we'll leave it, all right?"

In the moonlight, he saw her nod, and because she stood her ground, he took that as assent. Just as Joe could sing to his depersonalised pub audience, so Patrick found he could speak to this moonlit listener who was not quite either version of the Bobby he knew.

"I was onstage in Rome," he said. "It was part of the Debt Relief concert, all that African starvation stuff. Remember African starvation? Worldwide TV coverage. Big bands in every country. Link-ups going wrong and satellites screwing up right round the bloody globe. Do you know 'Wedding Vows'? My very own bloody awful song?"

She made no sound.

"Do you?" he said again, louder. Then he intoned it, resisting the terrible automatic pressure to sing it.

*A wife is there for leaving. Marriage vows are made to break.*
*Man's intended for deceiving, that's why Adam met the snake.*
*Adultery's for adults—faithfulness for fools.*
*Monogamy's monotonous—*

"Yes, I know it," she said, just to shut him up as his voice rose. "I've heard it. Everybody's heard it."

"Well, I really excelled myself that night. We had two hundred million viewers, they said. I wasn't going to sing it. I hated it before it was even released."

"But you sang it that night?"

"Oh, yes, I sang it. I'd had a bottle of tequila and God knows what else, and the organisers came in to say they didn't want it. They banned my song. Not in the spirit of the concert. That was why we did it."

"You sang it anyway?"

"Yes, I sang it, but that wasn't the point. I dedicated it live to Rachel. Live, in front of two hundred million people. Do you want to know what I said? This nice man who you're so sorry for? I said, 'Now this song is for my wife, Rachel.' I wasn't even supposed to have a wife. 'This is for my secret little wife back home,' I said, 'and I mean every single word of it.' I told two hundred million people that I meant every single loathsome syllable of it." He stared at her face, impassive in the moon-gleam. "I am not a nice man. You'd better get that idea out of your head."

"What happened afterwards?" said Bobby. "Tell me what happened. She left you, didn't she?"

"Left me? Oh, come on. You know. You must know. You've been looking me up. I know you have."

"Not again. Not since I told you. You don't like people prying, do you? So I haven't pried. You can't have it both ways. Don't complain when I don't know."

It was a moment when Patrick might very easily have poured it all out. Nighttime, in a strange place, to a strange woman—those things combined to eat away at his defences. He could easily let himself imagine this woman really was a fresh start, a second chance, instead of someone who merely happened to look like one. He only had to let that thought into the very edge of his mind for the ground to shift under him and for that irresistible tug of need to reach for him. Then, standing on the edge of that vertiginous slope, knowing that even one step meant demolishing the walls that were the only thing protecting him from the world, Patrick pulled back.

"I lost her," he said. "That's all that happened."

In the silence that followed she turned the silver mirror of her face slightly away, so that, like the dark part of half-moon, he sensed rather than saw her.

"I don't mean this cruelly," she said, "but you're not the only one. I've lost someone . . . a partner. I do speak that language."

How could she say that, he thought with fury. She didn't even know what he was talking about. He meant death, not separation.

He could have asked about it, but stepping further into her world felt like letting her step further into his. Having to say something, he came up with the wrong thing.

"A *partner*?" he exclaimed. "I'm not talking about a partner. You can lose a partner. You can find another one. It just takes time. There are far worse things than that. There are things you can't replace."

He might as well have slapped her, the way the impact of his words knocked her head back.

"I came here to try to help you," she said. "My mistake, maybe, but you can't bully me into thinking you're as bad as you say you are. I'll make up my own mind. I can't argue it with you now. I'm too tired. I have some farmwork to do as well as the food, you know. I'm going back home because I don't think there's anything else useful I can say right now."

She turned and walked away, leaving him right back in his homemade hell, knowing he had hurt someone who had gone out of her way to help, but unable to find the right words for an apology.

He walked away, too, needing to find a different space, a space not quaking with the vacuum left by Bobby's departure. He walked around the shoulder of the hill and sat down on a tree stump to prove to himself that she was wrong, that nobody else spoke quite the same language of loss. He deliberately set out to go over the events of that pivotal moment in his life—that half hour in Perugia when all his bills became due.

I T WAS THE HANGOVER MORNING, THE MORNING AFTER THE concert, the morning after his brutal dedication. They were on the road again, leaving Rome, the sun too bright, the swaying of the bus too sickening, and the phones in the tour bus ringing nonstop. Every rock and gossip writer in Britain was after the story of Paddy Kane's unsuspected little wife back home, all vengeful because they were fending off editors who wanted to know why their staff hadn't known. The press were out for blood and there was plenty of that promised in the way Paddy had revealed Rachel, revealed her and re-viled her in the same instant. Every PR person on Colonic Music's payroll was frantically trying to put the genie back in the bottle. Paddy's manager, Don Claypole, was being told to shut him up and make sure he stayed shut up, and while they were trying to decide how to contain the damage before they got to Venice, the bus stopped for a lunch break in the ancient city of Perugia.

There was no space for lunch in the emaciated, speed-racked frame of Paddy Kane, nor in his head. He craved only solitude, and he found it, as far as it was to be found, inside the Cathedral. There he saw the boy playing in the bright spangles of light, and there he caught his glimpse of how people with faith deal with their guilt in the formality of confession, and he envied them. When he came out and saw Claypole walking up the steps and Claypole told him Rachel and David were both dead, it didn't seem for a moment that it could possibly be true, and he thought for a merciful instant that it must be a childish trick dreamed up by the music company to teach him a lesson. When it dawned on him from Claypole's expression that it must be true, it still did not seem real, not told to him by this man he did not like here in this city he did not know, where there seemed no thread of a connection to anything he knew.

Perugia had not yet finished with him.

He stood on the Cathedral steps as Italians walked up and down past him, cut off by language from the drama happening in their midst. He heard Claypole tell the outlines of what he knew with a growing casual cruelty. Claypole's attitude revealed to that last gasp of Paddy Kane that the other man was already aware that Paddy was finished and that he would have no more need of a manager. He told Paddy that Rachel had never even made it down the drive of their house, that her car had hit the wall on the bend of the drive and ricocheted into the river, that David was found drowned in the backseat next to an open bag, messily stuffed with the few things she had grabbed before rushing out of the house, that nobody knew exactly when it had happened.

Paddy knew. Paddy knew it had happened within minutes of his song going out across the world's ether to sting the soul of its intended target. When it had all got through to him, all the strung-together words combining to explode inside him, he had run back into the Cathedral, run through the astonished sightseers and worshipers, into the gloom to the nearest confessional, and tried to tell all that had just happened to an astonished and uncomprehending priest who spoke not a single word of English. He had gone on and on, louder and louder, desperate to tell the story, until the priest in the next booth had broken off the confession he was hearing, leaned forward, and said, "Peace, dear man, peace, for your sake and our sakes. I will speak to you when I am able. Take yourself into the chapel there. I will find you."

Paddy had walked blindly into the side chapel with the full

dreadful horror of it all crystallising in his head into a sharper and sharper pain, filling his consciousness with its agonising edges, showing him that below all the surface scum of the past years he still had something that might have been the embers of love for Rachel. Far more acutely, he knew he loved David with his whole soul and that because of what he'd done the future held agony and guilt in huge and equal measure.

When he entered the empty side chapel he saw an immense carved crucifix towering over him, dark and threatening, angled down from the left-hand shadows. Turning his eyes quickly away, he found himself looking up straight into the wild face of God. High up on the back wall, light burst on him through a stained-glass semicircle: The image in the glass was a vengeful white-haired God in yellow robes who thundered down at him with an accusing finger pointed directly at Paddy and eyes that met his and tore right through him. When the priest came into the chapel five minutes later, all that he found was the black silk jacket Paddy had been wearing, abandoned on the floor. The priest kept it for a week, then he put the wad of lire notes that he found in its pocket into the collection, flushed a plastic envelope of white powder thoughtfully down a drain, and gave the jacket itself to the old man who usually slept in the Cathedral doorway.

That was the end of Paddy Kane.

The band and its manager never saw him again. He had a credit card and the clothes he wore. He took trains to get home, huddled in a corner seat, shivering in just a shirt while the God in yellow robes conducted a fierce inventory of his life, cauterising all that was Paddy and leaving Patrick in his place.

After the funeral, in the loneliness that followed, Patrick came to understand the full extent of what he had made Rachel suffer, and to remember the way he had once felt about her. But it was David's voice he would hear, time and time again, in the middle of the night. He would get out of bed as he sometimes had when David had his incoherent nightmares, and try to find David's bed so he could get in with him and wrap his arms round that frantic little body and sing the first few notes of a song that would send his son into deep, peaceful sleep instantly.

There would be no bed to find.

Before he went to sleep in his tent, he wrote a note to Bobby and left it on the gas ring where she would find it in the morning. It just said, *Thank you. I shouldn't have said that.* Then he climbed into his sleeping bag, looking out at the skyline and the square shape covering the ancient grave, trying to convince himself that it was not his own past that they had disturbed under that earth.

# CHAPTER EIGHTEEN

W HAT HAD BEEN PACKED,
moist earth deep below
the topsoil had now
been exposed to the air
all night and most of
the morning. It had dried out except in the
patch of clay where Gaye had been digging. It
was a hot morning; Dozer's shirt was damp
with sweat across his back. CD was working
away next to him, and Edgar was perched on
the edge of the finds tray, playing with a twig.

"Hello," Dozer said, raising an eyebrow
when Patrick came towards them, holding
his trowel. "Funny how directors only get
their 'ands dirty when you start finding the
good stuff."

Patrick knew that was how it must look.

"I'm only here to help. I'm going to give
Gaye a hand with the sword." He needed
to lose himself in the minute therapy of
digging, and the small exposed patch of what

looked like a sword blade offered a form of respite after a dreadful
night and a disconcerting morning.

"Wrong place for a sword," said Dozer, succinctly.

"Meaning?"

"Well, what's it doing right down there? Should be with the
body. Unless it's another burial, and that's too far down into the
ditch, I'd say."

"It could have got disturbed."

"Down there? Nah."

The small section of exposed blade looked absurdly smooth. The
surface of the exposed clay around it was crusting and cracking in the
sunshine, but a dribble of water at one corner of the patch showed
where a tiny spring had been keeping the clay moist all these years,
unnoticed under the turf. Gaye raised no objection to Patrick joining
her, but then he gave her no chance to. He needed distraction, because David had come to him in the night as he had expected, as he
always did when Patrick accidentally let him out of his tight box.
David, forever four years old with Rachel's huge eyes in a face that
was otherwise entirely Patrick's, had stood over him, soaking wet,
and David had skipped back, infinitely tiny, beyond his reach whenever he tried to touch him.

That was bad enough, but the worst of it was that Rachel had
been there, too, and they were a loving couple with nothing complicated between them, just the waves of simple, sweet, overpowering
love that was exactly as it had once been, so that he wanted to stay
there asleep, wrapped in that warm blanket. Rachel had her arms
wrapped round him, and David came and touched his shoulder with a
surprisingly large, strong hand, touched it and then shook him, calling him by name.

Rachel fled away back into her bitter grave and Patrick woke,
searching for David but finding instead Bobby's disembodied arm,
reaching in through the tent door, offering a mug of coffee, and he
groaned.

"You'd better get up," she said. The way he'd treated her the
night before came rushing in to panic him.

"Did you see my note?" he asked.

"That's why you get the coffee. One of the reasons, anyway."

"I shouldn't have said what I said."

"If you ask me, you should have said more."

"Well, I shouldn't have said it like that."

"No argument there."

"Is it late?"

"No, but there's a deputation here to see you."

"Who?"

"The vicar and the headmaster. That's the other reason I'm here. If you don't come soon I may have to take up Dozer's offer and hire his mate, the chiropodist."

"The vicar? Where?"

"Sniffing around by the grave. On my land. Without asking."

"Tell them I'm coming."

"I'm not telling them anything."

Patrick felt faintly grateful for the vicar's arrival, which at least put him and Bobby on the same side. Pulling on his clothes, he shot out into the sunlight and found the Reverend Augustus Templeton-Jones trying to undo the zip of the tent that protected the grave. A man in tweeds was standing behind him, the man Patrick had seen arguing with Bobby at their first brief meeting.

"Leave that alone, please," he called, irritated. "That's a protected environment." It sounded good, and it stopped the vicar in his tracks.

"I do beg your pardon," said the vicar. He was bald on top with white side whiskers, and he didn't look sorry at all. The other man stood back, embarrassed. In daylight, Patrick could see the vicar had a sharply hooked nose which swept down in an unbroken curve from his forehead. In profile, he looked like a piece of a clock mechanism, a circular cam with a gash for a mouth.

"What can I do for you?"

"Word has reached me," said Templeton-Jones, "that you have made a further find. A crucifix, I believe. If so, that rather supports the point I was making to you at our previous meeting, I feel."

"Who told you that?"

The vicar shrugged. "Is it true?" was all he said.

"A crucifix? No, I'm afraid not."

"Well, I apologise if I have been misinformed, but I understood that you had found a brooch in that form."

"The only brooch we have found is bent, broken, and generally pretty badly damaged. As far as we can see it's got three arms, but it will take a great deal of work to see what it's really like and—"

"If one arm was missing, that would make four. Four arms is a cross, young man."

"Four arms is also a swastika. That's an equally common symbol."

"There is nothing common about the cross."

"*Common* as in *frequently encountered*. At the moment, it's a broken brooch, that's all. Three arms. What does that make it? A Saxon Mercedes emblem?" The man made it hard not to be rude. "Ask me again in a month, when it's been cleaned."

"I also wanted to talk to you about another matter." Templeton-Jones looked behind him, down towards the tents, then at the man he'd brought with him. It was clear that the vicar was now getting to the real point of their visit. "The woman who is doing your cooking. Miss Redhead."

"What about her?"

"Just a word of warning, that's all. I feel it is my duty to say this. I understand that many people in this village have had problems with her attitude since her return. I'm afraid to say she has ceased to be a regular church-attender, and she has a reputation for causing trouble. I merely want to warn you. She can be a most unfortunate and occasionally malign influence."

Her return? Patrick wondered what he meant by that, but didn't want to discuss Bobby any more than he had to. "I haven't found that."

The headmaster broke his silence; his voice was peevish. "As a case in point, she is currently trying to start what you might call a civil disobedience campaign among the parents in the village."

"You're talking about the May Day parade?"

"If that's what you want to call it. Miss Redhead is going to get a lot of people into a lot of trouble, but then, that is the way she tends to behave."

"I don't quite understand your objection to it."

The vicar stepped in quickly. "It teaches the children a form of idolatry, Mr. Kane. In effect, they worship a graven image. Miss Redhead attempts to justify it in the name of tradition, but that, I fear, is a mere fantasy. This has every sign of a recent invention. The modern fascination with forces of nature is a whimsy, and a dangerous one at that. It is directly against everything the Bible teaches us."

"I thought Green Man images are found in carvings in quite a lot of churches?"

"Neglect of proper forms by long-dead wood-carvers is greatly to be regretted. Are you a churchgoer?"

"No." *Only at funerals.*

"Then I don't suppose you would understand the anguish of those who are practising Christians at the idea that such an act could be proposed as part of a child's education. May I urge you to have as little to do with her as possible?"

"She is a valuable member of our team."

"You will see the error of your ways."

"That's right," piped up the headmaster, "you will. Good day to you."

They turned away and the hill seemed to shrug them off with a chorus of birdsong and a sudden shaft of sunlight.

E DGAR LAUNCHED HIMSELF FROM CD'S SHOULDER AS THEY started digging and flapped down to the other side of the trench, staring at the earth with his head to one side. CD was labeling a finds tray with the context number when the bird hopped into the trench; he didn't notice it until it flew away.

"CD," Dozer said, watching it go, "that vulture of yours 'as got something in his beak."

"Ah."

"What? Your bird is flying off with something it's just nicked out of a trench and all you can say is 'ah'?"

"In this case, Dozer dear, 'ah' is short for 'I sincerely hope what's in that damn bird's beak is some totally uninteresting lump of crap because otherwise I am deep in the doo-doo and we're going to have raven stew tonight just for a change.' "

"It's gone to that tree again. The one where it took your bike keys."

"OK, I'll check it out later. Don't tell Patrick, OK? It's probably nothing."

It was far from nothing. It was something quite beautiful, a small saucer brooch, little more than an inch across. In shape it was similar to a thousand others found in Saxon graves. What set it apart was its decoration, a pattern made in garnet, white shell, and gold filigree. CD would have identified it at once as a great rarity, but CD never got the chance.

THE BROOCH HAD BEEN HILD'S BRIDE-PRICE, A GOOD DEAL,
CUTHWULF THOUGHT, CONSIDERING THE BOOT WAS ON THE
WRONG FOOT. HE WAS DESPERATE TO GET HIS DAUGHTER
MARRIED BACK INTO HIS WIFE'S CLAN, BECAUSE THERE
WERE STRONG MEN AT ABBANDUN, MEN OF CELTIC BLOOD
NOT ENTIRELY COMMITTED TO THE GEWISSE. WITH ALL
HIS SONS DEAD, CUTHWULF KNEW THEY NEEDED STRONG
MEN. HILD QUITE LIKED THE HUSBAND HE CHOSE FOR HER,
ÆTHELMUND.

"YOU MUST HAVE SONS," CUTHWULF TOLD HER,
EIGHTEEN MONTHS AFTER THE MARRIAGE. "THOSE BASTARD
MURDERERS WILL COME BACK ONE DAY WHEN THEY HAVE
LICKED THEIR WOUNDS. YOU MUST HAVE STRONG SONS
AROUND YOU."

THEY WERE STANDING BY CYNELM'S GRAVE, RAISED
HIGHER THAN THE MOUNDS COVERING HIS SIBLINGS. IF THE
BROTHER BAND HAD KNOWN HOW WEAK THEY WERE, THEY
WOULD HAVE UNDOUBTEDLY RENEWED THEIR ATTACK,
BUT AS A PRICE FOR THEIR FAILURE, THEY WERE FIGHTING
PENDA'S MEN SOMEWHERE TO THE NORTH. THAT WAS WHAT
STEAN SAID WHEN HE LAST CAME WITH THE HONEY.

HER DAUGHTER WAS NINE MONTHS OLD AND A WONDER,
BUT A DAUGHTER WAS A DAUGHTER IN CUTHWULF'S EYES,
NOT A MEANS TO EXTEND A DYNASTY. THAT EVENING, HILD
WENT OUT UNDER PRETEXT OF LOOKING FOR HERBS. SHE
WENT TO THE OLD ROMAN WALLS AND DUG IN THE
GROUND, HOPING FOR AN AMULET, A POWERFUL TOKEN
THAT WOULD BRING HER A SON, AND SHE WAS REWARDED.

The TV people hadn't shown up. The other diggers were getting on
with their exploration of the outer edge of the mound and Patrick
was losing himself in the intricacy of his work, troweling gently to
loosen the sticky clay soil around the horizontal surface of the sword
blade and scraping it to one side into a dustpan when too much
had accumulated. Nearby in the main trench, CD and Dozer were
painstakingly uncovering more of the skeleton, as precise and intent
on their task as surgeons. The exposed section of the sword blade was
six inches long and, brushing at the surface with a stiff paintbrush,
Patrick was amazed at its condition. It was an even mid-brown colour,

with nothing more than small irregularities on the surface to show what seemed to be corrosion, miraculous in this small patch of damp. He brushed harder, and all at once, on part of the surface of the metal, he thought he could see regular markings.

"Look at that," he said, and Gaye peered at it.

"What?"

"CD," he called, "you're the sword expert. Come and look at this."

"What have you found? Chicken feathers?"

"Patterning, maybe."

Patrick stood up to make room, and CD took a large magnifying glass from one of the many zip pockets of his bulging waistcoat. While the American stared at the blade for a long time in silence, Patrick looked around at the activity. The other trench had produced charcoal and two fragments of what looked likely to be Iron Age pottery, but the diggers had settled in to their work now and he was satisfied that they couldn't do any lasting harm for the time being.

CD pulled his trowel out of his back pocket, scraped at the blade, then made a face. He looked through the glass again and got to his feet as Patrick spoke.

"What do you think?"

Dozer had put down the toothbrush he was using and was staring up, waiting for the reply.

"You were hoping this was pattern-welded, right?" said CD.

"Maybe."

"What's pattern-welding?" said Aidan from the closer end of the other trench.

"Get back to work, you son of a dog," said CD. "This is not for your ears."

"Why not?" said Patrick. "It's about time for another sword lecture. Especially when there's a real sword to talk about."

CD gave him an inscrutable look. "You may regret that, but be it upon your own head. You may also want to stop uncovering much more until dear Kenny and his merry men are here . . . well, his merry man, anyway." He bellowed at the others with unnecessary strength. "All right, listen up. Leave your trowels and your shovels and come and soak up some wisdom, folks."

The shout reached Bobby in the catering tent. Patrick saw her come out into the sunshine, glancing down the hill towards her farm as she usually did, as if to check all was well. He watched her stride across the hilltop towards them and realized how glad he was that she didn't seem to bear grudges: He had given her grounds for plenty of them. She looked hard at him, enquiringly, as she joined them, and he turned his gaze quickly back to CD.

"The boss here wants me to tell you all about pattern-welding," intoned CD. "Pattern-welding in sword blades produces an interesting, curvy herringbone sort of effect in the metal. That was maybe valued for its own sake, but mostly it came from the way they put the blades together to get the right strength."

"Just like the song," said Aidan.

"Well, quite like the song. Now, for our current state of knowledge, we are indebted to a man named Anstee, about forty years back, who didn't believe all the complicated theoretical garbage the sword experts were writing back in the old days about how these patterns got there, so Anstee went and made a sword himself, using a pretty basic hearth and bellows. He twisted together different bits of iron, a sort of club sandwich of flat strips and square bars and then he—"

"Fed them to the chickens?" suggested Maxwell.

"Well, now, smarty-pants," said CD, "no, he didn't, *but* he did heat them up in a special paste, which if I recall rightly was made up of honey, flour, olive oil, milk, and . . . guess what?"

"Ostrich droppings, chicken poop, elephant dung?"

"No, no, no. Pigeon shit!" said CD triumphantly. "Anyway, to make a long story short, Anstee forged it all together and he welded on the cutting edges each side and ground off the crap, and lo and behold, he'd made a beautiful patterned sword."

"And that's what we've got here, is it?" said Aidan, looking into the trench.

"No," said CD, "I'm afraid not."

"It's not?" said Patrick.

"Definitely not."

"So why have you been telling us all about it?" said Aidan.

"I was asked to talk about pattern-welded sword blades. I talked about pattern-welded sword blades. Some people are never satisfied."

"But this isn't one," persisted Patrick.

"No," said CD happily.

"I thought I saw a pattern," said Patrick.

"Maybe you did," said CD, smiling in delight.

"Well, how do you know it isn't pattern-welding?"

"Because when you try to weld wood, all it does is catch fire."

"Wood?"

"Wood. Very fragile wood. I just scraped off a little lump by mistake."

"It looks like rusty iron."

"I grant you that, but it's not. It's very hard wood. Fragile as hell now, but if it hadn't been very hard once, there'd be nothing left at all. I guess it's only there at all thanks to that spring."

"Why's that?" said Aidan.

"Anaerobic conditions. No oxygen. That means the organisms that would normally destroy the wood can't survive. The wood must be completely waterlogged. We'll have to be very, very careful, because this is special. We've got to keep it wet."

"Why's it so special? If it isn't a sword, what is it?"

"Did I say it wasn't a sword? Did I?" CD turned to the others for support.

There was a scattered reply of "No" and "You didn't," except for Dozer, who said, "I can never understand a single bloody word you say, anyway."

"What is it, then?"

"My guess is it's a sword all right, but it's a little wooden one, kinda like a half-scale model."

"What use is a wooden sword?"

"You thought you could see a pattern," said CD to Patrick.

"Yes. What was it? The grain?"

"Some of it, sure. But the rest is something much much better. Can you guess?"

Something lurked at the back of Patrick's memory, something from a footnote in a book. "Runes," he said.

"Oh, come on. Runes?" Aidan was sceptical.

"I believe so." CD proffered his magnifying glass. "I can see two of them pretty clearly, and I'll make a prediction." He turned to the others. "Important professional waiver here, guys and gals. Archaeologists don't make predictions, because it's always too early . . ." He paused expectantly.

". . . to tell," they replied as one.

"Notwithstanding that," he said, "notwithstanding that, I predict that when we uncover the rest of this, one end will be burnt."

Patrick's vague memory was firming up.

"The only other wooden sword like this one I've come across," continued CD, "and if anyone's interested I do have copies of the appendix to my second doctoral thesis available at just nine dollars and ninety-nine cents, plus the movie rights are still up for grabs. Where was I? Oh, yes, the only other wooden sword had a runic inscription which ran something like, *Return messenger,* which fits the fact that it was burnt."

Patrick remembered. "Burnt arrows were a summons for help. It meant someone was in extreme danger. You sent a message back to say you were on the way. The other wooden sword, it came from Germany, didn't it?"

"Frisia," said CD, "on the coast." He waved vaguely. "Holland, is it? Dutchland, Deutschland, what's the difference?"

"There speaks a citizen of the country that was too busy to join in the first half of the big match," said Dozer, sourly.

"Ah, come on, Doze," said CD, and it sounded like a resumption of an old wrangle, "we're all Germans, really. You just have to go back far enough. Anyway," he said, "that sword had a burnt point and it was made out of yew, which you will all know was a very tough wood commonly used in ritual and magic."

Patrick took the magnifier and knelt over the exposed part of the surface. He could see the ragged mark where CD's trowel had nicked the edge and, enlarged, the terraced crumbling edge, paler than the surrounding surface, was quite clearly wood. It was drying out fast. He stared through the lens at the marks where CD was pointing, but his hand was trembling and he couldn't see clearly. He took a deep breath and his hand steadied long enough for a worm trail of drying, lighter-coloured earth to show through, embedded in the grooves. It needed little imagination to see the shape: a vertical line, with two parallel diagonals sloping down from its right—the "æ" rune of Old English. The other eluded him, too indistinct to be sure if it was the M shape that spelt "e" or had the two extra lines of the "d" rune.

"So what's with these runes, anyway?" asked Maxwell, but suddenly there was good reason to hurry.

"We'll talk about that this evening," said Patrick. "This is an amazing find. We need to protect it."

"It's been there long enough," complained Maxwell. "Surely it's all right for a bit longer?"

"It wasn't exposed before," Patrick told him. "It's out in the open air now, and that's the worst possible thing."

"Open air's good for wood, surely," said Aidan. "Isn't it true that wood doesn't rot so fast when it's got a good draught around it?"

"Pah!" said CD, and went on in a melodramatic voice, "Oxygen, the deadliest substance on earth. Do you know what we are, people? We're living miracles, fighting off the daily ravages of a gas that eats iron for breakfast, turns copper green, crumbles aluminum into powder, and makes potassium go bang. Our skin is armour plate, my friends. If it wasn't we'd feel like we were in an acid bath from the moment we're born."

"The thing about old wood," said Peter, "is that the cellulose turns into sugar and gets washed away. It's only the water that stops it falling apart."

"So what do we do about it?" said CD.

"Call an expert."

"First, we cover it up again," said CD, and Patrick scooped wet clay from each side of the exposed wood, patting it gently into place over the sword to seal it from the air.

Hescroft swung into action as soon as they made the call; a conservation specialist from the Pitt-Rivers Museum was on her way to them in minutes.

That was the upside. The downside was that Hescroft also alerted the TV crew, so the rest of Patrick's day was taken up satisfying them as much as superintending the painstaking removal of the wooden sword. Jack was there with his camera turning when the last of the soil was carefully removed from the sword's pointed tip and the black marks of old scorching were clear to see. The specialist was a forthright Danish woman who got straight down to it.

"Get that camera out of the way," she snapped. "You shouldn't have left it uncovered *at all*. Do you know how fragile this is? It could crumble just like that. There is no time to lose. Bloody archaeologists."

"So what do we do?"

"You do nothing. You stand still and *watch*. I take it out as a block. Slice down and under it, three inches at least below it so we support it from under, and lift it like that."

She did it under their anxious eyes, sliding a thin sheet of ply-wood under it and lifting it out with great care. When it was safely on the grass, she produced a roll of clear plastic wrap and swaddled the entire block tightly in it.

"I take it back now for proper treatment," she said. "Soak it in PEG probably. You know PEG?"

"I used to," said Dozer. "Barmaid at the Star and Garter."

"Funny man, I don't think," she said. "Polyethylene glycol. Wax soluble in water. Gives it strength. Or maybe I freeze-dry it. We'll see about that."

When she'd gone and the camera had packed up and left them alone, Patrick found himself standing next to an unexpectedly pensive CD. The American was normally boisterous when things went right, but now he was far from triumphal.

"What is it?" Patrick asked.

CD shrugged, and Edgar, perched on his shoulder, fluttered indignantly. "Hard to say. First he was a he, then she was a she, with a little one. Now there's this. The burnt sword. Her distress call. I guess she's not just bones anymore."

"That's what you wanted, CD. You wanted her to come to life. For the diggers."

"Sure I did. Not quite so fast, maybe."

"What do you make of the sword? Did she send it? Did she get it from someone else?"

"Speculation," said CD. "I only speculate after sundown, and even then only when someone crosses my palm with a bottle of Glenboggy."

"It's six o'clock," said Patrick.

"Sundown's a-comin'," said CD, squinting at the sky. "Just another couple of hours to get the Glenboggy in."

"My round," said Patrick.

"True, but I didn't like to say so."

Patrick got in his car, which took a long time to start, and drove down to the Stag. As he slowed down to turn into the pub car park, he noticed a little knot of people on the village green and saw with surprise that Kenny Camden and Jack were there, with the camera on a tripod. They seemed to be interviewing a group of people. Patrick parked the car and walked over to the camera. Camden was intent on what he was doing, asking questions and pointing the mike at each of the villagers in turn. He didn't see Patrick coming up behind him.

"So you agree with the vicar?" he asked. "If the woman does turn out to be Christian, you think she should be decently reburied as soon as possible?"

"I do," said a large woman with an improbably deep voice. "That would be the decent thing."

"And what about this wooden sword," said Camden, "the one they've found this afternoon? What do you make of that?"

Patrick cleared his throat loudly as the woman started to reply, and Camden said "Stop" in an angry voice and swung round on him.

"Do you mind?" he said. "We're—" Then he saw who it was.

"A word in your ear," said Patrick coldly.

"I won't be a minute," said Camden to the group, and glanced at Jack, nodding slightly. Patrick led him into the centre of the triangular green, aware that the whole group was staring after them.

"Who said you could do this?" he demanded. "I had an earful from the vicar this morning. I wondered how he knew about the brooch. I didn't realise you were going around egging everybody on. In fact, I think I specifically asked you not to mention it to him, didn't I?"

"I've got a show to make," said Camden. "Give me a break. I don't tell you about archaeology, you don't tell me about TV, OK?"

"No, not OK at all. You're letting all sorts of stuff out. We've got the security of the site to think about, let alone provoking the vicar. I'm not having you blurting all this stuff out about the finds."

"What harm can it do?"

"It can't do any good. You want their reaction, we'll lay on a show for them at the end. When we're finished. You go on doing it now and you prejudice the whole dig."

"To be frank, I think you're being a bit precious, Paddy."

"*Do not fucking call me Paddy.* I've told you—"

"Oh, come off it," said Camden, to goad him. "Big deal—Paddy, Pat, so what? I can't help it. It's the way I think of you."

Patrick's fingers were clenching into a fist and he fought to get back under control. "Yes, that's the whole trouble. Time you stopped. Look, I understand you have a job to do, but you don't have to do it this way."

"Nothing gets anywhere without a push," said Camden. "Life is a bicycle. Stop pedaling and you fall over. You didn't get big without people like me stirring up the public interest."

"Yeah. People *exactly* like you," said Patrick venomously, hissing the words into Camden's face.

"This Christian business is genuinely interesting," Camden said, "and as for that chick and her crusade, it's brilliant stuff."

"Chick? What chick?"

"Oh, come on. Who do you think I mean? You've noticed her, I know you have."

"Who?"

"I wasn't born yesterday. Bobby, of course."

"Are you saying there's something between me and Bobby?"

"Isn't there?"

"No, there bloody isn't."

"Calm down, Paddy. Everyone's staring at you."

He watched Patrick with the cold eye of a video editor, wondering if he had enough. The man was struggling with himself, taking deep breaths. He decided he had. It was time to crank down the pressure.

"Whatever. Anyway, Bobby and her May Day are a real gift. All this stuff simmering in the village, and you digging away on top of the hill. Past and present overlapping. That's just the sort of stuff we need."

"She's working for us, that's all."

Camden smirked, which got even further under Patrick's skin.

"I really don't need this. I'm trying to do a serious dig. We're getting good stuff for you. Why can't you be happy with that? Any TV channel would give their eyeteeth for what we're giving you."

"Come on, Pat. You and I understand each other. There's been any number of these shows on TV already. They pull in the top slice of the audience—you know, the ones with the education. We want to widen it. This story's got human interest. You understand that, surely. We're both entertainment professionals. You've been there."

"Look, I'm not there now. Don't assume you know who I am. I'm not your property, OK? I'm not here to be used, and I've just about had it with this. I'll do the job, but leave me alone, understand?" Patrick became aware that he was shouting.

"Understood," said Camden soothingly. "We'll stay out of your hair if you just play ball a little."

Patrick stalked across to the pub and Camden strolled back to Jack and the camera.

"You did get that, didn't you?" he said.

"Yes," said Jack, rather regretting that he had. "You won't hear much of it because I couldn't get that close, but you'll see all the arm waving and that. He was pretty worked up."

"That's my boy," said Camden, and he could have been talking about either Jack or Patrick.

SUPPER WAS STEW ON PASTA, THOUGH BOBBY CALLED IT *tagliatelle giardinièra*. It didn't matter. Six litres of the Stag's cheapest red wine chased the taste away, and it seemed the diggers could hardly wait for darkness and the campfire chat.

"Do you think Joe's coming tonight?" Dozer asked Bobby as they cleared the table.

"He's here already," she said, nodding into the gloom, and there was her brother, standing motionless on the fringe of the firelight.

"No git box?" said Dozer.

"What?"

"As Dozer's official translator," said CD, "I can reveal that what appeared to be a random series of unintelligible grunts actually meant, 'Well, goodness me, I have perceived the fact that the man in question has not come bearing his stringed instrument for making mellifluous music, namely his guitar.' That is an approximate translation, but the best I can do under the circumstances."

"When I want translating I'll tell you," said Dozer.

CD cupped a hand to his ear. "Sorry, I couldn't follow that one. Say it again more slowly."

"No songs tonight, then," Gaye said.

"Who knows?" Bobby said, smiling, and Patrick, remembering Camden's jarring description of her on the green, felt a flash of anger for her.

"So what do we think?" said Patrick when they'd all settled down in what were already becoming their accustomed places around the fire. "It's after sundown, CD, and your jackdaw's tucked in bed. You're allowed to speculate now."

"Raven," corrected the American. "All in good time. Let's lay out the facts and see what everybody makes of them. We have a pregnant Anglo-Saxon woman, probably seventh-century, buried in warrior style with a shield. And close by we have a half-size wooden sword, burnt at one end and inscribed with runes. All of this is very, very, very unusual. Our woman is also accompanied by grave goods typical of female burials, such as toilet items, plus we now think there is a real metal sword in the grave beside the skeleton."

"We do?" said Patrick, startled.

"Sorry, forgot to tell you. It's too early, et cetera. Just a sign of something bladelike so far. Discovered it while you were fetching the booze. Speaking of which, you seem to be clutching a bottle under your arm which I have not yet been introduced to."

"It's Teacher's. They didn't have any rotgut."

"I'll manage. So, speculate away, folks."

"I think the song's right," said Gaye, glancing behind her towards Joe, still motionless fifteen yards away.

"Come and join us, mate," called Dozer, but there was no sign Joe had even heard.

"He'll come if he wants to," Bobby told them.

"I bet she sent the sword for help at the last minute," Gaye went on, "and they didn't come in time, so she had to defend her children herself. Then when they did come, when it was too late, they buried the sword with her."

"Children? You said *children?*" Maxwell was curious. "You think she had other children?"

"Of course she did," said Gaye. "Trust a man not to know. If she was pregnant, she would have run and hid. Anything to defend her unborn baby. But she fought, didn't she? She would only have done that if she had other children to protect."

"Is that right?"

"I think it is," said Bobby. "I've seen that."

"Where?" said Patrick, surprised.

"Oh . . . that's another story. . . ."

She was looking into the fire and he could see her in profile. Then, seeming to feel his gaze on her, she glanced sideways at him, grimaced slightly as if to dismiss it, and went back to looking at the fire. Rachel had made that same face increasingly often as their life together turned sour. She made it when she pulled back from saying something she knew would lead to more confrontation, and Patrick knew now he should have taken note each time he saw that face instead of bullying her into silence. Seeing Bobby do it at this moment pierced him.

He came out of a trance knowing, to his embarrassment, that he was still staring at the silhouette of Bobby's face, that he had been doing so for far too long, and that this was bound to have been noticed. But it hadn't, because something much more remarkable had grabbed the attention of everybody else around the campfire. People were shuffling up, making room, and Joe, distant, silent Joe, was coming in to join them round their fire, and everyone was looking at him with fascination, holding their breaths as if he was some wild animal, unaccountably seeking out human company.

## CHAPTER NINETEEN

ITH QUICK, CERTAIN movements, Joe sat down on the log between Aidan and Gaye. As he sat, he was already looking all round the circle, nodding at each of them in turn as he met their eyes. His nods seemed unpractised—single sharp dips of his head like muscle spasms. There was a moment of silence in which no one seemed to know what one could safely say to a mute that didn't demand an answer, then CD reached across to him, holding out the whisky bottle, and said, "Nice to see you, pal. We'd been hoping you'd join us."

Bobby, watching Joe closely, looked as surprised as the rest of them. He took the bottle, lifted it to his lips in a token gesture, wiped it on a clean handkerchief from his pocket, and passed it on to Gaye, who flinched as he turned to her, then hastily put on a fixed smile. Joe was dressed in an army surplus sweater, green with leather on the elbows, and patched cord trousers. Patrick could see no trace of a family resemblance to Bobby. Her brother had a square, weather-beaten face; his temple over his right eye was marked by a scar, a slight depression the size of a pound coin. His grey hair was short and curly, and under bushy eyebrows his bright, pale eyes darted from side to side, making swift assessments. His arrival had put a stop to the natural flow of conversation.

Unexpectedly, it was Joe himself who broke the silence.

As they stared at him, he nodded as if to himself, took a breath, and sang three descending notes, softly and slightly quavering: "Ah, ah, ah." The hush intensified and drew in around them as they stared at him, but he just looked at them enquiringly and sang the same three notes again, this time more loudly. They all looked back blankly, waiting for him to go on, but now he stood up and held out both hands, palms up, in front of him, nodding at them.

Bobby sang the notes back at him, accurately, and he beamed with pleasure and gestured with his hands. The cadence sounded sad to Patrick, plaintive in a minor key.

"Our turn, folks," said Bobby. "All together. He wants us to sing the notes."

It was ragged at first. Joe, listening intently, kept shaking his head, then signing for them to start again. After five false starts, they sounded reasonably good, and at that point, Joe made a chopping, cutoff sign with his hands and held up two fingers. This time he sang six notes, starting low and soaring up, only to descend again. They'd got the idea now and it only took three tries to get it right. He confused them briefly by holding up one finger, but Bobby said it meant they should do the first one again, and he nodded, beaming. One finger for the first, two fingers for the second. They did them one after the other until he was satisfied, then he held up three fingers.

"Blimey, how much more is there?" grumbled Dozer. "If we're doing Handel's *Messiah* in bite-size chunks, we're going to be here all night."

Joe swung round and stared at him.

"It's all right, maestro, I'm only joking," Dozer said hastily.

They learnt the third and fourth sections quickly, each of them wondering where this was leading, but it seemed four was enough.

Joe made them run through all four twice in succession, then he beckoned them all to their feet with upward sweeps of his arms.

"I guess it's show time," said CD, echoing Patrick's thought. It seemed Joe considered them ready for the full rendition of this odd four-part lament he'd taught them, but that wasn't his intention, not yet, not here. Joe walked off into the darkness and they followed, urged on by his emphatic gestures as he led them up the gentle slope of the hilltop.

There was no doubt about their destination. The tent protecting the woman and her child rose against the skyline, a square nylon tomb, directly in their path. Joe went to it, holding one corner pole and looking towards Patrick. In the darkness before moonrise, it was difficult to read the expression on his face.

"You want us to move it?" Patrick asked, and he saw Joe give another of his sharp downward nods.

"OK," he said, "give us a hand to get the pegs out," and the diggers moved the big tent carefully out of the way so that the grave lay bare, a dark slash across the centre of the low mound.

*What now,* Patrick wondered, hoping Joe would do nothing unexpected that might threaten the trench, nothing that would force him to intervene and incur Bobby's protective wrath again. The man took a step closer to the edge of the grave and knelt as if in prayer. A log dropped into the distant campfire, and in the sudden flare of sparks, Patrick could see fire-painted bones and also see Joe's jaw working as he, staring at the shapes in the grave which were no more than the suggestion of a woman's frame, spoke soundless words. Then he got back to his feet, turning to them in the manner of a conductor facing his orchestra. He held up a single finger. Humming the first note as a guide, he looked round to check they were all ready, then brought his finger sweeping down.

There was no doubt in their response, no embarrassment, no hanging back. The descending notes made their sad stairway down the dark sky. All day the grave had been cluttered with the jarring gadgets of modern times—cameras, tape measures, plastic trays. The language of the day had been that of the archaeologist, concerned with measurement and with the science of conservation. Now the night had brought back simplicity. They were just fourteen living souls on a hilltop, honouring the dead with an ancient tune. Now it made no difference whether a year or a thousand years separated them. The last note ended and they looked to Joe for guidance, expecting him to signal the second sequence, but he was staring down at the grave again, and in the silence he half sang, half chanted:

> *The boda came to Abbandun at evening bell*
> *Brought by the child with sunset head.*
> *We left our looms to answer it as black night fell,*
> *That blood call on the summoning sword.*

An involuntary shiver ran through Patrick's body. Joe's voice, somewhere between song and speech, had a slight quaver, standing by itself, deprived of the accustomed support of a guitar. His pronunciation was precise and oddly foreign; "night" sounded almost like the German *nicht*, "blood" was *bloode*, "summoning" started with a *soo* sound. Majestic and intent on what he was doing, Joe held up a hand again and, swept along by the rhythm and the logic of the sounds, they all knew that the second part followed. The notes they sang into the night took on a true beauty beyond anything they had sung before, and when it ended, they stood without a sound, hanging on every word as Joe went on.

> *The mother river broke its banks that heartless night*
> *And slowed our feet in beds of mud*
> *When we climbed to your shattered hall at dawn's first light*
> *You'd taken ship on seas of blood.*

This time they needed no prompting at all, coming in unison into the third part; a female voice, unidentifiable in the dark, broke from the rest and harmonised the last note. Joe came in as they ended, and his tone contained despair.

> *Your husband-kin, who failed to pay the sword-blade debt*
> *Now stand before you with bowed head.*
> *We came too late to help in time of need, and yet*
> *We vow we'll keep your daughter fed.*

Above them, Venus drew Patrick's eye and he sang the final notes straight to the evening star, while real stars carpeted the sky. The same woman's voice soared above them all on two notes that were a final wordless "amen" and then, while Patrick went on staring up into the heavens, they stood in stunned silence. *Those stars aren't really there at all,* he thought, *although I can see them. What I see is just a message from where they were a thousand years or a thousand millennia ago, from where they were when this loved body was laid in the ground. If I can take that ancient light for granted, what then is so odd about doing the same for this ancient sound?*

He pulled his gaze back to the earth and Joe was gone and the rest of them were looking at each other as if shocked by what they'd done. No one spoke, as if they were loath to interrupt the faint echo of the music in their heads. After a long moment, Patrick shook his head to clear it, went over to the covering tent, and waited there in sad tranquillity until CD and Dozer joined him and, moving slowly, helped him walk it back into its place protecting the grave. Then they all moved off, drawn back to the fire they had left so short and so long a time ago.

As they settled back into their places around it, Patrick noticed that Aidan and Gaye left a space between them as if Joe might reappear. He knew the space would not be filled; probably they did, too. CD produced the bottle of scotch and it made the rounds. No one turned it down. Then the American said, in a voice that contained none of his usual bantering tone, "Before you ask, Aidan, *Abbandun* is the old Anglo-Saxon name for Abingdon, which is, I would say, four hours' hard marching away in the times before there were roads, and maybe six or seven hours if the river was flooded."

"Thank you," said Aidan, nodding. "I hadn't yet thought of asking that, but I suppose it saves time. I *was* going to ask about the unfamiliar word there at the start?"

"Sounded like *boda*?" said CD.

"That's the one."

"It means nothing to me. Peter? No? Well, I'll check it out tomorrow."

"It was clear what the sense was," said Maxwell, almost indignantly. "The *boda* was the summons, wasn't it? It couldn't have been plainer."

CD shrugged. "This is beyond my humble knowledge."

Dozer nodded slowly. "What gets me is that I'm the king of the cynics, but all the time I was listening to him, I was quite sure he wasn't just making it up. Come on, Bobby. Tell us what you know. You'd heard that tune before, the way you were singing. All those fancy bits."

Patrick had guessed that sweet sound came from Bobby, but it was good to know for sure.

"I've heard the tune," she answered. "That's all. Sometimes when we're washing up, Joe sings. Never words, just sounds like that. I join in. We sing bits backwards and forwards at each other and we sometimes work out the harmonies."

CD was cleaning his glasses on his sleeve and at that he looked up at her. "What sort of *brain* has he got? Could he make up stuff like that? Stuff that sounds real? I mean, stuff with Anglo-Saxon thought processes sticking out of it?"

"It sounds stupid, but like I said before, I just don't know. When someone doesn't talk, there's so little to go on—even when you're brother and sister. He listens to everything and he picks up all sorts of stuff and I know he's got an amazing memory. We were talking about that the other night, weren't we? Well, afterwards I remembered that there was a song my mother sang us, maybe three or four times, no more. She learnt it from my granny. That was, I don't know, twenty-five years ago. It's got fifty verses. It's some sort of Victorian music-hall doggerel, all about an explorer and his pet walrus. He sang it in the pub last year, and I can't be sure, but it sounded just the same to me, and he didn't falter once."

"Look at what he got us all doing," said CD. "Thirteen supposedly responsible adults—well, twelve plus Maxwell—and a man who doesn't speak got us all baying in unison."

"No, don't do that," said Gaye, indignantly. "I don't want you to start making fun of it. Whatever you say, that was *special*. In fact, I think that was more . . . oh, I don't know, there must be a better word than 'special' . . . more *wonderfully disturbing* than anything else in my life. Tomorrow, we mustn't laugh at the way that we all just felt. We mustn't feel embarrassed. Last time the grave was open, they were laying her in it. I'd really like to think those words were more or less what they were saying then."

"Yup," said Dozer.

That's quite a speech, thought Patrick, coming from Gaye, who seemed to feel strongly only about hygiene when she'd first arrived.

She sat there defiantly; the red lipstick had gone and what was left looked younger for it. In the firelight he could see the stains of grass and earth that had spread across her clothes like creeping camouflage.

"You can't say that, can you?" objected Maxwell. "You can't say those were the same words. What he said tonight, that was modern English."

"Oh, it's not so very different," said Peter. "All those Old English words just got a bit of French and a bit of Danish added to them here and there. That's why we've got so many different words for subtle versions of the same thing, but you know, if you just take the time to learn to pronounce Old English, the mystery disappears."

"Like what?"

"Well, for example, you see something that looks like a 'p' with a little spike sticking up, then that joined up 'ae' thing and a 't' on the end, and it looks completely unfamiliar, but the first letter is just 'th' and the second is the same as 'a,' so all it spells is 'that.' It's not so foreign when you know how to say it. It wouldn't be too hard to put together a pure Old English sentence that you'd understand with no trouble at all."

"*Boda,* with an 'a,' " said CD, who clearly hadn't been listening. "Idiot! I don't have to look it up. Maxwell, I hate to say this, but I owe you an apology. B, O, D, A—well, I should say *berkano, othila, dagaz, ansuz.*"

"Bless you," said Dozer. "That's a nasty cold."

"That's the runic alphabet names for them. I told you about the goddamn Frisian sword. That's half of what's written on it, the second word, *boda.* Wait. Do not move." CD leapt to his feet, ran to his tent, and came back with a heavy book and a flashlight.

"Bedtime reading," he announced, "and you get to give your pecs a workout at the same time. Bosworth and Toller's Anglo-Saxon dictionary. *Boda, boda, boda*—yup. Masculine noun, meaning *messenger, ambassador, herald,* et cetera."

"A summons to help," said Maxwell. "I told you."

"Oh, well, that explains it," said Aidan. "Joe must have seen it in a book."

"Excuse me," said CD, "and I don't mean to belittle him in any way, but Joe doesn't strike me as the type who would have Bosworth and Toller or Hilda Ellis Davidson on Anglo-Saxon swords lying around in his bookshelf. Is that what you're suggesting? Or maybe he has a subscription to *Archäologisches Korrespondenzblatt?*"

"What's the other half of the inscription?" asked Aidan. "On the Frisian sword?"

CD screwed up his face in concentration. "*Edda? Adda?* Something like that. Maybe a personal name? I can't remember."

"So if the runes on our sword say *boda,* that would be pretty strong support for the song," said Aidan.

"Runic characters," said CD. "Just to be really purist, runes were the sacred stones they were cut into, which is just a feeble attempt to postpone answering your archaeologically unacceptable question, but yes, I guess it would." He looked around. "I just hope no one who's deciding on my doctorate can hear me."

"Bet you a fiver it doesn't say *boda,*" said Dozer.

"That's a bet, my friend," said CD. "I just love placing a bet when the horses are halfway round the course."

"What do you mean?" asked Dozer suspiciously.

"You forget, I've already read two of the runes. *Dagaz, ansuz* is a pretty good start. That's the 'd' and the 'a.' "

"Oh, bugger," said Dozer. "If they were already under starter's orders, the bet's not valid, chum."

"Listen, my old mucker, how many runic characters are there in the *futhorc?*"

"The what?"

"The runic alphabet, you pig-ignorant earth-mover."

"You're just jealous 'cos the earth never moves for you."

The humour felt strained. No one else was laughing or joining in. They were still trying to hang on to what had happened, diminishing so rapidly down time's perspective.

"All right," said Dozer, "How many are there, then?"

"There's twenty-five letters, Doze, and—"

Peter coughed.

CD looked at him. "Twenty-six?"

Peter shook his head slightly.

"Twenty-seven? Twenty-eight?"

Peter nodded.

"Like I was saying, there's twenty-eight letters. So even if it's a four-letter word, the chance of the word being *boda* is about, oh, I don't do this multiplying stuff, about one in a squillion."

"What are these runes about anyway?" said Aidan. "I thought that was comic-book stuff. Hobbits and wizards."

"Ask Peter, the one-man database," said CD. "He knows everything. Me, I have a life instead."

*"Rune,"* said Peter, chuckling, "originally meaning 'mystery.' An early system of lettering, made up of straight lines, probably because the letters were incised into stone or wood and it's easier to do straight lines if you're using a knife. The alphabet is called the *futhorc* just like we say ABC, because that's what the first six letters spelt." He turned to Aidan and said, "Before you ask, I know *futhorc* has seven letters, but the third one is a combined 'th' sound."

"I think I'm starting to dislike this preemptive answering," complained Aidan. "It's taking away the fun."

"You have to imagine written words used not for communication but for symbolic purposes," Peter told them. "You might put a name on a valuable object to label it as yours, but more likely you put on runes to give it a certain power."

CD broke in. "You get runic inscriptions on real swords, but mostly not until later, the tenth century or so. They called them things like 'whirring death' and 'bringer of life's sleep.' Brilliant stuff."

"I always think of those poor Britons," said Peter. "There they were, used to Roman culture, history, poetry, and plays, and all at once it all evaporates and in come these crude foreigners whose entire literary heritage adds up to a row of grunts carved on a rock. They have to wait another six hundred years before there's anything else worth reading."

There was a scatter of appreciative laughter, then a silence that no one wanted to fill. Patrick realised again that none of them had the heart for it tonight, this dry dissection across the grain of the direct sense of time brought to them by Joe.

Gaye said it for all of them.

"I don't really care where that song came from. It's true enough for me. We should remember that's a burial over there, not just a dig. She was as alive as we are, that woman. If Joe's songs are the best way to remember that, then that's good enough for me."

There was a bit of whispering in the darkness then, as the bottle circulated. Maxwell went off to his tent and came back holding something behind him out of sight. Aidan seemed to be encouraging him to do something but the boy was reluctant. In the end, while the rest of them stared into the fire, deep in thought, it was Aidan who took the guitar Maxwell was carrying and went over to Patrick.

"Now, Mr. Director," said the man, momentarily demonic in the firelight as his eye sockets danced with reflected flames, "we have a favor to ask."

Patrick was used to Aidan the constant questioner, but this Aidan had a direct human quality in his voice. He looked at the guitar, appalled.

"What?"

"We know you have a fine voice, having heard it tonight, and we know you're an archaeologist through and through these days, which is all that matters and not anything else at all from whatever went before. It's just that some of us have an idea that you might also be rather good on one of these things and we wondered whether you might be persuaded to give it a shot, just among friends. Nothing rough, you understand, just some tuneful old things that we'd all know. It would be a kindness—this evening, it seems to me, should end in music, not in words."

So, astonishing himself, Patrick reached out and took the instrument, feeling the heft of it with a shock of old familiarity. He nestled the swell of its hip against his thigh and suddenly realised, as his fingers touched the strings through skin no longer tough from constant playing, just how long it was since he had last played a guitar, and how very much longer since he had last played one for pleasure. It was an old cheap acoustic with nylon strings, and that was a short-circuit back to his cleaner times, the times when young Pat had played in the clubs.

It was out of tune and he spent much longer than was strictly necessary getting it right, finding that even after a gap of years he could still tune it by the harmonics without any conscious thought. Without his thinking about it, his fingers itched into a fragment of a twelve-bar blues, then settled on the sliding introduction into "Wonderful Tonight," and there was no other sound but the crackle of the fire, and even that seemed to listen to him. The words came unbidden. *"It's late in the evening. She's wondering what clothes to wear,"*

then his mind caught up with the words to come, words of love
charged with memories he could not possibly sing. He brought it to
an untidy halt and, aware of sounds of regret from his audience, cast
around for safe ground. His fingers found a reggae beat and launched
him into "Redemption Song" instead. He hadn't played anything
plainly tuneful since before Nam Erewhon, but his conscious mind
was dealing with the inadequacies of this guitar and his subconscious, free to roam, brought the words and the chords back as if the
intervening years hadn't happened at all. It was good to play at being
Bob Marley by that fire; and he could have been alone, except that
when another log-falling leap of firelight made him look up, he saw a
circle of underworld, flame-painted faces all watching him.

"C'mon, Pat, give us something we can dance to," called Dozer.
"Me and Gaye want to rock and roll."

"I do *not*," objected Gaye.

Patrick did his best with a half-remembered intro to "Blue Suede
Shoes," which hardened up as he got into it until he was pounding it
out as loud as the tinny guitar would let him. Dozer got to his feet,
trying to pull Gaye with him, but she wouldn't, then Bobby smiled
and jumped up and she and Dozer went into a dance with as much
style as if they'd rehearsed it a hundred times, Bobby slipping in and
out of Dozer's grasp to twirl under his arm with fluid grace. Patrick
went on repeating the verses he could remember, over and over again
just to watch the two of them, until Dozer dropped exhausted and
Bobby danced on just as if he was still there.

He played her to a whirling finale and, not wanting her to stop,
slowed into a song that came out of his subconscious and only when
some of them joined in, did he realise what it was he was playing.

*I'm a young man, growing up in the world . . .*

He willed her to stop dancing before the chorus came, and perhaps
she recognised the tune, too, because she sat down suddenly. In the
firelight, her face seemed to carry the mark of the flames more
vividly than the rest, which puzzled him until he realised that her
cheeks were wet with reflecting tears. The chorus came—*"If you want
to know how she makes love, just look at the way she dances"*—and he was
glad she had sat down because it would have felt like an ambush and
he had not intended it that way.

She didn't want him to see and turned her gaze away down into the private flames, but he went on looking. After a while, knowing his gaze was on her, she stared straight back at him for a moment with her eyes still shining, got up, and walked off towards the farm.

The rest were intent on him and few saw her go, and he could do or say nothing to stop her, halfway through his song and the focus of so much attention. He brought it to a premature halt at the end of the next verse and rested, feeling the ends of his fingers tingling with the unaccustomed friction even though these were soft nylon strings, so much kinder than the metal ones of the Stratocaster he'd been used to.

They clapped for him and they wouldn't let him stop. Gaye wanted "Suzanne," while Aidan asked for something Irish Patrick had never heard of, but he settled for "Dirty Old Town." Dozer insisted on singing along with "The Boxer" but was howled down before he could get into the third line. By the time exhaustion settled on them, he'd been through all he could remember from Dire Straits to Dylan, shying away only from the songs that hurt.

He was happier at that moment than he'd been for as far back as he could remember. As he handed the guitar back to Maxwell, the boy looked at him and said, "That was just great. Famous you, singing all that just for us," and Patrick didn't even mind that.

Before he crawled into his tent, he looked down the hill at a single light burning in a dormer window at the farm and wondered what had caused Bobby's sudden flight.

## CHAPTER TWENTY

IF THERE WAS A SINGLE MOMENT that explained how Pat became Paddy, it was that first time he went out on-stage with the band. There was a huge darkness beyond the lights; he stood in the wings staring at a tiny slice of that darkness, and he was his father's son, cowed for years by a remote authoritarian. He was Rachel's lover, too, used to retreating from anything that troubled him into a universe of two. He was frightened, and all the small gigs he had ever played, all the applause he'd had in the clubs and the bars, helped not one bit.

"Get on," said Mig, the drummer, "or are we just going to stop here for the 'ole set?" and Pat went on into the lights, and the darkness beyond erupted with three thousand voices. In that moment of utter astonishment he found that he could play them like an instrument—a whirl of his arm doubled their volume, a flick of his head brought in the girls' screaming trebles. Fear disappeared and utter confidence in his mastery of this audience flooded through him. In their box seats, the management of Colonic Music breathed a deep collective breath of satisfaction as their fine-tuned creation generated a fresh chorus of howls. He had what his audience wanted and he played their hunger, letting it sweep him further and further down the path they wanted him to tread. It was the way he looked and the way he moved and the way he sang. He turned on something primeval in them with every movement. They responded with ecstasy, and Pat, who had always moved inside tightly set limits, even with Rachel, was swept away by it.

Now, waking to the unfamiliar tingle that the guitar strings had left in his fingertips, Patrick was back on that stage again for a moment and the future was not yet written. In the next second, the nylon-filtered green light and the shadows of grass outside the tent fabric right next to his eyes brought him back to a hard today in which all that mattered was long lost. He remembered the songs of the night before and wished the diggers hadn't listened with quite such reverence. He felt another unguarded morning pang, this one for David and for Rachel. People had told him he would get over it, but he wasn't even sure he would ever get used to it. But this was the first time he missed Rachel in the same way as David, with guilt in grief's background, not the other way around. And when he steeled himself to crawl outside, everyone else looked as if they had woken missing something, too.

In morning light, the bright clutter of the camp, the orange mesh strung from metal poles around the perimeter of the dig and the square tent covering the grave, spelt functional archaeology and blocked his ability to see this hilltop properly. He half closed his eyes and tried to see the burial mound again as it had been when Joe led him to it—time's thin residues layered and squashed between grass and rock, pressed flat by the remorseless weight of twenty miles of air. What they had done in the name of scientific curiosity was an invasion, but he knew that for all of them the dig now commanded a degree of reverence greater than it had before.

Patrick found his feet slowing on the way to the marquee for breakfast. Last night Bobby had danced like an angel and he had watched like a slave. Rachel had never danced like that, like a warm waterfall. That made it worse. *She's the cook,* he told himself. *I'm the director. I will go in and be polite and that will be the start and the finish of it.* She was busy frying eggs in a sour cloud of hot oil when he went into the tent, and she scarcely had time to look round when he said good morning. He took slices of bread and a scoop of marmalade, poured coffee, and went outside to sit on the grass where CD and Dozer were already eating their food in unaccustomed silence.

"It's good for us, this camping business," said CD as Patrick sat down. "Gets us closer to the mind-set of our ancestors, living at ground level. Grass with everything."

"Bet our ancestors didn't fry their bleeding eggs in diesel oil," said Dozer.

"Take a look," said CD. "They're early." He was pointing with his knife to where Camden's car was coming into sight through the gate.

"Maybe we won't mention last night," said Patrick.

"My thoughts exactly. You go and occupy them for a minute or two, and I might just spread the word round the gang. No mention of Joe. After all, we have our reputations to consider."

"I'll go," said Dozer.

"No, no," said CD, "we merely want to delay him, not frighten him to death."

"OK," said Dozer, happily.

The Toyota's tailgate was open and Camden was standing bent over, busy with papers in the back compartment, when Patrick walked up. Jack was sorting through his camera gear on the bonnet.

"Good morning," said Patrick. "You're bright and early."

He took Camden by surprise. The man stood up sharply, cracked his head on the roof, yelped, and dropped the cardboard file he was holding. It fell to the ground, and as Patrick went to pick it up for him he found himself staring, transfixed by the photocopy that had slid out of the folder. It was a page from a tabloid newspaper and he remembered it horribly well. Anger rose in him that Camden should have such a thing in his files. It didn't belong here. He snatched it from the ground and stared at the old headline, which still said, "Mad Paddy Broke My Camera Says Our Snapper." An irrational feeling came over him that there should be some statute of limitations, that when enough time had passed, old stories should be purged from the records, like old convictions.

Rachel had insisted. The argument had gone on for days, and he had given in because there was the whole summer to get through with no gigs planned and it might keep things quiet. He'd suggested going to one of the big names, someone like Audrey Maskell, someone the stars went to. Rachel put her foot down. She said it had to be Relate, just the ordinary local office in Maidenhead, that or nothing. He tried to explain that it wasn't a question of feeling he was too good for that, it was more that fame distorted things. He needed someone who was easy with fame, who understood the pressures, not someone who would treat him like a creature from Mars. He even said he was worried that Rachel wouldn't get a fair hearing if the counselor was overawed by his presence. She said he was just saying that, that it showed he really wanted someone who'd stroke his ego and that was the whole trouble, everybody all round him stroked his ego except her.

She wasn't entirely fair. His reluctance *was* to do with fame, but deep down, it was because he didn't want to have to explain himself. He wanted someone who already knew who he was, so that some things would be clear before they even started. He wanted someone who had read the articles, seen the profiles, someone who knew about showbiz. Rachel was not going to compromise.

"We've got to do this like real people do," she said in the kitchen when she got back from taking David round to Sally's house. "We've got to get back to being real people. I don't want any of this." She waved her hand at the stainless steel cupboard doors, at the walk-in fridge and the fake Lichtenstein mural filling the far wall. "I'd rather we were back in Wandsworth bloody starving than this."

It was so rare for Rachel to say even "bloody" that he had stared at her, astonished.

"I've made an appointment," she said, "whether you like it or not. One of us can go or two of us can go. I've already been twice by myself and I've met the woman we're going to. She's called Mrs. Wilcox and she's very nice. Now, it's up to you, but if I go by myself, don't expect me back. I'll take Davey straight back to Wales when I pick him up. Do you understand?"

So they drove to Maidenhead and she insisted he park the car miles away from the Relate office, though there was space to leave it on the forecourt.

"Turning up in this stupid great thing?" she said. "You've got to be daft. What sort of start would that be?"

"I don't want to walk there," he said. "Someone will see me, and you know what happens then."

"Oh, yes," she said, "I know very well what happens then. You do your 'I'm a rock star pretending he doesn't want to be recognized' bit and I have to go away and hide and lots of silly little teenagers wet their knickers running after you."

So they'd walked halfway across the town, and of course, a hundred yards from the building that housed Relate, three school-age girls shrieked "Paddy Kane!" and he smiled at them, because that was always his automatic response. The girls' faces took on that familiar besotted, feral look, and they chased Rachel and Paddy all the way into the building until the receptionist shut the door in their faces.

Mrs. Wilcox was a tall grey-haired woman with an austere manner, which changed once she'd led them upstairs into a small room with three chairs, a low table, a large box of tissues, and an alarm button. Then, when they sat down, she smiled, and Paddy felt suddenly that perhaps this wasn't just some stitch-up arranged between two of the great sisterhood of women.

"Now, Mr. Kane," she said, "as I'm sure you know, your wife has already seen me by herself. I understand you were away?"

*Was I?* thought Paddy. *Was I actually away, or was I just out of my head?* It seemed to come to the same thing.

"Yes," he said.

"You travel a lot, I hear. You're a musician, your wife told me."

"Yes."

"Would that be an orchestra of some sort?"

Christ on a bicycle, where had this woman been? Here he was dressed in artfully slashed leather, with the peacock haircut that was his trademark round the world, and she thought he was in an orchestra.

"No," he replied, "I'm a rock musician." There was a small window to his right, looking out to the front of the building. A car horn blared and he glanced out to see a group of five more girls running across the road towards the front door.

"Perhaps I can summarise what Rachel sees as the problem, then you can give your point of view." She glanced down at her clipboard and he could see Rachel's views stretched from top to bottom of the page.

"You met when you were quite young—students, I think—and

you were both very happy until three years ago. Then two things happened at once. You had a baby—" she checked the sheet "—David, and you began to be away from home much more often. I think it would be fair to say that Rachel feels you have changed a lot since then."

"Everything's gone a bit mad," he said. "Life's changed, not me." He looked at Rachel, sitting in her chair, staring at the floor. "Rache knows what it's been like. I've had a lot of, well . . . success, I suppose. We've been doing all right, I—"

"You say you've been doing all right? What do you mean? The two of you?"

"I mean, well, you know, financially, success, that sort of thing. I've had to do a lot of touring."

"I don't know you anymore," said Rachel, bitterly, looking up, and it hurt that she could say that in front of a stranger. "You're nothing like my Pat. He was sweet, you know." Now she was looking at Mrs. Wilcox. "I was so in love with him. Then this stupid band of his came along and suddenly he's on TV and in the magazines all the time and it's gone to his head."

*No, it hasn't,* he thought, shocked. *It hasn't.* It was just that he had to go along with it, he had to do the act.

"It's not like that," he said. "I'm a professional rock musician." He could hear far-off shouts and screaming from outside. "I have to do all that."

"I'm sorry," said Mrs. Wilcox, frowning. "Perhaps I should have heard of you. What is the name of your band?"

He quite liked this, the moment when she would realise what she was dealing with. "Nam Erewhon," he said casually.

She looked blank and shook her head. "Erewhon, after the Utopian ideal, I assume?"

She must be doing this to cut him down to size. She couldn't not have heard of them. Everybody had heard of them. They were every crusty old right-winger's greatest hate object. At least she must have heard people *complaining* about them.

"Well, yes, I suppose. Really, it's just that it's 'Nowhere Man' backwards, like we're the antidote to the Beatles."

"I didn't know the Beatles needed an antidote," she said. "But I take it you're a hit with the younger set."

He laughed. "Well, yes" was all he said.

"Listen to you," said Rachel. "Listen to the way you say it. You love every minute of it. I want to save you, Pat. It's going to your head, all this. It's not just me and David I'm scared for, it's you, too."

"Oh, you don't have to be scared for me," said Paddy Kane, thinking how far he'd come and how little she knew.

"Why are you scared exactly?" asked Mrs. Wilcox.

"I know how he works," said Rachel. "He's best when he doubts himself, then he drives himself harder. It's always been that way. When he used to write a song, it was usually pretty middling to begin with, then he agonised over it and he got really frustrated, then he sorted it out. He's not like that anymore. Everyone tells him he's fantastic, so he's started believing it. His songs are going to pot. They're all horrible. Well, they are! He thinks they're right first time."

"Oh, come on," said Paddy, "you can't say that. I—"

"She has said that, Mr. Kane. You must hear Rachel, because whether you agree with it or not, it is what she thinks, so please let her finish, then you can have your say."

"It's David that makes me really sorry about it all," said Rachel, "because I do believe that Pat does love him. It's just he doesn't know what being a father really is. He's never there, and when he is there he always gets him all overexcited and brings him stupid presents. He just treats David like a toy of some sort. He's not there for the messy bits. I know it's like that for a lot of fathers, but I thought he was going to be the best dad in the whole world, and instead of that he's a rock star."

"Tell me how *you* react to that, Mr. Kane," said Mrs. Wilcox calmly.

"I love David," he said, shocked. "When I'm home I want to spend all my time with him." A police siren could be heard approaching. "I think that's really unfair. He's . . . well, he's just great. I don't see why I shouldn't bring him presents. It makes up for me being away. It's only a temporary thing, all this. I'll be able to stop in a year or two when I've stashed away a bit."

"You won't stop," said Rachel sadly. "I don't know what it would take to make you stop. You're like a dog with three tails."

"People manage to live with fame and success," said Mrs. Wilcox.

"If they don't let it go to their head," said Rachel.

"Well, if they have a supportive partner and they talk it through, then they can often find a way to deal with it together."

"I'd be a supportive partner if I was allowed to exist," said Rachel savagely. "Ask him about *that*. Nowhere Man! That's a laugh. I'm the Nowhere Woman. He's single. Did you know that? Married since we were twenty and he's *single*."

"What do you mean?"

"It's what the record company says, see? So it doesn't damage his sex appeal. No one's allowed to know about me and David in case it"—Rachel put on a fake male tone, mocking the PR men—"in case it damages his profile with the target groups. We've got this London flat by Hyde Park that I'm not even allowed to go near. That's where they say he lives. When he comes home he has to check his rear mirror to see if the press are following him."

"Dear, oh, dear," said Mrs. Wilcox. "I can see life is a bit difficult, but sometimes people get these things out of proportion. I think maybe that—"

They never found out what she thought. The phone rang. They hadn't even seen a phone. It was out of sight on the floor behind her chair, meant perhaps as a second line of defence to the alarm button.

Mrs. Wilcox was clearly startled. "I'm so sorry," she said. "That's certainly not meant to happen. We have a rule against interruptions."

She picked up the receiver. "Yes?" she said, then she listened and looked astonished. "Really? And it's because . . . Oh, I see. Well, he did, but I . . . Are they?" She glanced towards her two clients and mouthed the word "police." "All right, if that's what they say." She put the phone down and sat collecting herself for a moment.

"Well, I suppose I have to say I do see what you mean about the effects of your, er . . . your *career*." She said it as if she were quite sure that was not at all the right word. "There are rather a lot of excited young women outside, causing something of a disturbance. The press are there now, apparently. Our receptionist has had to lock the doors, and the police are advising that you leave the building by the fire exit at the back."

"Oh, God," said Paddy. "The press. They mustn't see us here."

"What do you mean?"

"How can I be found trying to sort out a marriage I'm not even supposed to be in? Listen, are you the only people in this building?"

"No," said Mrs. Wilcox. "We share it. There's the Cat Protection League."

"Cats? Nothing else?"

"There's Thames Wheels. They're on the top floor."

"What are they?"

"Some sort of motor project, I think. A place troubled boys get sent to by the probation service, to learn about car engines."

"Thames Wheels?" Paddy was reaching for his cheque book.

"Yes."

He scribbled. "OK. Here's a cheque for them. Would you give it to them and tell any press who ask that's why I was here." He scribbled again. "Here's another one for you."

She looked at them as he stood up. "But they're a thousand pounds each! Our session fee is only twelve pounds, and then only if people can afford it."

"That's fine. I was here to give that to Thames Wheels, right? By myself, yes?"

"Yes," Mrs. Wilcox said faintly. "Go down the back corridor. Miss Green is waiting by the fire exit."

As Rachel brushed past her, the counselor said, "Poor dear. I do see what you mean," and was immediately overtaken by a wave of guilt at such a breach of professionalism that she didn't notice the cheque was written out to "Release" instead of "Relate" until Paddy Kane had left the building and it was too late. When she did, she wondered if it had been a Freudian slip.

Paddy sent Rachel out first, telling her to meet him at the car. It was just as well, because as soon as he reached the corner of the building, he heard running feet, and a short, fat photographer, a local agency man looking for an equally fat cheque from one of the nationals, raced up and fired off his camera in Paddy's face. It was an instinctive reaction to try to snatch the camera, and it was only an unfortunate movement by the photographer that took his cheek into the arc of Paddy's hand.

PATRICK STARED AT THE PHOTOCOPIED ARTICLE AND HEARD Kenny Camden say "Whoops."

He tore it deliberately into small pieces, stuffed them into his pocket, then turned to face Camden.

"Before you start," said Camden, "I forgot that was still there."

"Why was it there in the first place?"

"Because I was finding out about you. I didn't know all this would be so sensitive for you, did I? Of course I did my research. That's what you have to do when you're putting a show together. I didn't realise how you'd feel about it, OK?"

"What else have you got in there?" said Patrick, pointing at the folder.

"Lots of programme stuff."

"I want to see it."

"No, come on. It's private stuff." Camden glanced round at Jack, to see that the cameraman now had his gear ready; the camera seemed to be casually pointing in their direction.

"What are you looking at him for?" Patrick demanded.

Camden dropped his voice. "The stuff in the folder. It's all about his contract. I don't want him to know." He tried to sound conciliatory. "Look, Patrick, I know you've had a rough time, but I don't really know why. Maybe if you just told me a bit more, I could avoid treading on your toes."

"Or you could jump on them harder. Does it really make a difference to you?"

" 'Course it does. You've done nothing wrong."

"You know that for a fact, do you?"

"I know you lost your family. Car crash, wasn't it? No one can blame you for that."

"You know nothing," said Patrick, "nothing at all, and stop bloody prying into my affairs."

"Look, I can see that maybe it's tough for you here."

"What does that mean?"

"Well, a grave with a mother and child . . ."

"Hey, stay out of my head. That has nothing to do with it," said Patrick, stung by the fact that it had everything to do with it. "You shoot your stuff, but stay off that. This is just a dig, nothing more."

"Whatever you say."

"I'm going to work now. That's what it is, right? It's just work."

"We'll be down in a minute."

Camden watched Patrick walk away. Once he was out of earshot, he swung round to Jack. "Did you get all that?"

"No."

"What do you mean, no? For God's sake, do you mean you missed it all?"

"I had no idea you wanted me to shoot that. Sounded private to me."

"Get this, you dickhead. *Nothing* is private where he's involved, OK?"

"If you say so."

"I pay your wages, Jacko. I say so, *comprende?*"

"Oh, yeah. What was all that stuff about my contract?"

"Cover. That file's got his entire life story in it."

# CHAPTER TWENTY-ONE

THE DIGGERS, ENJOYING THEIR usual leisurely start to the day, were spread around the grass outside the marquee when Patrick arrived, randomly scattering his anger at Camden all over their breakfast.

"Come on," he snarled, striding through them. "You should have finished eating by now. Let's get on with it."

"It's only twenty past eight," said CD, who was sitting with Dozer.

Patrick turned to him. "If I say it's time to start, it's time to start." The words were out of his mouth before he could stop them. He saw CD's face and regretted them immediately.

"Easy, boss," said Dozer. "We're coming. What's the matter? Hurricane expected?"

"No. Sorry, guys. I had a row with Camden." Patrick made a big effort to smile and cancel out what he'd said, but it wasn't a complete success. The diggers worked in a baffled silence until the day's first find wiped the slate clean and gave them back a common interest.

"Take a look at *this*," murmured CD, as Patrick was working away at the exposed length of the sword blade which lay down the left side of the burial, parallel with the woman's leg bones.

Two small coins, one overlapping the other, lay next to the shoulder blade.

"I think there's more of them," said CD. He scraped away a little more soil. "Yup. Thought so. There's four, maybe even five."

Though CD hadn't raised his voice at all, the antennae of the other diggers had started twitching and the usual ring was quickly forming round the grave trench. Jack arrived with the camera.

Maxwell beat Aidan to the question. "What are they?"

"*Itett*," said CD.

"What's that?"

"Short for 'It's too early to tell,' " said CD, "but you've made me say it now, so I've wasted all that time I could have saved. They could be *sceatta*s, maybe." The word sounded like "shatters."

"What are *they*?"

"Peter?"

"Saxon silver coins," said Peter promptly. "Usually cast in clay molds, then stamped. But I'd say it's a bit early for them. Until the eighth century they're usually only found to the southeast of here."

"Do you promise that you're not going to suddenly turn out to be somebody I should have heard of and make me feel really stupid?" CD asked him.

"I'm afraid not," said Peter, smiling. "I *am* a bit of a coin specialist, though."

"As well as an everything specialist?"

"No, no. I'm a rank amateur in most things."

"I wish I was one of those," said CD, "instead of just not knowing anything."

"So what else might they be?" persisted Maxwell.

Peter considered. "Well, before that there were *tremisses*—Frankish coins—but they were mostly gold, and these are clearly silver." He bent to pick one of them up but stopped himself in time and turned to CD. "May I?"

"Give me a minute to get it on the record sheet. Couple of photos." CD busied himself with the camera and the paperwork, then he gently loosened the top coin. "OK, here you go."

Peter rubbed at the surface. "It's been pierced," he said. "There's a small hole near the rim. Condition's good, apart from that. Can I borrow your magnifying glass?"

CD passed it over, and the older man inspected it carefully.

"All right," he said. "It's one of the type called radiates. Do you see there? There's a crown which radiates round the emperor's head? Looks like an *antonianus* to me. You have to be careful because there are lots of inferior copies, but I'd say this one's rather fine, very probably the real thing."

"What emperor are we talking about here?" said Aidan. "I didn't know the Anglo-Saxons had emperors."

"Oh, they're not Anglo-Saxon. These coins are Roman. They could be as old as the third century. Can't be sure until they're cleaned up."

"So what are they doing here?"

"My guess is someone made them into a necklace. Look at the holes. You sometimes see them as pendants."

"Well, dear lady," said CD, looking down at bones. "Full of surprises, ain't you? You just love those old Roman things." He turned back to the others. "You realise maybe we're looking at the first archaeologist here, folks?"

Kenny Camden loved that and tried to make CD speculate on camera about it, but CD wouldn't be drawn too far in that direction.

"Why should we have the monopoly on digging up the past?" was all he would say. "Hell, this stuff was three, four hundred years old when she was born. That's like me digging up a coin from the Stuarts. Pretty damned exciting, I'd call that."

COINS MEANT LITTLE TO HILD. COINS WERE NOT YET USED TO COVER THE IMBALANCES OF TRADE. THE DISKS WERE HER AMULETS, FOUND IN THE ROMAN EARTH, A POWERFUL SOURCE OF CONCENTRATION FOR THE MIND AND BODY ON THE TASK OF MAKING A SON — AND THEY HAD WORKED.

In the afternoon, with the skeleton now exposed to more than three-quarters of its depth, and only the left side of the slumped-over skull still substantially buried, Dozer found two pieces of shaped bone which he pronounced with complete, unjustified certainty to be gaming pieces. Patrick, trying to keep the dignity of the dig intact, and aware that Jack's camera was catching the whole conversation, was arguing for caution in the identification. Dozer went on troweling away as they talked. In the middle of the conversation, with the lens sucking it all in as eavesdropper and judge, Dozer won hands down by exposing the surface of a flat slate and, wiping off the dirt, discovering the incised straight lines of a superb gaming board. That stopped everything for quite some time, Camden wanting to know what the game was and how it was played and even Peter not having an answer that satisfied him.

"We know a bit about Roman games, but this is Dark Ages stuff. It's a mystery."

They were into the bottom four or five inches of the grave now, and the finds were coming thick and fast: an amber bead and two large, square-headed brooches, one of which was very finely decorated and still had a delicate trace of mineralised cloth clinging to the back of it.

"We'll get a pattern of the weave out of that if we're lucky," said CD. "Hey, look what's here. I think I've struck iron."

In the next few minutes he uncovered several heavily rusted iron cleats, oblong plates in pairs, with the remains of rivets at each end holding them apart.

"It's the bed," said Patrick, oblivious to the camera drinking it all in behind him. "It's the bed, just like in the song. There were cleats like that at Swallowcliffe. They held the planks together. It's her wooden bed, and look, there's an eyelet. George Speake says cords went through those and held up a latticework support for the mattress. It's just the same."

" 'She lies there still on her wooden bed,' " said CD. "How does it go? 'The iron brackets are brown with rust.' Oh, hi, Jack."

Patrick whirled round and with dismay saw the cameraman. They'd been caught in the act. Jack looked around him, saw Camden was nowhere in the immediate vicinity, put a finger to his lips, and winked.

Patrick went on working away at exposing the whole of the sword blade, while the American uncovered more and more of the fragile remains of the bed, but it was Dozer, on the other side, who exclaimed next.

"I've found glass," he said, and that brought the crowd round.

"Can you get it out quite quickly?" said Camden, reappearing. "I've got to be in Oxford for a budget meeting at five."

"No, he can't," said Patrick curtly. "It's bad enough having to do things twice, but we won't do them fast, OK? This dig is not going to be prejudiced by your timetable."

"Hey, hang on. This meeting's in your interests—"

"Oh? In what way?"

"We're discussing putting in the cash to do a facial reconstruction on the skull. Wouldn't you like to see that?"

*Yes,* thought Patrick, *more than anything.* "No," he said. "It's old news, isn't it? They're always doing that on TV."

"We've got the chance of going a bit further," retorted Camden, stung.

"Really? How?"

"I can't say yet. That's what I have to go and talk about. So, how about it? I'd really like to get this in the can tonight."

"No. I told you, we don't take any risks. We go carefully and we record and we *don't* cut corners for the cameras."

As it turned out, they could easily have uncovered what they'd found in time, but by mutual, silent consent among Patrick, CD, and Dozer, they went very slowly indeed, making a meal of every aspect of the recording. This was more or less justified by what was emerging from the soil. It was an intricate beaker of pale blue-green glass, the conical cup part strengthened and ornamented by two tiers of curving glass arches, like flying buttresses. It was lying horizontally, and when the top half had been exposed and Camden had taken Jack and his camera away, Patrick called everyone over to see it. Bobby, who had been down at the farm since lunchtime, was walking back up the hill, and Patrick waited until she joined the back of the group before starting.

"Quite a day," he said. "We'll try and draw some conclusions tonight, but I just want to bring you all up to date on what we've found. First of all, there's the sword. We've got an excellent blade now, made of extremely good metal, and we're just starting to expose the hilt. It's clearly very fine work. There's Dozer's gaming board, which you've all seen; there are the coins, which are probably a necklace; and the brooches, one of which is very good indeed. We now know that she was indeed buried on a wooden bed, and the latest

thing to show up is a wonderful piece of glass, this clawed beaker."
As a joke, he called across, "Peter, I don't suppose you know anything about clawed beakers, do you?"

It didn't occur to Peter for one moment to take it as a joke. "A
bit," he said. "They're Saxon copies of a Roman style of beaker, but if
you look at those curved supports running up from the base, the
Saxon version is much cruder. The Roman ones often have dolphin
shapes, where the Saxons just used plain arcs of glass. A lot of them
seem to have been made in Kent, by the way."

"Thank you," said Patrick. He saw Bobby trying to crane round
the people standing in front of her.

"Now, the thing is," he went on, "these beakers are very often
found in pairs, so with a bit of luck we might even find its twin tomorrow."

Bobby had wormed her way past the others and had crouched
down by the edge of the trench, staring at the beaker.

"That's it for now," Patrick said. "Clear up your loose, get yourselves cleaned up, and after supper, we'll have the fireside chat again.
Plenty to talk about today." He watched Bobby walking away back
down the hill with a slight pang of regret. He'd wanted to share a bit
more of the day's events with her, especially the discovery of the bed.

An hour later, showered and changed into slightly cleaner jeans,
he was sitting outside his tent, watching the others playing with a
Frisbee, and brooding on the day. It should have felt like a success,
but instead, he could still trace the jagged edges of the morning's
brush with Camden and his file. A voice, Bobby's voice, broke in.

"Would you like a glass of wine?" she said.

"I would. Thank you." He took the glass she held out. "I wanted
to say something," he began.

"You're not very observant, are you?" she said. There was a curiously intent expression on her face.

It was the sort of thing Rachel used to say in their early days
when she'd had her hair done or bought new clothes. In their later
days, she hadn't expected him to notice. He stared at her. Not the
hair; she wore the same concealing woolen hat. Not the clothes, not
the face, the same disturbing face.

"What have I missed?" he said cautiously. She was watching him
like a hawk. He raised the glass to his lips and took a sip as he waited
for her reply but she just raised her eyebrows, and he realized the lip

of the glass was very thick and the stem was an intricate and bulky affair. He looked at what he was holding in his hand: The glass with the wine in it was the clawed beaker from the grave.

He stared at it, bewildered. "What have you done? You haven't taken it out? You shouldn't have done that! Why? Don't you realise—"

She was shaking her head. "It's still there," she said. "Just don't raise your hopes when you go looking for the matching one. I think you're already holding it."

"Don't be daft. This? This is the other one? How can it be?"

"I don't know."

"I mustn't drink *wine* out of it," Patrick said, torn between tipping out the contents and holding the beaker as carefully and upright as possible.

"Why not?" she replied. "That's what I've been doing for years. I had no idea what it was. It's even been in the dishwasher."

"Oh, no. You've been using it for years? How?"

"We've had it in the house ever since I can remember. I suppose it's something Dad found. I thought it was maybe Victorian or something, until I saw the one in the grave." She giggled. "If I'd known, I'd probably have been so nervous I'd have dropped it ages ago. I used to ask to have my bedtime milk in it when I was little."

"How could he have got it? He didn't dig this grave?"

"Ma told me he sometimes pulled stuff out of rabbit holes. Maybe it was that."

There was rabbit damage on the left side of the trench.

"Well, it could have been, I suppose. Maybe rabbits moved it near the surface and he saw it sticking out? Is that possible? It's a big thing for a rabbit to move. You must have realised it was special, surely?"

Bobby looked at him and shrugged. "The house is stacked with Dad's stuff."

"What sort of stuff?"

"Everything he ever found. It's all there. Joe spends a lot of time looking at it. You'll have to come and see it all, I suppose, then you'll understand."

"Definitely. When shall I come?"

"After supper? No, that won't do. After the fireside chat."

"Oh." Patrick imagined the two of them walking off together

into the dark and the whispering that would start all over again. He could suggest CD come, too, but he knew he didn't want to do that. He wanted the chance to look at all this stuff all by himself, whatever it was. He wanted the chance to see it all first, and maybe also the chance to hear its story from Bobby.

"Fine," he said, "after the fireside chat."

It came soon because dinner didn't hold anyone's attention for very long.

"Undercooked British root vegetable vindaloo," pronounced CD. "An unwise concept executed with a certain panache—or maybe it was potash, I couldn't be certain." He said it when he was sure Bobby couldn't hear.

Large quantities of the pub's best bitter, brought up in a plastic dustbin in the back of her Land Rover, helped a great deal.

Round the fire, Aidan spoke first, and it wasn't a question, it was an opinion. "Our lady there. Don't you think she was a bit of a sport, as well as being an archaeologist, of course?"

"How do you mean?"

"It wasn't just the sword and the shield. That gaming-board stuff. She was competitive, I think—someone who'd give the boys a run for their money. I like a woman like that."

Patrick sat in the dark listening, thinking of the women he'd turned to when life became exciting and Rachel seemed suddenly dull. Then he'd found there were women who egged him on, who played pool as snappily as he did, who drove as aggressively, predators who knew how to crank up the tension and how to make final surrender all the more delicious by it. They'd evoked a powerful response, all those sleek women whose clothes were foliage, not wrapping paper. He was astonished by how foreign all that felt now. That was not the nature of the buried woman of Wytchlow, this brave soul whose values were straightforward matters of life, death, and loyalty, whose vitality had reached out to touch them all from the grave where only bones remained.

"Aidan's right," said Maxwell. "She's like Zelda. A real warrior-woman. I bet she was beautiful."

"Who on earth is Zelda?" said Gaye, bewildered.

"Don't you know Zelda? The video game?"

"No, I most certainly do not."

"I didn't say she was like that," said Aidan, affronted. "She was a good woman, wasn't she? Not some kind of a cartoon. I just meant she was one to take on the world when she had to, and she enjoyed a laugh, or they wouldn't have put the game in there."

"Maybe she just liked to play quiet games at home," suggested Peter. "We don't have any idea what their games were like. If you found someone buried with a chessboard or a Monopoly set, you wouldn't immediately think they were a hell-raiser, would you?"

"Well, no, you wouldn't, but a set of poker dice, now, that would tell you something else." Aidan grinned and nudged his glasses up. "I agree with old Maxwell, though: I bet she was a beauty."

THERE WAS NEVER TIME TO PLAY GAMES AT THE HALL, AND WITH ALL HER BROTHERS DEAD, THERE WOULD HAVE BEEN NO ONE TO PLAY THEM WITH. HILD'S HUSBAND SPENT AS MUCH TIME OUT OF THE HALL AS HE COULD, KEEPING CLEAR OF CUTHWULF.

"I HAVE TO KEEP UP WITH THE TRAINING," HE TOLD HER WHEN SHE TOOK HIM TO TASK. "WE HAVE TO HAVE MEN WHO CAN FIGHT. LOOK WHAT I'VE GOT. SIX SLAVES WHO'D RUN AWAY AT THE FIRST CHANCE; OLD ALBRICHT, WHO MEANS WELL BUT NEEDS BOTH HANDS TO LIFT UP A SWORD; AND THE FAERPINGAS FAMILY. THEY'RE THE ONLY ONES WHO ARE ANY DAMN GOOD, AND THERE'S ONLY THE FATHER AND TWO OF THE SONS WHO ARE BIG ENOUGH."

CUTHWULF STARTED COUGHING AGAIN, BEHIND THE CURTAIN, AND THEY BOTH LOOKED TOWARDS THE SOUND.

"WE CAN'T RELY ON YOUR FATHER. I KNOW HE COUNTS FOR TWENTY, BUT HE'S NOT WELL."

HILD NEVER EVEN SAW THE GAMING BOARD IN HER LIFETIME, NEVER EVEN KNEW OF ITS EXISTENCE. IT BELONGED TO HER HUSBAND'S KIN, AND IT WENT INTO THE GRAVE AS A SURREPTITIOUS GIFT TO ATONE FOR WHAT THEY DID AND TO MAINTAIN THAT IT WAS ALL A MATTER OF UNFORTUNATE CHANCE.

"We might find out," Patrick said cautiously. "Kenny Camden's talking about doing a facial reconstruction."

"Does that take a long time?"

"Not so long as we get her skull out in one piece. They just scan it into a computer and build it up from that."

"Take her head off?" exclaimed Gaye, aghast. "You can't do that. That's horrible."

"I hate to tell you this," said CD, "but you may not have noticed. She's been dead for rather a long time. Her head's already off. It's just another disconnected bone."

None of them seemed to like that thought, and Gaye wasn't leaving it there. "Oh, but I was thinking we'd, well . . . we'd keep her together. Treat her properly, you know."

"We have to take the bones out of the grave. They need proper examination. They come out one at a time."

"I'm starting to see what that vicar means," said Gaye. "While they're lying there, she's still a person, isn't she? Her bones are the way they were when she was alive. Are we really going to take them apart?"

"I don't know how graphic you want me to get, guys and gals, but that ain't exactly right," said CD. "Those bones are where they dropped when she fell to pieces."

"You're not to talk about her like that," said Gaye crossly. Then, probably to change the subject, she said, "All those Roman things she had. Do you think she knew who the Romans were?"

"Ah, now that's an interesting question," said the American. "The British knew, didn't they? They'd been living with the Romans for four hundred years. The question is, did they get the chance to tell the Saxons their Roman stories or did they just get their heads chopped off? We don't have any clear idea yet of which way it worked, inter-marriage or genocide. I guess if our lady up there was maybe part Brit-ish and part Saxon, then she'd know about the Romans. It was only two or three hundred years back. That's not many lifetimes. If old Joe can still keep a song going that's a thousand years old, who's doubt-ing it?"

"Where is Joe?" said Dozer. He turned to Bobby. "Any chance of seeing your bro tonight, love?"

"I don't think so," she said. "He was loading up his backpack with food when I left the house. That usually means he's going to be off somewhere all night."

"Where does he go?"

"I haven't a clue. He's always back by morning to start work."

"Shame, that. I was looking forward to another surprise." Dozer spoke for them all.

"I know the surprise I'd like," put in Gaye. "I'd like to find that other glass beaker thing. I hope it's in my bit of the trench."

Patrick was about to say she couldn't because it was in his tent, before he realised he hadn't yet told anyone else about the surprise Bobby had brought to him. He exchanged a glance of complicity with her in the firelight. The talk seemed to run out of steam after that.

"Might go down the pub," said Dozer.

"Good plan," said CD. "Who's coming?"

Everyone was except Patrick and Bobby.

"I might come later," he said, "I've got a few things to do."

Bobby took the dirty dishes down the hill in the Land Rover, and when the others had all gone to the village, he walked down after her, every step heightening his anticipation. What he was telling himself was that it was all about her father's finds, stacked up and waiting. He felt he was about to strip away another layer.

## CHAPTER TWENTY-TWO

THERE WERE RAISED VOICES
from the farmyard as Patrick
came down towards the back
of the barn—Bobby's voice and
a man's. Then there was deri-
sive male laughter and a door slamming, and
as Patrick came round the corner into the
yard, he saw the taillights of a car swinging
into the road. Bobby was standing in the
middle of the yard, looking furious.

"What's the matter?" he asked.

"He is."

"Who was it? I didn't see."

"Roger bloody Little, our so-called Chairman of the School Board."

"Your friend and mine. What did he
want?"

She waved the letter she was holding.
"Do you know what this is?" She sounded in-
credulous. "He's given me notice that they're
applying for a court injunction to stop us taking the children out of school for May Day."

"That's a bit out of proportion."

"It's completely absurd. It's just vindictive, that's all."

"You can fight it, can't you? There must be a hearing of some sort. You can give your side."

"Oh, sure. Just imagine how that will be. Me and a few of the mothers, against three pillars of society? Can you imagine any judge taking the slightest notice of us? No judge is going to think it makes any difference which day we have it on, not when Little and Campling and Reverend bloody-double-barrelled are all claiming the whole thing's a modern invention anyway. I haven't got any evidence." She crumpled up the letter in her hand and he realised she was on the edge of tears. "Anyway, May Day sounds a bit left-wing to people like judges. We haven't a chance. They'll say I'm just a troublemaker."

"Is that the way the village sees you?"

"No, not the village. Just people like them."

"I'll help you."

"Will you? How?"

"In any way I can."

It was hollow but it was better than saying nothing, and he was genuinely moved by her plight.

She shook her head. "Come on in. Sorry, that's not much of a welcome. Would you like another glass of wine?"

"Out of an ordinary glass?" he said, to try to make her laugh.

"I can probably find something plastic if you're happier with it."

The wide front door led into a big, stone-flagged hallway with a beamed ceiling, running straight through the house to an equally large door the far side. The hall was lit only by a dim bulb, and she led him through to a big kitchen with an old Aga and a huge table. There were no pretensions to country chic here. The Aga had been roughly painted in dirty white and the surface of the table was covered in cracked Formica. He followed her through the kitchen to another room, a parlour perhaps.

"Have a look around. I'll get the wine."

A rug-covered sofa and two old brown armchairs, their leather upholstery roughened to dry, flaky sandpaper, almost filled the room, but the walls were completely lined with shelving, on which sat a myriad of objects. Patrick stood in front of them, staring. It was chaos, the sort of dusty jumble you'd find in an old-fashioned small-town museum. He picked up a tiny pottery oil lamp with a hand grip at one side, clearly Roman. Next to the lamp was half a medieval floor tile, inlaid with a fleur-de-lis pattern, and beside that, a heavily damaged double-sided bone comb which would need expert inspection to pin it down to any precise date in the last two thousand years.

"It's not great wine, I'm afraid," said Bobby, coming back in with two glasses.

"I'm sure it's fine," he said, taking a sip and discovering she was right. He was staring at what he had just spotted next to the comb: two small bronze pyramids, an inch or so across. He picked one of them up. It was finely made, decorated with some sort of filigree work.

"Look at these," he said. "They're Saxon."

"What are they?"

"I don't quite know, but they were part of a scabbard. I think they're the ends of the straps that secured the sword. Where did they come from?"

"I haven't a clue." She was preoccupied. "Have you any idea what happens if you break an injunction?"

"We could ask Peter," he said, and won a smile out of her. "I think it's pretty serious stuff if you do, because it's contempt of court."

"What does that mean?"

"Well, don't hold me to it, but I think it means the penalty isn't to do with the seriousness of what you do. It all turns into something else. You're offending the dignity of the courts, or something like that."

"So they lock you up?"

"I think so. Don't go *that* far, will you? It's not worth it."

"You don't know that. I keep wondering what *she* would have done."

"Our woman in the grave?"

"Yes."

"What she would have done about the May Day parade?"

"I'm pretty sure she wouldn't have let them stop her."

"I'm sure she wouldn't, but you're not going to take your sword to the vicar, are you?"

"Oh, just give me the chance. You would if you were me. I saw the way you went for Little after he trashed the site."

"I'm not proud of that."

"You should be. You came alive."

"A bit too alive."

"Patrick, the way I see it, if it's in a good cause, it's justified. Stop being frightened of yourself. Anyway, that's not why you're here. What do you think of our collection?"

"Extraordinary. You should get someone in to have a look at it."

"I have. You're here."

"I meant a professional."

"I thought you were one."

"Oh. No, I'm just a new boy. I'm not an expert on anything much. Get Peter up here. He'll tell you about all of it, I expect."

"Joe wouldn't like that. I know he approves of you. He wouldn't want lots of strangers going over this stuff."

"Why? Anyway, what makes you think he approves of me?"

"I just know it." She looked at him, so full of crackling life that he felt a spark would jump across if he stretched out a hand. "As for why . . . my mum used to say Joe appointed himself guardian of Dad's treasures, and she told me Dad always said that if a museum got their hands on them, they'd be put away in boxes and nobody would ever see them at all."

"True enough."

"I once broke a little bowl. I was tiny. Joe got so upset."

"Was it something special?"

"I don't know. He mended it. It's here somewhere."

She searched the shelves. Standing with her back to Patrick, her figure and her way of holding herself seemed to him so like Rachel's at the start of it all, in their love-soaked years, that he longed to get up and go to her and put his arms round her and bury his face in her neck as he would once have done. She turned round with the bowl and raised her eyebrows at whatever it was she saw in his face. At that moment, Patrick lost the ability to tell who she was or when they both were.

"Is something wrong?" she said. He took a step and his arms came out to her and he saw her eyes widen. He stopped then, recognising her as Bobby, and looked down at the bowl and took that instead.

"Late medieval," he said in a voice he didn't recognise.

"Um . . . is it? You can see where Joe mended it. It's the only time he's ever been cross with me that I can remember. I suppose breaking something that was Dad's was pretty unforgivable. Joe minded about it because Dad wasn't around anymore to mind. He was Dad's boy. He knew him properly. I was too young." She took the bowl back out of Patrick's hands and ran her fingertip against the crack in its surface. "We do mind, though, don't we? When something old gets broken, when a painting's destroyed, or an old house burns down."

It seemed safer to talk about huge ideas, about things that were outside this small room, which seemed to him to be vibrating with something very disturbing.

"It's all got to go someday," he told her. "Our planet's only got a finite life."

"It's a long time until the sun explodes," she said dryly, "or do you think we're going to get hit by a meteorite first?"

"Well, certainly a meteorite," he said, "but Europe won't last that long. There'll be another ice age long before that. They last eighty thousand years, you know. There's only ten or twenty thousand years in between them. The next one's coming whether we like it or not."

"My goodness, that's cheerful. Have I got time to sit down and finish my wine?"

They sat opposite each other in the armchairs.

"I mean it," he said. "The ice will come back. It always does. All of this England of ours and most of Europe is going to be scoured clean by enormous glaciers at some point quite soon in geological time, long, long before the sun eats us up. Mankind will have to move south again, and we won't be taking all this with us. The ice isn't going to spare the archaeology."

"Is that really how it is?"

"Yes."

"Well, I sometimes think I wouldn't mind," she mused. "The poor old land needs a rest. There's a place up by the wood where you can see the road going into Oxford, and now, when it's a clear night, you can even see the headlights on the M40, solid lines of light. All those cars, all those people, and we go on growing, more and more of us. Where it used to be dark fields at night, you can see the Oxford streetlights making the clouds glow. All the new developments they've built, and now these horrible houses up here, where Little's dug up the villa. I'm going to be looking straight at those every time I walk into the farmyard."

"I'm sorry about those houses," he said. "Maybe you could plant some trees."

"Maybe."

"The roads, they're just a spider's web. You shouldn't get it out of proportion. Suppose you were in a balloon, going up and up. They'd look pretty horrible to start with, then you'd go higher and you'd start seeing how big the rest of the country is. Then finally, those lights would get smaller and smaller until they disappeared."

"I'm not convinced," she said.

"Did you know that fifty years ago, you could get the world's population standing up on the Isle of Wight with the tide in and they wouldn't even get their feet wet? And did you know you could still do it today except you'd have to do it when the tide was out?"

"I never liked the Isle of Wight anyway. I can't make you out, Patrick. Are you a pessimist or an optimist? You started off threatening glaciers next Friday and now you say it's all OK."

"I'm not sure which I am," he answered. "It's a personal thing, isn't it? It's about how your chemistry lets you live your life. I don't expect the best or the worst. I think I've come to expect nothing. What does that make me?"

"A nihilist?" she suggested. "The worst of all."

"So tell me what was your father like."

"I didn't know him properly," she said sadly.

"How come he got so interested in all this?" He gestured toward the shelves.

"Ah, I do know that. That was the peas."

"Peas?"

"Come on, I'll show you."

He followed her out to the hall, where she took a big lantern from the bench and opened the heavy door at the back of the cross-passage. They stepped out into a walled vegetable garden, and she shone the flashlight on a well-dug bed with hoops of wire netting protecting it.

"They're not showing through yet, but those are the peas. They started him off."

"You'll have to explain."

"The story Mum told me was that when Dad was a kid, some

time in the 1930's, I think, a man turned up here to buy a horse from my granddad. Apparently, this man had been working in Egypt with Howard Carter on Tutankhamen's tomb. There, you see? You said you wouldn't laugh."

"I couldn't help it. Every archaeological tall story has Tutankhamen in it somewhere. Go on."

"Well, when this man was about to take the horse away, he saw Dad looking sad because he hated it when any of the animals went, and the man reached in his pocket and he gave Dad this tiny packet of peas, all dried up, and he told Dad they were very special because they came from a jar in a pharaoh's tomb and if he planted them in nice wet soil and looked after them carefully, they might grow."

"And these are them? I thought you were going to say he swapped them for the horse, like Jack and the Beanstalk. Was he very disappointed when they didn't grow?"

"These are them. Pharaonic peas, we call them. Dad harvested them every year and replanted them. They're never very big and they don't taste too good, but that's not the point. Mum always cooked a special meal every year at pea-picking time. If you come back in the summer, I'll cook you some."

"Kenny Camden would love *that* story."

"Absolutely not. Don't even think about it. I don't want him here, crawling all over this place. I've seen what he's trying to do to you. Joe wouldn't have it. You haven't been talking about Joe to him, have you?"

"No, of course not. You heard him in the tent. He knows Joe exists, and he's heard a bit about the song, but I don't think he realises Joe is anything to do with you."

"I really want it to stay that way. I hate it when people make fun of Joe. He's quite innocent in most ways. You won't tell Camden anything, will you?"

"I promise I won't breathe a word about Joe or the songs to Camden, OK?"

"OK. And you be careful. I've seen the expression on his face when he looks at you. You're just camera fodder to him. Remember that. He's made sure everyone in the village knows who you are."

"Has he?" That was an unpleasant thought. "You mean who I was."

"If you like."

"What happened to your mum?"

"She died three years ago. That's when I had to come back and help Joe run the farm. He couldn't do it on his own."

"Come back? Where from? I assumed . . ."

"That I'd always been a farmer? Other people have complicated stories, too, you know." She saw his reaction. "Sorry," she said, "but you asked for that. You shouldn't make assumptions."

"So where were you?"

"A long way away and another world completely."

"What were you doing?"

"I thought they would have told you in the village."

"I've hardly spent any time in the village."

She shut off abruptly. "It's not the right time for life stories."

"I didn't mean to—"

"You don't want to talk about yours. I don't want to talk about mine. Isn't that fair?"

"I suppose so." All at once, he could feel how it hurt to be shut out.

"Let's go in," she said. "You wanted to see something. The things Joe sang about. The axes and the carving."

He followed her back inside and to the shelves.

"Here's one of the axes."

She handed him a napped flint hand-ax. He took it and gave it a brief glance.

"I know I've probably been fairly unreasonable to you," he said.

"I think I've made a lot of allowances for things I can only really guess at," she said. "I have to admit it is hard when you suddenly treat me like your worst enemy, especially when it's in public. Can you tell me why you do that?"

"There's something I find very difficult to tell you, something that would explain it."

"I think you'd better try, then."

He looked at the shelves, searching for the right words to start, words that would explain the nature of the turmoil she had accidentally created in him at first sight. His gaze fell on a photo frame, down on the bottom shelf, a small photo of a man in some kind of tunic, smiling at the camera.

"Who's this?" he said, picking it up.

She took it out of his grasp, almost snatching, then stood still, seeming to weigh the picture in her hands.

"A deal," she said. "You tell me this difficult thing of yours, in full, with nothing left out, and if I think you've told me enough I'll decide whether to answer that question."

"Not much of a deal."

"It's the only one on offer."

"All right," he said, but he still didn't know if he could do it. "The thing is . . ."

She stood waiting.

"The really difficult thing, the thing that is the reason I have behaved rather, well . . . oddly towards you is that I find just looking at you is really disturbing. You look so like Rachel that I keep getting you muddled up."

"I look like your wife? The woman you left?"

"Not just a bit like her. *Exactly* like her. Well, not even that. Exactly like she would have looked by now if life had treated her better."

"Life?"

"Well, no. Me. If *I* had treated her better. If I hadn't drained everything that mattered out of her."

She was shaking her head. "So what does that mean? I'm having trouble here."

"Rachel is dead, Bobby. My wife is dead. So is David, my son. They are both dead because I turned into some sort of crazy person who forgot why I married Rachel and how I loved David."

"So I'm a painful reminder of that? Are you saying you can't bear to look at me?"

"No, not that. You just take me straight back to the last time life was good, to the time when I was really in love with Rachel. Every time I look at you, for a moment it's like life's given me another chance. And then I realise it hasn't."

She turned her face away. "That's a heavy responsibility to put on me, Patrick. I'm not her and I'm nothing to do with your guilt. I'm sorry, but I'm me and I can't do anything about that." She frowned. "Actually, I have to say what you've just said pisses me off a bit."

"Why? It's not really about you."

"That's why. I've been quite glad that I seemed to be someone you felt you could talk to. I wanted to see if I could help. I thought we had some sort of point of contact."

"Don't we?"

"No, it seems we don't. I've looked at you when you've been looking at me, and there's been something open there between us. Now you're saying it's all just an accident caused by the shape of my nose or something. That's just not very flattering."

His mouth almost betrayed him. His voice almost said there was much more to it than that, but his reason once again overcame his emotion.

"I'm not very good at dealing with this sort of stuff these days. I'm sorry if I've managed to upset you again."

"Part of your problem," she said, going to the fireplace and standing with her back to him, "might just be that you think you're the only person in the world who has been through it. Well, I don't feel like keeping my half of the bargain. I don't feel like telling you about this"—she waved the photo at him—"because I don't suppose it can possibly match up to what's happened to *you,* not for a moment." Her voice was sarcastic.

"I'd like to hear about him," Patrick said quietly.

"Well, I'll just give you the headlines, shall I?"

"Yes."

"He's . . ." Her voice caught. "He was somebody I was in love with. He got sick. I couldn't save him. He died. Right? Is that enough for now? One death for me, two deaths for you. You lead two to one. Thirty-fifteen to Patrick."

"Bobby, I am so—"

"No, no, no. Let's not get into who is sorrier than who. Let's just call it quits and get some sleep. I've got an early morning. You know the way out."

He was halfway across the yard with his heart in his boots when he heard an upper window open.

"Patrick," she called.

He stopped and turned; she was silhouetted in a dormer window. "Yes?"

Her voice was softer and a little hesitant. "I just wanted to say you should keep an ear open tonight."

"What for?"

"There's been a bit too much talk round the village. The TV people, really. They've been stoking it up. There's a few hotheads talking about all the stuff you're supposed to have found. They're saying there's some gold around. Things like that."

"Are you saying they might try to steal something?"

"I don't know. I'd be happier if I knew you were watching out."

*That's not why she's saying it,* he thought to himself. *She just wants the night to end on a different note, so she's picked on this because it's where we can find common ground.* He felt grateful to her for letting him walk up the hill with a lighter heart.

"OK," he said. "I'll listen out. Sleep well."

"You, too."

Of course, after that, however well he understood why she'd said it and why it was probably an exaggeration, it was hard to sleep. The others disturbed him coming back from the pub, even though they were quite subdued and seemed to go straight to their tents. Something clattered his tin plates outside in the grass an hour later and he came out of half sleep with his heart hammering. When he stuck his head out of the fly-sheet, there was nothing to see, but the noise continued and it was a relief to find the tiny hedgehog who was solely responsible. After that, he blew up his soggy air mattress and lay on his back thinking of the evening and wishing he'd found different words, words that might have gone down better. It was hard when he knew he mustn't let her think he was attracted to her. That wouldn't be fair. It wasn't her he was attracted to, it was just a ghost. Those thoughts became intolerable, going round and round in his head, and he decided to get out of the tent and walk round the hilltop.

There was a lot of cloud, and the remains of the moon shone through the fringes of it. In that tricky light, the square silhouette of the grave cover seemed to be moving against the sky, an illusion caused by the movement of the clouds behind it. He walked towards it and saw he'd been right the first time. It *was* moving. The moonlight faded as a cloud drifted across it, and he could no longer see clearly, but he started to walk as fast and as quietly as he could towards the trench. Moonlight broke through again. Now he could see that the cover stood to one side of the trench, and close to it there were two figures ahead of him, twenty-five yards away. They seemed to be rushing towards each other. He heard the sound of a fist landing on flesh, a cry, and another blow.

"Stop there, whoever you are!" he shouted, then both of the figures were running away and he was racing after them. He caught the nearer one easily, grabbed at the man's arm, tripped him with a sweep of his leg, and fell on top of him in the grass.

"Jesus Christ, get off me!" said a woman's voice. "You stupid arsehole. He's got away now."

"Bobby? Oh, shit. Sorry. Did he hurt you?"

"Not nearly as much as you did."

Flashlights were going on in the tents now.

"Who's that?" shouted Dozer.

"Me. Patrick," he shouted back. "There was a guy trying to nick stuff. He's run off towards the village."

"Right, mate. I'll 'ead 'im off at the pass," shouted Dozer. "Come on, CD, you ride shotgun." He lumbered towards his car with CD in pursuit as Aidan and Peter arrived, panting, shining their torches on Bobby. She was sitting on the grass feeling her cheek.

"No blood," she reported. "He almost missed, but his knuckles just caught me."

"I heard two blows."

"You did," she said, sounding happier. "The first one was me punching him in the eye."

"Did you see who it was?"

"I saw his outline."

"Did you recognize him?"

"I didn't have to, really, did I? Whoever's got the black eye in the village tomorrow might just be our main suspect."

"So you don't know who it was?"

"I didn't say that." Bobby sounded pleased with herself. "I know exactly who it was."

"Are you going to tell us?"

"It wouldn't surprise me if Roger Little keeps his face well out of sight for a few days."

"It was Little? Really?"

"Really."

"Why would he do that?"

"Because he's a greedy man who wants a bit of everything, and it's probably been driving him mad wondering what sort of things we might be finding up here. I knew it would be him. That's why I warned you."

"But why were *you* up here? You asked *me* to listen out."

"And I don't think you really believed me, did you? Was I right?"

"Well, I wasn't asleep—but I suppose you were. You're usually right about most things," said Patrick. He looked around. "Where were you?"

"In a sleeping bag. Over there on the grass."

"Well, you can go home and get some proper sleep now. Have you got something to put on your cheek?"

"Yes, but what are you going to do? He might come back. There's a few others might have a go, too."

"I'll move my tent up here in the morning," said Patrick, "right next to the trench."

"And the rest of tonight?"

He looked at the grave cover and felt a wisp of drizzle on his cheek. "If we put this back over it, there's enough room for me to sleep inside. I'll get my sleeping bag."

# CHAPTER TWENTY-THREE

IN THE HALF DARK, IVORY BONES gleaming from the grave next to him, Patrick sat upright, his hair prickling on the back of his neck, as an invisible voice sang.

*There came the time of the old King's death*
*And he blessed her with his final breath.*
*He gave his sword to be handed down*
*To the boy who would one day wear his*
    *crown.*

*They buried him at the battle stone*
*And the news went out that he had gone.*
*Far to the east, the traitors heard*
*Of the end of the King with the chicken*
    *sword.*

*The Queen again grew big with child*
*As it came to winter, cold and wild.*
*She woke one night from a warning dream*
*And heard the watchman's dying scream.*

Trying to sleep when the night's fuss had died down, Patrick had drifted instead into a trance, his mind teasing at the idea that there might be some simple trick to time. Here he was lying next to the woman and her child. Space was right, only time was wrong, and if he could only find that trick, he could clothe her bones in the right flesh with his imagination. Then he might bridge the gap to her just as easily as reaching out to touch the edge of the trench where she now lay.

He didn't know he had slept, but he woke to find the ground drumming against his ear. The earth was telegraphing solid footfalls coming at him out of the darkness. He was disorientated, immediately aware that he was in an unfamiliar place, then he remembered. He and the German Queen had been sleeping side by side. He sat up, holding his breath. The footsteps were coming from the other side of the hill, away from the camp, away from the village, away from the farm. Who was this being who was striding purposefully towards him in the darkness?

He thought of shouting, of getting out of his sleeping bag to prepare for whatever was coming. Propelled into fear by the speed of his awakening, he did neither. Instead, he stared towards the doorway as the seconds stretched out. Could it be another intruder from the village? The moon had not yet set, and the tent fabric was a screen on which a pale shadow now loomed up, just a head and shoulders at first, silhouetted at ground level, swaying with each step, growing and rising to tower over him as the steps came nearer. He could sense the open grave next to him, smell the thick richness of the earth, but he couldn't look at her bones because he couldn't tear his eyes away from the tent flap ahead of him. It was the flimsiest of barriers against an unknown intruder and he felt he was only moments away from violence or horror, he did not know which.

The footsteps stopped. The shadow collapsed to half its height, as if kneeling. There was a moment when he almost called out, "Who's there?" but he hesitated, unsure how to make the words come out strong and straight, and in that moment a man's voice began to sing quietly. Joe, back from his wanderings and unaware that he was overheard, was paying a visit to the German Queen.

The singing ended and Patrick wondered if Joe would open the flap and, if he did, whether he would be embarrassed to find he had an unexpected audience.

Then Joe spoke.

"I've come here to say I'm sorry, Queen," he said, and Patrick, astonished, strained to listen, knowing it was far too late to reveal his presence. When he thought no one alive could hear him, then Joe, it seemed, could find words.

". . . that is, I've come to say sorry if I need to, but the thing is, I don't know if I need to or not. I brought them here, it's true, and they've disturbed you, but they've let you see the daylight again and they know that you're special because I've told them. I've made sure they know your story."

He spoke slowly, with a heavy weight of thought in every syllable.

"Anyway, I can't help thinking that what was really you has gone into this whole hilltop now. They've disturbed your bones, but bones weren't what you laughed with and loved with and fought with. They were just, I don't know . . . I'd say they were just the easel on which your picture was drawn."

This was a Joe of unsuspected eloquence.

"All the other parts were what mattered—your brain, your heart, the muscles that made you smile and frown, the eyes, the skin—those were the parts that made you what you were. Oh, yes, and my dad told me what his dad told him, that you were really something. He said that when you died it must have been like a punch in the guts for all those who loved you, a punch that takes the wind out of you when you know that you shouldn't have taken all those other moments for granted and that now there is just the bitter ache of the lonely future. That's why they put you up here, where they could look up at your mound every day and remember you from down where they lived. My dad told me you lived where we live now. Anyway, my lady, when I look at you, I think those other parts that were really you have gone into the ground here, and they've helped make a million blades of grass and a great sprawl of flowers every year, and those have seeded and spread and carried you across all the hills, so I hope you don't mind what's happened too much. Because of my wish to see the great lady of the song, the brave Queen, these bones of yours will be taken out from their place here quite soon now and probably poked about and looked at one way and another. I really hope you don't mind. There is one more thing, which you might say is the good side, and I've put it in a little verse for you."

He stopped and cleared his throat and spoke his verse slowly and quietly:

> *It's not a time for shedding tears*
> *It's not a time to mourn*
> *For after waiting all these years*
> *You'll see your baby born.*

Then he walked off.

Patrick kept still long after he heard the last of his footsteps. Only then did he quietly unzip the tent flap and look out. On the grass in front of him was a bunch of spring flowers in a glass jar, another offering from Joe. Patrick went back inside, holding them, moved near to tears by what he'd heard and, looking down at the skeletons in the grave, the adult and the unborn child which would soon leave its mother's body for the first time, he put them on the grass at the head of the trench and said, "These are for you, and I, too, am sorry for the disturbance." That didn't seem enough.

"I'll do what I can," he added, "to make sure you are put back again, here, in this grave, when we've finished."

He stared at her and tried to imagine her, badly wanting to find that trick for looking back across the years to the brief flesh. Of course he failed. Instead, Joe's words on loss came back to him. *The punch that takes the wind out of you and the bitter ache of the lonely future . . .*

He'd learnt what that meant. Loss, when it came to Patrick in Perugia, had a shape and a feel to it, a long balloon inflating upward from his stomach through his chest cavity, driving a prickling blizzard of tears ahead of it. It had a sound, too, a shout that burst out of him, as loud as he could make it, but never loud enough to drown the pain that made it. He looked down at the dead mother and her dead baby and, for the first time, he really understood that he was not, after all, the first person to whom such a thing had happened.

"I wasn't any good as a father," he said aloud to the woman in the grave. "I shouldn't even be presuming to talk to you. I meant to be a good father. I was going to be better. I was ready to change. I was going back to say I'm sorry to them both, I'm sorry and I'll do it your way. For David's sake. No, that's not true. It was for *my* sake."

He stared down at her skull, slumped away in the earth.

"I would love to see your face," he said. "You might have stopped me, I think. I needed someone brave enough to stand up to me and strong enough to defend me. Poor Rachel. I broke her. There was no excuse for that. It wasn't her fault. I needed someone like you."

He stood there in silence for a while, staring at the fragile skeleton of the baby, still nestled above its mother's pelvis.

"We'll be very careful with you," he whispered. "I give you my word."

Next to her lay the sword, and he permitted himself to recognise his deep belief that it was indeed her father's great sword. Seeing the first light of dawn through the side of the tent and knowing there would be no more sleep that night, he went to get his trowel. In the next two hours, as all the creatures who go by the sun's clock woke and went about their business and only man slept on, he excavated the last hidden part of the sword, talking occasionally to the woman and her child while he worked.

"Oh, look at this," he said as the trowel revealed the first sight of the hand-guard. "Silver? No, silver inlaid into iron."

There were simple swirling patterns along the edges of a broad guard, a thick bar across the top of the blade, strong enough to catch an opposing blow.

"Did you really use this sword? It's a wonderful weapon, but it must have been heavy for you."

The tang of the sword blade passed through the hole in the guard; at the other end of the hand grip, it was clenched tightly into the pommel, a smaller bar with faint decoration just visible. There were traces of something softer on the grip in between, bone maybe, fragmented but still sticking to the rusty tang in rotting lumps. He thought back to the scabbard fittings he'd seen at Bobby's house. They could have gone with this sword.

"CD's got to see this before I do any more," said Patrick. "I'll go and get him. Bye for now."

"CD's snoring in his tent," said Bobby, behind him as if he had conjured her.

Patrick spun round and stood up. "Hello," he said. "How embarrassing."

"What's embarrassing?"

"Well, you know. To be caught talking to our friend here."

"It would have been rude not to," said Bobby, seemingly quite serious.

"Yes." Should he tell her of the night's astonishing visit from her brother? Was it trespassing into a private area? He saw the bruise on her cheek.

"Let me have a look at that," he said. He took a step towards her and held the flap of the tent up to let more light in as he inspected it. Across her cheekbone was a purple swelling that looked like exotic makeup. He reached out his hand and felt it gently, and his finger-tips tingled. "Does it hurt?"

"Only when you press it," she said, and he pulled his hand away sharply.

"Joke," she added. "Anyway, I came to say it was my turn to apologise. It was just a bad day yesterday, that's all."

"There's no need. It was very brave of you to go for our intruder. I hope you're right about who it was."

"I'm sure I am. Anyway, I'd better go and get the food on. . . ."

"Bobby. Wait a minute." He'd reached a decision.

She turned back to him.

"Joe was here before dawn."

"I heard him come back in very early. Did he disturb you?"

"Not at all. Well, yes, he did. He scared the hell out of me until I realised it was him. The thing is, he didn't know I was inside here, and he stayed outside."

"And?"

"And . . . he spoke."

She nodded. "He does sometimes, you know, in the pub. It's po-etry. He can do poetry. I suppose it's because it's a performance."

"No. There *was* a poem, but that was right at the end. I heard him. He spoke completely normally. Rather better than normally. He was kneeling outside here and talking to her. He was apologising for the fact that we're disturbing her."

"Did he speak for long?" she said incredulously.

"Well, yes. He said some very beautiful things. He said her bones were just an easel on which her body had been painted and that the grass and flowers on the hilltop were her real remains. You're crying."

"Stupid. I can't help it. I know he does do that. I've sometimes heard him when he thinks I'm asleep. I only *wish* he could talk to me and not just to himself."

"He was talking to her," said Patrick, pointing at the grave.

"Someone who's been dead for a thousand years? Well, that's talking to yourself really, isn't it?" She blinked the tears away. "No, I'm glad. I always knew there was a lot going on in there. I'm glad you heard it. Did he find out you were here?"

"No. I think he'd be horrified if he knew I'd heard. Bobby, that reminds me. The night before last, when they got me singing. You were crying then, too, weren't you? You got up and left and I never even asked you why."

"Oh, do you really want to know?"

"Yes."

"It's complicated."

"Try me."

"Well, first I was worried because I could see you started to sing something that was painful for you. Then you stopped and played that other stuff and I suddenly saw the real Patrick. You just lost yourself in the music and it was beautiful."

"And that made you cry?"

"Almost. Not quite. We farmers are made of tougher stuff. No, it was something you sang. It just happened to be a very painful song for me."

There was a long silence.

"Do you want to tell me?"

"No, some other time. I've got breakfast to make. Play for us again before this is all over, won't you?"

"Only if you tell me what songs I mustn't sing."

"No, we can't lead our lives that way. We just have to learn to hear them differently. By the way, when *will* it be over? There can't be that much more to do up here once you've finished in the grave."

"It depends on my boss and on Camden, I suppose. There's three or four days' more work here."

"Is that all? Well, I'd better get on."

EVERYTHING THEY BELIEVED IN TOLD THEM THEY
SHOULD BURY THE CHICKEN SWORD WITH CUTHWULF
BY THE BATTLE STONE, PUT UP ON THE SPOT WHERE
HE VANQUISHED THE KILLERS OF THREE OF HIS SONS.
CUTHWULF WOULD NEED A SWORD TO FIGHT THE DEMONS
HE WOULD MEET IN HIS JOURNEY THROUGH DEATH.

ÆTHELMUND DECIDED THEY SHOULDN'T. HE INSISTED THE SWORD WAS THEIR ONLY HOPE.

"MY BLADE GOES WITH ME TO DEATH" HAD BEEN THE LAST COHERENT WORDS, APART FROM OATHS, THAT CUTHWULF HAD SPOKEN BEFORE THE FINAL CONVULSION.

"IT'S BEEN DONE BEFORE," ÆTHELMUND SAID. "MY UNCLE WAS BURIED WITH A COPY OF HIS BEST SWORD. IN DEATH, IT'S THE SPIRIT OF THE SWORD THAT COUNTS, NOT THE METAL."

THAT NIGHT HE CARVED A WOODEN SWORD, THE SAME LENGTH AND SHAPE AS THE CHICKEN SWORD. THEN, IN A SOMBRE MOOD, HE ALSO CARVED A MINIATURE.

"IF YOU EVER NEED HELP," HE TOLD THEM, "AND I AM NOT HERE, THIS IS MY FAMILY'S SUMMONING SIGNAL."

THEY BURIED CUTHWULF WITH THE BIG WOODEN BLADE IN THE CHICKEN SWORD'S SCABBARD AT THE FOOT OF THE BATTLE STONE. HILD WAS SURE SHE SHOULD BE FEELING SORROW AT HIS DEATH, INSTEAD OF MERELY FEAR THAT THEY WERE NOW UNPROTECTED.

The stone stood there for more than four hundred years. Then, at the time of the Norman invasion, it was toppled by the undermining work of badgers digging their sett beneath it. Many years later, a patient farmer hollowed it out with hammer and chisel, and it now stood, unregarded, in Bobby's yard, the stone drinking trough on which Patrick had sat in the dark.

A CONVOY OF CARS BROUGHT HESCROFT, CAMDEN, JACK, and an unfamiliar iron-haired woman just as the diggers were ready to start work.

"This is Celia Longworth," announced Hescroft. "She's our bone person. Got a few things to chat about in a minute or two."

CD had already been gloating over the sword, and now Patrick brought them up-to-date with it.

"It's a very fine weapon, according to CD. He says there's one almost identical to it in the Ashmolean, and two in the British Museum." They collected the American and went up to look at it, and Celia Longworth gave a cry of excitement when she saw it.

"Yes!" she said, "I worked in the Ashmolean for a long time. My goodness me, you're quite right. It is very, very like the earlier of the Abingdon swords. The quality of the work on the hilt doesn't look quite as intricate, but the blade's in even better condition. What superb metal they must have used."

"Abingdon," said Patrick.

"*Abbandun*," said CD. "The *boda* came to *Abbandun* at evening bell."

Patrick kicked him surreptitiously.

"What's that?" asked Hescroft.

"Oh, nothing," said CD. "Just some old doggerel, or it might be catterel. I forget."

Edgar, who'd been left behind in CD's tent, flew up and landed on Camden's head, which distracted them enough to kill the subject. When order was restored and the bird was perched in his usual place on CD's shoulder, Hescroft revealed that he had other things on his mind.

"Patrick, Kenny here has some good news. He's picked up serious coproduction money from US Cable and Northern TV. We've got the green light to go from development into production, and what's more, we've got a budget that buys a few tricks."

Kenny Camden raised an eyebrow, and Patrick suspected Hescroft had borrowed the sentence wholesale from an earlier conversation.

"What it means, Pat," said the TV man, "is that we can do something pretty serious about your bones. That's why we've brought Celia along. She can not only give your woman back her face, she can also make her walk."

"How?"

"You tell him, Celia."

She looked at him with a knowing expression that said she was a professional and that she shared his clear distaste for the TV bullshit.

"Well, Patrick, of course you're familiar with facial reconstruction, building up muscle layers over the skull and working out the main dimensions that way. We don't have to do it with clay anymore; we've got very good computer scanning programmes that do that pretty fast."

"Yes, I've seen them."

"I'm sure you have. We've just gone one stage further in my unit. We've started analysing muscle attachment markings and joint articulation in the skeleton itself, and we're finding we can get a very realistic animation that will show just how a given individual would have moved."

CD whistled. "You can make her walk around realistically? Hell, I wish you'd done that for my last girlfriend. People used to double up laughing when she walked by."

"What does that mean you have to do to our skeleton?" said Patrick nervously, remembering the promise of care he'd made by the grave earlier.

"Nothing special. We just put all the bones through a three-D scanner. May I see the skeleton? I'll need to make a proper assessment as to whether it's practical. Of course, the condition of the bones is critical."

They moved the tent for her and Patrick quickly pulled his sleeping bag out of the way, but not before Camden noticed it and raised an eyebrow.

"Security," said Patrick shortly. "We had an intruder last night."

It felt oddly disturbing to see someone who wasn't directly involved get down into the trench, someone impersonal and detached.

"Bone preservation's very good," Celia Longworth said after a long inspection. "Everything's here except some toe bones on one foot. The foetus is amazingly intact, apart from the skull. Very good definition of the bone surface on the adult. I'd say this is the ideal candidate. When can we lift it?"

It? *Her,* thought Patrick.

"This morning, I suppose," he said. He hated the idea of putting her bit by bit into a box. "As you can see, we're just about ready. Everything's exposed now except the lower part of the skull. That shouldn't take long." Something needed to be said. He wondered if this was the wrong time, but he knew it might be the only time.

"One thing, though," he added. "We all feel we would like to bury her and the child properly afterwards."

"Yes, that's right," said CD, who hadn't heard a word of this before. "We all feel very strongly that would be the right thing to do."

"Where?" said Camden. "In the churchyard?"

"Absolutely not," said Patrick indignantly. "There's no evidence that she was a Christian. We'll bury her up here, where she belongs."

"Sounds like nonsense to me," said Hescroft. "What will the authorities say about that, I wonder?"

"Sounds pretty good to me," said Camden. "A touching ending, I'd say."

"Oh, well, fair enough, then," said Hescroft.

"We'll need to be very careful with the little one," said Patrick, and CD nodded agreement.

L ATER THAT MORNING, THEY FOUND OUT HOW THE GERMAN Queen had died. Patrick was lifting the bones, carefully and with a heavy heart, one by one into the padded boxes they had labeled and prepared, leaving the skull until last. He had taken the foetus out with extreme care, aware that its bones were little more than eggshells. Joe's poem kept ringing in his ears. It was a caesarean with no need for a scalpel, the saddest delivery he could imagine. Lifting the baby's crushed skull, a piece at a time, with tweezers was the worst of it and no one who was watching made a sound while he did it. Then, when he finally moved to lift the mother's skull gently from the earth, he wriggled his fingers delicately underneath and felt the gap in the bone that explained why they had laid her with her head to one side, so that the terrible injury that had killed her would be hidden from sight.

# CHAPTER TWENTY-FOUR

S HE DIED FROM A VIOLENT DOWN-
ward blow to the left side of her
head," said Patrick that night
when the circle had formed round
the campfire.

Joe was close to them, sitting within earshot but a little outside the circle.

"Would it have been . . . quick?" Gaye
asked, and although it was the sort of question usually only asked about recent deaths,
no one laughed at her.

"I would have thought so," said Patrick,
because he'd asked himself the same question as he'd held the skull. "Celia Longworth
says she thinks the baby must have been near
full-term. At least eight months." He spoke
loudly so that Joe could hear.

"What's happened to them?" Gaye went
on. "It really doesn't feel at all right, not having them here."

There was a general murmur of agreement.

"I asked her from all of us if she would take special care," Patrick told them. "Celia's laid them out, side by side, on the examination table. It didn't feel too bad to me."

"So what happens now?" said Dozer. "Is it just a wash-up job? Clean up and fill in?"

"No. It's a bit more than that. Camden wants to keep us all together here for just two or three days more while the labs do their work."

"Why?"

"To be honest, it's really for the TV. So he can have us responding to it all on camera, I suppose. There's the message sword and the real sword to be cleaned and all the other small finds. Then there's this reconstruction they're going to do on the skeleton. Plus the fact that he needs a lot more footage and he wants us to do some sort of presentation of what we've found in the village. He said he wants to talk to you all about how the dig's made you feel."

There was something else Patrick couldn't bring himself to tell them about, the uncomfortable hole Camden had put him in, revealed to him in a quiet corner of the Oxford lab that afternoon. Patrick didn't yet want to share that with anyone.

"I've got a bit of a dilemma you can help me out with, Pat," Camden had said. He reeked of stale tobacco, and his leather jacket seemed to Patrick to have the evil sheen of old engine oil. "Let's get a cuppa and talk it through."

Hescroft had disappeared somewhere and Patrick smelt another attempt at a setup.

They got plastic cups of not-quite-tea from a machine in the hallway, and Patrick sat down on a hard chair by the window. Outside, traffic was stationary on the Cowley road. His flat was less than a mile away and the thought that he would soon be spending his nights in it alone filled him with despair. He knew all at once that he'd become very fond of his bunch of diggers, of CD, Dozer, Peter, and Aidan—even of Gaye and Maxwell. A short distance away, the solitary life and the cheerless flat were rushing at him, and this unexpectedly precious now would turn sad as it crossed the frontier into memory. Maybe he should just go on camping in the field, he thought. It was much nicer than the flat.

Camden perched on the windowsill so that he looked down on him.

"You know the way it is with networks," said Camden as if Patrick was an old colleague. "It's all right doing the highbrow stuff for BBC Two and Channel Four, but they've got their bone-shows already. This has been a mass-market gig from day one, right?"

"If you say so."

"Well, the thing is, Pat, that got to be more of a problem since the coproduction money came in. We've got the Yanks and the Aussies in it now, and they both want human interest, you understand?"

"All too well," said Patrick wearily. "You're telling me you still want to do the rock star angle, right? You want to put my past life in the middle of this, yes?"

"No, no," said Camden with an expression that said he was astonished that Patrick could ever have thought such a thing. "You made it quite clear you wouldn't do that. It would have been great, sure, but I've had to respect your wishes. I understand your point of view. No, I've been looking around for something else in the human interest line, and I think I've found something that's nearly as good. Well, three things, really."

"Oh? What are they?"

"OK. First there's the vicar and all this business of burying the bodies with a Christian burial. You wouldn't have any objections to making that part of the film, would you? We'd have to film a bit of a dingdong between the two of you."

To Patrick, it seemed a relatively small price to pay for his continued anonymity.

"No, I don't think I'd mind that. I'm sure he hasn't got a leg to stand on. All the diggers think they should go back in the same grave, not in the churchyard."

"So far so good. Then that leads on naturally into a little sidebar story on this business about the vicar and the headmaster and the chick who's cooking for you."

"The May Day parade? How could that fit in?"

"Oh, you know, village traditions. We'll find a way. While you're waking up the past on top of the hill, the headmaster's trying to put it to bed down in the village, something like that."

"That would be up to Bobby. I don't know if she'd want to do it. It's nothing to do with me."

"You could help persuade her. Everybody says she listens to you."

"Really? Somehow that had escaped me."

"Anyway, it's not her decision, it's a story, it's out there. It's public property. They're in court tomorrow or the next day, aren't they? But leave that for now. Neither of those are the real business. It's her brother I really want."

*Her brother? Oh, no.*

"Why's that?"

"Come on, Pat. I'm talking about Joe. You know who Joe is."

"I know Joe."

"Yeah. Now that's a *really* powerful story line. Anonymous archaeologist, down on his luck, listens to a song sung in a pub by the local weirdo, and lo and behold, it all turns out to be true. You dig up the woman, you dig up the sword. Bingo, I've got a story the Yanks will love. The German Queen comes out of the grave—and there's the added attraction for you that Paddy Kane stays safely buried."

"Who told you about the song?"

"Give me a break, Pat. I'm not wet behind the ears. We've been filming in the village. We heard all about it. You weren't the only one in the pub. Anyway, what's the problem? It's brilliant. I can see why you didn't choose to mention it yourself. It does sound a bit flaky, but it'll be great TV. Thing is, I need you to persuade the bloke to sing it again so we can film it. We'll use it as a soundtrack."

What Camden was thinking was that in an ideal world, he'd get Patrick to sing part of the song himself; then, when it came to the final cut, he could just mix from that into Paddy Kane onstage. That would get the show into all the "Pick of the Day" columns without him having to do another thing.

*Bobby will flip her lid,* Patrick thought. *She'll think I put them up to this to get myself out of the hole.* All at once he saw the full elegance of the trap the TV man had sprung. Patrick or Joe: It was his choice. One way or the other, Camden was going to have his blood.

"There's something else you could do instead," he suggested with a degree of desperation in his voice. "This local builder, Little—the guy who wrecked the first site. Why not bring him into it? People shouldn't be allowed to get away with that sort of stuff. I think you'll find he's got a black eye. Bobby thumped someone who was trying to nick stuff from the trench last night. She's sure it was Little. Apparently he's been keeping inside his house all day today."

"Oh, please. You must know a bit about the laws of libel. You got any proof at all that it was him who did the damage?"

"No, but who else would it have been?"

"Not good enough, Pat. It's a local issue. That's not going to play too well in Peoria."

"Where?"

"Just an expression. Cleveland, Boston, Wollongong, wherever. What do they care about a builder and a few square yards of flooring? A mute farmer with a direct line to history—now, that's something else. You like all that stuff, I know you do. Local history and place names and all that."

"Is that everything? I'd better get on."

"Think about it. If we're going for Joe, we need to start shooting something with him tomorrow. Oh, and that reminds me, we're going to do some DNA testing, too."

That was when Celia Longworth came looking for them.

"You wanted my first impressions," she said, leading them back to the table where the bones were laid out. "She was in the prime of her life. Maybe twenty-five. Quite tall, about five foot nine, and in good health, judging by the evidence here. No sign of infections, breaks, or disease on the bones."

"And the wound?" asked Patrick.

"There's no doubt at all that was what killed her," replied Celia. "That's hardly surprising, from the scale of it. There's no new bone growth around the edges. It looks like a single blow, but I'll have a better idea when we've done a full examination. I'll let you know."

After that, Patrick went to his flat to get another pair of jeans. There was only one letter on the mat, a blood-money royalty cheque from his old agent, revealing the unwelcome news that two of Nam Erewhon's remixed albums had taken a new lease on life in Japan. It only made him more depressed. He left the cheque on the kitchen table. When the dig was over he would have to decide which charity to send it to.

That evening, relieved to be back around the campfire, he passed on most of what Camden had said, leaving out only the bit about Joe.

"So what do we all do now," asked Aidan, "just sit around here, twiddling our thumbs?"

"If anybody's dying to leave, they can," said Patrick, "but Hescroft's agreed that we should do a bit more work to date the original mound, and we might widen the grave trench to check for anything we've missed."

"And what might be the point of this DNA testing stuff?" said Aidan.

"It doesn't really help the archaeology," said Patrick, "but apparently it's the sort of stuff that makes good TV. The idea is, you usually find families who've always lived round here. People didn't move around much, that's how the theory goes, not until recently, anyway. Camden says he's done some research. There's four families here who go back generations. There's the Parslowes, who used to run the pub, and the Hawkins down at the bottom farm, and a couple of others."

"So just explain it a bit, will you?" said Aidan.

"I think they first did it in Somerset a few years ago. They got DNA from the tooth of a skeleton that came out of a cave in the Cheddar Gorge. It was dated as nine thousand years old, and when they did the tests, they found a local history teacher who turned out to be a direct descendant."

"It's a great story," said CD. "The really weird thing is that they weren't even going to test the guy, on account of the fact that he came from somewhere else. They were only doing the school kids whose families were long-term locals, but some of the kids got nervous, so this guy took the test himself just to show it didn't hurt."

"Does it?" said Gaye.

"Nah, it's just a cheek swab."

"So are they going to test us?" said Dozer.

"Not much point testing you," said CD. "You've clearly got no human ancestry whatsoever."

"It's all very well saying people didn't move away," argued Maxwell, "but that's not true, is it? The Saxons came and the Britons moved away."

"We don't know that for sure," said CD. "They might have stayed as slaves or wives or whatever. Those Britons just didn't leave many tracks."

"So there could be people still living in Wytchlow who are the great-great-great-times-a-hundred-grandsons of our Queen?" said Maxwell.

Peter cleared his throat and a reverent hush fell. "It does have to be mitochondrial DNA. That means it comes down the mother's line, so there could be a man living in the village but the ancestry would have to be through his mother and her mother and so on."

Maxwell turned to Peter. "And it survives that long?"

"Oh, they've got DNA from Neanderthal man dating back over fifty thousand years."

"Cool," said Maxwell, "but our Queen's baby died with her, surely? So how could she have any female descendants?"

"She might have had other kids before," said Roy.

"She *did* have others," Gaye said indignantly. "We know that, don't we? From Joe's song-thing. You know, the one we all did by the grave."

They turned to look at Joe, still sitting outside the circle, and he inclined his head and, in that same half-chanting, half-singing style, repeated the opening lines:

> *The boda came to Abbandun at evening bell*
> *Brought by the child with sunset head.*

The words came to them across the night air between them, filtered thin.

"It doesn't say it was *her* child," said Aidan.

Joe nodded downwards, just once, in that emphatic way of his, and nobody felt like arguing.

"And what do you suppose those words mean, that 'sunset head' thing?" said Aidan. He was looking at Joe but the man just looked back impassively.

"I'd like to think it means the child had hair like a sunset," said Gaye. "Wild hair, sticking out like rays of light, probably golden. That sounds more like a girl than a boy, so you see Peter's mito-whatever-it-was could easily have come down from her, couldn't it?"

"That's reading quite a lot into a single word," said Peter carefully.

"Well, I think I'm right," replied Gaye defiantly.

"That's my girl," said Dozer. "You tell 'em."

"I'm not your girl and I never will be."

"I'm proud of old Gaye here," said Dozer. "Do you know why?" he asked the circle.

"Stop it," she said. "You promised you wouldn't tell anybody."

"Dropped her hairbrush down the khazi this morning. Reached in and got it out. I found her giving it a wash."

"Dozer!"

There was a round of applause and Gaye gave a shrug and a little smile. "It's the only one I had," she said.

"Sorts out the women from the girls, this kind of thing," said Dozer. "Hey, speaking of women, have you heard about Bobby and her court case? Day after tomorrow, she's got to stand up and stop these bastards ruining the May Day thing. Wish there was something we could do to 'elp."

"Let's all join her on the march," said Gaye to a chorus of agreement.

"Where is she?" said CD. "A campfire ain't a campfire without our Bobby."

"She's down at the house. She said she'd be up soon," Gaye said. "I asked her to pick up some wine. Tonight it's on me."

There was a cheer, which disturbed Edgar down in CD's tent. He cawed indignantly.

"You got your keys back from that tree yet?" Dozer asked CD.

"I'm borrowing a ladder tomorrow," the American answered grimly.

"Look for my ring while you're up there," said Gaye. "He flew off with it this morning."

"Raven burgers," said CD. "Imagine how tasty they would be. . . ."

Bobby's old Land Rover groaned out of the twilight, and moments later she came over to Patrick. "Special request," she said. "Time's running out, isn't it? If I find you a guitar, will you play for us again?"

He found to his astonishment that something had changed. He could think of playing without any of the old overtones of association. "Only if it's not Maxwell's," he told her. "My fingers are still recovering. There's enough airspace between the strings and the frets to crawl through."

"I think I might just be able to do better than that," she said. "Wait a moment."

She walked back to the Land Rover and produced a padded guitar case. The instrument that came out of it shone deep golden-brown, and she passed it to Patrick, holding it out flat with both hands like an offering. He took it carefully and could tell at once that this was nothing ordinary. It was a classical jazz guitar, exuding handmade quality, and when he rippled his thumb across the strings, the sound they produced was exceptional.

"Eat your heart out, Maxwell, this is something else," he said, then he noticed the way Bobby was looking at the guitar and at him and he knew that this was an emotional moment for her, a bridge of some sort she had decided to cross.

"Who made it?" he asked, tilting it against the firelight to try to see if there was a label inside.

"A Canadian," she said. "A French-Canadian in Quebec named Maillette. It's supposed to be very good."

"Benoit Maillette? This is one of his? Do *you* play it?"

"I've never played this one."

He looked into the darkness where Joe sat. "Is it his?"

"No. Stop asking questions. Just go on. Play."

"What would you like?"

"I don't know. Something traditional."

So after a few solos, Patrick got them all singing with Bobby's pure voice and Joe joining in with a deep bass and his own voice leading them like the Pied Piper through an evening spun from magic. When, at last, the wine was gone and the fire was dying down, Patrick walked back to the Land Rover with Bobby, carrying the guitar. He put it back carefully inside.

"Thank you for letting me play it," he said as she got in. "It's got a story to it, hasn't it?"

She nodded.

"Would you tell me?"

"Why do you want to know?"

"Because I think you might want me to. Isn't that why you let me play it?"

"Perhaps. I don't know what I can say about it. I'm a bit like you, maybe."

"It's up to you."

"I'm not sure I shut up the chicken house," she said, looking away from him, down to the farm. "I've got to go back and check."

He thought that was the end of it, but she turned back. "Give me ten minutes. I'll meet you."

"At the house?"

"No, Joe will be there. Where the track takes you down to the yard, don't turn in left at the gate, follow it on. There's a slope up into an old orchard above the vegetable garden. There's an open shed there, a sort of field shelter with a bench in it. I sometimes go and sit there."

It seemed a long ten minutes before he followed her, and as he did so he warned himself to be very careful. This was his chance to give her something in return, for the times she had listened to him. But he felt that he was heading for uncharted waters.

"He came from Quebec, like the guitar," Bobby said without a word of preamble, when he found her sitting on the bench in the dark. The shelter in which it stood had an open front looking through a handful of old fruit trees, down the lane towards Wytchlow. Patrick sat down beside her, close to her because the bench was short, and she shivered. He could feel the warmth of her breath as she exhaled.

"He was called Gilles and he worked with me and he died." She was looking straight in front of her. A light in a window of the farmhouse showed him her profile.

"It was his guitar?"

"I thought you'd ask me how he died," she said wryly.

"We'll get to that."

"Yes, it was his guitar."

"Has anybody else played it since?"

"No."

"Why did you let me play it tonight?"

"For at least two reasons," she said. "Because you can play it nearly as well as he could, but more importantly because this is all about attitudes to life."

She hesitated. "When something goes really wrong you have the choice, don't you? First there's the suicide option. By the way, that's easy for farmers."

"Because you've got all the stuff lying around? The chemicals and the guns?"

"No, that's what people say. It's true that we know how to make a good job of it, but it's not just that. Farmers see a lot more of life coming and death going than most people. We know it's not really such a mystery. It's quite a simple business. That's one of the things I think is so amazing about the Queen up there. She lived in a time when life wasn't so ridiculously precious as it is now, but her death was still such a big event. . . ."

She fell silent and he waited. "So, leaving out suicide, you can either curl up inside your shell or you can go out and get on with it. What do you see when you look at me? I mean, when you look at me—Bobby—not at some awful old memory."

He did look at her next to him but she stared resolutely at the house.

"I wish I had a candle," he said. "I see someone who gets on with it, someone who all my diggers would happily go to jail for if the vicar got in her way."

"When I look at you," she said without doing so, "it seems to me that you're somewhere between the two, the curling up and the getting on with it. With a bit of a heave from your friends, you're just starting to come out of your shell, and I think it's time you started thinking about other people more."

He was shocked. "What do you mean?"

"I mean that nobody lives on this earth in a vacuum. You can be as miserable as you like by yourself, but when you do it in company, you take other people down with you. I don't think anyone has the right to be such a misery as you are. You've had the whole lot of them—CD, Dozer, everybody—tiptoeing round you for most of this dig, not sure whether you're going to fly off the handle or burst into tears on them."

"God almighty. I'm not that bad, am I?"

"Even worse. Well, you were, anyway. I have to admit there are slight signs of improvement."

"Look, if I am that bad, I'm sorry, but I'm not sure I can always help it. You know why. I told you."

"Because your wife and your son died."

"Yes."

"Patrick, you didn't put a gun to their head and pull the trigger. You got stoned or drunk or something and you said something you shouldn't have and *she* drove off the road. *She* did that, not you. It was a tragedy, but it's time to get it in proportion. You can't trail it around behind you for the rest of your life, because it keeps knocking other people over. Now, how did Gilles die, Bobby? Oh, thank you for asking, Patrick. I thought you were never going to get round to it." She paused. "No, sorry, that was a bit heavy-handed."

"I want to know. Tell me."

"We were working together. In the southern Sudan. There was a

French-Canadian medical charity that linked up with Médecins sans
Frontières. Gilles was one of the doctors."

"What were you doing, nursing?"

"Oh, sod off, Patrick."

"What have I said now?"

"I was a doctor, too."

"I see," and he thought he did, because from the first moment,
there had seemed too much to her for this narrow stage.

"No, you don't see. I was a farmer's daughter at the village school
and I *wanted* to be a doctor so badly I bullied them all into letting me
try—my mother, the teachers, then the Comprehensive. That's why
some of them down in the village think I'm a bit of a pain in the back-
side, a bit full of myself for a farmer's daughter. Anyway, Sudan . . . We
were cut off for a long time in a village, Gilles and me. There was
fighting going on all around us. It wasn't like you ever knew what was
really going on, because it was a civil war inside a civil war. Do you
know anything about the Sudan?"

"No."

"The north is all Arab, Muslim. The south is black, either Christian or traditional religions. We were in a Dinka village. The trouble
was, the rebels in the south had had a big split a few years earlier. One
side stayed under Riek Machar and the other under Garang and they
were fighting each other all round us. One lot would appear, then
the others, and sometimes they'd accept that we were there to help
everyone, and sometimes we thought maybe they were just going to
shoot us, anyway. We had a radio, but a soldier put an ax through it
and we were running out of everything, and then Gilles got sick."

She fell silent and Patrick prompted her gently. "And you couldn't
help him?"

"If I'd had a hospital lab, I could have. If I could have found out
what it was. If I could have got him to Khartoum, which was completely impossible. All I had to go on was what I could see, and I just
couldn't tell for sure. He'd been on a trip out with one of the Dinkas.
When he came back, he was in big trouble. He was confused and
drowsy. I couldn't get any sense out of him. The guy he was with
thought maybe he'd fallen over. He had this bruise and swelling. He
got worse. I thought it was a subdural haematoma. Bleeding under
the skull."

She was off somewhere terrible, far away from him. "I did all the tests I could. His pupils were different sizes, but he had a fever. He shouldn't have had a fever. I decided it was cerebral malaria, that went with the fever. Also it was one of the few things I still had drugs for. Maybe it was wishful thinking."

"Did they work? The drugs?"

"No." She sounded so sad, frightened. "He just went on getting worse."

"There wasn't any way to get help?"

"We were supposed to have a supply plane once a fortnight. I was going to fly him out on it. It didn't come on the day it was supposed to. I waited all the next day. I was beside myself. I was watching him die, and all I could do was try to get liquids into him and sponge him off. Normally, with other people, I felt like a real doctor. I knew they needed me to feel like that. With Gilles, I couldn't. I felt so ignorant. He would have known what to do, but I couldn't ask him. The malaria drugs should have been having an effect. In the early evening, one of the village boys came running in and told me he could hear the plane. I can't tell you how that felt. It was going to be OK. I went outside and we could see it, maybe half a mile off over some scrubland. I remember it so clearly. It was the silver Piper, but the sun made it look golden. Then I saw sparks flying up towards it like a firework and it veered away, and two or three seconds later I heard a burst of machine-gun fire from the scrub. There were little white specks showering down, I think they were bits of the Piper's tail or something."

"The plane was shot down?"

"No, it was just damaged, but it turned away and I could see it was flying strangely and then it just gradually disappeared into the distance. The pilot didn't know Gilles was ill. He said afterwards he would have tried to land if he'd known." She was speaking slowly and distinctly, as if making a report. "So then I knew it was up to me. I went over everything to make sure I hadn't got any other alternative. I thought it must be the haematoma after all. In the end, there's only one thing to do with a haematoma."

She didn't sound as if she was going to say what it was, so he asked. Only then did she turn and look straight at him.

"You have to drill a hole in the skull," she said. "To relieve the pressure of the bleeding. I drilled a hole in my lovely man's skull, and I didn't feel like a trained doctor. I felt like a child who was using a tool she'd stolen from her father's workshop." She sighed. "There was no haematoma. Before the plane finally came back five days later, he got meningitis because of what I did, and . . . and he died."

"Oh, Bobby." His overpowering instinct was to put his arm round her, but she was far away with her dead lover and he knew he could not. "There wasn't anything else you could do, though, was there?"

"Do you think that helps?" she cried. "Do you think when you love someone with all your heart and you're making plans to go back to Quebec together and you don't care about the heat and the shit you're living in, do you think it helps to know that? I was supposed to be able to heal and I *didn't know* enough. I was used to having backup, specialists I could talk to, labs to analyse things for me. It was just me and I wasn't enough and all I could do was something that killed him. Do you really think it helps to know that there wasn't anything I could do?"

"No. I'm so sorry."

"That's not the point." Her tone changed, became brisker. "I didn't tell you so that you'd be sorry. The point of my little story is that life goes on. I got out a week later."

"Did you come back here?"

"What's the saying? Good things come singly, but troubles arrive in legions? Yes, I did. I was back in Khartoum trying to make sense of it, with lots of people I scarcely knew saying all the wrong things. I'd tried to put a phone call through to Mum, then they came to my room and said there was a call from Wytchlow, and it was Jean Anderson down in the village telling me Mum was in hospital. So I came back and I was just in time to see her before she died, and then I realised I had to stay for Joe, so now that's what we do. We farm, day in, day out. When I heard about the dig, I thought, Great, I'll have some fun, this stuff's in my blood. I didn't realise it was going to turn into all this crap about sorrow and loss because the dig director was going to come fitted with his own personal thundercloud. All these people who came on this dig, they all deserve something a bit better, not just me."

"Oh, shit." The weight of it hit him. "You weren't real people to start with, none of you. I'd been living in my head for too long. This is the first time I've been out in public for ages. I'm doing better than I was, surely?"

"Most of the time. What was bugging you tonight?"

"While we were singing? Nothing."

"Before that. When I arrived. I could see it in your face."

"I'll have to start wearing a mask. It wasn't much. I had a difficult time with Camden, that's all."

"Why?"

"He wants me in his programme. Me, as Paddy Kane, punk rocker. Just to boost the ratings."

"And you've told him to take a running jump."

"It's not that simple. He fixed the money that let us do the dig, after all. I owe him something. He says he needs a human-interest angle and if it's not me, it's going to have to be something worse."

"Worse?"

"He's threatening to use Joe."

She sat up straight. "Joe? How could he use Joe?"

"He's heard about the song and how we found the grave."

"You told Camden that?"

"No, of course not. I didn't tell him. I promised you I wouldn't. He says someone in the village told him."

"Oh, come on, Patrick. If you've put him on to Joe to get him off your back, I'll never forgive you. I'm not having my brother turned into a figure of fun just for some fucking television programme, do you understand?"

He realised how good it had been feeling to sit there, now that the atmosphere had so abruptly gone.

"It wasn't me."

As he had found before, where her brother's interests were concerned, Bobby was a terrible foe.

"I don't see that it makes much difference whether you're Paddy Kane in the programme or not. They're going to call you Patrick Kane anyway, aren't they? Big deal! Anyone who's interested is going to figure it out. I'm sure you don't look that different. What does it matter? I don't understand why you did such crappy songs when I've heard how you sing really, but that hardly adds up to a reason. Just be Paddy Kane if that's what they want. So what? Listen, you get Camden off Joe's back. Don't you dare off-load this onto Joe, OK? I hold you responsible. Good night."

She got up and walked quickly to the house, and the door slammed in the bitter darkness.

# CHAPTER TWENTY-FIVE

OON AFTER FIRST LIGHT, CD
was forty feet up an oak tree,
roping himself carefully to the
trunk, when he looked through
a gap in the branches and saw
Patrick in the far distance walking purposefully down towards the farm. The American
had got up at the crack of dawn to get his
tree-climbing out of the way before anyone
else was up and about to laugh at him. He
wondered briefly what Patrick was up to, but
the tree and the problem of the final six feet
to where Edgar had dropped his keys drove
other thoughts away. He stretched out for
the next handhold, hung precariously by his
hands for a moment, then swung a foot onto
a safe branch. Three feet left. Before he had
fallen out of the tree last time, he had
marked the crook of a branch where Edgar
had taken his finds. Now he could see that in
that crook was an old bird's nest.

He climbed up a little farther and the rope stopped him, snagged round a branch below his feet and stretched tight. He reached up as far as he could and his fingers touched the edge of the nest, but couldn't grip it. He moved to untie the rope, then looked down at the drop. A sudden total understanding of the savage power of gravity and the frailty of the human body came to him, and he thought better of it. Common sense said he should climb down and untangle the rope, but common sense, unfortunately, failed to reign. Instead, CD lunged upwards with his fingers outstretched, shoved the nest sideways out of the crook of the branch, and watched it fall, shining objects spilling from it, into the thick leaf mold far below.

When he finally got down to ground level again, he saw his ignition keys lying on the ground and Patrick's pen near them. A bit of searching turned up Gaye's missing ring, and he was about to depart, pleased with his success, when he just caught the glint of something metallic, almost completely buried in the vegetation.

PATRICK HAD THOUGHT ABOUT WHAT BOBBY SAID FOR AN hour or two before going to sleep, and when he woke up soon after dawn, he went straight to the farm and sat quietly in the yard until he saw a light come on downstairs in the kitchen. Then he knocked on the door. A voice inside called something he couldn't catch but no one came, so he turned the knob and pushed it open. The kitchen door from the hall passage was ajar.

"Coffee's on the table," called Bobby from inside.

He walked into the kitchen and she was standing at the Aga, with her back to him. He guessed she'd just had a shower; she was wearing a dressing gown and she had a towel wrapped round her head.

"Bobby?" he said, and she spun round, staring at him.

"I thought you were Joe."

"I knocked."

"He sometimes does that so he doesn't startle me. What are you doing here? After what I said to you last night, I'm surprised." She turned back to stir a saucepan.

"I'm here *because* of what you said. I'll not be long, but I've come to sort out a couple of things. First, I know you're right about me wallowing in it. You've made me look at myself and you've set me quite an example. I needed it."

"And second?"

"Second, I want to say you don't need to worry about Joe. I've decided I'm going to talk to Camden. I'll tell him that so long as he stays completely away from Joe, I'll do it the way he wants. He can have his punk rocker. I've just realised there's no reason it should matter anymore."

"Thank you," she said. "Now go. I'm making Joe's porridge. I'll be up at the camp in fifteen minutes."

When Kenny Camden's Toyota appeared after breakfast, Jack was at the wheel and there was no sign of Camden. Patrick walked across to the cameraman.

"Morning," he said. "Where's your boss?"

"Please," said Jack, grimacing. "I'm a hungry freelance trying to keep my standards up. I prefer to think of him as my paycheck."

"Are you two not seeing eye to eye?"

"Have you tried getting Camden to meet your eyes? Look, I'm out of line here, but watch out for him. He's not a nice man."

"Thanks. I'd sort of guessed. Where is he?"

"Down on the village green. They're setting up the testing down there."

"The DNA test?"

"That's it."

Patrick walked down to the village, leaving CD to deal with the trench. He used the walk to steel himself for what he was going to do. There was a white tent on the green and Camden was standing outside it, talking to the villagers.

"We'll be ready to start about one o'clock," Patrick heard him say. "We'll have the cameras back down here by then. Get all your friends to come, too. We'll stay open until about seven to catch anyone who's been at work." He turned round. "Morning, Pat. Good to see you. What can I do for you?"

Patrick led him over to the base of the big beech tree that stood at one corner of the green. "I've changed my mind," he said.

"Er, about what?"

"About your programme. You can bring me into it any way you like."

"Ha," said Camden. "Thought so. There's still a performer in there, eh? Well, thanks for that, Pat, but no need, really. Truth is, I've gone off the idea. I think this farmer guy is a really good story."

"Hang on," said Patrick. "Joe's not going to do it. I will. Come on. I don't mind what you say."

"Look, Pat, let's face it. Four years is a long time. People have short memories. Sure, I was keen on it to start with, but then I thought a bit and, well, it's old hat, really, isn't it?"

"You're not listening to me. Joe won't do it."

"It's not actually for him to choose. We've already got shots of him."

"What shots?"

"You know the way he hangs around the fringes of the dig. I got Jack to watch out for that. It's great. It looks like some animal circling round a water hole because there's too many others already there. Then I've managed to put together a few bits and pieces of the song from people who were there. We can do it somehow. That's what I'm good at."

"I think you're making a mistake," said Patrick with a sinking heart, imagining Bobby's reaction.

"Maybe," said Camden cheerfully. "Gotta get some stuff together. See you back on the hill."

He walked away, privately laughing to himself. He had Patrick just where he wanted him, and Patrick wasn't going to have any choice. His past would be in the film whether he liked it or not; Joe was an added extra. It was all coming out well. After all, this was a one-off, not a series. He didn't need any of them again, ever.

Patrick couldn't bring himself to tell Bobby what had happened. He spent the rest of the day avoiding her, sitting in his car, writing up the paperwork on the trenches while the diggers found nothing but two possible Bronze Age potsherds in the barrow ring-ditch. The shards were potentially helpful as dating evidence, but hardly exciting artefacts in their own right.

As suppertime approached, it dawned on him that there was no sign of anything happening in the food tent. He went over and found the diggers inspecting three heaped trays of sandwiches.

"Bobby said she hoped we wouldn't mind," CD explained. "She's got some meeting down at the pub about her protest thing. I said it would be OK."

"What's in them?" said Dozer. "It's not stew, is it?"

"Close," said CD, picking one up and sniffing it. "It's definitely organic matter, but I'd need a lab report to get closer than that."

"You coming down to the pub?" Dozer turned back to Patrick. "Joe's singing, yeah?"

"Is it Friday?" Patrick realised he'd lost track of time.

"No, it's, um . . . Wednesday? He's doing another special, apparently. I thought you knew. Anyway, we're all going to get our DNA done just for a lark. CD's having his changed for something better, like a cockroach."

"Hey, respect where respect is due, man. Remember, you're looking at a highly successful primate with amazing tree-climbing abilities."

"You got your keys back?" Patrick asked.

"Yup, forgot to tell you, plus your pen, fairly undamaged." CD reached into his pocket. "Also Gaye's ring, and one more thing I am very embarrassed to show you."

"What?"

CD took out something that glittered dull silver. "An Anglo-Saxon silver coin, namely one *sceatta,* almost certainly late seventh century."

"Which would probably have been extremely useful dating evidence," said Patrick, "if we had the remotest idea where on the site it had come from, instead of finding it in a bloody jackdaw's hideaway."

"Ravens do not steal archaeological items," said CD, "because if they did, I would have to wring their neck. As it is, he's confined to my tent until we're off the site."

Back at the base of the oak tree, deep in the leaf mold where it had buried itself by its heavy fall, lay Hild's bride-price, the unique and colourful brooch, buried with her, stolen from the grave by Edgar, dislodged from the tree by CD, and now lost all over again.

THERE WAS A LONG LINE OF LATE ARRIVALS AT THE DNA TENT, but the tests were quick. Each person was handed a tiny brush on a stick. It was a simple process. All they had to do was swab the inside of their cheek, then the brush was put in a sterile bag and labeled.

The pub was packed, and the first thing Patrick saw was a large group of women clustered around Bobby in the far corner of the L-shaped bar, all talking intently. She saw him come in and beckoned to him. The others around her didn't stop talking and he couldn't get right up to her, but she craned her neck towards him round the back of her neighbour and said, "What's going on?"

"How do you mean?"

"They're saying you asked Joe to sing tonight."

"No, I didn't. I haven't seen him."

"I heard you sent him a note." She was frowning.

One of the others turned to her and said, "Bobby, we all think it should be you who speaks in court," and Bobby shrugged at Patrick and went back into the conversation.

Joe did sing, but not for long. He came into the bar from the back room, dressed in his hat and red waistcoat, and a little cheer ran through the crowd. He tuned up and sang a song about May Day to the tune of "Greensleeves."

*For centuries, we've decked the mask,*
*with flowers arranged most carefully,*
*performing this most ancient task*
*as it's been done traditionally. . . .*

The song went on to be savagely witty at the expense of the headmaster and the vicar. Joe made no mention of Little. There was a service hatch to the kitchen set in the wall, where the lunchtime food could be ordered. It was opposite Joe's microphone, and Patrick, listening uncomfortably while he leaned against the same wall, wondering how Bobby had got the idea that he'd sent Joe a note, noticed one of the flaps was half open. As the song came to an end, he saw movement by the hatch, and for a moment, the business end of a camera lens came into view. He knew then that Camden's man Jack was filming Joe from an oblique angle, hidden inside the kitchen. And he also knew, beyond a shadow of a doubt, that the note to Joe must have come from Camden in Patrick's name.

Joe started the introduction to another song and Patrick realized it was the song of the German Queen, and though he wanted with all his heart to hear more of it, he did not want the camera to have it. He started to get to his feet with no clear aim except perhaps to go to the hatchway and force the flap shut, but Joe glanced at the hatch, stopped playing abruptly, and marched across to it himself, holding his guitar in one hand. He reached in trying to grab something, probably the camera. Whatever it was, it was out of sight. Everybody started talking at once in the bar and there were muffled noises from the other side of the hatch. Joe slammed the hatch shut, turned round to hang his guitar on a hook on the wall, then strode past Patrick, straight out of the pub door. Patrick saw Bobby rise, trapped on the far side of the room by a tide of people, but the look she gave him was sheer, cold hatred. Then he ducked out of the door into darkness, and it felt like a replay. He would pursue Joe across the green and Bobby would be on his tail like a fighter plane before he could straighten this out. Except this time, there was no sign of Joe striding away into the distance. Instead, a hand shot out and grabbed his wrist, and Joe, who'd been standing waiting for him just outside the porch, set off round the corner to the car park, towing him along. The thought dawned on Patrick that he might be heading for a beating.

"I didn't send that note," he protested. Joe turned his head, gave an unexpected grin, then put a finger to his lips to silence him. Patrick heard the pub door open again and Bobby's voice call "Joe!" but the man took no notice.

Joe led him round to the far side of Camden's big four-wheel-drive, parked next to the pub dustbins. He knelt down. He fiddled with the valve cap, and Patrick heard the hiss of escaping air. Joe knew who the real culprit was, and he was taking appropriate action.

"Why not, indeed?" said Patrick quietly, and went to the other tyre, but Joe grabbed his arm again. He held up one finger and nodded, then two and shook his head. Forcing them to change a wheel was one thing, he was clearly saying, but leaving the men stuck here would be going too far. When all the air had gone and the wheel rim was squelching the rubber down into the gravel, Joe went round to the windscreen and wrote, in reverse writing on the dirt, CHECK YOUR TYRES. Then he slapped Patrick on the back, indicated both of them in turn, and mimed walking with his fingers.

"You want us to go for a walk?" Patrick asked.

The other man nodded and set off into the darkness.

"Where are we going?" called Patrick, but Joe's only response was to urge him on with a sweep of his arm. They walked, and it was soon obvious this was no mere stroll. Joe's long stride took them rapidly through the churchyard, over a stile, and down the side of the field beyond. For him it might not have been dark at all. For Patrick, stumbling on ruts and over stones, uncertain of every footfall, and panting to keep up, it soon turned into a marathon. They took an old overgrown pathway down through the wood to the lower ground by the river, crossed the lane there, and climbed another stile onto a signposted path. Joe was striding easily along, silhouetted against the skyline. Ten yards ahead, he waited where the path forked, to make sure Patrick made the right choice. They walked as fast as Patrick could go for an hour and a half without ever taking to a road except to cross it. There were occasional clues to where they were— light aircraft on night-flying training descending into Kidlington airport, a footpath sign off left to Woodstock, illuminated by the chance sweep of headlights of a car turning into someone's drive. Finally their general direction became clear. A bank of low cloud crept in ahead, lit from below by the loom of reflected light from the bright streets of Oxford.

Joe started to climb another stile into an old sunken pathway enclosed between high banks, but when he was on top, he stayed where he was, straddling the rail, turned to Patrick waiting below, and declaimed,

> *Down Yarnton Lane, King Charles's men*
> *Crouching, crept on June the third*
> *Between the Roundhead ranks and then*
> *Escaped the siege, not seen nor heard.*
> *Five thousand men crept down that lane*
> *With Waller left and Essex right.*
> *The King's men crept between the twain*
> *And broke the circle in the night.*

"Down this lane?" said Patrick. "This is how they got out of the siege of Oxford?"

Joe, up against the sky, nodded with Orion's belt behind him, and swung down into the lane. For the next quarter of a mile, Patrick imagined silent Royalist columns and their horses with carefully bandaged hooves, creeping towards him in the silence on which their survival depended, along the bottom of the old hollow way. He wondered for a moment whether Joe was leading him to some new archaeological discovery, and in a sense, he was.

KING CHARLES'S MEN USED IT FOR THEIR ESCAPE IN 1644,
BUT THE HOLLOW WAY HAD BEEN IN USE FOR A THOUSAND
YEARS BEFORE THAT. WHEN HILD'S DAUGHTER MELA
RACED TO ABBANDUN WITH THE SUMMONING SWORD,
SHE SHUNNED THE TRACK, TAKING A PARALLEL ROUTE, A
HUNDRED YARDS TO THE SOUTH. SHE LEAPT THE HEDGES
AND RACED ACROSS THE GRASS, WATCHING FOR STRANGERS
WHO MIGHT TRY TO STOP HER.

IT WAS ON THE WAY BACK THAT SHE RAN INTO TROUBLE,
AND THAT WAS NOT WITH STRANGERS, IT WAS WITH HER
FATHER'S OWN KIN, THE UNCLES SHE WAS DRAGGING TO
HIS AID.

"YOU MUST BE ABLE TO GO FASTER THAN THAT," SHE
IMPLORED THEM. "RUN, CAN'T YOU? WE'LL BE TOO LATE."

"WE'LL NEED OUR BREATH TO FIGHT," THEY REPLIED
BRUSQUELY.

"WE SHOULDN'T HAVE GONE ROUND THAT WAY," SHE
SAID. "I TOLD YOU THE FLOODS WEREN'T BAD. WE'VE
WASTED SO MUCH TIME."

THAT WAS EXACTLY THEIR INTENTION. HILD'S DAUGHTER
WAS MUCH TOO LIKE HER MOTHER. BOTH WOMEN HAD TOO
MUCH OF CUTHWULF IN THEM. BEING AMONG THE GEWISSE
BUT NOT BEING TRULY OF THE GEWISSE, THE ABBANDUN
FAMILY HAD LEARNT TO KEEP THEIR EAR TO THE GROUND.
HILD'S ATTACKERS HAD GEWISSE BLESSING. ARRIVING TOO
LATE TO SAVE HER MIGHT BE NO BAD THING.

Beyond Yarnton, Joe climbed a wall and on the other side stretched
his hand out to stop Patrick from blundering into a barbed wire
fence, hidden by darkness and foliage. He put his foot on the middle
strand and pulled the top one up to make a space for Patrick to climb
through. The wood ahead looked impenetrably gloomy, and Patrick
said again, a little nervously, "Where are we going?" but Joe had already gone on into the wood on a narrow twisting track, and Patrick
had to hurry to catch up. They crept through the trees like poachers.
Twice, Joe held up a warning hand and they both froze. Whether
there were gamekeepers about, Patrick never discovered. He had
learnt early on that Joe was more at ease in the countryside in the
dark than he himself would ever be in daylight. In the end, after

many minutes of slow, careful movement along what seemed no more than an animal's trail, they came to a bank and climbed down it to a wider track, surfaced with gravel and rough stones. Joe stood listening carefully for some time, then nodded and turned left along it. The track curved and ran downhill for a hundred yards between high banks, and then, in the darkness, rising above and surrounding them, Patrick made out dim cliffs of rock and guessed they had arrived on the floor of a quarry.

Joe took him to the far end of it, picking his way between old fridges, piles of tyres, and mounds of rubble. Then he crouched down, took a little torch out of his pocket, and shone it on the ground, waving to Patrick to come and look. What they were looking at was the edge of a huge pile of earth, apparently tipped from some other access up on the quarry's lip. Small fragments of colour glinted in the torchlight. Roman tesserae, bright fragments of mosaic, tumbled into the heap of soil that had been dragged here from Little's field.

Patrick scrabbled through the soil with his fingers. It was thick with broken roof tiles and with the sad pieces of the ruined floor, the artistry of their arrangement lost. All it amounted to now was useless builder's rubble.

"My God, what a waste," he said, turning to Joe. "Have you been out searching for this every night?" He got a single emphatic nod.

"Well done, Joe. There could be other artefacts in here. We need to come and check through this lot. It won't do much good, though. We'll never prove it was him, will we?"

Joe nodded two or three times.

"We will? How?"

Joe was bursting to convey something to him.

"You've got proof?" said Patrick.

Joe waved his hands around in the dark, then held up a finger in front of Patrick's face as if to say wait a minute. He shone the torch on himself and passed it to Patrick like that, then in the torchlight he held out his hands as in a game of charades, making the symbols for book, film, and play in quick succession. He was smiling.

Patrick laughed. This was an unsuspected Joe, playing games. He was clearly in high spirits.

"You're going to act it?"

There was a quick nod.

"Two words. First word?"

Joe brought his two hands close together.

"Small? Something like small?" Joe was encouraging him. "Oh, got it. Little?" That wasn't quite right. "Something like Little? Yes. You're going on. Second word?"

Joe stuck his arms out, tilting and banking and making a droning noise like a child playing war games.

"Aeroplane?"

Joe egged him on, then held up an admonitory finger again and mimed with a flat hand, something curving down to a horizontal halt.

"Aeroplane landing? Yes? Yes. Landing. Shorter than landing. Land? Okay, land. That's it? Little land. What? I don't get it."

Then he did.

"Little's land? This is Little's land. He *owns* this place? You're kidding."

Joe mimed somebody taking aim with a gun and firing.

"He keeps it for shooting? And you knew that, so you came and searched? Oh, clever Joe, bloody well done, mate. We'll get him now."

Joe held up both thumbs then tapped his watch and mimed sleeping. They walked back and Patrick was even slower on the way back, because the night was now very black indeed and he had the greatest difficulty finding his way, though Joe loitered along so that he could stay in his sight. It was one o'clock in the morning before they reached the village, and Patrick, completely exhausted, waved good night to Joe where the track to the hilltop turned off the lane.

CD woke him in the morning.

"It's late. Hate to wake you, but we've got a tiny little rebellion on our hands."

"I found where Little dumped the stuff. Joe showed me."

"Good, good. There's more important things than that going on."

"Like what?"

"Like breakfast, or rather it's not going on, and there's the problem."

# CHAPTER TWENTY-SIX

A NOTE WAS PINNED TO THE flap of the marquee. It said, *Milk and bread inside. Make your own breakfast. I've had to go. Pub will do lunch if you tell them you're coming. Maybe supper. B.*

"What does 'maybe supper' mean?" said CD. "Does that mean maybe the pub will do supper or maybe she will?"

"This is all about me," said Patrick, reading it ruefully.

"Yeah, I know. Well, partly, I guess. She was pretty angry last night after you guys went out. She had a go at Camden, too. He couldn't get away because he had a flat tyre. She used the word 'conspiracy.' It was not nice to hear."

"I'll go down and see her."

"You want reinforcements?" asked CD. "I wouldn't go in there without backup, the way she sounded. Two platoons of Marines and air support. Even better, take Dozer. Well, no. Normally that would be a good plan, but believe it or not, he's otherwise occupied." CD turned and stared at Dozer's tent.

"How?"

As if in answer, the zip opened and a face looked out, but it wasn't Dozer's. Seeing them staring, it vanished again.

"Gaye? Was that Gaye?" said Patrick. "No, it couldn't have been."

"Believe it, baby. It's that end-of-the-dig, last-days-of-Rome atmosphere. They decided last night they were made for each other. In different factories maybe, but there you go. She may need therapy this morning."

"I've got to go down and sort this out with Bobby. She thinks I tricked Joe into being filmed. All she's got to do is talk to Joe."

"So long as he answers."

"He's a genius at charades. He'll explain."

There was nobody at the farmhouse with whom Patrick could sort anything out, but there was a note on the door. It said:

*Louisa: I've gone to check a few legal things at the Citizen's Advice Bureau. The hearing's at ten-thirty at Oxford court. They've got some big-time barrister. See you there. B.*

His mobile bleated.

"Patrick. It's John."

"Who?"

"John Hescroft. Are you still asleep? Look, Kenny Camden says there's a lot to do today. Sweeping up, you know. Kenny asked me to give you a call. Can we meet at the conservation lab, the one where they've got the metallic finds? You know the place? Out by the ring road? They've got some of your stuff from the trench cleaned up, ready for the cameras. Done a very quick job for us. I'm sure you'll want to see it all, and Kenny's man Jack needs to shoot some pictures. Thought it was a good chance for us both to fly the PSC corporate flag a bit. You know, make sure we both mention the name in the interviews? We could meet there in what, fifteen or twenty minutes?"

Patrick almost laughed. He'd known Hescroft would pop up when the hard work was done and try to get his face on the programme. "OK," he said. "I need to talk to Camden, anyway. But listen, John. There's something else. Last night we found the dumped soil that was stripped from the Roman site, chock-full of the remains of a mosaic floor. Can you have a word with the County council and tell them? The beauty of it is that it's been dumped on a bit of private land belonging to Roger Little."

"Oh, that's a dead issue, surely."

"No, it isn't. Will you tell them or will I?"

"Can you prove *he* dumped it there?"

"Come on. Who else would have?"

"Well, someone trying to cause trouble for him, perhaps?"

"Why don't you just tell the planners and see what they say?"

"It's very embarrassing, Patrick. I see him at the golf club."

"You've got a conflict of interest?"

"Oh, no. No, no. Nothing like that."

"So you'll do it?"

"We'll talk about it later, old boy. I'll see you at the laboratory."

Kenny Camden and Jack were waiting in the foyer of the lab with the camera gear. Patrick walked right up close to Camden and stared straight at him.

"I'd like to know what you think you were doing last night?"

"Last night?" said Camden. "Well, I had an excellent meal at the Luna Caprese, then—"

"In the pub."

"We were filming, Pat. Perfectly within our rights. We had the landlady's permission."

"You didn't have Joe's permission."

"Didn't need it. He was performing on her premises under her licence. That puts her in charge."

Patrick had no idea whether he was right or not.

"Well, he made it pretty clear he didn't want to play. I'm glad he walked out on you."

"So am I," said Camden. "You should see it. It makes a really great sequence. The Wild Man of Wytchlow rushing up to try to grab the camera. We'll get two or three more like that and the audience will be pissing themselves laughing."

"I won't allow this. This is really dishonest. You sent Joe the note, didn't you? You pretended it was me asking him to sing?"

"I might ask *you* who let the air out of my tyre?"

A red mist started to rise in front of Patrick's eyes, but before he could do anything regrettable, John Hescroft came in through the door, spraying a foam of obviously false bonhomie on the flames.

"Morning, old boy; hello, Jack. You look a bit bushed, Patrick. Suffering from the under-canvas syndrome? Never mind, it'll soon be over."

Patrick breathed heavily and Hescroft looked at each of them in turn, frowning.

"Is there a problem?" he asked.

"Forget it," said Patrick. "What happened with the planners?"

"The planners?"

"About Little? About the fact we've just proved he wrecked the site. Remember?"

"Calm down, Patrick. I left a message. We'll have to see."

"OK, what do you *think* they'll do?"

"If you've really got proof, they might take him to court."

"Will it affect the planning permission?"

"Separate issue, I would have thought. There's nothing on the site to save now, is there? Not really my bailiwick. Nor yours, come to think of it. Perhaps it would be better to stick to the job in hand. Have you told anyone we're here yet? Paul McGovern should be expecting us. Let's give him a shout."

McGovern, a ponderous man, came out to meet them and, waddling, led them into a side room where various familiar objects were laid out on a table, dominated by the sword.

"We've finished all the cleaning," he said. "No particular problems."

Patrick crossed to the table and bent over it, studying the sword intently.

"This is very fine," said Hescroft, joining him, "very fine indeed."

"In the song," said Camden, "your pal Joe called it by some funny name, didn't he? The chicken sword? What was that about?"

"I haven't a clue," said Patrick. He ran through a mental checklist. The coins were there and the shield boss. But there was something missing. The heavy disk of Roman work that had been one of the earliest finds.

"There's something else," he said.

"I was saving that for last," McGovern said. "I think you'll like this. It's cleaned up quite nicely."

He lifted a plastic cover at the end of the table and an astonishing sight was revealed. What Patrick had only seen as an encrusted lump was now a disk of bronze, with an intricately cast man's face at its centre. It was a curious object, perforated with holes at intervals all across it, but what commanded Patrick's complete attention was that he knew this face already—the face of a man with a beard made up of leaves and fruit and with two birds flying out of his mouth, a face later carved in wood, a face worn in the dark by the little demon, Mikey, at the painting of the cart, a face central to a tradition kept alive down all the years to the present day. A tradition, he realized, that was about to be put through the processes of modern law.

"Um, I need to borrow this for an hour or two."

McGovern blinked. "Well, of course, it's yours to take, but—"

"What for?" demanded Camden, as Patrick picked up the bronze disk. "Where are you going? We need you. We need to get pictures of that."

"I'll be back."

"No, come on, Pat, you can't just rush off like this. We need to shoot that and we need to have you tell us all about these finds on camera. You can't just piss off. We're expected at the other lab."

"Phone me on the mobile when you finish here. I'll join you." Then he was gone.

"What was that about?" said Camden, worried that he was missing something. "Can anyone tell me why he's suddenly . . ." He snapped his fingers. "Bloody hell, I know what it is! It's the chick. Joe's sister. It's her court case this morning. It's about that, I bet. Come on, Jack. We'll shoot this later. First things first."

"I really wonder whether it was wise to employ that young man," said Hescroft. "If I'd known about his background, I would have thought twice."

By that time, Patrick was already starting his engine. He drove the old Peugeot down the Banbury Road into Oxford as fast as the traffic would allow, looking at his watch every time he was forced to slow down. It took far too long to find a parking space, and when he ran into the court building with the bronze face under his arm, it took further agonising minutes to find out where Bobby's hearing was taking place. When he finally walked into the courtroom, it was already well under way.

The man who was addressing the judge was a stranger to him, a barrister in wig and gown whose every syllable sounded expensive.

". . . in accordance with that. It is therefore the contention of the school authorities, in seeking this injunction, that the parade is not in fact an old tradition at all, and that there is no record which can be produced in evidence of any such tradition going back before the Second World War on the basis suggested by Miss Redhead and her supporters. We ask, therefore, that the injunction be granted to prevent a serious disruption to the work of the pupils."

Patrick couldn't spot Bobby, then he realised she was the woman in unfamiliar smart clothes, wearing a hat like a turban, who was sitting at the front of the court. He started scribbling her a note. *I've got something that will help,* he wrote, *so can you call me to give evidence or something?* It was too late to get it to her. She was already standing up and he heard her trying to answer that accusation. All she could do was explain the strength of local feeling about the tradition.

"In the village, we know it's been going on for years and years," she said, "since time immemorial." It sounded vague and anecdotal and he knew instantly that in this place of precise, provable argument it was not going to wash. What could he do? Could he just stand up and say something? He thought he'd probably be ejected from the court for that.

In a corner, under a gallery at the back of the chamber, a large white board stood on a stand, and hanging from a string was a marking pen. On the board someone had drawn a road map, the details of some traffic accident—a previous case, perhaps. He got up and a few people looked at him curiously. He went to it, wiped the board clean, and started to write. A man in a suit standing on the other side of the courtroom was wagging a finger and shaking his head. Patrick saw the vicar, the headmaster, and Roger Little—complete with a bruise just under his eye—staring at him, frowning. In big block letters, he wrote BOBBY, CALL ME AS A WITNESS. Bobby didn't turn round. The judge was now peering at him owlishly over his glasses, and Patrick knew he was pushing his luck with the dignity of the law.

"Miss Redhead," said the judge. "For reasons that are not at all clear to me, a young man at the back of the court appears to be attempting to attract your attention."

Bobby twisted round sharply and finally took in Patrick and his message.

"Do you know what this is about?" the judge asked her.

"No, Your Honor, I don't. The, er . . . the young man is an archaeologist."

"He is perhaps an expert on local history?" suggested the judge.

"Perhaps," said Bobby vaguely. "I don't, well, I'm not sure . . ."

"May I suggest you call him as an expert witness? You do seem a little, well, undersupported," said the judge kindly, so she did.

Then there was a curious moment while Patrick sat in the witness box and she stared at him, unable to tell what he could be doing there.

"You are Patrick Kane, an archaeologist, yes?" she said.

"Yes, I am."

"And you have been digging on an Anglo-Saxon burial site in the village of Wytchlow?"

"Yes, I have."

"And . . ." There was a long silence, while she stared at him and he tried to get her to notice the bronze disk which he was holding as obviously as he could, but her eyes were fixed above it, staring at his face in a sort of desperate trance. "And," she said again, more decisively, "what question would you like me to ask you?"

"I'd like you to ask me about the disk-shaped Roman artefact that we discovered buried in the Anglo-Saxon grave."

"Mr. Kane," she said, "would you tell us about the, er . . . the disk-shaped Roman artefact?"

He held it up, and as she finally focused on it, her eyes widened.

"Yes," he said, "as you have no doubt already told the court, the May Day observance centres on the procession around the village of an old Bath chair decorated with flowers and carrying a very distinctive wooden mask, in the shape of a Green Man face with two birds flying out of the mouth. The issue today seems to be whether this has or has not been a long tradition. As you are probably aware, spring rituals and the Green Man tradition certainly go back to pagan times, and were widely celebrated in the Roman world. While we were digging in the Anglo-Saxon grave at Wytchlow, we discovered an earlier Roman object buried with the body. Sorry, am I going too fast?"

"No, no," said the judge. "Most interesting."

"The object was obscured by an encrustation of dirt, but I have just collected it from the laboratory where it has been cleaned. This is it. It has been in the earth for nearly fourteen hundred years, and it was made perhaps three hundred years before that. It is possible to date it with a high degree of confidence to the third or fourth century."

Patrick looked across at the vicar; the Reverend Augustus Templeton-Jones had his mouth tightly shut. "It is virtually identical to the wooden mask used in modern times in the parade."

The judge broke in. "And from that, you would infer, would you, Mr. Kane, that this is indeed an ancient tradition?"

"I would infer, Your Honor, that there must be an unbroken tradition based around this particular facial form, going back at least to the burial of this mask."

IN THE CORRIDOR OUTSIDE, PATRICK EXPECTED BOBBY TO BE grateful at his Lone Ranger act, riding to her rescue at the last moment, but her anger ran far too deep for that.

"I suppose you think that was clever, crashing in like that! I suppose you think I couldn't have done it without you!" she said. "And I suppose you think that makes up for your truly disgusting behaviour over Joe! Well, it doesn't."

A voice behind him said, "Mr. Kane. A word," and the vicar was suddenly in between them, spitting his anger at Patrick while Bobby turned on her heel and walked off.

"Not now," he said to the man, but Templeton-Jones held on to his arm.

"You have no idea what damage you have done," said the vicar.

"Not nearly as much damage as I'll do to you if you don't let go, and not nearly as much damage as your man Little did to our Roman villa," replied Patrick. "Why don't you ask him who gave him that black eye?"

The vicar let go and Patrick started to follow Bobby, but his phone rang at that moment. Two of the Wytchlow mothers who'd been in the court stood there looking at him with sheeplike admiration. At least he'd pleased somebody. Hescroft's voice in his ear said, "Where are you?"

"In town."

"Look, Patrick, do pull yourself together. There's a change of plan. Kenny and Jack had to shoot off. Will you nip along to Celia Longworth at the computer place? She was expecting all of us. Can you give her a message? If she's got the face reconstruction stuff ready, Camden wants her to bring it out to Wytchlow on a laptop this afternoon so we can film all the village people looking at it."

Bobby had disappeared round the corner towards the EXIT sign.

"Where is it?" Patrick said wearily.

"Thirteen, Mortlake Street," replied Hescroft. "Get moving. I don't want to keep her waiting."

"Thirteen?" he repeated, but Hescroft had hung up. "Do you know where Mortlake Street is?" he asked the two women.

"I think it's off the Iffley Road," said one. "Just after a pub, isn't it? You were great in there."

"Where did Bobby go?"

"Outside."

He caught up with her at the front door and he chased her through the door, still intent on putting things right, straight into camera shot. Jack wasn't allowed into the precincts of the court, but they couldn't keep him off the pavement outside, and he was following Bobby's every move with the camera. Camden was sitting in his Toyota at the kerb. He had his phone to his ear, talking hard. Bobby stopped dead and Patrick ran into her from behind.

"Call your bloody dogs off," she snapped.

"They're nothing to do with me."

"So why are they following me and not asking you all about yourself, Mr. Paddy bloody Kane?"

"Will you stop and listen to me?"

"No. Piss off."

He gave up and went to get his car. She strode round the corner to her Land Rover, and Jack followed. As she climbed in, the cameraman came right up to the driver's door and tapped on the window.

On the way up Iffley Road, Patrick spat all the things at the windscreen that he wished he'd said to Bobby. He hissed bits of sentences out loud and the rest of his words bounced round his head with the rattle of shrapnel.

"You ask your brother who got him to sing. He'll tell you. Somehow. You go off like a bloody firework because you jump to bloody conclusions all the time. Well, I've had it. I can't be bothered with it. Go back to your bloody farming and leave me alone. I've got other things to think about.

"I'm bloody glad the dig's nearly over. I'll be pleased to see the back of you. You're so sodding ungrateful. You've got your bloody parade, and that's because of me. You wouldn't have obeyed their bloody injunction. I've kept you out of jail. How could I do it any other way? There wasn't time. You think you're so brave about life and I'm so spineless. Well, you don't know me at all. Get out of my bloody way."

He blew his horn at a cyclist who'd done nothing worse than travel on the same bit of tarmac.

He built a barricade in his mind and put Bobby the far side of it, then he thought instead of the other woman—the German Queen. She was so much simpler, so much easier to understand. He could safely let himself feel things for her, poor, dead her, that were far too powerful to be turned on anyone alive. She was a real woman, a brave, straightforward woman, and he let himself love the idea of her. She had commanded love. That was what her bones said, and the tributes they'd piled round her. They'd put her in her mound on the skyline and they'd sung a song which had come down all the years in between and in a few minutes he would see her face.

The impact of that hit him. Her face. They were going to give her back the flesh the years had stripped away. An electronic Lazarus, she was going to get a new chance, and Patrick knew that it was all he needed, the sight of her face to put together with everything he knew in his heart about her from the song and from the feel of her bones in the soil.

THIRTEEN, MORTLAKE STREET HAD BEEN AN ORDINARY TER-raced house quite recently, judging by the nursery wallpaper in the upstairs room that Celia Longworth took him to.

"This is overspill," she said. "I think it would be better if your people didn't actually film here. I'm not really quite sure we're meant to be using it for this. It's only temporary, you see."

"They're not *my* people," he said, "but I'll tell them if I see them."

There were three tables crammed into the room, carrying a mass of monitors, keyboards, and cabling. A young man who looked no more than a teenager was working at one of them. His hair was streaked blond and he had two silver rings in one ear. "This is Nick," said Celia. "He's my right-hand man. He knows how all the buttons work. This is Patrick. He's come to see his Saxon woman."

"Great," said the youth, giving them a cursory look. Then he did a double-take. "Patrick?" he said.

"Yes, that's right." Patrick said it firmly, but Nick kept staring at him.

"I know you, don't I?" he said.

"Yes, I think so," answered Patrick. "Someone's party, maybe? Do you know Lisa?"

"No."

"Alice?"

"Yeah, Alice. Was it there?"

It seemed to work. Patrick filed that one away for future use.

"We scanned all the bones back at the lab where you saw them," Celia explained, "but they're still building our new extension. This is where we do the clever stuff. Now, do you know how all this works?"

"Vaguely." *Get on with it,* he wanted to say.

"The skull gives the face its main shape, of course," she said. "About ninety-five percent, you might say, but it's the other five percent that matters and that comes from the soft tissue, the muscle and the flesh. That's what makes it tough to get it just right, because our eyes are tuned to tiny differences in face shapes. Get the soft tissue five percent wrong and you wouldn't recognise your own mother. Even then, the last one percent can make all the difference between beautiful and ugly. You need to understand this because we're going to need some input from you to decide the final version. Do you see?"

"Yes," Patrick said, though he didn't.

"Can you put up the skull, Nick?" On a huge monitor, the familiar scanned-in skull of the woman from Wytchlow came up against a neutral grey background, slowly revolving. Patrick would have known it from any other, even before it turned to reveal the great jagged hole across one side.

"There you are. There's our starting point. We'll just fix the damage."

Keys clicked and the skull healed over. Now she was not dead, but neither was she alive.

"When reconstruction first started, the major problems were the mouth, the nose, and the ears, because that's where the human eye really does identify the tiniest differences. In the early days, they couldn't be precise about any of that. Now we've learnt how to work it out by analysing how the muscles attach. The marks on the skull tell us which way the muscles pulled and how powerfully, and that's just as important as the depth of the soft tissue. It makes all the difference to how lifelike it is. They used to build them up with strips of clay on a cast of the skull. Now we do it with this thing."

Celia was an enthusiast lost in the wonders of her world. He was unable to stop her, although all he wanted was to see the outcome.

"So, take the mouth. You might ask how we get the right size."

He might, but he hadn't.

"There are two giveaways. If the teeth are still there, the outer edge of the canines gives you the width of the mouth, and that also tells you exactly how the eyes were set, because it's the same as the width between the inner edges of the iris. The general shape of the nose is quite easy. Do you want me to explain that?"

"No, I've got the general idea. Where do I come in?"

"OK. Nick, give me the average face."

On the screen a flattened mask appeared and wrapped itself over the skull. It looked like a shop-window dummy. Nothing in it stirred Patrick in the least.

"Right, that's using average soft tissue depths superimposed on the skull. Now, the clever bit with this software is that we've built in different average values for various ethnic groups, and that makes this much more accurate. So now we'll try the same thing with Saxon averages instead."

"How do you get Saxon averages?"

"By going to Saxony," she said as if it ought to be obvious. Maybe it was a joke.

The face that formed on the screen now had a strikingly familiar look, but Patrick couldn't quite get it. Nick added some brown hair and suddenly he did. It was very like the cloaked woman in a long-running insurance commercial, blandly beautiful, but it didn't look at all like someone who would have picked up her father's sword.

"She doesn't look the hero type," he remarked, and Celia laughed.

"Supposing she'd been a Roman instead?" suggested Nick. "Would you like to see that?"

The face on the screen changed quite remarkably, narrower over the cheeks, more pointed around the nose. It was an unconvincing mixture.

"No, she was Saxon," said Patrick. "Of course, she might have been the result of intermarriage. Her mother could easily have been a Briton. We have no real idea how much that happened."

"I could do you a bit of Celt?" said Nick, and got busy on the keyboard, calling up menus onto his screen. "I'll try sixty-forty, Celt and Saxon, yes? What about a bit of heroic red hair for the full Celtic experience?"

"OK."

It took a little while to process, the face on the screen flickering, and then a new face was scanned down a strip at a time over the old one, and as it emerged complete, this face tore a response out of Patrick, taking his breath away. This was a lively, living face framed by a cascade of deep red hair. The song had come to life before his eyes.

"Oh, yes," said Patrick. "Oh, yes, that's her. That's definitely her."

He felt absurdly happy, absurdly hopeful. This was the woman who took up her father's sword, the woman so valiant that she had been given the privilege of a warrior's burial. This was the woman he had slept a night beside. This face had every right to be remembered long afterwards, and it triggered an echo somewhere deep in his heart. Her death was the world's loss, and now here she was again. They had retrieved her from oblivion; they had given her a second chance at life.

"How about that?" said Nick. "Isn't she just something. I reckon your telly people are going to love her, don't you?"

Patrick found he loathed the idea of sharing her with Camden.

"That's sixty-forty, is it, Nick?" said Celia. "Try it forty-sixty, the other way round."

"No," said Patrick, more vehemently than he meant. He couldn't bear to lose her.

"OK," said Celia. "Now, do you want to see her walk? This is the bit nobody else has done before. Show him, Nick."

The wonderful woman on the screen moved far away, down a stylised country lane with hedgerows on each side, and began to walk towards them with a swinging, athletic stride. Was that a suggested bulge of pregnancy? It was extremely lifelike, and Patrick gazed at her, lost in love. Nick pressed another button, and she began to run with her hair flowing out behind her. She ran towards them, then on, as if she had passed right through the camera. The screen went blank.

"Did you see how she threw her weight forward and her feet turned out a little when she ran?" said Nick proudly. "It's all from the joint- and muscle-marking analysis."

"Now, the really clever bit," Celia added, "is that we've managed to analyse the force and the direction of the blow that caused the damage to the skull. It was probably a single-edged weapon like a scramasax, definitely struck downwards and from behind, something like this."

Before Patrick could prepare himself for it in any way, the wonderful woman appeared again running towards him, but this time, she was being overtaken by a huge man with a blade raised behind him, a blade that slashed down as she came closer, biting into the side of her head, and blood sprayed out. Electronic it may have been, but it was intensely realistic. Patrick cried out as the German Queen collapsed to her knees, then pitched forward to lie facedown on the grass in her own spreading lifeblood.

"I'll play it again," said Nick. "Good, yeah?"

To his horror, Patrick found his eyes flooding with tears. "No," he said, choking, knowing he had to get away from that screen, and lunged for the door.

"Are you all right?" Celia called, but he ran down the stairs and out onto the pavement, overflowing with illogical grief. Death had been defeated in there, but only for a moment.

He heard someone shout his name, and there, coming down the pavement towards him through the blur, was another stranger, who called out again in Bobby's voice. She saw him and broke into a run, and a gust of wind took away her turban, releasing the hair he had never seen before in daylight, a cascade of deep red curls that tumbled around her lively, living face in unsuspected glory. She was running towards him with her weight thrown forward, her face framed entirely anew, a counterfeit Rachel no more, and she was so like the picture he had just seen on the screen that he searched the pavement behind her, heart pounding, looking for the giant swordsman. She was running towards him, and she was bringing with her the news that there was no longer any need to mourn the dead.

She stopped in front of him and looked at him quizzically. His eyes were drinking her in.

"What's happened to you?" she said.

"Everything."

He hugged her.

"Wow. What's this for?" she gasped.

"For being alive," he said, and kissed her hard.

She went tense for a moment, then she kissed him back. When she broke away, breathing hard, she looked at him wonderingly and said, "Jack told me."

"Told you it wasn't me?"

"Yes."

"How did you find me?"

"You asked Louisa where to go. Patrick—I need you. Jack says they're going straight back to Wytchlow and they're going to corner Joe. Jack can't stand Camden. He says Camden gave Joe a note this morning saying if Joe didn't do the song for them, he'd have to do all the stuff about you instead. He thinks Joe's going to agree to do it."

"Well, let's go and stop him, shall we?"

"Yes. Your car's faster."

In the car, he looked sideways at her.

"I can't believe I haven't seen your hair properly before. Why do you always wear that horrible cap?"

"That's just a farmer thing," she said, dismissively, trying to scoop it all up to put the turban back on. It got out of control and she let it all tumble down again. "Well, actually, that's not the main reason. Can you imagine what it's like to be called Redhead and have hair like this?"

"Rather wonderful, I should say."

"Rather dreadful. People make jokes all the time. I went to Africa to be with people who wouldn't understand my surname."

He could hardly drag his eyes away.

"You see?" she said. "Now bugger off. Watch the road. Does this thing go any faster? You look nice when you smile."

"I'll do it more often." He took her hand.

"Don't you need to change gear or anything?"

"Only sometimes."

"What on earth happened inside that building? Was that the DNA results? Why did you come rushing out like that?"

"It was the face reconstruction. You'll see it later on. Forget the DNA. It takes ages. I'll tell you something, though." He looked at her and a warm glow of certainty about the future flooded his body. "There's not much point in waiting for it. I know the result already."

He wouldn't tell her any more.

As they tore into Bobby's farmyard they were greeted by an unexpected scene. A grinning Joe, wearing his red waistcoat, was walking into the house carrying a guitar, but he turned when he heard them approach and waved cheerfully. Kenny Camden, looking like he'd lost his wallet, was scrawling something on a clipboard while Jack, whistling aimlessly, folded his tripod.

"They've done it," exclaimed Bobby. "We're too late."

"Yes, but *what* have they done?" said Patrick.

They got out of the car and Jack nodded at them.

"What's happened?" demanded Bobby.

"Ask him," said Jack, and winked, jerking a thumb towards Camden.

"What's happened?" said Camden. "I've just *wasted* the last hour, that's what's happened. All this bullshit about your brother. I suppose everyone thought it was very funny."

"Do you want to see it?" said Jack. "I can run it back through the viewfinder."

"Yeah, that's right, let them have their laugh," said Camden and, punching numbers into his mobile phone, he climbed inside the car.

Jack ran the videotape back for them. Bobby and Patrick shared the headphones, their cheeks touching.

The camera was moving towards Joe in the yard at the start, as though they feared he might run away and they wanted every last frame. He was washing off his boots with a hose.

"Mr. Redhead?" said Camden's voice. "Can we talk to you?" Joe looked up and smiled, then he walked into the house. They heard Camden's voice, off-mike, say, "Damn. We'll have to go in after him."

Before they could move, however, Joe came back out wearing his red waistcoat.

"Could we have a word?" said Camden again. "Actually, I understand it's difficult to have a word, because you don't speak at all."

Joe looked surprised, shrugged, then said perfectly clearly, if a little slowly: "Well, whoever could have told you that, I wonder?"

Camden, out of shot, seemed to have been struck dumb himself. Joe waited for a long moment, then asked politely, "Was there anything else?"

Camden said, "Um . . . yes. Er . . . there was a song you sang in the pub . . ."

Joe nodded helpfully. "I often do that."

"Would you sing it for us?"

"Which one would that be?"

"The one about the German Queen."

"Oh, well, you see, I make them up as I go along. Can't say I remember that one."

"Right," said Camden. "Well, thank you."

"I have got one song I can do for you."

"Er . . . all right."

"Wait a minute."

There was a long pause while Joe disappeared into the house again. The camera stayed on, and they could hear Camden, off-mike, say, "I think someone's been pulling my plonker."

Joe came back with his guitar, tuned up, and launched into a basic folk melody.

> *There's a man they call Little who lives in this village,*
> *And all that he's good for is plunder and pillage.*
> *When they came to dig up what the Romans had left*
> *He saw a threat to his profits so he turned to theft.*
>
> *For the past it is yours and the past it is mine*
> *And the man that destroys it is naught but a swine.*
> *He brought lorries and bulldozers late in the night*
> *And he wrecked the old villa as he dug up that site.*
>
> *He'll make a small fortune as he sells off each house*
> *But that won't change the fact that he's simply a louse*
> *For the past it is yours and the past it is mine*
> *And the man that destroys it is naught but a swine.*

"Did you like that?" said Joe to the camera, and there was no reply.

Jack switched it off. "That's it," he told them. "Deeply satisfying."

Patrick followed Bobby into the kitchen, where Joe was standing by the Aga waiting for the kettle to boil.

"Joe?" said Bobby, hugging her brother. "You old bastard. How did you do that? Come on, say something to me," but Joe just smiled and put a finger to his lips. Then he held Bobby's shoulders at arm's length and gave her a searching look. Turning the same intense gaze on Patrick, Joe took Bobby's hand, led her over to Patrick, and wrapped his hand round hers. As he felt their fingers intertwine, he smiled, kissed Bobby on the forehead, and left the room.

"Ah," said Bobby, "that's odd. I seem to have just been . . . well . . . *given* to you, I suppose. Not even gift-wrapped."

"The wrapping's perfect," said Patrick, running his fingers through her hair and pulling her gently towards him. "Joe knows best."

"God, I hope so," she murmured.

# CHAPTER TWENTY-SEVEN

THE NEXT MORNING, PATRICK
woke, curled in the nest of a
soft bed, soaked in the butter-
scent of Bobby, with his arms
wrapped round her and one of
her fingers tracing a gentle pattern on his
cheek. She was smiling into his eyes with a
hint of wonder, and he knew his penance was
over.

"Hello," he said. "It wasn't a dream, then."

She kissed him. "Time to get up," she
said. "It's May Morning. We mustn't be late."

They walked out into the freshest day
of Patrick's life and took the lane to the
meadow by the river. There were families
converging on it from every direction, small
children running ahead to pick flowers out of
the hedges. Bobby took a small bottle from
her pocket and held it up to show him.

"Roman glass," he said. "Perfect."

They gathered the dew together, kneeling down to harvest it drop by drop from the

leaves. Patrick ran his hand through the grass and reached out to anoint Bobby's cheeks with wet fingers.

"We can start being young now," he said.

They joined the children in gathering armfuls of flowers, then trooped back from the field to decorate the cart together. It was then that Patrick remembered the priceless object he had left unlocked in the car the day before, forgotten as the night had caught fire.

"Would your wooden man mind if his ancestor took his place round the village this year?" he asked Bobby.

"Why don't they both come?"

So all together, they wove flower stems into the holes in the face of the bronze man and then, with the May Queen crowned and all the children in the village singing their hearts out, Patrick and Bobby took their place in the procession.

ON ANOTHER MAY MORNING, TOLD BY THE ALIGNMENT OF THE SUN AT DAWN, NOT BY ANY PRINTED CALENDAR, THE FAMILIES WHO NOW FILLED THE HALL AND THE HUTS OF HILD'S DEAD BROTHERS TOOK UP THE MASK THEY HAD MADE AT HER DAUGHTER'S FIERCE URGING AND REPEATED THE CEREMONY SHE HAD INITIATED. IT WAS THE FIRST OF THE LONG SERIES OF WOODEN MASKS.

"YOU DO IT LIKE THIS," SAID MELA, THE GIRL WITH THE RED, RED HAIR. "HE IS THE WOVEN GOD, AND THIS MORNING'S FRESH FLOWERS MAKE HIM LIVE JUST AS THIS MORNING'S DEW MAKES US LIVE. MY MOTHER SAID THIS WOULD MAKE SURE OUR WHOLE VILLAGE WOULD LIVE."

SHE BROKE OFF AND FOUGHT DOWN A SOB. IT WOULD NOT DO TO LET THESE PEOPLE, WHO WERE ON HER SIDE ONLY WHEN IT SUITED THEM, SEE HER CRY. SHE WAS STILL ANGRY THAT HER MOTHER WAS UP ON THE LONELY, WINDY HILL, NOT DOWN AMONG THE RUINED WALLS WHERE SHE HAD WANTED TO BE. NOW IT WAS UP TO HER TO MAKE SURE HER MOTHER'S WAY WOULD CARRY ON.

"WE WILL WALK WITH IT AROUND THE EDGE OF OUR HOUSES JUST AS SHE DID, AND WE WILL SING A SONG FOR HER."

"WHAT SONG?" SAID HER OLDEST UNCLE, WHO HAD COME TO LIVE IN THE HALL.

"A SONG I SHALL TEACH YOU," SHE SAID. "IT IS NOT YET
A LONG SONG, BUT IT WILL GET LONGER."

Five months later, at the end of a beautiful Sunday in October, they buried the German Queen and her child again, laying the woman's bones out tenderly just as they had found them and nestling the fragile bones of the baby, wrapped in a shawl, into the space between her arm and her ribs. Joe had spent weeks at the forge in the barn, beating and grinding away to make a copy of the chicken sword, and he'd also put together a new wooden shield for her. In a series of heated debates in stuffy rooms in Oxford, they'd given up hope of re-burying most of the grave goods with her, but Bobby had drawn the line at the Green Man mask.

"I know how she felt about it," she said, and anyone who tried to persuade her otherwise came away shaken by the experience. The mask was carefully recorded and a casting was taken from it and then the original face went quietly back into the grave just as they had found it, a secret known only to the diggers.

All the diggers were there on the hilltop; Jack, the cameraman, arrived by himself, with no camera, and asked if he might join them. They buried the bones with enormous care, sieving the heap of fine soil down over them so that the earth packed around the bones in loving protection as it had before, then they rolled the turf carefully back into place over the grave and laid their flowers down.

The tents had blossomed again in their old places, and with the campfire blazing and wine bottles passing, it was what they all wanted, a recreation of past times, except now, as Dozer said, lying with his arm round Gaye, it seemed a whole lot nicer.

They talked about this and that for a while, about how the vicar had resigned from the school board, about the amazing moment when they had first seen the reconstruction and Bobby had seemed to run out of the screen at them.

"I was sure they were going to find your DNA was the same as hers," said Gaye to Bobby. "They must have got it wrong."

"Not necessarily," said Peter. "It could go all the way down the line to Bobby's grandmother, then if it came down her father's side instead of her mother's, it wouldn't show up, see?"

"Well, we all know who she's descended from, don't we?" said Gaye, and Patrick agreed.

"What did you think of the show?" said Jack diffidently.

"Could've been worse," said CD. "I was glad to see Camden let old Patrick here off lightly."

"Funny, that," said Jack. "Bit of a technical problem with some of the videotapes. I don't suppose I'll be working for him again."

"You came out of it pretty well, mate," said Dozer to Patrick. "I mean, at the end of the day, all it really said was you used to be a rock singer and now you weren't."

"Well, it's past history now," said Patrick. "Only thing is, I have to keep turning down gigs."

"Can you tell us what happened about that builder?" asked Aidan.

"Roger Little?"

"That's the man."

"Have you seen the field?" said Bobby.

"Well, I couldn't help noticing there hasn't been any building on it."

"That's because the Woodland Renewal Trust bought it to plant trees," said Bobby.

"So did he not get his planning permission, then?"

"Yes, he did. Then he sold up. It's all a bit of a mystery."

"No, it's not," said Dozer, and he was too far away for Patrick to kick him into silence. "I went and had a word with him. Made him an offer he couldn't refuse."

"What with?" said Bobby, staring at him in amazement. "I didn't know that."

"Spare royalties some pop star had hanging around, weren't it, Pat? Mind you, I got it for a rock-bottom price, having all the evidence, you might say. Evidence of the whereabouts of a large pile of Roman flooring. He saw my point of view quite quickly. Got out ahead and with no fuss. I was quite reasonable, really."

"Where's Joe gone?" asked Maxwell. "I didn't see him go."

"He was here," said Bobby. "I think he went down to the barn. Have you seen it? He's made a great job of it. We said he didn't have to move out just for us, but you can't argue with him."

"Well, you could, but it might be a bit one-sided," pointed out Dozer. "Here he is."

Joe walked up out of the darkness with two guitars, and they made space for him in the circle. He gave one to Patrick.

"There's only one song I want to hear tonight," said Bobby, resting her head on Patrick's shoulder, and there under the stars, next to the fresh grave of a long-dead woman, Joe finally sang the whole story as the two guitars met in perfect understanding.

> *I sing you the song of the German Queen*
> *With her hair dark red and her eyes so green.*
> *I sing you the song of the way they cried*
> *On the dreadful day when the fair Queen died.*
>
> *The eldest child of her father's line,*
> *A slender shoot from a sturdy vine,*
> *She kept his house from her early days*
> *Once her well-loved mother had passed away.*
>
> *Her father wore the golden ring*
> *From the German lands where he'd been a king*
> *And, dreaming of what once had been,*
> *He called the girl his German Queen.*
>
> *There came a time in that peaceful land*
> *When their peace was marred by a roving band,*
> *New arrived from the Saxon shore*
> *With a grudge from home and an old, old score.*
>
> *They climbed the hill on an autumn morn*
> *And the first light gleamed on the swords they'd drawn.*
> *High on the hill, that glint was seen*
> *By the chieftain's girl with her eyes so green.*

"Sorry about the eyes," Bobby whispered in Patrick's ear.

"You can't have everything," he whispered back. "Given the choice, I'd take the hair any day."

> *She ran to the wall with the warning gong*
> *And she made it sing its arousing song.*
> *Her brothers leapt from their wives' warm arms*
> *At the first loud cry of its harsh alarm.*

*They met the raiders, blade to blade*
*In a spray of blood at the old stockade.*
*Outnumbered by them five to one,*
*The fight was led by the oldest son.*

*At the moment when they saw him fall*
*And his soul took flight to the warriors' hall,*
*The hills rang out to a chilling cry.*
*Their father saw the young prince die.*

*He burst on them, this wrathful lord*
*And he whirled the blade of his iron sword.*
*They fell at his feet like stalks of corn,*
*Harvested for his dear firstborn.*

*That robber band, they quaked and ran,*
*Before the wrath of a righteous man,*
*Leaving their dead where they'd been laid*
*By the slashing edge of that chicken blade.*

*A month went by while they mourned the son*
*And marked the bold deeds he had done*
*By laying his shield across his chest*
*As they put him in the grave to rest.*

*That was when they came again*
*In the hooded night, those murderous men,*
*Feet wrapped in cloth and swords honed keen*
*But they didn't allow for the German Queen.*

*She stayed awake while her brothers slept.*
*Moon-shadows moved in the watch she kept*
*And when she heard a skittering stone,*
*She beat the gong with a great leg bone.*

*Three brothers only faced the foe*
*And they made their stand by the witch's low.*
*They stood surrounded, back to back,*
*Against the waves of the night attack.*

This was here, where they lay, and they all looked at each other in a shared electric moment in which more than thirteen centuries were set aside. Seeing their reaction, Joe played a long instrumental passage to give them space and Patrick improvised a countertune, winding its way through it. They came out of it on a slower, sadder note.

> *Their sister raced to summon aid,*
> *To bring the King with his chicken blade.*
> *But the King's old legs brought him there too late.*
> *His last three sons had met their fate.*
>
> *The King's hot blade was slaked in blood.*
> *Six traitors lay in the hillside mud.*
> *Down that hill they carried their own*
> *And buried them round their valley home.*
>
> *The King turned to his daughter dear*
> *And spoke to her of his dreadful fear.*
> *"You, my Queen, are the only one*
> *Left of my line. You must bear a son."*
>
> *She was wed by the light of an autumn moon*
> *To a noble lord from Abbandun*
> *And twelve months on, she was brought to bed*
> *Where she bore the girl with the sunset head.*
>
> *The girl was made in her mother's mould*
> *Her hair was a weave of red and gold,*
> *It flowed from her head like a river spun*
> *From the crimson rays of the western sun.*
>
> *She was bold as a wolf and fast as a hawk*
> *And she learnt to run before she walked.*
> *When more years passed, a son was born*
> *And the old King knew that his line went on.*
>
> *At the village under the witch's low*
> *The Queen and her children came to know*

*A time of peace, a time to mend,*
*A time they thought would never end.*

*She filled their home with the things she found*
*Given up by the riven ground,*
*Sharp axes chipped from ancient stone,*
*A stag's head carved from an old thigh bone.*

*When others shunned the Romans' stones*
*She dared inspect their resting bones*
*And there, when winter turned to spring*
*She found what proved her favourite thing.*

*He came to her from the deer-delved earth*
*As if the land had given birth*
*And what she saw beneath the sod*
*Was the leafy brow of the woven god.*

*That year she set herself the task*
*Of weaving flowers in the leaf god's mask.*
*So he led them as they'd dance and sing*
*To celebrate the return of spring.*

*There came the time of the old King's death*
*And he blessed her with his final breath.*
*He gave his sword to be handed down*
*To the boy who would one day wear his crown.*

*They buried him at the battle stone*
*And the news went out that he had gone.*
*Far to the east, the traitors heard*
*Of the end of the King with the chicken sword.*

*The Queen again grew big with child*
*As it came to winter, cold and wild.*
*She woke one night from a warning dream*
*And heard the watchman's dying scream.*

*Her husband left their bed so warm*
*And summoned men to brave the storm.*
*There were six who fought that fight*
*But just three lived when it grew light.*

*Before the dawn, to aid her lord*
*She took the wooden summons-sword.*
*She roused her eldest child from bed,*
*The fleet-foot girl with the sunset head.*

*"You must now run your swiftest race,"*
*She told the child, "and at the place*
*Called Abbandun, you'll find our kin.*
*Without their help, we cannot win."*

*She raced away like a blaze of light*
*But even as her feet took flight,*
*The Queen saw two defenders fall.*
*Lone stood her lord against them all.*

*She dressed herself in a warrior's cloak*
*And the chicken sword from the wall she took.*
*She went to stand at her husband's back*
*To share the weight of that foul attack.*

*When he saw the blade she wielded*
*The first attacker turned and fled.*
*She killed the next and then two more*
*And her husband matched her lethal score.*

*Two hours they fought on that bloody hill*
*And the chicken sword's blade drank its fill.*
*They stood their ground in the Bury Field,*
*Outnumbered, they refused to yield.*

*Three to two, they stood at last*
*On the burying place from a distant past.*
*There she fought like a bear for her children's life*
*And for one unborn in the midst of strife.*

*The traitors struck a mortal blow*
*That felled her lord on the witch's low.*
*She whirled the blade like an iron fan*
*And two more fell to join her man.*

*Right to the end on the blood-soaked grass,*
*She would not let those traitors pass.*
*Just one more faced her, towering tall,*
*The villains' leader, worst of all.*

*From down below she heard her son*
*Cry out, and then she turned to run*
*Fearing foes had reached her hearth.*
*That action brought about her death.*

*He cut her down with a coward's blow*
*Struck from behind, and it laid her low*
*But, dying, one last stroke she made*
*And she spitted him on the chicken blade.*

*Her kin came late to the slaughter, led*
*By the grieving girl with the sunset head.*
*They found her there, still holding tight*
*To the chicken sword in its final fight.*

*Up on the hill on the sacred ground,*
*They dug a grave in the ancient mound.*
*They laid her there with her sword and shield*
*In that older tomb in the Bury Field.*

*Amber beads were round her head*
*And she sleeps there still on her wooden bed.*
*Her cloak secured with the royal jewel*
*That had marked the years of her father's rule.*

*Now leather and wood have turned to dust.*
*The iron brackets are dark brown rust.*
*The bed has lost its strength and weight*
*But the burden on it's no longer great.*

*The years and the plough have flattened the land*
*Which she saved with a stroke of her valiant hand.*
*Now silence and shadows mark the scene*
*Of the glorious grave of the German Queen.*

Joe's voice sang the final words and the two guitars played together in a sweet finale as the song settled around them all, and for Patrick, an unsuspected future stretched ahead.